THE SCORPION TRAP

Harold James is the author of:
A House in Kathmandu
Across the Threshold of Battle
Tales of the Gurkhas

And the co-author of:
The Gurkhas
The Undeclared War
A Pride of Gurkhas

The Scorpion Trap

Harold James

JANUS PUBLISHING COMPANY
London, England

First published in Great Britain 2010
by Janus Publishing Company Ltd,
105–107 Gloucester Place,
London W1U 6BY

www.januspublishing.co.uk

British Library Cataloguing-in-Publication Data
A catalogue record for this book is available from the British Library

ISBN 978-1-85756-716-8

Cover Design: Three Dots Design
www.threedotsdesign.co.uk

Printed and bound in India

Dedication

To my devoted Tamang family:
Karna, Santi, Santosh James, Ngima Dolma,
who have cared for me so selflessly.
With love from Harold *Baje*.

… And in memory of the gallant Gurkhas,
who served with me in Burma.

Note for the reader:

Many readers will probably be unfamiliar with military formations and the system of ranks in the Indian Army up to the end of World War II, and the following paragraphs are included as a general guide.

Forming the old "Gurkha Brigade", each with traditions and customs of its own, were ten regiments. A regiment was divided into two battalions, except during the emergency of the war, when two or three additional battalions were raised. With reference to a particular battalion it is customary to give its number first, followed by that of the parent regiment. Thus: 1st Battalion of the 4th Gurkha Rifles. Abbreviated, as used throughout this book, this becomes 1/4th Gurkhas.

Generally speaking, a battalion was about 1,000 plus. It was split into four rifle companies, each of three or four platoons. In turn, the platoons were divided into three or four sections. In addition, there were specialist groups such as the pioneer platoon, commando platoon, mortar and medium machine-gun groups, and signals.

A battalion had eleven or twelve British officers, assisting them, and the backbone of the battalion, were Gurkha officers, who held the Viceroy's Commission. The senior of these was the subedar major, a man of great power in the battalion. Under him were the subedars and jemedars. As a rule, the former were second in command of companies, while the latter commanded platoons.

The non-commissioned ranks consisted of havildars (sergeants), naiks (corporals) and lance naiks (lance corporals). There were also senior non-commissioned officers such as the company havildar major. The other ranks were known as riflemen.

Moulmein-Yenangyaung

Yenangyaung

Magwe Yin Chaung
Taungdwingyi
Kokkogwa

Salween River

IRRAWADDY RIVER

Pyinmana

Allanmyo
Thayetmyo Kyaukpadaung Yedashe
Dayindabo Bawlake

Tamagauk Wettigan
Nawin Chaung Toungoo Mawchi
Prome Hmawza
Padaung Shwedaung

P
E
G
U

Y
O
M
A
S

Pyu

Sittang River

Thailand

Nyaunglebin

Letpadan
Tharrawaddy

Henzada

Waw Sittang
Mokpalin
Kyaikto
Hmawbi Aby Bilin
Pegu
Hlegu Tawa

Taukkyan

D
a
w
n
a

R
a
n
g
e

Mingaladon

Rangoon Pegu River
Syriam

Martaban Gyaing River Kawkareik
Kyondo
Moulmein

Gulf of Thailand

N

Miles: 0   25   50

Burma and surrounding countries

Chungking •

C H I N A

I N D I A

Himalayas

Brahmaputra R.

Dimapur •
Kohima •

Chindwin R.

Myitkyina

Imphal •

•Kunming

Kabaw Valley

Kalewa
Yeu

Lashio •

Mandalay

Salween R.

Meiktila

Kengtung •

Akyab

B U R M A

Loikaw

Toungoo

Prome •

Irrawaddy R.

Sittang R.

B a y
o f
B e n g a l

Sittang

INDO - CHINA

Rangoon •

Gulf
of
Martaban

Moulmein

Thailand

Tavoy

• Bangkok

Tenasserim

Mergui •

G u l f
o f
Thailand

Saigon •

Victoria
Pt.

Thailand

Thailand

0   100   200

Miles

Contents

Prologue
Burma, February 1942

The Sapper Company had worked all through the hot Burmese day preparing the three centre spans of the Sittang Railway Bridge for demolition. If the bridge was not destroyed, two Japanese divisions could cross over to the west and attack Rangoon, precipitating the fall of Burma and placing India in a grave position.

More than 4,000 British, Gurkha, Indian and Burmese troops of 17 Indian Division were still on the east bank of the river, held in a fierce battle with the Japanese, and nothing seemed to be going right for Major General Jackie Smyth, VC. Each crack of a rifle, each staccato burst from a machine-gun, was like a rivet being driven into his body. Yet, he had told himself many times before that it could have been so different; though, he now knew with absolute finality that there was nothing more he could do except sit it out.

As darkness fell, Smyth at last drove back to his Ops Room at the village of Abya some 5 miles west of the bridge. He felt faint from lack of food, weary in mind and body. A body which he had kept so fit throughout his career and which now threatened to let him down at the most vital moment of his life. A bite to eat and a few hours sleep were needed to revitalise him, to help him fight the pain, but it seemed as though he had hardly closed his eyes when he was awakened by Brigadier "Punch" Cowan, his chief of staff, to take an urgent telephone call from Brigadier Hugh-Jones, the bridgehead commander. As the general was handed the receiver he sensed that his worst fears were about to be realised; he had, after all, stressed upon Hugh-Jones that on no account must the enemy seize the bridge intact.

Hugh-Jones reported, 'I have had a word with Captain Orgill of the Field Company and if the bridge is not blown now, he cannot guarantee to do so in the morning.'

'Why is that?' Smyth asked.

Hugh-Jones explained that there was not enough fuse and electric cable, so the firing point had to be located on the bridge itself and some distance from the west bank. 'The enemy has now established a machine-gun post on the railway cutting. We tried to dislodge it but failed. In the daylight, the sappers will be dangerously exposed as they touch off the fuses.

'I have spoken to the commanders of the bridgehead troops and they are both of the same mind, sir. Our bridgehead is holding off the enemy at the moment, but a more concentrated attack in the morning is inevitable.'

Smyth lowered the receiver, holding it against his chest. The bridge must not fall into Japanese hands. Yet, some two thirds of his division was still on the wrong side of the river. Wireless communications had broken down, but obviously his men must be fighting desperately to restrain the enemy, so they could cross the bridge themselves before it was blown.

The only way across for miles, the iron bridge was 500 yards long, of eleven spans, each 150 feet, and recently decked over to take road traffic and marching troops. The river widened below the bridge to 1,000 yards, a formidable obstacle, even to strong swimmers, because of the treacherous current. A considerable number, probably the majority, were non-swimmers and as for boats – only the day before some 300 sampans had been bought by the Royal Engineers from Burmese villagers on both sides of the river and then destroyed to deny their use to the enemy.

The Japanese could have bombed the bridge at any time, but it was much more important to them intact as the shortest route to Rangoon; to find a suitable alternative further north would have meant a long delay. With this in mind, Smyth had hoped to have his complete division across the river and the bridge destroyed well before the enemy reached the area. He could have organised a stout defence on the west bank, supported by 7 Armoured Brigade, which was due to arrive shortly from Rangoon. But because of a clash of opinion with higher command, he now found himself in this hopeless situation, caught with his division split, the enemy attacking fiercely and the bridge still intact.

What a horrible decision to make, Smyth thought. He had gone over the pros and cons many times and he knew that there was really only one decision to reach. But he hesitated, allowing himself another few minutes of deliberation, seeking despairingly for an alternative solution.

Lieut. General Sakurai, commanding the elite *33 Division*, was handed an intercepted radio message which had been transmitted in clear, and at once he realised that the British were pulling back to the Sittang Bridge.

'We must reach the bridge before the British. Catch them in a scorpion trap!' He curled his hand like the claws of a scorpion and then snapped the fingers together, closing the hand into a fist. 'And hold them for the death sting.'

It was The Scorpion Trap, a Japanese manoeuvre established in ancient times. The scorpion, with claws outstretched, reaches to seize its prey from behind so that it can be held and stung to death.

Acting on the general's immediate orders, *215 Regiment* moved out: around 5,000 ruthless and experienced soldiers advancing at top speed towards the bridge, fired up by hunger for more action and for victory. Meanwhile the rest of *33 Division*, together with *55 Division*, stood by to give the death sting to 17 Indian Division once it was caught in the scorpion trap like some fragile grasshopper.

Across the river, Brigadier J. K. "Jonah" Jones, of 16 Indian Brigade, had that evening set up a defensive position around Mokpalin village, about a mile short of the bridge. A sort of fort in the jungle, where he hoped to hold out overnight and break out from in the morning through the block the enemy had placed between him and the bridge. The perimeter was manned by a mixed bag of units from the division's three brigades, which had been dispersed in the confusion caused by surprise Japanese ambushes and roadblocks earlier in the day.

One of the units was C Company of 4/15th Gurkha Rifles, commanded by Captain Paul Cooper. Separated from his battalion when it was ambushed, he had led his company to Mokpalin and been allocated a position on the perimeter.

His men dug in, while Paul waited anxiously for what the night might bring. How many more men would he lose? He was 20 years old, an Emergency Commissioned Officer, short of military experience and propelled into command. But he had brought the survivors of his company some 300 hazardous miles in the past five weeks as 17 Division withdrew towards Rangoon, pressed by the Japanese invasion forces. Now, he was in a trap from which it would be difficult to escape.

Suddenly, the night was rent apart by artillery flashes, the blast from exploding shells reverberating around the village, mortar bombs plunging in from their high trajectory. Fierce machine-gun fire opened up, the tracer threading the darkness with stitches of red, green and white to indicate the various enemy formations. There was also the usual rattle of the cracker guns to try to locate the defenders' machine-gun positions. Then the first line of enemy infantry hit the perimeter.

Part One
The Hungry River

Chapter One
Journey to War

Lieut. Colonel Lionel Osborne, Commandant of 4th Battalion, the 15th Gurkha Rifles, looked over his officers as they settled down in an assortment of chairs in the officers' mess, where he had called a meeting at short notice.

A tall man in his mid fifties, he was lean, wiry and brown from his long service under an Indian sun. After several years of rising through the various regimental positions, he had at last been given a battalion of his own. A few weeks earlier, the battalion had moved into camp in the centre of Poona Racecourse. Now, the colonel had received exciting new orders.

'Right,' he said abruptly and the officers sat up straight, eager to hear his news, '46 Brigade, which was due to sail for the Middle East, has been diverted to Burma and we are to accompany it and become part of 17 Division under the command of General Smyth.'

A reaction of surprise, expectation, delight and fear crackled like electric sparks under the canvas and the colonel paused to let everyone settle down again.

He had known most of his senior officers before the battalion had been raised because they had held regular commissions. Best of all, he knew his 2 i/c, Arthur Kennedy. They had almost been brought up together in the regiment from their earlier days and their families and children had grown up together. Arthur was a self-made man, but he was not the sort to throw his weight about and because of his understanding manner he was respected by his Gurkhas. He was also respected by the other officers, although he was a silent man, not given to unnecessary conversation. Robin Hutchings, the adjutant, was a younger man, much more intense, a strict disciplinarian, not an easy man to get to know, and he seemed to live for the regiment. Osborne felt he would be better off for more outside interests. Still, he was an excellent administrator and the colonel found his help invaluable.

Of his four company commanders, three were professional soldiers. Martin he knew vaguely and was satisfied with the opinion he had formed. Todd and Sanderson had been transferred from the regimental centre and he had not had an opportunity to really sum them up. But they both came with good reports. The fourth company commander was Davidson: suave, always well turned out, he looked as though he would be more at ease in a cocktail bar than on the parade ground. Normally, Osborne would not have made him a company commander, but there was no one else as senior; although, he had to admit, even Robin could find nothing wrong with his handling of his company.

Osborne was also very short of junior officers. The battalion was a new one and had been taken unawares by the sudden order to join 46 Indian Brigade. Most of the action was in the Middle East, so formations in that war zone had priority. Of the few subalterns he had managed to purloin, two were on courses and one was in hospital. He looked at Hunter, his intelligence officer, almost straight out of officers' training school, which should not be held against him; after all, soon, the army would consist largely of emergency commissioned officers and most of them would do very well. But although Hunter was a presentable, young, intelligent man, he had an obvious inferiority complex and Osborne hoped that enemy action would shake that out of him.

Doc Green, the MO, was just the opposite; impressive, reliable and an excellent doctor, if somewhat eccentric. This left Paul Cooper, whom the colonel sensed was a good officer in the making. Young, dark-haired, pleasant bearing, very tanned, athletic, about 5 foot 10 inches tall; from a distance he would blend in well with his Gurkhas under the probing sights of a Japanese sniper. He also had an advantage over most of the officers, because he could speak Nepali fluently as he had been brought up on a tea garden near Darjeeling in the Himalayas. But he seemed to be rather friendly with Davidson and the colonel hoped he would not be led astray.

With the officers more settled, Osborne continued, 'You will be given details of the movement order shortly, but first, while you are all gathered here, I felt that I should just remind you that we have been concentrating our training with the Germans in mind as the enemy. Now, we will have to switch to a completely different enemy – one who, I might say, in spite of all the misleading intelligence put out to belittle his capabilities, is an enemy to be respected. I spent a few months in Japan before the war as guests of some Japanese military friends. Take it from me, the Japanese soldier is tough, dedicated, utterly ruthless,

often barbarous and fanatically devoted to the Emperor and he believes
it is his duty to sacrifice his life for his country.'

Osborne paused for a moment. 'I don't want to sound defeatist,' he
continued. 'The Japanese are not supermen but very good warriors,
superbly trained and experienced. I know we are a very young battalion,
untrained in jungle warfare, and, of course, we are still well below our
official establishment in both officers and men. But our Gurkhas have
a reputation of courage and I am sure that the battalion will maintain
the highest traditions of the regiment. It will be up to us to give the
right leadership and I am sure you won't fail me there.'

Paul awoke with a start as Rifleman Gopiram Gurung shook him out of
a deep sleep. The Gurkha orderly handed him a mug of life-saving tea
and struck a match to light up his first cigarette of the day.

It had been Tony Davidson's idea to have a night out at some club in
Poona Cantonment. 'Could be our last chance before we leave for
Burma,' he'd said. Paul had not needed much persuasion, but now he
sat on the edge of his camp cot in his crumpled uniform, suffering the
effects of a monumental hangover. A sip or two of the hot, sweet tea and
some drags on the cigarette and he began to feel better. There was a
broad grin on Gopiram's face.

Paul said defensively, 'I was not drunk.'

The young orderly's shoulders shook. 'Ho! Ho! Is that why you slept
in your uniform, sahib?'

Paul ran a hand over the Gurkha's shaven head. 'Get along you, *badmash.*'

Still grinning at being called a troublemaker, Gopiram poured hot
water into a canvas bowl. Paul shaved, took a shower in the ablution
tent, changed into a clean uniform and wondered if he could face
breakfast. To his surprise, he was able to make a reasonable meal before
walking over to C Company's lines.

The men were already on parade and Subedar Tilbir Gurung
called them to attention as Paul approached. Returning the salute,
Paul stood the men at ease while they awaited the arrival of Captain
Mike Martin, C Company Commander.

'What do you think of the news, Subedar Sahib?' Paul asked.

'It is good, sahib. We have been idle too long.' Tilbir was a slim man
in his late thirties, but with all his years of service he had little
experience of action, apart from a skirmish or two as a young man on
India's North-West Frontier. War would give him the chance to win a
medal, perhaps, and secure a larger pension. He was a quiet-spoken

man, giving an impression of softness which quite belied the steel which ran through his body. His soft brown eyes could change in an instant to the paralysing glitter of those of a snake, making tough Gurkha NCOs wish the ground would open to devour them and young riflemen wish they were back on their snowy mountains. But he was also fair in his judgements and he was certainly loyal to both Crown and Regiment.

Behind him, the men of C Company, waiting in their three platoons and the headquarters' section, looked smart, but most of them were only just beyond the recruit stage. It was going to be straight into the deep end for them – and me, Paul thought. But they were Gurkhas and that, he knew, made up in courage for whatever they lacked in military skills.

They were a long way from their homeland in the high mountains of Nepal, the small, independent Hindu kingdom tucked into the Himalayas on India's northern borders. A rough, poor country with no roads outside the capital of Kathmandu, just a switchback of paths up and down the hills and across perilous, rickety bridges over mountain streams which became raging torrents in the monsoon. Small hamlets perched on the hilltops and back-breaking fields tumbled into the valleys. A hard country of rugged beauty which had produced a tough people – but a beautiful people – with a great sense of humour, a determination to live and a joy of music and dancing. They were as warm and hospitable as they could be cold and ruthless if the occasion warranted and, above all, loyal to a cause and steadfast to an oath.

Tilbir coughed a warning as Captain Mike Martin approached. Paul admired his company commander, a regular officer in his early thirties, a strict disciplinarian but a fair one, whom the Gurkhas respected because he had learned their language and he understood them. Paul called the company to attention.

After a brief moment, Martin said, 'Fall the men out, please. I want to see the order group in the company tent at once.'

He entered the large tent a few yards away where, presently, Paul joined him, accompanied by the senior members of the company. Sitting behind the trestle table which served as his desk, Martin picked up a pencil and twirled it between his fingers.

'C Company has received orders to be the advance party, the rest of the battalion following in a day or two. We are moving out at 23.30 hours tonight to catch a train at 01.00 for Calcutta, where a ship will take us on to Rangoon. Which, I am afraid, does not give us a lot of time, so let us discuss the quickest and most efficient way to proceed.'

The order group consisted of experienced men and within the hour the meeting had worked out priorities and a general scheme for the journey.

The remainder of the day was a mad rush, organising fatigue parties to help the quartermaster with stores and ammunition, the packing of the men's personal belongings, arrangements for the care of the handful of sick men and transport to Poona Railway Station. Then the RTO had to be telephoned to make certain the company was booked all the way to Calcutta and that feeding arrangements were organised for the long journey across the Indian Continent. Someone also had to check that Calcutta had been advised of their pending arrival and was laying on transport to the docks; goodness knows how many other things had to be tied up before they left. By the time their evening meal was prepared the company was ready.

'I'll see you later in the mess,' Martin said.

Paul took a shower before going to the officers' mess for dinner. As he entered the tent, his friend Tony said, 'You look as though you need a Scotch.' He clicked his fingers at the mess orderly.

'I could certainly do with one. It's been a very hectic day. God knows how we managed to get everything done in time. We are sure to have forgotten something, I suppose.'

At that moment, Osborne came in followed closely by Major Arthur Kennedy. 'Pay attention, please,' the colonel said abruptly. 'I am afraid I have bad news. Mike – Captain Martin – has been injured in a car crash. I believe he is badly hurt and in hospital. We are waiting for further news.' He turned to Paul. 'Please let your subedar know.'

After Paul had left, the colonel said, 'Now, what are we going to do about a replacement?'

'One of the other company commanders will have to take over,' Kennedy suggested.

'Normally, perhaps,' Osborne said. 'But we are short enough of officers as it is without interfering with the other companies. I think Cooper is capable of taking the company to Calcutta. After all, it will only be a few days before the rest of us join him. Meanwhile, we'll have to see if we can raise a replacement from the regimental centre.'

When Paul returned, the colonel came straight to the point. 'Right, Paul, I want you to take over temporary command of C Company. I presume the company is ready?'

'Yes, sir.'

'That's fine.' He turned to the bar to collect his drink and carry on a conversation with Kennedy as though everything was as it should be.

Paul was surprised that the colonel had not given him a lot of advice or told him how much was expected of him. But then, Paul thought, the colonel was not that sort of man. The adjutant, however, was an authoritarian and he took Paul to one side later, quizzing him thoroughly, to make certain he knew what was expected of him.

A few hours later, C Company was ready to move out of camp, the lorries loaded with the stores and kit, the men just waiting for the final order. The colonel eventually gave permission to move out and at the blowing of a whistle, the Gurkhas clambered into the backs of the lorries, chattering and laughing more than fully trained soldiers would have done, but on this occasion the NCOs restrained themselves from enforcing firm discipline. They were going to war, to new places. But how many of them would come back? And how many would be seriously wounded, carrying their scars and their disabilities for life? But that was far from their thoughts.

The drivers started up and the lorries rolled out in convoy past the cheering, laughing men of the other companies. Then the lights of the camp vanished and they were on their way to war.

As the flying boat approached Rangoon, Major General Jackie Smyth felt a growing excitement. At last he was to command a division in the field. But if there was excitement, there was also a touch of anxiety at the similarity between the situation in Burma and at Dunkirk, where he had commanded a brigade.

The events at Dunkirk were still vivid in his mind: the appalling difficulty of retreating from superior forces, continuous attacks from land and air, units widely separated, communications cut and only the miracle at Dunkirk to save them. What miracle would save them at Burma?

A realistic appreciation made it all too clear that with his scratch division, well short of full strength and not trained in jungle warfare, all he could do was try to hold the crack Japanese divisions long enough to allow reinforcements to build up behind him. He had to find some place to make a real stand – there was to be no shambling retreat without coordination. The enemy had to be given a few body blows as well as being held in check. With his long years of service and his experience gained in two world wars, he felt confident of making a good show.

He looked out of the aircraft window, down to where the Bay of Bengal sparkled silver in the sunshine, lapping against the Burmese coastline where the mangroves were almost black against the sand. And further inland the dense jungle, fissured by countless streams, climbed over hills – the sort of terrain which demanded fitness. But he had always been fit, with no excess weight. A slim man of average height, with a heart-shaped face and growing prematurely bald, he had always led an active life from the trenches of World War I, where he had won his VC, to the beaches of Dunkirk. And he was still fit – or was he? For a moment there was a hint of guilt. After the operation at Quetta was he now fully fit to command?

It was the first time in his life that he had become really ill. The doctor had diagnosed an anal fissure and an operation had been necessary. Then, to make matters worse, a few days after the operation Quetta was struck by the most severe earthquake since the terrible disaster of 1935. The hospital shuddered and swayed, and there was screaming and shouting and nurses running around evacuating everyone into the open. Those who could walk had to help their less fortunate fellow patients. It appeared that he was one of those who could walk and he did his bit, but all the time he was conscious of his recent operation, certain that he would do himself some damage. And he did: his wound opening up again. And the blasted hospital hadn't collapsed, after all!

About two months after his discharge from hospital, he took command of 17 Indian Division, stationed at Poona and ready to leave for the Middle East. He had never thought of refusing on medical grounds. Had he been right? He looked down at the Burmese coastline. He reckoned he had, because by now he was near enough fully recovered from the operation.

He had joined the division at Poona on 8 December 1941, the day the Japanese attacked Pearl Harbor and invaded Malaya. But his thoughts were concentrated in the opposite direction: his operational theatre would be the Middle East and not the jungles of South East Asia. Shortly after his arrival, the division began to move out: first 45 Brigade, sailing for Basra, the men complete with thick battle dress against a winter in the desert, and next 44 Brigade. But while at sea both brigades were diverted to Malaya, where they arrived in time to spend the rest of the war as prisoners of the Japanese.

Smyth wondered where this sudden turnabout left him. Then, on 28 December, he was given his new orders. He was to take his headquarters and 46 Brigade – his sole remaining unit – to Burma, where 16 Indian Brigade and 2 Burma Brigade would come under his command to form the new 17 Indian Division. But first he was to report to the commander-in-chief, General Sir Archibald Wavell, in Delhi.

Smyth cast his mind back to his interview with Wavell in the latter's library at Flagstaff House, New Delhi, on Sunday, 28 December 1941.

The commander-in-chief was a tough, stocky man, who had lost his left eye at Ypres in 1915. He did not know fear and he looked as though he had been hewn out of stone. He was a man of strong principles, but behind the stern exterior was a kindly man, a man of poetry, a man of literature. Unfortunately, he was also a man prone to long silences. Anyone in conversation with him had to be prepared for moments when he seemed to gaze into space. Now, in between the silences, he gave Smyth a résumé of the war and his opinion of the Japanese.

'I have recently completed a tour of Burma and Malaya,' he told Smyth.

But he did not say that it had been his first visit to these countries. Like many regular officers of the British and Indian armies, at no time in his service had he been east of Calcutta. He did not know Burma, Malaya, Thailand or the Dutch East Indies and he knew nothing of Japan or China.

He believed that a Japanese attack was not expected. Anyway, personally, he could not see how a Japanese force would make very quick progress down the peninsula towards Singapore. As for Burma, he had been horrified by the complete lack of organisation, intelligence and planning generally to meet a Japanese attack. On the other hand, he assured Smyth that there was no real need to worry too much about the Japanese because he considered them as second-class soldiers.

There was another period of silence, broken by Lady Wavell summoning them to tea. There was no further talk about Burma or exactly what Wavell expected Smyth to do to resolve the situation, but the general became quite voluble and excited as he turned the conversation to pig-sticking.

'Have you done any pig-sticking, Smyth? I wish I had the time to try it. I have read a most interesting book. And then I had the good fortune to meet an old district officer who gave me a first-hand description. You need to be a good horseman and have a cool judgement, because the boar is a fast mover, wild and savage and resolute to the last extremity. It is obviously a great builder of confidence and character, which helped the old district officers in their arduous tasks. Perhaps,' he concluded with a sudden sense of humour, 'we should introduce it into our military training.'

After tea, Wavell saw him out and said, with a confidence Smyth did not share, 'I'm sure you'll have no trouble in handling the Japanese.'

*   *   *

Looking after Burma was not going to be easy, Smyth considered. Wavell had recently been appointed Supreme Commander of the newly constituted South West Pacific Command – ABDA (American, British, Dutch, Australian) as it became known, and Burma was included in this command.

From a military point of view this was likely to prove a mistake – maybe a costly one – Smyth reflected. Wavell had his headquarters in Java, 2,000 miles from Rangoon, and to make matters worse, there was no reliable means of communication, even by wireless, between Burma and Java and all communications had to be routed through Delhi. So most of Wavell's instructions were going to be based on out-of-date information. What effect is that going to have on the way I fight the battle? Smyth thought anxiously.

'We're about to land, sir.'

Smyth came swiftly back to the present. 'Oh, yes. Thank you.'

Below, the Irrawaddy looked like a small, sparkling stream meandering through green forests, but as the aircraft descended it grew larger and larger, wide enough to take several flying boats, and the magical sparkle changed rapidly to a muddy brown.

As the aircraft came to rest on the wide reaches of the river, air-raid warnings screamed across the city. Near the jetty the boats, already on their way to the plane, turned sharply about and returned to shore. The flying boat was trapped in the middle of the river, a shining silver beacon for the Japanese bombers. How ironic to be blown to smithereens only minutes after arriving in Burma, Smyth thought wryly. But on this particular day the Japanese were interested only in Rangoon Docks, where flashes of flame and billowing black smoke recorded the fall of their bombs. When the all-clear was sounded at last, the boats scurried out again.

Shortly after landing from the flying boat, Smyth reported at Lieut. General Tom Hutton's headquarters in Rangoon. 'I see you received the usual warm greeting the Japs reserve for welcoming British generals,' the army commander said.

'I'm glad it wasn't warmer, sir,' Smyth said.

'Well, the supreme commander had a much hotter reception when he landed at Mingaladon on Christmas Day. He had to dive for shelter in a trench. And seventeen bombs fell within 50 yards of him.'

'That was obviously in deference to his higher rank,' Smyth remarked with a grin. 'The flying boat was much more comfortable than a trench; although, I must admit, it didn't feel as safe at the time!'

Hutton said, 'Well, come along; let's fill you in with the situation.'

The army commander was a tall, tough and wiry man with a rather droopy moustache and a lantern-shaped face. A man who had proved his courage in World War I, being awarded the Military Cross and Bar. Previously, he had been Chief of General Staff at AHQ Delhi, a position which he had enjoyed and to which he had brought considerable administrative talent. He had begged Wavell not to appoint him as Army Commander in Burma, but the C.-in-C. had been quite adamant. Now, Hutton gave Smyth evidence of his chief-of-staff attributes with a clear and correct appraisal of the situation.

On the wall was a large map of Burma: 250,000 square miles of long hill ranges, winding rivers, dense jungle split apart by patchworks of paddy fields and a dry zone near the country's navel, which bubbled with oil. Everything seemed to run south: hills, rivers, railways, main roads. Elsewhere, the lines of communication were sparse to nil.

Burma was tucked in between India on the west and China, Indo-China and Thailand on the east. The western and eastern boundaries were marked by high hill ranges covered in dense jungle and stretching all the way down to the sea. To the north towered the eastern massif of the Himalayas. Burma's long coastline stretched from India's borders along the Bay of Bengal, through the Arakan, to Rangoon in the delta of the great Irrawaddy River. Beyond Rangoon, the coastline fringed the Sittang Estuary and the Gulf of Martaban, dropping like a monkey's tail for some 500 miles to Victoria Point. This part of Lower Burma, called the Tenasserim, was bounded by the sea to its west and Thailand to the east and south.

Hutton ran his pointer down Burma's eastern frontier with Thailand, which stretched for some 800 miles from Chiengrai to the Kra Isthmus. 'That's our front line because, feasibly, the Japanese, with their military camps established in Thailand, could use any of the many routes across the hill ranges.' Hutton tapped the map again, defiantly. 'But my bet is that they will concentrate at Raheng, the Thai border town, and then cross the border and make for Moulmein.'

Hutton told Smyth that 16 Brigade had been dispatched to Kawkareik to block the immediate threat. But the brigade, as Smyth was to learn all too soon, had not been long in Burma and Brigadier J. K. "Jonah" Jones had assumed command only a few days before its embarkation from India. Like a great number of units in India, the brigade had suffered from "milking" – many of its best personnel being transferred to other formations in the Middle East. A large batch of recruits was rushed in to make up its numbers three days before embarkation for Burma. The brigade was untrained in jungle warfare, it lacked suitable equipment and its main transport consisted of a small pool of lorries.

Hutton continued, 'Although I feel certain that the main action will be in the south, we need a long stop in the Shan Hills. There could well be a Japanese division there, so I had to keep General Scott's Burma Div. to guard that part of the border with Thailand. If the Chinese can be persuaded to take over the responsibility of that area it would release Scott's division.'

A few weeks earlier, Wavell had flown to Chungking to meet Chiang Kai-shek. What actually happened during their conference only history would decide. It was alleged that Wavell had refused the offer of two Chinese divisions to help in the defence of Burma, but Wavell always stoutly denied this.

There was now the possibility that the Chinese generalissimo would prove cool to subsequent requests for help. But Burma was important to his own survival and the supplies moved north to his forces from Rangoon were vital. He would obviously not be able to stay out of the fight. Smyth had an uncomfortable feeling that he was about to relive his Dunkirk experience.

At the crack of dawn the following morning, Hutton and Smyth arrived at Rangoon's Mingaladon Airfield on their way to visit detachments at Mergui and Tavoy. The air officer commander met them, but was most concerned for their safety, and the paucity of air transport was soon made clear to Smyth when the AOC apologetically confessed that he could only supply one old Blenheim Bomber.

'I can't really say I'm happy about this trip, sir,' he said to Hutton. 'There are some 150 Japanese aircraft within striking distance of Rangoon and you could easily run into some of them.'

But Hutton was insistent. He climbed into the front seat of the Blenheim with the pilot, while Smyth had to lie down in the bomb rack. When the aircraft took off, it was escorted by two antiquated fighters.

They flew to Mergui, at the extreme south of Burma. After a flight of some three hours, a very cramped Smyth climbed down to inspect the Burma Rifles battalion which was defending the town. They then returned north, along the Tenasserim coast, to Tavoy, which was within 300 miles of Bangkok, the main Japanese base in Thailand. The garrison consisted of a Burma Rifles battalion and a police battalion, just converted to a regular role, very raw and untried.

From Tavoy, they continued north to Moulmein, where Smyth's divisional headquarters was to be located, arriving around 16:00 hours. Hutton continued his journey on to Rangoon, leaving a somewhat depressed Smyth behind.

Moulmein was around 100 miles from Rangoon by air and about twice as far by land. Several of Smyth's staff had already arrived and he was soon discussing the situation with them.

They all looked at the map of Burma. 'It's quite obvious, Simmy,' Smyth said to his GSO1, Lieut. Colonel Simpson, 'that there has been an awful balls-up. And we've got to put a finger in the hole in the dyke to stop the water flooding out.'

'There are a lot of holes, sir,' Simmy said.

It was an enormous area of jungle country to cover: some 400 miles from Papun in the north to Mergui in the south; 16 Brigade was in the dense jungle of the Dawna Hills at Kawkareik, 80 miles east of Moulmein; 2 Burma Brigade was scattered over some 300 miles of rough country including Tavoy, 170 miles south of Moulmein, with Mergui another 120 miles beyond that.

'And we have only two brigades,' Smyth said. 'Ekin's 46 Brigade is on its way from Poona, but I'm sure we'll be at grips with the enemy before he arrives. It looks as if we'll be forced to fight in batches. Just what I had hoped to avoid. I wanted to concentrate the force in a tactical position, say behind the Salween, in the Martaban–Bilin area to begin with. Intelligence is so bad it's almost non-existent and we have no real idea of the enemy's strength; one division is the guess, though I would put it at around two.'

'Air cover is not so hot, either, sir,' remarked a staff officer.

'You can say that again,' Smyth snapped. 'I had that brought home to me most forcibly during my flight to the south yesterday. While I lay in the bomb rack, for a moment I felt real despair; and if it hadn't been for my sense of humour I could have burst into tears at the ludicrous situation.'

The RAF consisted of some sixteen Buffaloes and six Blenheims based at Mingaladon, Rangoon's airfield. Fortunately, a squadron of twenty-one Curtis P-40 (Tomahawk) pursuit fighters from Chiang Kai-shek's American Volunteers Group was also based at Mingaladon.

Smyth looked at the map again. 'You know, the ideal ploy would be to break up the Burma Rifles into guerrilla units to harass the enemy in front of a strong base held by our regular battalions. We could hold the enemy, giving time for reinforcements to come into Rangoon. And, if necessary, we could make another move back to the Sittang, which would be a good place to stand.'

'We'll have to ask for more reinforcements, sir.'

'I'll send General Hutton a report and stress the urgency for at least one division – I very much doubt we'll get more – otherwise, we'll be unlikely to stop the enemy. And as a start, I'm going to ask for 48 Brigade.'

'What about Mergui and Tavoy, sir?'

'I tell you, Simmy, I felt really sorry for their garrisons. Leaving them out on a limb. The airfields there are important, but the strength of the garrisons hardly equates with the importance. I'm sure we'll lose both, but I suppose it will look better on the report if we're seen to go down fighting.' Smyth paused for a moment. 'No, Simmy. I don't believe they have a chance.'

Chapter Two
Ambush at Kawkareik

C Company arrived in Rangoon after a long and tedious rail journey to Calcutta, followed by a rough sea crossing. But there was hardly enough time to disembark before Paul was given new instructions to move the company almost at once to Kyaikto in Lower Burma.

The Gurkhas loaded their belongings and stores onto lorries, which took them to Rangoon Railway Station, where they had to unload everything and manhandle it onto the train. Within half an hour, the train pulled out of the station, heading north for Pegu where the line branched, the main line going north to Mandalay while C Company's train followed the track to the east, across the vast paddy fields through Waw to the Sittang River.

As the train rattled over the Sittang Bridge, Paul could see no evidence of a strong guard on the bridge. It was the gateway to Rangoon from Lower Burma. If the Japs blew it up we'd be trapped, he thought. He looked down to the broad river. It had a dark, ominous look about it as it flowed out to the sea, rippling with a powerful current. For a moment he felt an anticipation of fear, as though the river was a serpent waiting for its prey.

Beyond the bridge the line turned sharply south-east to Kyaikto, where the company was to detrain. But when the train pulled up in the station, with squealing brakes and a loud hiss of steam, a young staff captain poked his head through the open window of Paul's compartment.

'Hello. You Cooper? Grant's the name. Sorry to mess you around. Change of orders, I'm afraid. Please tell your men to stay on the train. I've asked the station master to delay departure.'

Paul sent Gopiram to advise the subedar and then Grant opened out a quarter-inch map of the Kawkareik area and spread it across the seat. 'Let me explain – 16 Brigade is up in the Dawna Hills guarding Kawkareik. We are laying our heaviest bets on the Japs choosing that way to cross the border from Thailand. It's wild, hilly country, with dense jungle and close-knit bamboo. Used to be the old trade route from Raheng, the Thai border town, into Burma through the pass and 39 miles on to Kawkareik. Those 39 miles are motorable, but you can imagine what it is like: some positively scary, rickety bridges on the way.'

Grant moved his finger along the map. 'Then beyond Kawkareik the road continues westward for about 15 miles to Kyondo, a small village on the river route to Moulmein or Martaban. But at this time of the year it is possible to motor cross-country the 80-odd miles to Moulmein, although it means crossing the Haungtharaw on a ferry.

'Brigadier Jones has instructions to hold the enemy for as long as possible, but not at the expense of getting trapped. He is drastically short of troops to cover all the area around the pass. With two rivers behind him, including a car ferry, he certainly does not want the Japs to infiltrate and cut off his line of withdrawal.

'Now, we have just learned from a local source of a rough path which bypasses Kawkareik and comes out near Kyondo.' He pointed to the small quarter-inch map which, to Paul, seemed all jungle and closely ringed contours. 'While we don't think it will be used as the main push, it could still be an ideal route for a small group to slip through and lay an ambush between Kawkareik and Kyondo. The brigadier is keen to keep a watch on it, so your arrival at this time is a stroke of luck. If you stay on the train for the rest of the journey to Martaban, arrangements have been made to ship you upriver to Kyondo, where you'll be met by a guide. Now, have you any questions?'

'If I may make a point,' Paul said. 'There's another 70 miles or so to the railhead at Martaban and it will be dark by the time we reach it. The men have not eaten since this morning and there's our gear to be sorted out – we have rather more than ordinary marching order.'

'Ah, yes. You'll have to dump any surplus stuff at Martaban and leave someone to guard it. And as for a meal, you're right. Yes. OK, I'll get word to Martaban and arrange for rations and cooking facilities. Anyway, it is safer on the river at night because the Jap aircraft are a bit active during the day.'

Grant returned his map to its case, climbed down to the platform, saluted and marched briskly away. Paul walked along the platform to Tilbir's four-berth compartment which he shared with Jemedar Dilbahadur Gurung, the commander of 10 Platoon, Thandraj Limbu, the quartermaster havildar, and Ganesh Thapa, the havildar major. A runner was sent to bring the other platoon commanders and when they had all gathered in the compartment, the guard blew his whistle and the train moved out of the station on its way to Martaban.

Tilbir made sure Paul was comfortably seated on one of the lower berths, while the others settled themselves on the opposite bunk or cross-legged on the floor. Tilbir's orderly produced mugs of tea and Paul passed round his cigarettes. When they had all lit up, he told them of the change of plan.

Havildar Amarjit Limbu of 12 Platoon, the youngest of the commanders, seemed the most excited. 'Will we be fighting soon, sahib?'

The others laughed at Amarjit's enthusiasm. 'You should be more careful,' Jemedar Dilbahadur Gurung suggested.

Dilbahadur was a tough, squat man in his early thirties, with a short, thick neck and powerful shoulders.

'Why should Amarjit be more careful?' Paul asked.

It was Tilbir who answered. 'Because in Nepali terms he is a rich man. Of course, as the sahib knows, in Nepal a man does not need large sums of money to be rich, but his *kaakhi ama* has plenty of land and property in Darjeeling.'

'She was my father's younger brother's wife,' Amarjit explained. 'She and my uncle had no family. When my father died they adopted me as their son. My aunt is the clever one with the money – it was through her prodding and skill that my late uncle made his fortune.'

'She did not wish Amarjit to join the army,' Dilbahadur said. 'And if she knew he was about to go to war … My God!'

'She would certainly have much to say,' Amarjit agreed with feeling. 'She would also spend much time worshipping at the temple doing *puja* and giving the priests handfuls of money to say prayers and weave lucky spells to keep me safe from Japanese bullets. But I had to join the army, sahib. My father and his father before him were military men of some distinction.'

'His father was decorated twice in the Great War,' the subedar added. 'But he was badly wounded. He never really recovered and he died quite young.'

'And what about Jemedar Tule?' Paul asked, looking at 11 Platoon's commander, who was sitting cross-legged in a corner of the compartment; he was a quiet man, in his thirties. 'Has he a rich aunt?'

'He has somebody he calls his aunt,' Dilbahadur said quickly. 'But she is not rich and she is not his aunt!'

Jemedar Tule Pun took the general laughter with good humour. He rubbed his shaven head, his forehead creased in great lines, his eyes crinkled and his mouth stretched in a wonderful smile which brought a shine to his moon-shaped face. In the general repartee which followed, and at which Nepalis excelled, Paul sat back and relaxed. He was glad of this opportunity to be with his commanders in an atmosphere not stifled by strict discipline. He realised he was fortunate to be able to speak fluent Nepali and to have been brought up in a tea garden surrounded by Nepalis. Of course, there were differences between the peasants who worked on the gardens and the disciplined men of the regiment, but the basics were the same. After all, the platoon commanders had once been peasants themselves. As they talked, the compartment began to grow dark, signifying that a long day was coming to an end, the jungle merging into a dark mass of green as the train rushed past on the last leg of the journey to Martaban.

'This is as far as the lorries go,' a staff officer from 16 Brigade told them. The lorries had come off the narrow, bumpy cart track into a large open space surrounded on all sides by dense jungle rising high into the sky to blot out any view.

Earlier, the officer had met C Company on its arrival at Kyondo after a night trip up the Gyaing: a cold journey, the river enveloped in mist, and with daybreak came the eerie calls of birds and animals from behind the mist which thinned slowly in the sunrise.

The men debussed and then the lorries reversed and rumbled back onto the cart track like a herd of elephants, swaying more now that they were empty, and they were soon swallowed up in the jungle.

Paul turned to Tilbir. 'We will have a fifteen-minute break before moving off.'

The Gurkhas seemed to be in good humour. There had been time at Kyondo that morning for a meal of rice, dal and hot tea; now, the men smoked and chatted as though unconcerned about the dangers the next few days might bring. Armed with .303 Lee Enfields, a Bren gunner in each section, and the section commanders who had tommy guns, they looked tough, as though they could handle any enemy. But it worried Paul that they had not had time for more sessions on the rifle range.

Of course, they all had their khukuris, the national weapon of Nepal: 17 inches long from the top of the handle to the pointed tip of the 12 inch angled blade, honed to a sharpness that could behead a man with one stroke. The blade is usually made from steel railway tracks and even vehicle chassis and springs. Attached to the back of the sheath are two pockets, containing two small knives, one the *chakmak* or sharpener and flint maker, the other the *karda* for skinning, peeling and slicing. On the blade, near the handle, is a notch shaped like a half moon and jutting out of its middle is a small erection of metal like a penis, because this is a symbol of Hindu fertility and it is called *kaudi*. It also serves a useful purpose by allowing the blood to drip off, so the user does not make a bloody mess of his hand after removing his enemy's head – or maybe even a chicken, because the khukuri is also an everyday tool in the hills of Nepal, from cutting wood to decapitating a goat for the family meal. A Gurkha has probably had his own khukuri from boyhood, developing the skilled technique which has made the khukuri such a terrible weapon at close quarters in the hand of a Gurkha soldier who wears it sheathed in a frog on the waist belt.

'All right, fall in.' Paul swung his pack onto his back; it felt like a ton.

Everything he wanted he would have to carry, because the bulk of the company's kit, including the bedrolls, had been left at Martaban with the other company stores under the charge of Thandraj, the quartermaster havildar, and a small squad who had not been at all happy at staying behind, but there was really little choice. Everyone had to find room in his own pack for a blanket, a change of clothes and any personal belongings which seemed essential. Rations were a problem, solved by dividing it into small loads and distributing it among the men.

Paul was dressed like the Gurkhas: khaki shirt and shorts – the long, wide shorts which were the hallmark of the Indian Army at that time – thick stockings, puttees and black boots. Besides his pack, he had a haversack, a water bottle, a khukuri and a .38 Smith & Wesson, a weapon which he had fired on the range at OTS and although he proved fairly competent, he would have preferred something with more power. He was a good shot – there had been plenty of game in the tea garden and beyond in the wooded hills. He had also been able to fire a tommy gun on the range, near battalion headquarters, where the British sergeant major in charge had taken him under his wing as he had recognised promise, and Paul had proved a natural. You need to have control of a tommy gun; otherwise, your bullets could fly sky high and at a tangent in all the wrong directions. It was the weapon of choice Paul felt he should have in the jungle against the Japanese, but at that time it was considered ill-advised for an officer to carry one, in case he concentrated more on killing the enemy than moving his men tactically. Paul was determined to get hold of one as soon as possible – and when out of sight. When he had left the luggage guard at Martaban he had purloined two of their tommy guns, which he gave to Gopiram and Tilbir's orderly; the latter's he would no doubt take for himself at a later date.

The company moved out in single file, two men ahead with khukuris drawn, ready to cut a way through the jungle, followed by Paul and his orderly, Gopiram, and the leading unit which was Dilbahadur's 10 Platoon. They were soon in dense jungle, but the path was fairly clear as it wound its way through the bamboo and undergrowth. Now and again, the jungle encroached on the path and the Gurkhas slashed an opening with their khukuris.

As the day grew rapidly warmer, Paul's chinstrap was like an iron band and he could feel the sweat trickling down his back. Soon, the path became quite steep, the change in movement catching his calves, making the pack on his back seem even heavier.

He noticed that the jungle to his left was thinning out sufficiently for him to see that the path was skirting the back of a narrow *chaung* or stream. Then the path dropped into a hairpin bend and brought the company out onto the *chaung* bed. A bird rose with a sharp cry and flew up the *chaung* with a flash of colour. On the opposite bank there was a crash of bodies through the trees, followed by the whooping of a family of monkeys fading into the distance. Paul halted the column and Dilbahadur came forward to join him.

'Let us take a look a short way up ahead,' Paul said.

They scrambled over the rocky surface. The *chaung* bed was dry, except for small pools of water where swarms of butterflies hovered, dipping from time to time to drink. After a few yards the rocks gave way to sand and the path reappeared, winding up the right bank for about 50 yards along the top before swinging sharply away and into the jungle. The *chaung*, Paul noticed, was by now choked with undergrowth.

About 100 yards further on, the path dropped abruptly again into the *chaung*, having cut off a bend. Now, it was clear of undergrowth and once more the path crossed over to the left bank. Paul halted there and sent Gopiram to bring forward the subedar and the other platoon commanders.

When they arrived he said, 'Can you see a large force using this route?'

Tilbir suggested, 'Large enough, I should think, sahib, to come down behind Kawkareik and cause trouble on the road.'

Paul agreed. 'However, this path must continue for several miles to the top of the range. I do not think we need to go any further, so let us place 10 Platoon to watch the path here on the right bank. There is a good view as the path comes down off the other bank and the platoon could catch the Japanese in the *chaung*. Then, we will have HQ and 11 Platoon between here and where we first crossed it. And 12 Platoon further back on the left bank.'

Leaving Dilbahadur to place his platoon in its ambush position, with a listening post a short distance in front, Paul moved back about 50 yards and indicated a position for his HQ. Jemedar Tule of 11 Platoon then placed his three sections around Company HQ.

Paul returned along the path and across the *chaung* to where Amarjit was organising 12 Platoon. There was not much room because of the thick jungle, but one section had somehow climbed up the steep hill above and was digging its weapon pits beneath the undergrowth, completely hidden and in a great vantage point.

Paul returned to his HQ, where the construction of canopies from groundsheets, camouflaged by branches, to protect against the heavy overnight dew, was well under way. Later, when everyone had eaten an evening meal, he called a stand-to for half an hour after darkness, every man in the position he would occupy should there be an attack. Then he ordered a stand-down, apart from the sentries. There was nothing else to be done, so like the Gurkhas he turned in for the night.

With darkness the jungle grew cold. Paul, already wearing his army-issue jersey, wrapped a blanket around himself, but he still shivered and he hoped it was not from fear. Would he be afraid? He had been concerned about his young Gurkha recruits, but what about himself, just as much a recruit? Yes, what about himself – the first sight of the Japs, the first sound of a shot – how would he react? Oh, snap out of it, he reprimanded himself, go to sleep! His eyes pricked with tiredness, but still he could not sleep. Around him the jungle and the night mingled like lovers into one dark shape, but without any sound. The silence surprised him; he always believed that night in the jungle was full of sound, but apart from the cry of what he believed to be a tree lizard, and a cough from one of his men, nothing stirred.

Then there was a different call. A single cry from the depths of the jungle. A jackal? Or could it be a Jap imitating an animal? He reached involuntarily for his revolver, but none of his men moved. Then he relaxed a little, confident in the sentries. Or should he be? Should he go round the platoons to make sure? After all, like himself, none of the men had heard a shot fired in anger. But he was beginning to feel comfortably warm at last and suddenly he slipped happily into sleep.

The following morning after stand-down, Paul patrolled forward with a section from Tule's platoon. After a short distance the path turned away from the *chaung* and wound its way into the jungle-covered hills, widening out beneath a forest of tall teak trees and almost hidden beneath the brown leaves strewn over the forest floor. Paul saw no sign of human life and he returned to the company for the morning meal.

The next few days passed quietly and uneventfully, although every day the distant sound of Japanese bombers was heard as they carried out sorties on the main positions and machine-gunned the lines of communications.

On 19 January 1942, Paul decided to accompany the fatigue party to the lorry terminal to collect the much-needed rations the staff officer had promised would be there and he proved true to his word. In return, the Gurkhas brewed tea for the lorry driver and the staff officer, who was a friendly and talkative person.

'The Japs have captured Tavoy,' he said.

This was a small town on the Tenasserim coast some 170 miles south of Moulmein, isolated and an easy prey for the Japanese. Another 120 miles beyond Tavoy was Mergui, now in grave danger.

'We're in grave danger ourselves, come to that,' said the officer. 'Poor old "Jonah" Jones is in a terrible situation. He's got three battalions stretched over that wild country. Only one motor road through those hills. I doubt if we'll be able to hold out for long once the Nips attack. Incidentally, your 46 Brigade has arrived in Rangoon, but God knows if it will move up here in time.'

Gopiram asked if the sahib would like some more tea.

The officer drained his mug. 'Never say no to cha.' He held out his mug for a refill. He drank it quickly and then said, 'Well, cheer up. Things can't possibly get any worse,' and climbed into the lorry and looked out of the window. 'But if I were you I'd keep my ear to the ground. When the brigade moves out, it is going to move out very fast. See you around.'

Paul returned to the company and passed the information on to his platoon commanders. Then, early the following morning, Amarjit hurried over to report shots from the east, but Paul and Tilbir could hear nothing: sound in the jungle was not only deceptive as to distance, but sometimes shots could be heard several miles away and yet not within a few hundred yards. When they moved to Amarjit's position, however, they could hear what sounded like rifle fire, spasmodic, as though some current of air blew it across in gusts of sound. But was it rifle fire? Surely, Paul thought, the first action would be fought on the far side of the range, down on the Thaungyin River, which separated Thailand and Burma. Even allowing for the quirks of sound in the jungle, he did not think it possible; more likely burning bamboo a good deal closer.

In the early hours of 20 January 1942, the Japanese had crossed the border into Burma. A company from 1/7th Gurkha Rifles took the first fierce enemy onslaught and became isolated into groups that managed to fight their way out and rejoin the brigade several days later. The enemy was now poised to advance along the main road to Kawkareik, which was evacuated in the early hours of the twenty-first, Jones' HQ moving back to Milestone 12.

As no British reinforcements were immediately available, if 16 Brigade was overwhelmed there would be little to stop the enemy from sweeping into Moulmein. So, when that evening the brigadier was informed that his forces, positioned in the hills further up the road, could not guarantee to defend much longer without being cut off, he ordered a general withdrawal to Kyondo.

Meanwhile, C Company, out on a limb in its ambush position, had no idea at that time of what was going on in the rest of the area. But as the day was punctuated by distant "crumps" and machine-gun fire, it seemed that the action must have reached the vicinity of Kawkareik.

The company spent another cold, wretched night disturbed by periodic loud explosions and occasional bursts of machine-gun fire and with daybreak of the twenty-second, Paul decided to take out a small patrol.

'Listen,' Paul said to the naik in charge, 'we will have two men forward, then four – including you and me – and then two men further back. If we meet the Japanese, the two at the rear must turn and run straight back to the camp and alert the subedar sahib.'

The little naik nodded his head vigorously and gave the two rear men definite orders. The patrol moved out of the company position, across the *chaung* and past the listening post. A couple of Gurkhas scouted ahead, next came Paul followed by the naik and two men, and then there was a good gap to the runaway men.

The patrol followed the path which wound through dense jungle until, just before reaching the open teak forest, it gave a final twist and for a moment the first scout was out of sight. There was a shout, followed by a burst of machine-gun fire, and screaming metal cut the sides of the jungle and ricocheted off the path. The second scout turned the bend to look and then cried out, his rifle flying into the air as he spun and collapsed into the undergrowth.

Paul turned to the naik. 'Have the back men gone?'

'Yes, huzoor.'

Paul doubled forward to the second scout who was still alive, pulling him back out of sight of the enemy. Then he dropped to the ground and crawled on his stomach to look round the bend. The first scout was obviously dead. About 50 yards above on the open ground, positioned behind the huge teak trees, he could see the shadowy Japanese and hear their excited shouts. Then there was a sound like corks being drawn from bottles, followed shortly after by mortar bombs exploding on either side of the path. And all the time the machine-gunner fired bursts, with rifle shots now added.

'Back to the company on the double,' Paul ordered, hoisting the wounded scout over his shoulder.

The naik picked up the wounded man's rifle. 'Quick, sahib!'

They ran back along the path, the Japanese machine-gunner still firing blindly into the jungle and mortar bombs exploding at intervals. Further along the path, two riflemen crouched to give cover as they passed through before following on behind. The wounded Gurkha was a small man, but as Paul jogged along the path he seemed to get heavier with every stride. Paul felt himself swaying into the jungle wall, the undergrowth ripping at his legs, finding the gap between stocking tops and shorts, spreading thorns like claws with feline fury.

Then somebody was saying, 'Leave him to us, sahib,' and it was Dilbahadur who had come forward with a few men to see him safely back.

Paul reported to the subedar, 'I do not know how many there were. I saw nine or ten; but they could have been an advance group.'

'How far behind, sahib?'

The firing had stopped. 'I should not think they have moved forward at all. Do you think we should attack them?'

Tilbir hesitated for a moment. 'No, sahib. We are in a strong position here. Let them come to our guns.'

'Agreed. Keep everyone in their firing positions.'

Paul returned to his headquarters and only then did he feel himself begin to shake; a tremble in his legs, a slight twitching in his fingers as he fully realised what had happened in the last quarter of an hour. He had not panicked under the pressure of fire, but now he was feeling shit-scared. Hell, this would not do at all. He made a big effort to pull himself together.

The company waited for the anticipated attack. An hour passed in silence, except when a soldier tried to stifle a cough, or monkeys called in the distance, or some birds sang among the trees. Once, Amarjit came across to say he could hear fierce firing towards the south. Paul still believed the main push was there and they had only bumped a marauding group.

He was standing in his headquarters, looking towards Dilbahadur's platoon, when the silence was shattered by rifle shots and a Bren gun. Almost at that same instant, a machine-gun and rifles opened fire from across the *chaung*, from the densely covered far bank where Paul had thought it would be impossible for the enemy to infiltrate.

There was a sound like an axe hitting a tree trunk and a Gurkha signaller was on his back, a bullet through his head, the chinstrap snapped, the hat lying on the ground, filled with brains and matter spewed out by the force of the bullet. Paul stood like a statue for a moment and then he felt himself being hurled to the ground, lying with Gopiram restraining him, bullets a few inches from their faces, hacking divots out of the ground like a bad golfer.

Paul knew he must force himself to his feet and organise a counter-attack, but as he fought to overcome his fear and put his thoughts into action, the weight of fire around him eased and stopped. He scrambled to his feet, the subedar running to join him as the din of battle now raged out of sight, behind the dense jungle which covered the far bank of the *chaung*. The Japanese had not seen Amarjit's section, well dug in and hidden, and were paying for their mistake as the Gurkhas raked them with deadly, close-range fire. Shouts and screams intermingled with shots and the blast of hand grenades. Amarjit threw in another section and then the fight moved towards 10 Platoon. Paul, running forwards, saw three or four enemy soldiers hurl themselves off the path into the *chaung*, only to be massacred by Dilbahadur's men.

Then there was silence, until from behind the jungle opposite Dilbahadur's position, Amarjit called out, 'It is all right. Do not shoot. It is me. Havildar Amarjit.'

'Come out,' Paul called.

Amarjit stepped down into the *chaung*, a look of triumph on his face which was marked with the dirt of battle. Even his aunt would be proud of him now, Paul thought, as he gave him a "well done". Paul and Tilbir returned to headquarters, where they sat on a groundsheet to discuss the situation.

'I need your help, subedar sahib. Your military experience is greater than mine,' Paul observed.

'But in this kind of war, I am no wiser than you – and the sahib has already done very well.'

'The sahib has had too much good luck ... what should we do now? I feel we should move out of this position.'

There was something comforting in Tilbir's calm appearance, looking smart in spite of the conditions. 'Yes, sahib, we must move. The question is when and where? My feeling is that the Japanese would not have sent two separate groups down the track. And for the moment we are in a strong position over here.'

Paul agreed and the subedar continued, 'And if I may suggest, the men have not had a hot meal since yesterday.'

'Then let us put that right straightaway. Meanwhile, I will take a patrol up the track.'

Tilbir looked alarmed. 'But you are in command of the company. Jemedar Dilbahadur should go.'

A few moments later, Dilbahadur took out one of his sections and followed the path out to where the Gurkha scout had been killed, taking great care in case of ambush, but there was no sign of the enemy. The dead scout lay in the undergrowth; he had obviously been searched and his rifle was missing. They carried his body back to the company position, where Paul decided to have an order group and soon the platoon commanders were gathered around.

'How many casualties?' he asked.

Company Havildar Major Ganesh Thapa told him that three riflemen had been killed and three wounded. 'The wounded scout is a stretcher case, but I think he will be all right for the moment; the medical orderly has given first aid. The others are walking wounded.'

Regarding the enemy, fifteen bodies had been counted. There were also several Arisaka 6.5 bolt action rifles, an LMG – 6.25 Nambu, similar in appearance to the Bren – a mortar, a Jap sword, several ugly looking bayonets, a Jap flag and various documents.

'It will be dark in a couple of hours,' Paul said. 'My plan is that with darkness, we will withdraw to the lorry terminal and wait there until daybreak. The brigade has orders not to become trapped and I am sure is already on the way out. The explosions we have heard are probably demolitions to delay the enemy.' They then discussed and agreed the order of the march for the move out. 'Is there anything I have forgotten?' Paul asked finally.

'What about the dead men, sahib?' Ganesh asked.

God! What do we do about the dead?

Tilbir saved him. 'Of course, as Hindus, they should be cremated, but I think the sahib will agree that we cannot risk the fire; it would also take some time. May I suggest, sahib, that we bury them temporarily, so that no wild animals can savage them? We should make a note of the map reference, in case at some future date the bodies can be recovered.'

'I seem to remember, subedar sahib, reading that in World War I, many Gurkhas were never properly buried or cremated. But they were not forgotten, their names listed on monuments for posterity. So, all right, we will leave them, but I hope not forget them. And as for the captured weapons, much as I would like to, we cannot take them with us. Who knows what obstacles lie ahead of us? And we must also carry the wounded man and our own weapons, so render them useless. But we will keep all the documents found on the bodies and the Japanese flag.'

He was very pleased with the way the men had behaved in the heat of battle, in spite of not being fully trained and being in action for the first time, and he told his platoon commanders to pass on his words of praise to the men.

After the order group had broken up, Paul tried to settle down, but the last hour to nightfall seemed to drag. He could not stop himself from being tense, waiting for a sudden shot from behind the jungle wall to signal another full-blooded attack. He could not have welcomed darkness more when it came at last and after a half-hour stand-to, he was able with great relief to give the order to move out.

Dilbahadur led his platoon back quietly, first through Tule's platoon, next Amarjit's and then down the path for about half a mile, where he was to take up a position. Next, the wounded party moved out. The scout was carried past on a stretcher made of a groundsheet and stout branches and was covered with a blanket against the cold, which was beginning to sweep through the *chaung* in the first makings of a light mist. Paul put a hand out to touch him as encouragement and he found it seized fiercely for a moment. And then the Gurkha was gone, carried off into the night.

After Company HQ had moved out, Tule's men tagged on behind and through Amarjit's platoon. Lastly, Amarjit moved his sections out. Paul marched with his headquarters. It was too dark to see, but he took a final look at the far corner of the bank where his men now lay. Then he forced his mind back to the present, negotiating the rocky section of the *chaung*. The stretcher-bearers almost stumbled but recovered with a clatter of loose stones and Paul held his breath, but the noise was swallowed up in the night.

They came out of the hills about three hours later after a number of false alarms, which had left Paul's heart beating like mad, and a strength-sapping trudge down the winding jungle path, forever stopping and starting as happens when some sixty men are moving in single file in the darkness. At last they reached the lorry terminal point and somehow, Paul managed to indicate where the platoons should take up their positions before he sank into a restless sleep and finally into a deeper one.

When he awoke it was with a start. He blinked because the day was bright. And it was quiet. He had slept in a crouched position, enveloped by the undergrowth, and he felt stiff, his boots and puttees soaked by the dew. There was a blanket over his shoulders, damp on the outside but warm on the inside. Gopiram, without a doubt. He struggled to his feet and looked around at the sleeping forms lying everywhere. Must be Sunday, he thought.

He rubbed his hand over his face, which felt only slightly prickly, and was thankful that he didn't have to shave every day. Then, as he stood there, a memory flooded his mind and he remembered where he was. It was not some training exercise. If the Japs came now!

Paul shook the bundle that was Gopiram. The Gurkha sat up, bleary-eyed, looking like a little ornamental gnome in a suburban garden in his woollen cap comforter. Then he came awake and Paul said, 'Rouse them, but quietly.'

As Paul stumbled out of the small circle of bushes which had concealed Company HQ and onto the jungle path, he saw Amarjit's platoon sprawled in sleep. My God! He walked quickly up the path, stopping himself from breaking into a run, and to his great relief he found the sentries awake. A Bren post was manned, the gunner and his number two giving him a half smile.

The time was dead on nine. Why had they not awakened the company for a stand-to? He decided not to ask, as it would be better coming later through their own platoon commander. Instead, he asked, 'Any sign of the enemy?'

'No, huzoor,' replied the Bren-gunner. 'Only a tiger calling out from the far valley. Hungry and sounding bad-tempered, so I think we must have driven off his game. For a moment I thought I was back in the Terai.'

He was talking about the belt of tropical forest below the colder ranges of Nepal. Paul almost wished he were there, too.

'Right, now wake up your platoon.'

By the time Paul returned to his HQ everyone was awake. Tilbir looked a bit sheepish, Paul thought, as the Gurkha's soft brown eyes met his. There was no glint in them this morning, but no doubt that would be put right quite soon.

'I think, sahib,' Paul said, 'now that we are all refreshed from our Sunday morning lie-in, that we will have a stand-to, so that everyone knows his position.'

In a few moments men were flying in all directions and half an hour later, after stand-down, Paul called his order group together. While they talked, the men cooked rice and brewed tea, Paul having decided to risk the chance of the smoke being seen.

'Brigade must have pulled out by now,' Paul observed.

'This must be so,' Tilbir agreed. 'We can hear no firing from their direction. In fact, no firing at all since yesterday.'

'They must have pulled out before becoming involved,' Paul suggested.

'But no one has come to warn us,' Amarjit complained.

'Who knows what may have happened,' Paul defended the brigade staff. 'Somebody sent to tell us may have been killed on the way. We must take it that no one will come now.'

He looked at his quarter-inch map, which was not of much help, but, recalling the lorry trip a few days earlier, he reckoned that they were about 10 miles from Kyondo. His officers agreed they should make that village their destination. After they had all eaten he gave the order to march, deciding to follow the cart track, although the danger of ambush would be greater, because he just did not relish cutting through the jungle or sorting out a maze of path to find the right way. Besides, he wanted to reach the village before nightfall.

They made good progress along the cart track. The two walking wounded – their section comrades keeping a close watch – managed to keep up. The little Gurkha on the stretcher was being very brave."

Paul could hear no sound of any distant activity and he could see no further than the man in front or to the next bend in the track. The dense jungle wall made him feel like a caterpillar in a cocoon and what world he would emerge into when the jungle cocoon burst open was anyone's guess. He just hoped that part of 16 Brigade would still be at Kyondo and that there would be a chance of river transport and rations, because the last of the rice had been finished with the morning meal.

When the leading platoon reached the road, Paul went forward to where the scouts were crouched, looking through the foliage. He stepped carefully out onto the road. The same stillness. No sound of traffic in the distance. About half a mile to his right were the rooftops of Kyondo village. Above the rooftops, rising into a hot blue sky, was a column of thick black smoke.

'What do you think?' Paul asked Tilbir, who had come up to join him.

The subedar took off his Gurkha felt hat and rubbed the stubble of his shaven head. 'That is a bad sign, sahib. I think equipment is being destroyed.'

'Well, the only thing to do is find out. I will go forward with Tule's platoon. You keep the rest of the company here, sahib.'

The platoon moved forward gingerly, two sections up, one each side of the road, with instructions to dive into the jungle at the first sound of traffic. As they neared the village, Paul could see no sign of movement; the villagers had probably run away to hide in the jungle and no doubt some were watching him now, out of sight behind the thick cover.

At Tule's order, a section doubled forward to the edge of the village to take up positions underneath and around the houses, which were raised off the ground on wooden piles in the traditional Burmese style. Paul saw the section leader stand up suddenly and look further into the village as though he were at attention on parade. Then he turned abruptly and waved. Paul and Tule ran forwards to join him, staring in horror and disbelief at the wreckage of more than a dozen vehicles, some set alight by petrol, the canvas black confetti, the metal framework twisted out of shape, engines smashed beneath crumpled bonnets by pickaxes or charges of explosives. All around the graveyard of vehicles the ground was littered with equipment, from personal belongings to military material, burnt to smouldering rags, and a large dump which was still sending up the column of black smoke.

My God! What was the transport doing here? The vehicles should have taken a turn-off further back along the road from Kawkareik, leading to the Kya-in ferry across the Haungtharaw River, some 8 miles south-west of Kawkareik. The ferry was antiquated and could take only one vehicle at a time. Then there was another stretch of rough track to a second ferry, before meeting up with a fairly good dry-weather road to Moulmein. Meanwhile, troops would take boats down the Gyaing to Moulmein. But something must have gone drastically wrong.

What Paul did not know was that the withdrawal had turned sour. All the transport had been brought into Kawkareik just before dark on 21 January 1942 and the convoy got away from the town at 20.00 hours. The drivers were very nervous, raw and alarmed at the slightest sound. When they reached Kya-in in the dark, the first vehicle onto the ferry was a heavy sappers' truck but, on reaching the far bank, the ferry was not properly tied up and when the truck was being driven off, the moorings gave way. As the truck slipped into the river it took the ferry with it and so marooned the brigade's transport north of the river.

Meanwhile, the brigade carried out its withdrawal, the most forward troops moving back from the crest of the range to Kawkareik. There was a great deal of noise all along the road as kit and ammunition was set alight and the sappers detonated road and bridge demolitions to delay the enemy. Spread throughout 22 January, the brigade arrived at Kyondo in groups and the last of the transport and surplus kit was destroyed.

Brigadier Jones sent his wounded downriver in the only two boats available in the village. Then the brigade followed the Gyaing southwards in groups along the left bank, through rough country, eventually meeting up at Tarana, a steamer station, after a long, weary march with nothing to eat. They had to wait until 04.00 hours on 24 January, when three paddle steamers arrived to take them on to Martaban, where they disembarked some five hours later.

As Paul stood in Kyondo village, on the afternoon of 23 January, not knowing at that time what had happened, he could only surmise the worst: that the Japanese had cut off most of the brigade back at Kawkareik and only a few had managed to escape.

His thoughts were distracted by a slight scuffle and then Tule appeared with a Burmese villager. The man was very frightened, crying out in Burmese, waving his arms. When Tule brought him up to Paul, the man pointed frantically towards the river. But none of them could speak Burmese or even grasp the meaning of his sign language.

At that moment an Indian appeared, in Burmese clothes, wearing a sun hat. 'Sir! Sir!' he called out. 'I speak English jolly good. They went down the river.'

'Who did?'

'The Breetish Army. Many thousands. All yesterday. They came at different times. Blowing up lorries and much goods as you can see. Then they left – towards Moulmein, I think.'

'Downriver, in boats?'

'No, sir. Only two boats in the village and they put the wounded in them and sent them off down the river. Then the army marched off along riverbank.'

'And the Japanese?'

'No sign as yet, sahib. Thank God! Although Japanese planes came over yesterday to bomb the village. But I think they are not too far behind now. You should get away quickly.'

'Where are the villagers?'

'All gone. Run away. The government officer – the SDO Thakin – told us to go hide when he was passing through on his way out.'

'Why did you not go?'

'I did, sir, but had to come back for one or two things I forget.'

'When did the British Army go?'

'All gone by yesterday.'

The villager pointed out the route which, apparently, the brigade had taken the previous day. Dusk was near as C Company crossed the village ford and took a well-defined path to a bend in the Gyaing. Then they followed a rough track along the left bank for about half an hour, before moving well into the jungle to hide up for the night.

It was a miserable night, cold and wet, the mist swirling across the river into the jungle, and Paul was worried about the wounded scout and some of the men with a history of malaria; the dampness could bring on attacks during the night. There had been no reviving mug of hot tea, because there was no way he could have risked fires that night. In time, experience would teach him that it was safer to have fires at night in the jungle rather than in the day.

The river was much noisier than the heart of the jungle, every bird cry sharp across the water and the undergrowth rustling as animals of all sizes went down to drink. He just could not fall asleep, every sound jerking him awake, to hold his breath, wondering if it were Japanese, until at last daylight began to show through the mist like sunlight through the slits of a blind. He immediately sent a patrol upriver and on its return, about an hour later, they reported no enemy movement, so he ordered the company to march at once. He wanted to put a good distance between themselves and Kyondo.

After a hard two hours' march along the jungle path, Paul called a halt and let the men brew up. Thank goodness there was no shortage of tea bags and powdered milk – the hot tea and a cigarette made him feel a good deal better and the men also, no doubt. But, as he had feared, two of the men had suffered attacks of malaria. With the help of other riflemen they had managed to keep up and some aspirins from the medical orderly helped them to sweat it out.

The company continued its march until an hour before nightfall, but not covering any great distance because the path became less distinct and the jungle encroached across it, having to be cut aside so often that Paul was certain the brigade had not used this route. The Indian in the village must obviously have sent them the wrong way.

Paul again moved the company deeper into the jungle for the night; another difficult one, he expected. But through sheer weariness he nodded off quite quickly, only to be awoken by urgent shaking.

'Careful, sahib,' Gopiram warned in case he spoke loudly in the confused moment of awakening. 'Dilbahadur Sahib is here.'

The tough, stocky jemedar crawled forwards. 'Sahib, I think there is a fire not far from us. One of my sentries saw a faint gleam of firelight for a moment and called me. I looked for a long time, thinking he was mistaken, but suddenly I, too, saw just a glimmer as the wind blew the leaves apart for a moment. It is only one camp fire, I think.'

Paul accompanied Dilbahadur stealthily through the jungle to the forward post. The mist was beginning to creep up, slowly filling the hollow which lay beneath them, ascending the slope on the other side which was a dark mass of jungle. The sentry had placed two sticks as pointers towards the place where he had seen the fire. Paul looked along the sticks, but there was now only a wall of jungle. He waited about half an hour, but no flame revealed itself and then the mist finally curtailed any further chance.

Telling the sentry to keep a close watch, Paul returned to his HQ. There was or had been a camp fire, of that he had no doubt; Dilbahadur's sharp eyes were sufficient proof for him. But who had lit the fire? Some stragglers from the brigade seemed the most likely. But Japanese? He knew enough about the enemy now to realise that it was possible.

Dilbahadur agreed with him, but Paul said, 'We must wait till the morning. It would be foolish to attempt anything in the dark.'

In the morning, when the company had stood-to quietly, Paul sent a section on patrol about a mile back towards Kyondo, while he took out another section and moved forward. The hollow, he found, was full of elephant grass and it hid a small stream about waist deep but easily waded. The far side the path was free of jungle and was more defined. But the section leader, experienced in hunting wild game, declared that the brigade had not come this way. After another half a mile, Paul turned back to the camp. The second patrol returned at about the same time, to report no sign of any close enemy pursuit.

Calling the platoon commanders together, Paul said, 'We can either continue along the path and leave whoever is up on the hill alone or we can investigate.'

'Sahib,' said Tilbir, 'could not a boat have been taken from the river, pulled up the stream and hidden in the elephant grass?'

Paul agreed. 'But it must be a very long chance.'

'But worthwhile sparing a little time to look.' Tilbir was concerned about the wounded scout who had become delirious and there had been another case of malaria that morning.

'Then we will have a look,' Paul said to his men's obvious relief. 'We will move out in a few minutes, as though we were continuing our march, until we pass out of sight round the far side of the hill. I shall then take two sections and return through the belt of thick jungle I noticed on my patrol this morning and down into the elephant grass from that side. Meanwhile, I think we should leave a section in position here; in fact, where the sentry was when he saw the fire. And in hiding, in case somebody tries to escape that way.' He turned to Dilbahadur. 'As your section is already in the right place that is the one I shall leave behind and I think you had best remain with it. As for the other sections …' Paul looked at Tilbir because he did not want the men to think he favoured any particular platoon.

Tilbir designated two sections from 11 Platoon.

'And I must come with the sahib,' Tule said quickly. His platoon had suffered the most casualties but had still to fire a shot in anger.

They moved out of camp, Amarjit's platoon leading, and waded into the stream, the mist clearing rapidly. Beyond the *chaung* they came into thick jungle again and after a short distance Paul halted the company, leaving it in Tilbir's command. Then, with Tule and his sections, Paul retraced his steps to the edge of the jungle and climbed through the tall trees with low shrub interlaced and groups of thicker, prickly undergrowth. The mist, which he had hoped might give him some cover, was thinning out quickly in a warmer morning than usual.

Paul struggled through the thick undergrowth, trying not to make much sound. The tommy gun he had armed himself with for the occasion began to feel heavy. On either side of him, the Gurkhas moved quietly and much more easily.

As he fought his way through a shrub, the ground fell sharply from under his feet and he slithered down a fall of red earth where a large tree had once stood, the clatter of loose stones sounding like a landslip. He came to his feet quickly, bursting through a thin screen of jungle and out into an open space with a Gurkha at his heels.

As Paul came through the tangle of creepers, which snapped under his weight, he took in the scene before him: the still-glowing embers of a fire and around it four men. They looked at each other for a moment, Paul hesitating in case they should be Burmese villagers. But one of

36

them jumped to his feet and fired, and Paul heard the Gurkha coming up behind him give a low cry. Then Paul was firing, raking the man with a burst, sending him sprawling into the fire. The other three were seizing their weapons. Paul's tommy gun clattered in the confined space, echoing between the trees. He saw another man fall. Shots whined past him. Then a fusillade of fire from his right dropped the two remaining men in their tracks.

Tule was shouting, 'Sahib! Are you all right?'

Paul glanced over his shoulder. The little Gurkha rifleman was sitting on his haunches, holding an arm but grinning to show he was not badly hurt. In great relief, Paul walked over to the camp fire.

'Look, sahib,' Tule said excitedly, opening a bundle which contained Japanese uniforms.

One of the men called out, 'There is a path down here to the stream.'

'Wait!' Paul shouted in alarm. 'Dilbahadur's men are on the far side. We do not want anyone shot by mistake. I will go first and call out, so he knows who it is.'

He led the way, helloing across to Dilbahadur, who answered. Following the path as it wound into the elephant grass, he found four boats, well concealed from the view of anyone approaching along the riverbank. They were large craft, each equipped with an outboard motor and capable of taking about twenty men. It would seem that the enemy had infiltrated men in disguise to station boats at various points along the river for the oncoming army to use in its attack on Moulmein.

But they were not going to use these boats.

Chapter Three
Siege of Moulmein

When Paul and his company reached Moulmein their arrival caused quite a stir, because it was feared that they might be part of a Japanese invasion. Fortunately, they were identified before becoming the target of a fusillade of bullets. Steamers had picked up 16 Brigade two days' march from Kyondo and ferried them to Martaban, so no one knew of Paul's whereabouts.

The little Gurkha scout received immediate medical attention before being evacuated to hospital in Rangoon – the doctor in Moulmein holding out high hopes for his complete recovery. The walking wounded refused to be evacuated after receiving first aid. The man with the head wound said he had once been hit by a coconut without any ill effects, so a bullet graze was nothing to worry about. The Gurkhas with arm wounds said they were still able to wield their khukuris with their good hands, which was all that mattered. Paul was quite moved by their courage; the other Gurkhas seemed to take it as a matter of course.

The company was royally treated – able to bathe, do some laundry and have a decent meal – and that fine battalion, 4/12th Frontier Force Regiment, took them under its wing.

Next day, Major General Smyth arrived on a visit from his headquarters, which he had moved to Kyaikto. Inwardly, he was still fuming. The blame for the shambles at Kawkareik had been laid squarely, but not fairly, on Brigadier "Jonah" Jones and his men: he had withdrawn too early; they had not fought with true spirit. This was the verdict of General Hutton, the Army Commander, and Wavell, the Supreme Commander, conducting the war by remote control, the one at Rangoon, the other 2,000 miles away in Java.

They ignored the fact that Jones had taken command of the brigade only a few weeks earlier, that he had a Burma Rifles battalion switched with his more experienced Frontier Force Regiment and that a large percentage of the soldiers were raw recruits. The knives were out to skin him, but Smyth managed to divert the blades.

The telegraphic air between Java, Rangoon and London was hot with messages, all trying to apportion blame elsewhere and at the same time indicate that the situation was not really as bad as it seemed. The enemy had been allowed "a cheap victory", according to Wavell, who estimated the Jap invasion force as "comparatively small"; in fact, two thirds of a division. But there would be no more withdrawals – 17 Division was to stand firm!

Smyth was told to defend Moulmein with 2 Burma Brigade, which consisted of four small battalions and a mountain battery, but looking around the town, he knew that at least two brigades would be necessary to make a reasonable defence of the place. Its vital points were widely dispersed over a 12-mile perimeter: the airfield, the supply depot, the ammunition dump and the river quays, which were Moulmein's line of communication to Martaban and Rangoon.

If Moulmein was to be held for a space of time, even for appearance's sake, then a skirmishing force of say, battalion strength, would have been sufficient. A brigade was a third of his command and it could so easily be lost.

He noticed the small group of Gurkhas and a staff officer reminded him of C Company's action and escape to Moulmein in the Japanese boats.

'Oh, yes,' the general said, stopping to talk to Paul, listening with great interest to his account of the action. It made the general feel a lot better. He told Paul, 'I visited the Kawkareik area a few days before the Jap invasion. It was certainly very difficult country – wild, closed in. The night I stayed there a hungry tiger roared in the vicinity and I thought at the time how appropriate it was to the environment.'

'It was still there some nights later, sir. Or its mate – and it still sounded very hungry,' Paul said.

The general smiled. 'Let us hope it has since satisfied its hunger by devouring a Jap or two.

'Now, what's happening to you? I take it your battalion has arrived in Kyaikto.'

'Can we stay here, sir? My company could give a boost to morale and provide an extra hand.'

Smyth looked at Paul for a moment and the young lieutenant felt a little chilly, wondering if, for a 20-year-old, he was being too forward. But he remembered that the general had not been much older when he had won the VC in 1915.

Smyth said at last, 'I think you are right; a little bit of experience would not go amiss.'

Later, when Paul led his company onto the sharp ridge above Moulmein, he had a superb view of the town which jutted out like the single horn of an Indian rhino into the mouth of the Salween, facing – 4 miles northwards across the river – the promontory of Martaban, whose low hills stretched north and west towards the high-rising Thaton Hills.

The town, with its timber, saw and rice mills, and over half a dozen jetties, extended some 2 miles across the northern tip of the horn and then along the west side in a narrow front for some 3 miles. The ridge, running through the middle of the horn, dominated the town. Atop the ridge, the great pagodas gleamed in the sunlight, the magnificent Kyaikthanlan Pagoda reaching 152 feet into the sky: Kipling's old Moulmein Pagoda, where his soldier first saw the Burmese girl on the *Road to Mandalay*.

Evidence of enemy air raids was clear: the blackened framework of burned-out huts in the bazaar and the crumbled shells of houses dotted among the various governmental and residential parts of the town. There had been seven air raids between 3 and 23 January, mainly on the airfield, which was a few miles from the town, although there was nothing hostile to destroy. Following the raids on the town itself, most of the Burmese population had fled to the surrounding countryside. Some had stayed behind to loot, but the town was under martial law and several looters were shot. The last air raid had been on the twenty-third, when nearly thirty bombers and fighters had attacked the airfield.

Away from the town, to the north-east, spread vast paddy fields and beyond these loomed the jungle-coated Dawna Range, a constant reminder to Paul of his first conflict with the enemy. Southwards, dense jungle and rubber plantations extended towards the Taungnyo Hills and disappeared into the far horizon.

It was a beautiful sight, and a peaceful one, the tinkling in the wind of the hundreds of little bells which festooned the pagodas emphasising its tranquillity. Yet, somewhere out there, probably in that stretch of dense jungle and close order rubber plantations to the south-east of Moulmein, lurked the ruthless soldiers of *55 Division*. Soon, the pagodas which crowned the ridge could be blasted by shell fire, the whole place erupting in the frightening war cries of the advancing enemy and the screams of the wounded and the dying. The sharp tang of cordite would mingle with the smell of fear and sweat.

Paul shook the thoughts from his head as he entered the compound of a large bungalow where he had been told to position his company. There had been a general evacuation some days earlier of British officials and civilians, so Paul was surprised to see someone on the veranda. Because the bungalow was raised on high teak piles in the typical Burmese style, he could not see the person distinctly. At first he thought it was a boy and then he realised it was a girl as she moved to the front of the veranda – or maybe a young woman in khaki shorts and blouse, with long, suntanned legs, a slim figure and blonde hair. She was quite attractive. Could be eighteen, maybe more.

'Hello!' Paul greeted her.

She remained silent. No answering smile.

From within the bungalow a woman called, 'Who is it, Sue?'

'The Gurkhas, Mummy. Come to commandeer our bungalow.'

Her mother came out onto the veranda. A tall, good-looking woman in her early forties.

Paul approached and saluted. 'Sorry. I was told the bungalow was empty.'

'It will be, tomorrow.' She smiled, but it seemed a sad smile. This lovely bungalow had been her home for several years and now she would be leaving it to face a life which would never be the same. 'I'm Mary Whitcomb. And my daughter, Sue.'

Paul introduced himself.

'Well, don't mind us,' she said. 'You've got your job to do. I don't suppose the Japs will take care to avoid the herbaceous borders, so just dig your trenches where you must. We've had a go ourselves, as you can see.'

Paul noticed a couple of slit trenches.

Mrs Whitcomb explained, 'They were well used during the air raids, although luckily no bombs fell nearby. Well, you must get on. Afternoon tea in about an hour. Perhaps you'd care to join us.'

Paul did not know whether to smile at – or admire – this attempt to keep life normal.

She disappeared into the bungalow and Sue melted into the shadows on the veranda. Paul hesitated for a moment, attracted by this strange, shy girl. Tilbir coughed apologetically and Paul took the hint.

They walked across the compound and beyond it to the eastern edge of the ridge, looking down to the Ataran River, about 2 miles away, winding into the Salween.

'That is our front, subedar sahib. We will have two platoons forward and one in reserve near the bungalow, where I will have my headquarters.'

Paul turned back towards the bungalow. The men were soon digging their trenches, working out fields of fire, their shirts off, chattering away, laughing. It pleased him to see that their morale was high.

At the bungalow, Gopiram and the rest of Company HQ were standing about, not seeming to know where to go or what to do. Paul quickly explained, 'We will move into the bungalow tomorrow, when the *memsahibs* have gone. Meanwhile, spread out beneath the house.'

Paul continued on his way a short distance west of the bungalow, where the men of 10 Platoon were also digging their trenches. Apart from being in reserve, this platoon would watch the western approach to the ridge in case the enemy infiltrated from the south and then attacked up the ridge from that direction.

He was talking to Dilbahadur when the jemedar's eyes flicked expectantly to a point over Paul's shoulder. Paul turned quickly and saw Sue approaching, but a different Sue, in a frock now, looking like a young woman. And she actually smiled.

'Tea is ready if you'd like to come up to the bungalow. Mummy says your men can use the kitchen.'

'That's very kind of her. I'll just pass that on and then I'll join you for tea.'

A few moments later he followed Sue up the stairs to the veranda and into the cool interior of the bungalow. The large sitting room was furnished with a three-piece suite separated from the dining room by a folding Japanese screen, with a design of black dragons cavorting in an orange sea. Mrs Whitcomb was seated on an occasional chair near a small table, which supported a tea tray and a large tin of Huntley & Palmers biscuits.

'Do sit down, Mr Cooper – no, Paul. Yes, Paul will be friendlier. I'm afraid there is no bread for sandwiches. It is all rather chaotic as you can imagine. And no servants, either.' She poured the tea.

Paul passed a cup to Sue, and the biscuits, and then helped himself.

'They never would have deserted us,' Mrs Whitcomb said.

'Who is that?' Paul asked.

'Why, the servants. But George, my husband, thought they should go while they had the chance. They all came from around here, so they left yesterday for their villages, taking their families with them. They went reluctantly. Didn't they, Sue?'

'Poor Aung Tin cried a lot. He'd been with us the longest and he probably knew we would never meet again.'

'We mustn't be too pessimistic, Sue.'

'Oh, Mummy, it's no use closing our eyes. Moulmein cannot hold out for long.' She looked quickly at Paul. 'Oh – I am sorry.'

'That's all right, Sue. I know it as well as you do. But I don't think the intention is to fight to the bitter end. Just to hold the Japs back for a while before evacuating to Martaban.'

'Do you really think so?' Mrs Whitcomb looked slightly relieved at the possibility that this good-looking young man's life might be spared.

'No one's told me so in my orders, but I am sure we cannot afford to lose a whole brigade. We are heavily outnumbered as it is already.' He drank some tea. 'I must say, though, that I was surprised to find you still here. I thought all the British civilians had been evacuated a few days ago.'

'It's my husband. As you must know, intelligence reports have been scarce, so George has been trying to help General Smyth. George is manager of the Pagoda Timber Company and he has elephant camps in the hill forests near the border. He delayed his evacuation while waiting for some information from his men and we wouldn't leave without him, so he had to give in and let us stay. But he is very anxious because there has been no news from the camps. And now the general has told him that he must leave.'

'There's Daddy, now,' Sue interrupted as she heard a car draw up outside.

Mrs Whitcomb stood up. 'Excuse me.' She hurried out to the veranda.

'She is very worried,' Sue said. 'Daddy's been to Brigade HQ. And she's always afraid that he will volunteer to go up into the hills himself. Daddy has a strong sense of duty – all the same, I think he knows it would only be a futile gesture.'

Paul stood up as Mrs Whitcomb returned with her husband: tall, slim, early forties, burnt almost black from the sun, balding.

As he shook hands with Paul he said, 'So you're the young man I've been hearing about today.'

'What's this?' Mrs Whitcomb looked surprised.

'At Brigade HQ, Mary. Heard about Paul's adventures. Is there a cup of tea for me?'

'Now don't be a tease, George.'

He smiled. 'All right – but I really could do with a cup.'

'I'll pour you one while you tell me.'

'You'd think Paul wasn't here,' Sue said crossly.

'Oh, Sue! Can't you see? Paul wouldn't say a word. He's strong, silent, like most young officers.'

Paul was taken aback.

44

George said quickly, 'I'd better tell you. It appears Paul killed several Japs near Kyondo and used their boats to get his men down the river to Moulmein.'

'Somewhat exaggerated,' Paul protested in the truculent manner of a young man who is embarrassed.

'Then you have actually fought the Japs. We haven't met anyone else so far who has,' Mary remarked.

'I shouldn't think that record will last long, Mrs Whitcomb.'

Mr Whitcomb helped himself to an assorted biscuit. 'Were you in the Dawnas?'

'Only the foothills. Not to the top or the border. Is that where you have your elephant camps?'

'A few. I understand the Japs were seen riding elephants. Could have been mine. God knows how they are being treated or, for that matter, my *oozies* – elephant riders – and *sinoks*. I was relying on the *sinoks* – they run the camps – for information. But it was too much to expect and I only hope they have not suffered. We not only have the Japs to contend with, but the Burmese fifth column is very strong and it is often difficult to tell who is on the side of the enemy and who is not.'

'Are the people going to welcome the Japs?' Paul asked in surprise.

'I am not sure – well, not at first – just trying to keep out of the way of bullets and bombs. But if we lose Burma, that would be a different matter. A case, no doubt as they see it, of changing one master for another. But not the Karens or the hill tribes like the Chins and the Kachins. I am sure they will remain loyal. The Thakins, however – that's the powerful group of young, educated Burmese who are avid to win independence for Burma – well, I think they have gone too far. Mind you, I sympathise with their wish for independence. I fear they will probably burn their fingers by encouraging the Japs, welcoming them, giving them important information on our troops and on the topography of the land: the forest tracks, for example, which have helped the Japs to infiltrate. I think the Thakins will come to earth rather quickly when they find that the Japanese idea of independence does not match up to theirs.

'Anyway, they have organised a fifth column and you should take care whom you trust. They are quite likely to tell the enemy of your presence or light fires to indicate targets for Jap aircraft.'

'I haven't come across any as yet, but thanks for the warning,' Paul stood up. 'Thank you for the tea, Mrs Whitcomb. I really must see how my men are getting on.'

'If you are short of rations, we've got a large supply of rice,' George said. 'Or anything else, if your men wish to rummage. We'll be travelling very light tomorrow.'

'And dried milk,' Mary said. 'That is something that will be very useful. There are several large tins in the pantry.'

'Shall I show you the pantry?' Sue jumped to her feet and led Paul through the dining room and into a small room at the back of the bungalow. The shelves were laden with tinned food and there were sacks of rice, lentils and vegetables on the floor.

'I'm sure they'll enjoy the tinned fruit and fish. And the condensed milk, well! they are rather partial to that.' Paul returned the tin to the shelf. 'I don't know what army rations are available, but my havildar major went down an hour or so ago with a fatigue party to see what there was. And we don't want to eat you out of house and home.'

'We really are travelling light,' she said. 'Daddy thinks we may have to fly out from Rangoon and there is sure to be a crush. In fact, he feels we may have to travel north to find a plane to India. So we won't be carrying large tins of food. Just a small suitcase each, with some clothes and bits and pieces, and a rucksack with some essentials.'

'He has got it well organised.'

'Well, he has lived in Burma for over twenty-five years – so has Mummy, come to that. And he has to tour a lot.'

Paul felt Sue's closeness quite strongly in the small room, wondering why he had initially thought her strange and shy. There was no gawkiness about her and yet, on the veranda earlier, she had seemed a child.

'Would you like to see the kitchen?' She opened a door leading out onto a small veranda at the back which overlooked the kitchen and outbuildings. She stood in the doorway for a moment, as though she had read his mind. 'I … I've been meaning to apologise for my behaviour when you arrived,' she blurted out. 'Couldn't find an opportunity to do so before now.'

'There really is nothing to apologise about.'

'Oh, but there is. I was rude. But you must understand how much I love this place and the life I have led. And I always hoped that our going away would turn out to be a bad dream. But seeing you made it all real for the first time.'

'Please don't worry about it, Sue. You've more than made up for it.'

They stepped out onto the veranda and below in the compound Paul saw Tilbir and Ganesh and a crowd of Gurkhas in and around the kitchen. Tilbir looked up as Paul attracted his attention.

'Ganesh has returned, sahib,' Tilbir called out. 'He managed to buy a goat.' That would please the men, Paul thought; they had not eaten meat for several days.

'There is more food up here,' Paul said.

Tilbir climbed the stairs and looked into the pantry. He shook his head. 'Ah! Sahib! Goat curry and rice. Tinned pineapples and condensed milk. We will have a real feast tonight!'

After dinner, the Whitcombs and Paul stepped out onto the front veranda for a nightcap as the light began to fade from the sky.

They had all eaten the Gurkha curry. Mary was only too glad to avoid opening tins and putting together a scratch meal and she said it was excellent. The Gurkhas had also enjoyed their meal, but they mixed rice, dal, curry, pineapple slices and condensed milk all together in their mess tins and pronounced it the best meal they had eaten for a very long time.

George had two bottles of rum left and he gave these to Paul for the Gurkhas. Tilbir accepted them with pleasure and Paul knew that the subedar would ensure that the contents were spread as widely as possible and that no one would have enough to make him drunk.

While Paul and Sue sat on a two-seater cane settee, George and Mary stood at the veranda railings, looking out at a view which no longer had any shape as the fingers of night had quickly changed outlines into blobs and finally into a dark mass. But they had looked at the view so many times that they could still see it in the daylight of their minds: every house, tree, pagoda, paddy field, river. And they would take the scene away with them in their memories, to be drawn on from time to time in remembrance of this day and all those other days.

'Let's go in,' Mary said suddenly.

George squeezed her hand in understanding. 'Well, we do have to get up early,' he said.

'I'll follow you shortly,' Sue said.

'Oh – all right, darling,' Mary said as though she would rather have said no, you must go to bed at once. 'Good night, Paul. See you in the morning.'

When they were alone, Paul asked Sue, 'How are you going, tomorrow?'

'By ferry steamer to Martaban. Then a train to Rangoon. We'll probably stay in Rangoon with my Uncle Jack – Mummy's brother – until we know what's happening.' She paused for a moment. 'You'll still be here, I suppose.' Then, hurriedly, anxiously, she said, 'Oh, Paul, you will take care.'

47

The night was growing colder, a mist creeping across the river. Paul put an arm around Sue, drawing her closer and she came willingly. He felt the warmth of her body and there was excitement in the pressure of her lips. But he knew he shouldn't take it any further. He would probably never see her again; he'd be dead within the next few days.

He moved gently away from her so their bodies no longer touched. 'I think I should go now,' he said. 'Have to inspect the sentries,' he added lamely.

He helped her to her feet and they walked slowly towards the sitting-room door, arms around each other's waists. They paused at the door.

'Good night,' she whispered, stretching up to reach his mouth, the kiss almost making him lose his self-control.

Reluctantly, he released her and she stepped quickly into the sitting room.

Hidden in the darkness, Mary saw Paul run down the stairs. Should she have watched? She felt guilty. And yet – well – Sue was young and the soldier's future was doubtful. As she returned slowly to her bedroom, the thought came into her mind as to what she would have done had they gone into Sue's bedroom. She had a feeling she would have done nothing. Ridiculous! And yet the times were so strange, so unreal. They would be away in the morning and she knew they would never come back. And after the Japs seized Moulmein, the bungalow, her home, could be destroyed or perhaps commandeered by some filthy Jap pig! This won't do, she reprimanded herself and hurried into her bedroom.

As she climbed into bed, George asked, 'Well, was he the perfect officer and a gentleman?'

'Of course,' she said.

'Well, I'm no gentleman ...'

She felt the comforting warmth and safety of his nearness. And she turned to him willingly.

The Whitcombs left the next morning, while the mist still hung about in the valley and over the river, the Gurkhas cheering them off as the car moved away. Sue and her mother were both wearing trousers and each carried a little suitcase and a rucksack, a sight which aroused pity and sadness in Paul, because it seemed to mark so clearly the end of an era. For the women, the end of a life which had seemed destined to move slowly, happily along, until it was chopped off so abruptly. For George, all the years spent in building up the timber company, the elephant camps, the training of the elephants, finished – although logs recently slid into the river would probably reach Moulmein a year or more after he had gone.

And for Paul, he hoped it was not just the end of a moment. So unexpected when he had led his men onto the ridge. Although it was a dangerous time – who knew whether he would last out the war – he was sure he would remember those lips till the day he died.

Suddenly, he realised that the car was no longer in sight. He turned quickly towards the bungalow, glancing out of the corner of his eye at the men, but they all kept straight faces, not daring to smile. Even Gopiram, who seemed for a moment to be about to grin and make a joke, stopped in time, knowing that on this occasion there was no knowing how the sahib would react.

When the Whitcombs arrived in Rangoon from Moulmein, they were met by Mary's brother, Jack Stevens, and were driven to his bungalow on the outskirts of the city. The servants were taken aback at the small amount of luggage when they came out to unload the car; in their experience, the English always seemed to travel with a great number of suitcases and appendage.

Jack's wife, Celia, was surprised as well. 'Oh dear! Is that all you were able to bring with you!'

The residents of Rangoon were still not fully aware of the dire conditions east of the Sittang.

'I am afraid we are refugees now,' Mary said. 'It is about all anybody was able to bring out of Moulmein.'

'You are not refugees,' Celia said quickly, putting an arm around Mary. 'Come on in and get cleaned up and I am sure we will be able to find you some fresh clothes.'

After a luxurious soak in hot water and once fitted out with clean clothes, the Whitcombs joined the others in the sitting room where drinks were served.

'The news from the front is very sketchy,' Jack said.

'Are there no plans for the evacuation of Rangoon?' George asked.

'Evacuation!' Celia was horrified. 'Oh, surely not!'

'I think we have to be realistic,' George insisted. 'From what I have seen, I doubt very much if we will be able to hold Rangoon.'

Celia looked at Jack, for a moment an expression of fear on her face, and then she said quickly, 'Oh, let us forget the war for a moment. You have had a long journey. Take the opportunity to relax.'

George and Mary were only too glad to relax in comfortable chairs with drinks in their hands. But Sue's mind was still in turmoil, thinking of Paul and dreading how he might have fared in the raging battle for Moulmein.

In Moulmein, the first sounds of battle crackled early on the morning after the Whitcombs had left and before the mist had burned up in the rising sun. On the east perimeter, about 2 miles forward of the ridge, beyond the paddy fields, the enemy soon overran the forward posts of the 3rd Burma Rifles.

At the southern end of Moulmein, the Sikhs of 8th Burma Rifles foiled an attempt by the Japanese to break through the perimeter. A full-scale attack then developed and soon the whole of the southern perimeter was the scene of a desperate battle to keep out the enemy, who was flaying the area with automatic and rifle fire and grenades. A section of 12th "Poonch" Indian Mountain Battery brought its 3.7-inch howitzers into action, inflicting many losses on the enemy. It was late afternoon before the attack died away to a brief respite, punctuated by snipers.

At the airfield, splendid resistance by the Kokine Battalion detachment beat off the first enemy attack at 07.30 hours that morning. Once again, the "Poonch" Battery gave useful support and the airfield defences held out. Later, the enemy cut the telephone line to Brigade Headquarters.

The Kokine Battalion resisted throughout the day, but in the late afternoon the Japanese seized a hill overlooking the airfield and only 1,000 yards from its centre. Enemy mortar and gunfire blasted the area until, as darkness fell, and with the situation quite hopeless, the remaining troops withdrew, some making their escape through enemy lines to Martaban, others into the Moulmein perimeter.

Paul, on the ridge, was at first only an anxious sightseer. All that morning of 30 January, he could hear rifle and automatic fire crackling backwards and forwards from the east and the south, the dull thud of mortar bombs, the louder explosions of Japanese artillery and the answering blasts from the "Poonch" Battery.

It was the *55 Division*, which had marched on Moulmein, approaching from Kawkareik and from the south. They had launched five infantry battalions, supported by 75 mm mountain guns, against the 2,000 or so strong force on the British side.

Around midday, Brigadier Ekin of 46 Brigade arrived in Moulmein. It had been arranged by Lieut. General Hutton that in the event of an attack he would assume command of the garrison, taking over from

Brigadier Bourke of 2 Burma Brigade. Ekin found that although 8th Burma Rifles had valiantly kept the Japanese at bay to the south, it was a different story along the Ataran, where the much reduced 3rd Burma Rifles had been faced with an impossible task. Following a visit to its headquarters, Ekin ordered the battalion to move back just after 13.00 hours to a north–south line through Myenigon village. He also brought forward his reserve battalion, the Frontier Force Regiment.

Paul was glad to see the Indians climb up onto the ridge alongside him and dig in. It would not be long, Paul thought, before the enemy attacked his position and he knew it was going to be a great deal tougher than his initiation at Kawkareik.

He watched through binoculars to just over the mile where the paddy fields and the village of Myenigon were streaked by continuous flashes. The chatter of small-arms fire and the deep-throated oratory of mortar bombs were heard clearly – 3rd Burma Rifles was no match for the ruthlessly efficient Japanese. Poor sods, Paul thought sympathetically. The Indian artillery gave more practical help, silencing an enemy battery near Ngante.

But at last the Burma battalion disintegrated before the onslaught. Figures scurried in all directions like ants, growing larger into gasping men, khaki shirts stained with sweat and here and there streaks of blood, with the occasional soldier supporting wounded comrades. Some of them came through Paul's lines and down the other side of the ridge. But a group of soldiers and battalion headquarters gathered themselves together and took up positions on the ridge.

Paul moved back to his headquarters, which was slightly behind Tule's platoon. He had decided that the trenches were safer and he had cleared his HQ men out of the bungalow.

'It will be our turn, soon, Subedar Sahib,' Paul said.

'But everybody is ready, sahib,' Tilbir assured him.

Paul checked his tommy gun, removed the magazine to see if it had been filled correctly and then clipped it in again. He jumped into the slit trench with Gopiram, who was also armed with a tommy gun and who had placed some hand grenades on a ledge beneath the rim of the trench. Gopiram looked as if he could hardly wait for the expected affray.

At that moment there was a whooshing sound, followed instantly by the roar of an explosion and a fountain of earth as a 75 mm shell landed just beyond the company. Shells also exploded across the ridge, where the FFR were in position. The ground shook and the afternoon air was crushed in the grip of the killer sound.

More blasts of air enveloped C Company as shells struck the bungalow, rendering it apart. Great beams spun in the air, landing with frightening thuds around the Gurkhas. Deadly splinters flew out of the middle of the explosion like flights of arrows. Above the din of the barrage a scream sent a shiver down Paul's spine as in Dilbahadur's platoon a splinter ripped open a Gurkha's throat, while another rifleman died without a sound as a splinter pierced his heart.

By now, 12th Indian Battery was returning the fire with great effect. The brave, cool Indian gunners, smart in their puggarees, khaki shorts and shirts, brought their howitzers to bear with the ease of much training and almost as though it were just a practice shoot.

The Japanese infantry had moved forward under cover of an artillery barrage and with a frightening cry of Banzai! they had rushed the ridge, bayonets fixed. Several were cut down before the rest reached the defenders' positions. The main attack went in against the FFR, but a group swung over towards C Company. Both of Paul's platoons were out of their trenches, meeting the enemy in hand-to-hand conflict. Attackers and defenders were shouting, the dust whirling about them. There were cries of pain as a bayonet went in or a khukuri slashed a Jap into oblivion.

It seemed as though Amarjit's platoon was gaining the upper hand, but Tule's men were being pushed back. Paul scrambled out of his trench and ran forward, Gopiram close behind. A Japanese soldier appeared in front of Paul, who dropped him with a short burst. As the man fell aside, Paul could see more of the enemy and he emptied the magazine into them. Making a quick change to a full magazine, he doubled forward, put his foot into a pool of fresh blood and sprawled onto the ground. A Japanese was charging down, screaming, bayonet pointed at Paul's body. Then the man was blotted out of view as a bulky form sprang between them. Bayonets clashed and there was a scream of pain. The momentum threw the Japanese onto Tule and they both fell to the ground. Before the Japanese could get to his feet, Gopiram's khukuri swung onto the man's exposed neck, almost severing the head. Then Gopiram kicked the still-shuddering body aside and reached for the rifle and bayonet, still affixed to Tule's chest, but the Gurkha jemedar cried out, 'No! Leave it! Leave it!'

Paul scrambled to his feet and bent over the jemedar. 'Tule!' he cried. 'Oh Tule, why did you do it?'

Tule opened his eyes for a moment and tried to say something, but the blood gushed out of his mouth and he was dead. Poor, amiable, gentle Tule Pun.

'Are you all right, sahib?' It was Tilbir, making an anxious enquiry. And when Paul nodded his head, too moved to speak, the subedar said, 'The enemy have retreated. But they will be back.'

'Check our casualties,' Paul somehow managed to say.

He was told that six Gurkhas had been killed. There was one seriously wounded and, unfortunately, he was the battalion's best footballer, who would never play again.

'He has been carried down the ridge to the advanced dressing station, sahib.'

All along the ridge the Japanese had been thrown back, the FFR, who had taken the main brunt of the attack, fighting with great skill and bravery, but the defenders were hopelessly outnumbered and all their valiant efforts could only be delaying tactics. For the moment, the enemy had pulled back to lick its wounds and no doubt to reorganise for another attempt to push the FFR off the ridge. Further south, there was the occasional rattle of fire as 8th Burma Rifles still held firm.

Using the cover of the sunken road, Paul walked over to the nearest FFR unit for a word with the company commander. By the time Paul had returned to his own position, the covered bodies of Tule and the other Gurkha dead had been neatly laid out to one side of the company's position. He again felt the pang of Tule's loss and was grateful to be distracted by Gopiram handing him a mug of hot tea.

'Where did you get this?'

'Down the hill, huzoor. Somebody has organised a kitchen.'

'Have all the men had tea?'

It was Tilbir who answered, 'Yes, sahib.' And he continued, 'Jemedar Tule – I have asked Havildar Major Ganesh to take over 11 Platoon. Although the senior naik is a good man, the present situation is too dangerous and I think a steady, older head would be better. Does the sahib agree?'

'Yes, that will be fine. Thank you – I should have thought of it myself.'

'The sahib has enough on his mind without worrying about such minor details.'

The situation was causing Smyth more concern and after receiving Ekin's wireless report, he requested permission to evacuate the garrison. General Hutton agreed, leaving the timing to Smyth.

In Moulmein, with darkness, boatloads of the enemy were reported approaching down the Salween. Meanwhile, the men of 8th Burma

Rifles, who had held on grimly to the southern perimeter for twelve hours, were reaching the end of their tether.

Weaponry flashed all down the east side as the Japanese kept up a spasmodic fire, red, green and white tracer curving in out of the night; and as the defenders replied, the ridge burst into a bright, flickering light like the broadside from a ship. The Japanese bombarded the town and the ridge with their infantry guns and mortars; in turn, the Indian battery's howitzers hurled accurate shells into the enemy's positions, while the FFR's 3-inch mortars put down a deadly pattern of bombs, exploding in the distance with satisfying crumps.

Ekin, who had moved his HQ further back to the PWD Bungalow in Salween Park, decided with nightfall to shorten and so strengthen the perimeter and to counter any penetration into the town. The weary men of 8th Burma Rifles were pulled back some 1,000 yards to new positions on an east–west line, joining up south of the ridge with the river front. The defences were now in a rectangular shape, some 3 miles north to south and around 1,500 yards east to west. Except for those on the ridge, all the troops were in the town and would now have to meet the enemy at close quarters in the streets.

The 8th Burma Rifles broke contact with the enemy, who tried to follow up but were kept at arm's length by patrols throughout the remainder of the night, the narrow streets and houses becoming the scene of bloody clashes and echoing with rifle and automatic fire.

It must have been about an hour after nightfall when Paul was startled from a half sleep by a sudden outbreak of fighting on the northern perimeter, where the enemy had made a landing from boats. The whole area seemed to break apart, the houses lit up by the flashes of grenades and mortar bombs, the river beyond catching the glow of the flames. Shouts and cries mingled as 7th Burma Rifles fought desperately to keep the Japanese out. All along the line of the ridge, the FFR and C Company held firm, but in the town, 7th Burma Rifles was being pressed back, slowly but surely, the fighting still fierce among the houses.

By now, Ekin had reported to Smyth that he doubted if Moulmein could be held during daylight of 31 January. Smyth told him to draw up plans for evacuating the town and to put them into effect when he thought the time was right. Ekin immediately sent word for the fleet of fifteen river steamers of the Irrawaddy Flotilla to be brought across from Martaban.

By 02.00 hours, 7th Burma Rifles on the northern perimeter had been driven back from the timber yard to the police lines and the troops of 3rd Indian Light Anti-Aircraft Battery – stationed in the northern area to give cover to the jetties and the ridge – now found themselves on the front line. Japanese, posing as Burmese soldiers and apparently knowing the password, mingled with the withdrawing Burma Rifles until reaching the Bofors. Several of the gunners were bayoneted before the rest became aware of the ruse. The survivors fought back fiercely until forced to withdraw, abandoning their Bofors, and they were able to remove the breechblocks from only two of the guns.

By the early hours of 31 January, Ekin realised that the situation was very serious and he knew his men could not hold Moulmein for long after daybreak. At 03.30 hours he issued orders for a withdrawal to begin at 08.00 hours.

Shortly before dawn, a lieutenant from the FFR came across to Paul to pass on the withdrawal order. 'It's going to be a tricky operation, so please make your way independently straight down to the jetty. We'll disengage and leave rearguards.'

The withdrawal plan was simple, but a good deal depended on the men remaining calm and on acts of sacrifice – many of which would go unnoticed. The perimeter was to be gradually diminished into smaller boxes, the units maintaining close contact with each other as they fell back to the jetties. The Mountain Battery and the FFR were to form a bridgehead covering the jetties at Maingay Street, Mission Street and the Post Office Jetty, at each of which five river steamers had berthed to take off the troops. Each unit was detailed to withdraw on a particular jetty and the embarkation was controlled by specially appointed officers. The wounded, together with the medical and supply units, had been evacuated as soon as the decision to withdraw had been made.

Coming off the ridge, Paul led the way past the jail and into that part of the town adjacent to the Maingay Street Jetty, taking up position for a while in the new perimeter, which Ekin had drawn tight to cover the jetties. The first of the troops were boarding the fifteen twin-screwed ferry steamers of the Irrawaddy Flotilla.

Above came the sudden roar of aircraft and the steamers were moved out into the middle of the river, but the Japanese bombers, flashing streaks of silver as they were caught by the sun, flew straight overhead to Martaban. In fact, throughout the evacuation, the bombers concentrated their attacks on Martaban. There seemed no good reason for this: if they had bombed the jetties and the steamers in Moulmein, the evacuation would have been much more hazardous, if not impossible.

Back came the steamers and the evacuation resumed. The forward troops had disengaged shortly before the Japanese made an attack on all fronts and at first, the rearguards were not heavily pressed. But there was a great din: the continuous crack of rifle and machine-gun fire all around the perimeter, the sappers blowing up the power house, the telephone exchange and other vital installations, the Mountain Artillery putting down a final barrage over open sights, the steamer crews shouting at everyone to be quick and at each other to keep up their courage.

At last it was C Company's turn to board a steamer and as the vessel pulled away from the jetty, Paul had a wider view of the town: smoke and flame billowing among the houses and the flash and rattle of weapons as the FFR contained the perimeter area into a final shallow bridgehead covering the two southern jetties.

By 10.00 hours the FFR and the Brigade HQ had managed to board the last steamer at Mission Street Jetty, but the situation was more desperate at the Post Office Jetty, where the enemy, who had landed earlier on the north shore, pressed into the embarkation area. Among the streets and houses a bitter, last-ditch effort was made by 60 Field Company and 7th Burma Rifles to clear the approaches to the quayside. When the last steamer from the post-office jetty moved out into the Salween, a great number of these men were left behind. There was, however, no thought of surrender and many escaped on rafts, while others found country boats and a few even swam.

Meanwhile, as the evacuation fleet moved slowly across the estuary towards Martaban, the Japanese opened fire from the ridge, where they had now established their artillery. The shells and machine-gun bullets followed the steamers almost the whole way across to Martaban, but only one of the smaller vessels was sunk.

Above the smoke of the town, on the ridge and not far from where Paul's company had been in position, the magnificent Kyaikthanlan Pagoda still towered against the sky. Many centuries past, the original pagoda had been destroyed by Siamese invaders, but a new one, raised on the same site, had managed to withstand the shells and automatic weapons of the twentieth century. Not far from it lay the bodies of Tule and all the others who had died on a foreign ridge many thousands of miles from their homes. Paul felt a moment of sadness. If only, he thought wryly, they could have had the benefit of the same "curse" which had protected the many pagodas crowning the ridge.

On the great bell of the Kyaikthanlan Pagoda was an inscription in English:

> He who destroyed to this Bell, they must be
> in the great Hell, and unable to coming out.

Chapter Four
Marking Time

The road wound its way through dense jungle. In the warmth of the cab, Paul could not stay awake and he nodded off again. Tony Davidson did not speak. He drove steadily and Paul had vague recollections of passing through Thaton, a rubber estate near Bilin, and then over the Thebyu River. Tony had met Paul in Martaban with transport to take the company to Kyaikto, where the battalion had arrived from Calcutta.

'We are nearly there,' Tony said at last.

Paul forced himself awake as they entered the outskirts of Kyaikto; it seemed 100 years since he had passed through it on the train. Tony turned off the road onto a cart track, where he drove past a sentry post and stopped by a cluster of wooden houses, which suddenly came alive with rushing Gurkhas, surrounding the trucks, laughing, cheering. Paul knew he was home again.

The next morning, Paul gave Lieut.Colonel Osborne a verbal report of C Company's actions since its arrival in Burma; but the colonel made no immediate comment, just standing up suddenly when Paul had finished, and walking to the window to look at the other huts, at the jungle which twisted and turned between them and beyond, to listen to the sound of his men's voices. After a moment he moved away from the window and sat down again at the bamboo table which served as his desk.

Now he said warmly, 'You did a fine job out there, Paul. Not so easy at your age and with limited experience.' He laughed, but not, Paul thought, with much mirth. 'Although, even at my age I could have brought no greater experience of jungle warfare into the situation. In fact, I suppose you now have more practical knowledge than I have – or Robin.' He glanced at the adjutant who kept a stern face; he was not the kind of person to admit that anybody knew more than he did.

Paul said, 'I could not have achieved anything without the help of Subedar Tilbir and the other commanders and men – all of whom were quite superb in the circumstances, even to making the ultimate sacrifice, like Jemedar Tule.'

'Yes, I know how you feel,' the colonel consoled him. 'And I am well aware of the way the company worked together as an efficient fighting machine. Later, you must let Robin have the names and citations of those who did particularly well. Although, during a retreat, I don't suppose decorations will be awarded generously. Anyway, I shall be giving the men my personal *shabash* when I inspect them presently.' He looked at Robin for a moment and then back to Paul. 'There is first the question of what happens to the company. What is the strength now?'

'Fifty-seven, sir – and that includes five slightly wounded men and myself. Of course, 11 Platoon took the bulk of casualties and is down to ten, including three of the injured.'

'The trouble is we are so damnably short of men in all of the companies.' He looked at Robin again.

The adjutant said, 'For the time being, I think 11 Platoon should be split among the other two, making them twenty-five each. Then there is also the question of the company commander.'

'Yes,' the colonel agreed.

And Paul thought, here it comes – some bloody more senior officer to take over.

Covering a smile, the colonel said, 'If you looked like that at Moulmein, Paul, the Japs must have been scared out of their lives!'

'Sorry, sir.'

'I am not going to put anyone else in charge. It is your company, now.'

It has always been my company, Paul thought, but if he wants to make it official, that's fine.

The colonel picked up his hat and swagger stick. 'Let's go and see your men.'

Paul followed him out of the office, down the rickety steps leading to the dusty track between the houses. By the time they reached C Company's lines, Subedar Tilbir had drawn the men up on parade. The regiment had a tradition of smartness to uphold and C Company was determined to maintain it: after a night to relax in safe sleep, the morning had been hectic as the men bathed, did their laundry, polished their boots and sorted their equipment.

Paul felt real pride as the subedar called the company to attention and the colonel took the salute. He could sense the adjutant breathing down his neck but, as Robin passed no remark, even he must have been reasonably happy about the company's presentation. He could be quite a martinet when it came to drill and turnout.

The colonel spoke to the men; his Gurkhali was excellent. He praised them for their fine work and the very high standard they had set for the rest of the battalion to follow. He expected them to continue to give of their best under their company commander, Captain Cooper Sahib. Then he told Paul to carry on and walked away, accompanied by the adjutant.

Not by a flicker of an eyelid had any man revealed his thoughts at the colonel's indirect announcement that Paul was to continue as company commander with promotion to captain. But after the men had been dismissed, Tilbir asked if it were so and he nodded his head in satisfaction, just for a moment letting his guard down to show his approval. After that it was back to business.

Paul and Tilbir walked over to the Regimental Aid Post to see how their slightly wounded men were getting on. Captain Alex Green, always called Doc, was a tall, thin man with large, bony hands which somehow were able to bring comfort by their touch. Sensitive in performing delicate, intricate surgery, they were also great hands for directing a basketball into the net from all angles and his added height made him an indispensable member of the battalion's basketball team.

He came out of the wooden hut he had turned into a temporary hospital. 'You are too late for sick parade,' he said. 'If you want to be excused from parade you'll have to come back tomorrow. Only tomorrow you'd better look a lot less healthy than you do at the moment.' He appeared to be very serious, his large mouth tight in a line of thin lips. Only his blue eyes flickered in amusement.

'Well, Doc, the subedar sahib and I had thought about scrounging a few days off. But I see you're still as sharp as ever.'

'And so are you, young Paul. You've come about your men, I presume. Well, they're not all that bad – just a few minor wounds which I have treated. Lightish work for a day or two, if things are quiet that long. The little man with the arm wound is very lucky – your medical orderly did a good first-aid job on him – but I'm going to keep him under observation for a day or two. I don't know why you didn't send him back from Moulmcin with your seriously wounded men.'

'He wouldn't hear of it,' Paul explained. 'Frankly, we needed every man. And he performed as good a job on a Jap's head as you would have done in taking off somebody's leg.'

A large hand gripped Paul by the back of the neck. 'It is just as well that I like you, Paul; otherwise, you'd find your head being used as a basketball.'

'Thanks, Doc – for looking after my men and for sparing my head.'

'Go on, bugger off! I've got a lot of work to do. And you owe me a drink!'

On 6 February, General Wavell flew in from Java. He was met by Hutton and Smyth and was driven around the divisional area. He was tight-lipped and in a furious temper at the loss of Moulmein, coming, as it had, on top of the withdrawal from Kawkareik. He had been looking for a scapegoat and had settled on Brigadier "Jonah" Jones, deciding to replace him with Brigadier "Punch" Cowan. But on Smyth's insistence and strong recommendation, Jones was kept on and Cowan was appointed Smyth's brigadier general staff.

During his visit, Wavell spoke a few encouraging words to some of the troops, but he ignored Smyth for most of the time, unable to understand how it had not been possible to withstand the Japanese who he still, it seemed, stubbornly believed to be second-rate soldiers.

But he did ask Smyth one very important question. 'Any scope in this type of country for the use of light tanks?'

'Yes, sir,' Smyth confirmed eagerly.

'I'll cable the Middle East for an armoured brigade.'

The subsequent arrival in Rangoon of 7 Armoured Brigade, consisting of two regiments of light cruiser tanks, one RHA battery and one anti-tank battery, was to prove one of Wavell's most important decisions.

Wavell flew back to Lembang on 9 February. But the situation in Singapore was so grave that he flew to the island the next day, where he discussed the situation with General Percival and then decided to return to Java.

He was driven to the pier head through the darkened city which was already echoing with the stray shots of looters, where he waited in the car while his staff searched for the boat to take him to the awaiting Catalina Flying Boat. Wavell became impatient and he stepped out of the left-hand side of the car. That was his blind side and he had failed to realise that the car was parked on the edge of the sea wall. He fell some 6 feet onto rocks and barbed wire and lay there in great pain, his back badly torn by the barbed wire. The officers had found the motor boat and lifting him into it they took him to the waiting Catalina.

He was still conscious when they carried him aboard the Catalina, but he was in considerable pain. He was given several aspirins and a glass of whisky and in a few moments he was thankfully asleep. But Singapore was in its death throes and the harbour was overflowing with motor cruisers, yachts and sampans as the civilian population attempted to escape from Singapore, so Wavell's party could not take off under cover of darkness and had to wait for daylight. Meanwhile, the oil tanks at the naval base had been set on fire, the flames illuminating the area. Some five hours later, at daybreak, the Catalina at last lifted off, getting clear without being spotted by any patrolling Japanese aircraft.

On arrival at Batavia, Wavell was taken to a Dutch military hospital, where the doctors wanted to keep him in for a fortnight, but the tough and determined general would have none of it and he insisted on being taken to his headquarters, where he was then transferred to a British hospital in Bandoeng.

He had left behind him a desperate situation in Singapore: the island was only days away from surrender.

After Moulmein, the Japanese infantry had kept a low profile. Knowing that the Salween River would be a difficult obstacle, they were reorganising their forces for the next step in their thrust towards Rangoon. The crack *33 Division*, veterans of the China War and commanded by Lieut. General Sakurai, had been brought forward to take over the main impetus from *55 Division*. As far as Sakurai was concerned, it would be the old Japanese tactics which had worked so well: a frontal assault across the Salween River and then the sweeping hooks to draw the enemy into his trap.

Meanwhile, Major General Smyth believed that the situation had the makings of a monumental disaster. He had received orders to stand fast along the Salween, to hold the road and railhead at Martaban, to make bold counter-attacks against any Japanese forces that crossed the river – the sort of orders that read well back in Whitehall. In reality, he just drew the thin line even thinner, so that no one point was strong enough to withstand any great pressure for long without snapping; the section of the Salween most likely to see a Japanese crossing extended anywhere from Martaban upriver almost due north for more than 100 miles. All Smyth's instincts still warned him to find ground of his own choosing on which to make a firm stand, but he knew that Hutton and Wavell would not agree.

The only good news for Smyth was the arrival at Kyaikto of Brigadier Hugh-Jones' 48 Indian Brigade to stiffen the division; although, like everyone else, the brigade had been training for war in the Middle East before the sudden switch to the Burma front but it consisted of three redoubtable Gurkha battalions which, in spite of heavy casualties, were to prove invaluable during the long retreat across Burma.

Once the enemy had crossed the Salween, which Smyth was certain they would eventually do, then his division would be isolated by a hook beyond the Bilin River. He promptly called a conference of his commanders to discuss the deteriorating situation.

'To my mind,' said Smyth, 'and you know I have stressed this all along, we should be well on our way to the Sittang by now in order to cross and build up a strong defence on the far side.'

All the commanders agreed with him regarding the dangerous situation of the division. Their unanimous view was to concentrate at once on the Bilin and then without delay proceed to withdraw behind the Sittang. Somehow, they would have to persuade Hutton.

'The answer,' said Smyth, 'is to send someone to see the army commander and put the case to him personally.'

"Punch" Cowan was chosen as the messenger and he set off at once for Army HQ in Rangoon. He was able to see Hutton and put the case as forcibly as he could, emphasising that all the division's commanders were in full agreement. But Hutton was unmoved and he was quite adamant regarding his orders for Smyth to stay in his present position. Hutton had Wavell behind his back consistently drumming into him his view of the Japanese; he was not going to fall foul of the C.-in-C. But he did agree that Cowan should stay with Smyth as his brigadier general staff.

On his gloomy way back, Cowan could not help but believe that the delay would lead to disaster.

Meanwhile, in the early hours of the twelfth, two Japanese battalions crossed the Salween and attacked the 7/10th Baluchis. The Baluchis, most of them recruits, held on with great courage for eight long, terrifying hours against heavy odds in fierce hand-to-hand combat, but by the time darkness had given way to daylight, three companies had been practically annihilated, the colonel dead and the ammunition exhausted. The remnant was forced to surrender. The Indian battalion had lost fifteen officers and some 400 men. Only five platoons out on patrol escaped.

With the enemy across the Salween, Smyth was sure he would be isolated by a hook behind the Bilin River. Regardless of orders, he ordered his battalions back to the Bilin on 15 February. When Hutton heard of this he was furious and he sent a letter reprimanding him. The next day Hutton came forward to see Smyth personally and Hutton was forced to agree that the move had been made in the nick of time.

'But that is as far as you go, Smyth. On no account are you to withdraw one step without my permission. You must hold the line at Bilin.'

This left Smyth in a most dangerous position. At that time of the year, the Bilin was just a dried-up river bed, which a man could almost jump across without much difficulty. But Smyth had seen it as a good forming-up position for his division before the next move back to the Sittang. Now, he found himself in a situation which offended every principle of warfare: a major battle to be fought by tired troops against a numerically superior enemy who had the advantage of air support, with a dusty track behind the front line leading to the broad Sittang River, spanned by a single bridge.

And to top it all came the news that Singapore had surrendered. So much for a second-rate enemy, Smyth thought cynically. But he knew that this was an order he could not disobey without risking a court martial. All he could do was make certain his division fought with skill and courage.

Strengthened by 48 Brigade, the men of 17 Division fought hard to hold the line, keeping the seasoned enemy in check. Then it was discovered that a strong enemy force had infiltrated and established a roadblock behind the British line.

This was the situation when, in the afternoon of 17 February, there was a buzz of excitement around the 4/15th Gurkhas' position with a rumour that the battalion was to move forward. Then came confirmation that two companies were to attack. The colonel would be in command and he had decided to take A and B Companies. Tony, who commanded D Company, was disappointed.

'It's because I am not senior enough. Todd and Sanderson, being regulars, must have the chance to further their careers, I suppose.'

Maybe he was right, but personally Paul was glad that Tony would be remaining in Kyaikto.

The lorries pulled into line and the two companies embused quickly, with just a buzz of excited voices because they had been told there was to be no cheering. The colonel moved off first, giving a sort of half salute, half wave. It was quite a moment for him. After all his years of service, time had at last brought him to the possible fulfilment of his career. Paul wondered if he would see the colonel again or how many of the others would return. Then he walked over to his company lines, where the men were just starting their evening meal.

Gopiram brought him a plate of curry and rice. Paul sat cross-legged on the matting which had been rolled out over the wooden floor of the house and tucked into the meal. A few paces away sat Tilbir, looking casual without his boots and Gurkha hat, and perhaps a little older than Paul had imagined. In a little half circle sat the other senior Gurkhas.

Dilbahadur seemed quite calm, scooping balls of curry and rice with his fingers. Havildar Major Ganesh ate carefully, wiping his pencil-thin moustache after every mouthful – and as he was the only one who sported a moustache of sorts, he no doubt needed to keep it in good order. Because the survivors of 11 Platoon had been split up among the other platoons, Ganesh had returned to his position of CHM.

Tilbir rose to his feet and walked over to the open veranda of the house. His orderly poured water from a jug and the subedar washed his hands and rinsed his mouth. When he returned he asked, 'Sahib, what is the situation at the front?'

The others looked up, although carrying on eating. Paul, who always used his hand when eating with the men, rolled some rice and curry into a ball with the tips of the fingers of his right hand and guided it into his mouth with a flick of the thumb. He chewed on it while he arranged his thoughts into order.

'The situation is not very good. It is no use telling you anything else to raise your spirits; besides, you are experienced soldiers now and would see through any falsehood on my part. The fact is we are obviously outnumbered and neither do we have command of the air.'

'We are not outnumbered in courage, sahib,' Dilbahadur said pugnaciously.

'But we need more than courage,' Tilbir said. 'Courage and determination are all right if, say, you are holding a mountain pass, where only a few men at a time can attack along a narrow path. With courage, a small group could – as indeed proved in past history – hold out for many hours. But I am thinking that the position we defend at the moment does not cancel out the enemy's advantage.'

He looked at Paul again and the officer explained, 'According to our Colonel Sahib, General Smyth would like to move behind the Sittang River, where we could hold up the Japanese – like your men in the pass – until 7 Armoured Brigade and other promised reinforcements arrive.'

'We are doing that now, sahib,' Amarjit said. 'Are we not? Holding the Japanese back for a few days more. Is not every day they are held back precious?'

'Only if there are enough of us left to face them on the Sittang,' Dilbahadur said.

Paul said optimistically, 'Whatever happens, I am sure the time will come when our troops of all nationalities – British, Gurkha, Indian, American – will beat them at their own game and send them hurrying back to Japan.'

'But how do we survive the in-between period, sahib?' Amarjit asked.

Paul looked at him for a moment: the young Gurkha now proudly wore the badges of the rank of a jemedar, having been promoted to the vacancy as a reward for his action at Kawkareik. 'How can I give you an answer? I am not Buddha or some god.'

'But have you not led us out of a demon's inferno, sahib?'

Paul gave Amarjit a searching look. Was the young Gurkha being derisive? Paul did not reply at once. He walked over to the veranda, where Gopiram poured water for him to wash his face and hands.

Amarjit looked genuinely concerned. 'Have I offended you, sahib?'

Paul returned to the room. 'No, Amarjit, not at all. But you have bestowed me with too many powers. Had I been a man of such heaven-sent authority, I would have brought all the men back to safety from the demon's inferno as you describe it. But I think of Tule and the others – no, I am not blessed with divine powers. As your company commander I will do my best to help you to stay alive, but only through the few military skills I possess, backed by the courage of all the men. But in the end, Amarjit, it is like drawing the winning number of a lottery.'

'It is the only way, sahib,' Dilbahadur agreed. 'That is the way I live. Anyway, sahib, we Gurkhas have our own secret weapon,' he grinned, his teeth white against his brown face.

'And what secret weapon is this?' Paul asked, glad that Dilbahadur had taken the conversation away from the stark reality of what lay ahead.

Dilbahadur tapped his shaven head. 'This, sahib; is it not said that a Gurkha's head is as hard as a rock?'

'So I have heard,' Paul agreed, playing along with Dilbahadur.

'Ah! You do not sound convinced, but there is evidence that our heads are bulletproof. It was a long time ago, more than fifty years past, when the 44th – as the 8th Gurkha Rifles were called in those days – were taking part in the Relief of Chansil on the North-West Frontier. During the fighting, a bullet hit the head of Rifleman Gorcy Thapa but just glanced off and killed his commanding officer, one Swinton Sahib. Quite true, sahib, it is in the history books.'

The jemedar continued, 'This Gorey Thapa was soon famous in the regiment and the next year the 44th were at Manipur, where they attacked the rajah's palace. In the fierce battle this same Gorey Thapa was again hit in the head, but he was only a little dazed and he carried on as though nothing had happened.'

'Well, Dilbahadur Sahib, the next time we are in action I must remember to stand well clear of you,' Paul said amidst much mirth.

After this, the Gurkhas dispersed to their platoons. Paul walked over to the window and looked towards the east. Somewhere out there were A and B Companies and the colonel. Now and again he could hear the rumble of distant guns and in the sudden darkness of nightfall he could see flashes of light against the sky and intermittent glows that spread across the horizon and then faded away like the slow opening and closing of a fan.

Early in the morning of 18 February, Lieut. Colonel Osborne brought forward the two companies of his battalion in an attempt to break through the Japanese roadblocks. It was a tough task. The Japanese were well dug-in, determined to hold out to the last man and kill as many of their enemy as they could. With dense, jungle-covered hills on either side of the road and a clear field of fire across the open valley floor, there was not much room for manoeuvre.

With B Company giving covering fire and the battalion's mortars putting down a barrage, A Company made a frontal assault. Fierce counter-fire scattered the Gurkhas' ranks, like snooker balls after a hard break, and sought out the men even when they tried to find cover at the roadside. Captain Todd received a full burst of machine-gun fire and expired along with several other men. The company's survivors pulled back, leaving several bodies sprawled across the road.

Grim-faced, Osborne turned to Sanderson and gave him the opportunity to retrieve the situation. But Sanderson spilt his lifeblood on the road next to Todd and although his men fought fiercely and courageously, at one stage getting to hand-to-hand combat, in the end they were forced back again, suffering many casualties. Compassionate orders from brigade then directed Osborne to withdraw his men from the firing area and take up a position in a village about 3 miles to the south.

That morning, Smyth had visited the front line to assess the situation. During the past few days of fierce action the men of 17 Division had faced great odds and they were now reaching the limits of their endurance. It was clear to Smyth that the longer he remained on the Bilin, the more he was playing into Japanese hands, so he signalled to Hutton that the troops had fought to a standstill and his last reserve had been used to hold the left flank.

On the nineteenth, Hutton arrived from Rangoon to see for himself. He did not stay long – the situation was all too clear and so he gave Smyth permission to pull back to the Sittang at his discretion.

The danger to 17 Division was growing more serious by the hour and after dark, Smyth issued his operational orders. During the early hours of the twentieth, under cover of a heavy mist, the brigades broke contact with the enemy and moved back to Kyaikto. In less than twenty-four hours, Smyth succeeded in breaking contact and withdrawing the whole division some 17 miles, moving into position to the west of Kyaikto. The Sittang Bridge was now only 15 miles away.

Major Arthur Kennedy, the 2 i/c, moved 4/15th Gurkhas out of Kyaikto, early on the morning of the twentieth, to take up their bivouac position near the Boyagyi Rubber Estate, a mile or so north-west of the town. Space was left for A and B Companies who, it was understood, would be returning later that evening.

Apart from a brief account that the colonel and his group had run into trouble resulting in many casualties, the full story was still awaited. Ambulances returning with wounded was stark evidence of the stiff fight put up on the Bilin and the price that had been paid. Ambulances then arrived carrying more than a score of wounded from the battalion. Many were seriously hurt and with a tough journey ahead to the bridge, their chances of survival were slight.

In the early evening, lorries brought in the colonel and his companies. When the colonel stepped out of the leading vehicle, he looked very tired, dusty and grimy as Paul had never seen him before. And he also looked much older. He seemed to totter for a moment and then pulled himself together, adjusted his Gurkha hat to the right angle and, with a great effort which moved all who watched, he walked smartly up to the officers. When Paul saluted it was not just the crown and pip on the colonel's shoulders, but the man as well.

The Gurkhas stumbled out of the back of the lorries. Subedar Major Dhanbahdur Gurung stepped forward and called the survivors of the companies to attention in a voice that carried a command matured through years of experience. It brought instant obedience from the tired, sweaty, bloodstained Gurkhas.

The colonel was obviously moved when, at a nod from the adjutant, the subedar major marched smartly forward and said, 'Four Battalion, 15th Gurkha Rifles, ready, sahib. We shall not be found wanting.'

'That gives me new heart – although I really should expect no less from our battalion,' said Osborne. Then he added, 'We will probably be moving tomorrow. I await orders. Meanwhile, dismiss the men to their evening meal.'

Ahead of them lay the journey to the vital Sittang Bridge, which was defended only by the 250-strong 3rd Burma Rifles, in whom Smyth had little confidence, and a company of the Duke of Wellington's Regiment. The remaining companies of the British regiment had arrived from Rangoon that day, but had crossed to the east bank and moved down to Kyaikto to join 46 Brigade as rearguard.

The all-weather road from Martaban, which had served as the main line of communication for the division, ended at Kyaikto. From there to the Sittang Bridge stretched 15 miles of dusty, unmetalled road, cut up by motor traffic, full of bomb craters and deep in ruts, winding through dense jungle. From Kyaikto, the road headed sharply north, across the paddy fields and past the eastern edge of the Boyagyi Rubber Estate, continuing due west through dense jungle to the Meyon Chaung before turning due west towards the Mokpalin Quarries and Mokpalin village.

At Mokpalin, the railway, which followed the riverbank from Kyaikto, came into close proximity with the road for a mile, before turning westwards to the bridge, while the road swung north-east to Sittang village and then to the bridge, thus enclosing Pagoda Hill – crowned by a pagoda – and Buddha Hill, which bore a great image of the Buddha. The railway emerged onto the bridge by way of a cutting through a bluff overlooking the river.

Smyth had to get his division across the river before the Japanese arrived and then destroy the bridge. He could only pray that it was now not too late. He ordered his division to move off the next day, 21 February. Ahead would be the Malerkotla Field Company – sappers to complete preparations for the demolition of the bridge – and the 4/12th FFR to strengthen the bridgehead. The order of the march behind these two formations was Division HQ, followed by 48 and 16 Brigades, with 46 Brigade as rearguard.

On the evening of the twentieth, Osborne called the British officers and senior Gurkha officers into an order group to tell them of the arrangements for the morrow. He looked drawn and there was a pale tinge to his normal sunburn. Paul knew how the colonel must be feeling; he had gone through the same experience himself of losing men who had served with him for many months. It would have been much worse for the colonel, seeing two companies devastated and losing Sanderson and Todd.

For Osborne it was a difficult moment, facing his officers. Perhaps they would be blaming him for the disaster at the roadblocks. He was not to know the respect they all felt for him. Well, he had to get on with it, pull himself together. He remembered the meeting in the officers' mess at Poona only a couple of months past. He had been short of officers then and now he had lost two more; Sanderson and Todd would be hard to replace. He was down to six, including Doc and himself, so he asked Kennedy to take over A Company and placed Jack Hunter in charge of B Company.

'We will be marching with the rearguard brigade,' the colonel told them. 'All transport will be moving within its own brigade and in advance of the infantry. It's a single road through dense jungle. With transport and mules interspersed with marching troops – and no doubt Burmese refugees – progress will be slow. In fact, I don't believe we will start marching ourselves until quite late tomorrow.'

After more detailed orders, the colonel dismissed his officers. Paul and Tilbir wandered back to C Company in the darkness to brief the platoon commanders. When they, in turn, had dispersed to tell their men, Paul settled down on his groundsheet with a long-desired cigarette and a mug of hot, sweet tea which Gopiram had produced with the air of a magician.

Gopiram repeated the trick when Tony came over from his company and sat down beside Paul, who offered him a cigarette. They smoked for a moment in silence. Around them the night was, for once, devoid of any noise of battle. With the whole division spread out in harbour for some 4 square miles north-west of Kyaikto, there was a murmur of voices rolling backwards and forwards and across, with now and again a cough, sharp in the night air, and the harsh bark of a jackal scavenging somewhere along the Kadat Chaung or waiting to see what could be picked up from the leavings in the morning. Pinpoints of light glowed for moments all over the place like fireflies. A shadowy figure appeared out of the gloom; tall, well built, Jack Hunter looked confident, reliable, but he was plagued by uncertainty and lack of confidence in his ability. He asked in a stage whisper if he could join them.

'Of course, sit down.'

And shortly after he had done so, Gopiram appeared with another mug of tea. He must have quite a brew going, Paul thought.

'Unsettled,' Jack murmured aloud. 'Rather unsettled.'

'Understandably you are,' Paul agreed.

'Me? Yes, me too, of course, naturally. I have never commanded a company and I don't know how it will work out. But I meant the men: jittery and seemingly uncooperative. I don't know ...'

'Only to be expected after what they have been through,' Paul said. 'But I shouldn't worry about it. They will be all right when the time comes; you'll see.'

Jack sipped his tea absent-mindedly while Tony fidgeted, from discomfort or irritation. He had never liked Jack.

'The trouble is that we have been thrown straight into the deep end,' Jack said. 'I've been the IO for so long that I've hardly had any experience of running a rifle company. I have the feeling that they haven't enough confidence in me to see them through another ordeal.'

Paul hesitated for a moment and then said, 'Oh, they'll watch you all right. But they will give you the benefit of the doubt. From then on it will be up to you. It was drummed into me that all leadership is to set an example. That's the best advice I can give you, Jack. I suppose it's what I always try to do. Anyway, you have a good subedar. Win his confidence. Work together. As a team. That's what I found with Tilbir. I could never have managed without him.'

Tony shifted his position and Paul hoped he would not say anything to upset Jack, but Tony said, 'There's a lot of truth in that, Jack. Example does play a large part. Take Paul, for instance. I had a long talk with his subedar and his men are further evidence; they all talk of his coolness and courage.'

'That's enough,' Paul said with a mixture of annoyance and embarrassment.

'OK. But that's the real answer. You'll have to prove yourself to your men in a positive way.'

'So will you, Tony!' Jack said sharply to Paul's surprise. 'So will you!' He got to his feet. 'Thanks for the tea, Paul. I do feel so much better and I think it will work.' Then Jack was gone, into the darkness.

'So will I,' Tony repeated softly. 'Yes, so will I.' He stood up. 'Guess I'll have to return to the bosom of my company. Unfortunately, only a platonic bosom, but I suppose even Casanova had moments of frustration and enforced celibacy. See you in the morning, I guess. Look after yourself – I am sure you will; and very efficiently. You have changed a lot since the Poona days,' he said, disappearing into the night after Jack.

Paul stretched out on his groundsheet and wrapped himself in his blanket – the nights were still a bit chilly. War did a lot of things to people in a lot of different way, he thought. Perhaps he had changed, but was it for the better?

He did not reach an answer as sleep overtook him almost at once. But he awakened with a start shortly before daybreak as small-arms fire crackled from the direction of Kyaikto. There was a general stir as the Gurkhas took up positions, weapons at the ready. From the town came a crescendo of wild firing, but it was soon over: a small enemy patrol had slipped in from the direction of the sea, but a Sikh company from the FFR had soon driven them off.

After the excitement of an early skirmish, everyone began to prepare for the journey to the Sittang. Paul's battalion would be staying in its positions for some time yet, but he wanted to make certain that every man had sufficient water and so he arranged for extra *chagals* – the portable canvas water containers which could be tied onto the side of the packs.

With daylight, the FFR and the Malerkotla Field Company set off for the Sittang Bridge, Division HQ following at about 10.00 hours, while 48 Brigade, next in line, had to wait until later in the day when the earlier formations were well clear along the winding jungle road.

Everyone hoped that the division had broken away from the Japanese, certainly with at least sufficient time for the troops and transport to reach the safety of the west bank. But what they did not know was that two days earlier, when Smyth's withdrawal orders from the Bilin were being passed to the units at the front, the Japanese had intercepted a radio message which had been transmitted in clear.

Lieut. General Sakurai, commanding the renowned *33 Division,* was about to send his *215 Regt* on another attempt to turn the British left when he was handed the intercepted radio message. 'What inexperienced fools these British are.' He smiled at this senior staff officer. 'Not something our commanders would do.'

The smile gave the staff officer a shiver of fear. He would hate to be one of the general's commanders if he had sent such a message in clear.

'Now, we must move quickly,' Sakurai said, 'and reach the Sittang Bridge before the British.' He would catch them in a scorpion trap. He curled his hand like the claw of a scorpion and then snapped the fingers together, closing the hand into a fist.

So the vital race for the Sittang Bridge was under way, but it seemed as if the Japanese had the edge.

Chapter Five
The Road to Sittang

The road to Sittang was no more than a rough, winding track hewn out of the jungle, lying in thick red dust and pitted by previous air attacks. The transport column moved forward slowly, bouncing in the bomb craters, which was agonising for the scores of wounded in the ambulances. The long line of lorries, gun limbers, jeeps and ambulances raised a stifling cloud of red dust which grasped the marching infantry by the throat and brought on raking coughs. Mouths were soon as dry as desert sand, eyes red and sore as after a long night of debauchery. Brushwood from felled trees had been laid down to counteract the dust and the weary infantry cursed as they stumbled over both it and hidden tree stumps. That morning of 21 February 1942 was dry and hot, growing hotter by the minute along the airless track as the soldiers, hemmed in by the jungle, choked by the dust, weighed down by their packs, gasped for air and quite soon their shirts were black with sweat.

Out of that harsh blue sky came the Japanese aircraft. Bombs plunged down into the jungle and onto the track, disintegrating a supply lorry into a tangled mess of metal and matchwood and crackling flames. The soldiers flung themselves into the dense jungle, regardless of the sharp undergrowth, while the lorry drivers abandoned their vehicles and disappeared into the jungle. In the deserted ambulances, the wounded lay immobile, hearing the inferno of noise, clenching their fists in anticipation of a bomb striking the ambulance, opening up wounds in their anxiety as they called wildly for help.

Then the aircraft had gone as suddenly as they had come and the blue sky was clear apart from the scorching sun which was relentless. The lorries began to rumble forward again and the infantry plodded on through the dust, mouths still parched.

But the relief from the air was short-lived and as the sound of more aircraft built up in the sky, the soldiers hurried back to the dubious shelter of the jungle, while the transport drivers jumped out of their vehicles almost before the wheels had stopped moving. The air was filled with the roar of aircraft and an officer, his voice harsh with fear and despair, shouted, 'My God! They are British aircraft!'

With terrible accuracy, the Blenheims dropped their bombs, more lorries burst into flames and a gun limber was lifted like a model toy and hurled into the jungle. The mules, their eyes bulging with fear, broke away from their muleteers and stampeded through the trees, growing increasingly terrified as the undergrowth slashed their skins. Precious wireless sets were smashed or lost forever as the mules disappeared into the jungle. On the road, one of the wounded from an ambulance lay face down where he had fallen trying to scramble out of the vehicle and his lifeblood was flowing into the dust.

As the Blenheims turned away, a new sound filled the air. The tops of the trees shivered and the hot wind swirled madly as American P-40s roared over the terrified column, machine-guns flashing on the wing tips, flaying bullets, beating up the dust, igniting the petrol in a lorry which disappeared in a ball of black smoke. The Tomahawks searched out the infantry like bloodhounds, seeming to smell the fear that impregnated the jungle as the men hugged the ground or crouched behind trees.

When the aircraft turned away at last and headed back to Rangoon, the noise of their engines was replaced by the cries of the wounded, interspersed with shouts of officers and NCOs herding the men back onto the road and the lorry drivers into their vehicles. Men did what they could for their wounded comrades, applying bandages, trying to stem the flow of blood.

The wounded were carried to ambulances or were put as comfortably as possible in the back of lorries. Here and there a battalion doctor hurried to bring relief, to minimise the pain for the last moment of life in the most impossible cases.

With more shouts, orders and persuasion, the transport columns began to move forward again and the men trudged onwards. The heat seemed more oppressive, mouths were drier and swarms of flies settled on bloodstained, soiled bandages or buzzed exasperatingly around the heads of the marching men.

Everyone was tense, listening fearfully for the sound of returning aircraft, ready to hurl themselves into the jungle or out of the driving seat. The officers and NCOs drew on untapped sources of energy to keep the men moving, to give them encouragement.

But worse of all was the loss of valuable time. It was like a team scoring an own goal and left with only a few minutes to retrieve the situation before the final whistle.

While Division HQ and 48 Brigade dragged their weary feet towards the Sittang Bridge, 16 and 46 Brigades remained static. With the leading sectors of the column having to stop every now and then because of the air attacks and the nature of the road, there was no room for these brigades to tag on behind.

From his position to the north-west of Kyaikto, Paul could hear the distant hum of aircraft and the explosion of bombs beneath a sky now clouded with black smoke. He was thinking how lucky he was not to be caught in that jungle trap when aircraft swooped out of the smoke. He shouted to his men to take cover as the aircraft circled over the Boyagyi Rubber Estate, their bombs twisting down to explode in the estate where 16 Brigade had bivouacked. A bright light flashed among the rubber trees, like a vehicle's windscreen catching the sun for a moment, blinding in its sudden brightness. Then the boom of the explosion travelled across the paddy fields to Paul's clump of trees. Above the rubber plantation another column of black smoke curled into the sky.

Paul brought his binoculars into play and saw to his horror that the aircraft had British markings. A moment later a flight of P-40 Tomahawks flew over the rubber estate, strafing the area, their bullets slashing the rubber trees and the liquid from the trees flowing like tears.

As the Tomahawks passed overhead, Paul tensed. But they did not attack, although for a moment he was almost tempted to order his men to open fire. Then the aircraft banked over Kyaikto and vanished into the heat haze above the Sittang Estuary and out across the bay.

A long period of comparative silence followed, broken spasmodically by what sounded like the rattle of shots somewhere in the distance but which was probably burning bamboo. The only attack on Paul's position was from the flies, which evaded all attempts to kill them. He just had to sit and bear it, the hot sun slanting through the trees, drawing up the air to leave it stuffy and close, the sweat running down his face and welling under his arms.

'It is much too hot,' Tilbir said, mopping his brow.

'The only thought that relieves it,' Paul suggested, 'is that it must be a good deal hotter towards the Sittang.'

'But our turn will come, sahib.'

Jemedar Dilbahadur walked over from his platoon position, restless at having nothing to do. 'When will we be moving, sahib?'

'I doubt if it will be before tomorrow morning,' Paul told him. 'But there is always the chance that we might march through the night.'

'That would be a much better idea.' Dilbahadur removed his Gurkha hat to wipe away the sweat with a large, colourful handkerchief.

Paul remarked on the fine handkerchief. 'Oh, it is from Kalimpong, sahib. See the picture on it of a *natch* group?' A Nepali boy, one of the dancing group, in jodhpur-type trousers, jacket and the traditional hat which looked rather like one from a Christmas cracker without the frills, was dancing to the music of drum and flute.

'Oh! to be there now,' Paul said with feeling. 'In the Himalayas, drinking hot rum to keep out the cold beneath the snow-capped mountains.'

'Please, sahib.' Dilbahadur raised a hand. 'Spare us those memories. The heat is bad enough without having thoughts of the mountains.'

'And thoughts of the person who gave him the handkerchief,' the subedar said with a droll smile.

The jemedar folded the handkerchief carefully and put it away. 'It is true; I did not buy it in the bazaar. But it is always good to have some token that was given by someone dear to you.'

The tough, solid, pugnacious Dilbahadur seemed the last person to have such romantic notions. Paul supposed that at times like these everyone had to give a different impression. Even Dilbahadur had his dream to cling to – the wife and family in Nepal – to give him a greater determination to live, to fight harder, to destroy his enemies before they destroyed him. And especially because so far he only had daughters, three of them, and he so desperately wanted a son, like all Nepalis, to perpetuate his name.

Gopiram said suddenly, 'The Colonel Sahib is coming.'

Osborne, with Robin, the subedar major, and a couple of bodyguards, came out of the sunlight into the relatively cool shade of Paul's headquarters. 'Everything all right, Paul?'

'Thank you, sir. Though a bit concerned at being bombed by our own aircraft.'

'It's very difficult in jungle warfare. Especially when wireless communication is so poor and the tactical situation so fluid. I'm sure it won't be the only time we get strafed by our own planes.'

At that moment a whistle was blown to warn of an approaching aircraft which sounded in trouble. They rushed out into the open as a fighter appeared over the trees to their left, only just clearing them, branches and leaves scattering in all directions. The aircraft was losing height rapidly, enveloped in black smoke. And through the smoke Paul saw the grinning mouth and sharp teeth of a tiger shark painted along the aircraft's nose: one of the American Volunteers Group, The Flying Tigers.

The Tomahawk hit the paddy field, bounced off the mud ridges and came down again with a splintering crash, pieces of the plane breaking off, to cartwheel along the field. Then the wheelless plane slithered across the ground like a sledge. And Paul was running towards it, boots crushing the stubble of the paddy field. Ahead, what was left of the plane at last came to a grinding halt and in a moment was almost concealed in black smoke.

Paul's breath came in gasps and he could feel the sweat running into his eyes. The pilot was struggling to release his safety harness. Paul got him free, but the pilot was a big man and he seemed injured, so it was a struggle to pull him out of the cockpit. Paul caught hold of him roughly in his anxiety to get him away from the plane as the pilot cried out in pain, 'My hand! My bloody hand!'

'OK! OK! Got to get you out.'

Gopiram came running up and with his help, they pulled the pilot out. The American collapsed onto his knees, groaning, dazed. Paul hoisted him to his feet and started to stumble away from the aircraft. By now, Amarjit had reached the plane.

'Run for it!' Paul shouted, expecting the plane to blow at any moment, but the Gurkhas ignored his orders, coming up on each side to help support the injured man. They half ran, half stumbled away from the aircraft.

From the corner of his eyes, Amarjit saw a flash of flame. 'Down, sahib!' They fell flat, the pilot crying out again as he was pressed roughly into the ground. Then the Tomahawk blew up with a searing flash of heat that Paul could feel along the back of his neck. Paul pressed himself further into the ground for what seemed an eternity, until all of a sudden he realised that there was silence, except for men shouting excitedly in the distance.

Paul staggered to his feet, helping the pilot up. He saw that the man's face was smeared with oil and smoke, his eyes screwed up in pain. He was wearing a zip-up leather jacket with a huge eagle embossed on the back, a painted Hawaiian scarf, Levis tucked into Texas boots and a 45 Colt automatic in a holster at his hip.

They helped him towards the Regimental Aid Post, passing some British soldiers who had come across their position. One of them called out, 'Bloody Yank bastard!'

'Get back to the USA and shit on your own lot,' shouted another.

The pilot was startled, a puzzled look on his face. 'What the hell?' he muttered. 'What the hell?'

'Take no notice,' Paul said.

The voice of a sergeant major bellowed across the field. 'You lousy, idle layabouts! Come back here!'

The soldiers froze for a moment, a look of horror on their faces. Then they turned and doubled back in the direction of a red-faced sergeant major, hands on hips, waiting for them at the far end of the field.

At the Regimental Aid Post, Doc Green said, 'Right, let's have a look at you. Hmm. Yes.' He ran his hand down the pilot's left arm to the wrist, which was badly swollen. The pilot winced. 'You're lucky,' Doc said. 'I'm pretty sure nothing is broken. To be absolutely sure I'd have to see an X-ray and needless to say, I don't have one of those with me! Painful, is it?'

'Yeah.'

The American looked rather green, Paul thought.

'I'll try to ease the pain,' Doc said, giving him an injection. 'That should help.'

The pilot was tottering and Paul grabbed him just in time. When he came round a little while later Doc was adjusting a sling.

'Here, drink this,' Paul said.

'What is it?'

'Hot, sweet tea. Do you a power of good.'

'A slug of whisky would do me more good.'

But he drank the tea and the colour began to return to his face. He looked to be in his late twenties, a touch below 6 feet, with fair hair and hard blue eyes, lean and probably tough, Paul guessed. At the moment he looked a bit weary and there was still pain in his eyes; it wasn't every day that he crash-landed a Tomahawk and walked away from the wreckage with just a badly sprained wrist and a few cuts and bruises, which Doc's medical orderly was now treating.

'What's your name?' Paul asked.

'Dean. Ray Dean. You the guy who pulled me out?'

'One of them.' He told Dean his name.

'Thanks, Paul. My recollection is it was just you. But I know you British like to play everything down, so I won't say any more.' He grinned over the medical orderly's head.

Paul felt a hand on his arm. It was the colonel. He just squeezed it lightly to say well done and then he spoke to the pilot.

'Mr Dean, or is it Captain?'

'I guess captain would be appropriate, Colonel.'

'Doc tells me that apart from your wrist, you have suffered no other injuries. I am happy to hear it.'

'Look, sir. You're all being very polite, but I sense something isn't right. The way those two Limeys welcomed me – that wasn't just the usual Anglo-American friendly banter.'

'I am afraid your squadron and the RAF bombed and strafed our troops on the way to the Sittang Bridge earlier today. They probably caused frightful damage which we can ill afford at this stage.'

Ray was startled. 'First, let me say that I was not with the group this morning; two of us were on a separate mission, later, when we were jumped by several Japs. My wing man was shot down and I was hit, but I managed to get away and I thought the plane would keep going long enough to get home. But no such luck. And when I crashed it really surprised me to find British troops. I thought the Japs would be waiting for me.

'You see, we had a report from an air reconnaissance this morning that a column of some 300 vehicles was moving through Kyaikto. All available aircraft at Rangoon were put on alert and given the Kyaikto–Mokpalin road as the western limit for the bombing operation. Before I took off on my mission, the pilots returned and said they had found a long column of Jap transport and troops and given them hell. My God, if they knew ... When they find out, they'll really be cut up, Colonel. I guess I know now why those British Tommies called me a bloody Yank bastard. All I can say is thank God it was not my finger on the button. Which is no way of trying to get out of the mistake.'

'Think no more of it, Ray,' the colonel assured him. 'I'm afraid in jungle warfare this sort of terrible error is going to be difficult to prevent. Now, what are we going to do about you?'

Robin said, 'I'm afraid there is no way we can contact your base. Wireless communication with Rangoon is rather temperamental at the moment.'

'We should be moving towards the bridge tomorrow,' the colonel added. 'We'll find room for you in one of the brigade ambulances. Meanwhile, I'm sure Paul will look after you.' The colonel glanced at Paul.

'Of course, sir'

Ray got to his feet and swayed for a moment. Paul caught hold of him. 'Steady.'

'You sure there wasn't any Scotch in that tea, Doc?'

Doc smiled. 'Not even a medicinal tot. You'll be all right in a while. Stay in the shade. A cold compress would have done a world of good, but we are completely out of ice!'

'I've had a couple of *chagals* lying in deep shade,' Paul said quickly.

'Fine, I'll leave it to you. See you later, Ray.'

Paul helped Ray back to C Company HQ, where Gopiram made up a comfortable bed of grass and a groundsheet. A *chagal* – a canvas water container so useful as a reserve and easily attached to a pack – was brought out and Gopiram bathed the pilot's hand and wrist with the ice-cold water.

'That is great,' Ray said with a sigh of relief.

Afterwards, Ray sank back onto the makeshift bed. But Paul guessed he was determined to prove he was as tough as any Brit.

'Your clothes are in a bit of a mess,' Paul said. 'I'm sure you'd feel better in something clean.'

'I didn't pack a weekend bag,' Ray said with a grin.

Subedar Tilbir said, 'Would it not be better for the American Flying Sahib to change into British uniform?'

Paul knew the subedar was right. The sight of Ray in his leather jacket would be like a red flag to other troops who may have been victims of the bombing. Besides, it was not the best of attires for the jungle.

Thandraj, appropriately, like a real quartermaster, spoke up. 'He is about the same size as Captain Sanderson Sahib. I understand that the sahib's belongings are still in the care of the B Company QMH. If you were to ask Hunter Sahib ...'

'I will write him a note and you can deliver it and bring back the items,' Paul explained to Ray who liked the idea. Paul could not resist asking, 'I presume you come from Texas?' just to see the pilot's reaction.

Dean laughed. 'That's what everyone thinks. They believe the AVG is made up of Texans, but we come from more than forty states. I'm from California, myself.'

'That just shows my ignorance. And I probably know even less about your squadron.'

'The AVG? Well, the AVG is one man's dream: Claire Lee Chennault, probably the world's leading expert on fighter aircraft, is a great, dedicated man who tried for years to convince the American Air Force that the fighter was the tactical aircraft of the future. But he was considered too revolutionary, so when an opportunity arose they retired him early – physically disqualified at forty-seven from flying duties because he was partially deaf.

'Then Madame Chiang Kai-shek persuaded him to take a job, training and organising the Chinese Air Force. That was in 1937, the year the Japs began their undeclared war against China. And while the rest of the world stood back, the Japs forced Chiang Kai-shek deep into the interior of China, to the province of Yunnan, where he made his headquarters in the main town of Kunming.

'The Old Man – that's Chennault – was convinced that a world war was imminent, so he prepared for the future by building airstrips, storing huge quantities of gasoline, bombs and ammunition on fields in Eastern China.'

Ray shook out a couple of cigarettes from a pack of Camels and Paul lit the pilot's and his own. Ray then told him that when World War II began, although the United States kept out of it, Chennault knew that they would have to enter the affray in the end and he also knew that China could play a major role in keeping large Japanese forces occupied. But to do this, urgent supplies were needed from the West.

According to Ray, in the spring of 1941, the States committed itself to Lend-Lease for China, and Britain allowed supplies to move up Burma from Rangoon to Lashio, north of Mandalay, to the start of the dangerous Burma Road over the mountains to Kunming. At the same time, President Roosevelt gave Chennault the go-ahead to look for volunteers at the air bases of the army, navy and marine corps for his fighter force. Ray was a lieutenant in the Army Air Corps when one of Chennault's men visited the air base.

'I was going through a bad patch at the time. Won't go into details, but the usual thing, woman trouble. Also, I liked the idea of flying fighter planes.' He laughed. 'And there was money in it, too – 600 bucks a month: 675 for flight leaders, 750 for squadron leaders. There was also an unofficial bonus of 500 dollars from the Chinese Government for each Jap plane you shot down'.

They assembled at San Francisco in the summer of 1941, 200 of them – an equal percentage of pilots and mechanics – and then they were shipped to Rangoon, where they were put on a train to Toungoo and lodged in old British barracks on Kyedaw Aerodrome.

'I suppose Chennault put you through a tough course.'

'That he did, Paul. But it was all worth it. And he also gave us a good fighter: the P-40, which the British had turned down in favour of the Brewster Buffalo – a decision they have regretted. But Chennault believed in the P-40 and he was proved right.'

'So you have been involved in quite a few dogfights over Rangoon?'

'A few.'

'How many Japs have you shot down?'

'One or two.'

Paul laughed. 'And you accused the British of being modest.'

Ray smiled, shyly. 'As it's you, Paul, I'll tell you I have claimed four to date and there may have been a few more who did not make it back to their home base.'

'And how did you get the name of Flying Tigers?'

'That's what the Chinese called us after the sabre-toothed tiger of Fukien, China's national symbol. And we embellished it by painting a tiger shark along the nose of each P-40 under the prop spinner and covering the gap of the prestone radiator – also a blood-red tongue and a fierce eye, just aft of the propeller and forwards of the exhaust stacks.'

'You certainly seem to have been giving the Japs a bloody nose over Rangoon!'

'The trouble is the shortage of P-40s. Chennault says even ten million dollars could not get a replacement for every one shot down or damaged, because of the lack of spare parts. We've destroyed a lot of Japs, but in proportion, our own ships are dwindling dangerously fast.'

'But you say the Japs have had to pay a heavy price?'

'Sure. It seems that the Japs' brass decided to knock out the weak Allied air force rather than give their own *15th Army* more close support on the ground. Their first air raid on Rangoon was on 23 December and as there was no anti-aircraft defence, it all rested on the fighters. I guess the Japs lost a dozen or so on that day. But rather more on Christmas Day, close on twenty, I would guess, and we lost two AVGs and six RAF – they were still flying their Buffaloes then, poor shits!

'We did quite a bit of attacking ourselves: Jap shipping … airfields they had captured. I think the Jap's air force chief got rather overheated about the general failure of his bombers to flatten Rangoon and his fighters to knock us out of the sky. They came at us like wild dogs for six days at the end of January, over 200 of them, and mostly fighters. By the end of the week, they had lost over 50 by our reckoning and they switched to nights, just a few bombers slipping in for quick raids.'

'I suppose most of them fell to the guns of the AVG.'

'We had the advantage over your RAF's 67th Squadron, although give their pilots their due, they never hesitated to go up in their flying coffins. It's different now, that is in the past week, with the arrival of their 17th and 135th Squadrons, equipped with Hurricanes. We've worked well together. And your bomber boys, two squadrons of Blenheims, 45th and 113th have been out over the Jap airfields.'

Ray offered Paul another Camel. 'Is this your only pack?' Paul asked.

Ray unzipped his leather jacket with his right hand and revealed two large pockets on the inside. 'Another six packs,' he said, laughing. 'Now that is my idea of a survival kit!'

They lit up.

'Ever been to 'Frisco, Paul?'

Paul shook his head.

'No? Then I guess we'll have to put that right after the war. That's a firm invitation. Mind you keep it.'

Just then, Thandraj returned with the items of clothing and a short while later, Ray looked like a British officer of Gurkhas. He was almost the same size as the unfortunate Sanderson, so the khaki shorts fitted perfectly.

'You'll never get that shirt on,' Paul protested. 'You'll have to keep your own shirt on.'

Ray laughed. 'Lucky I am not wearing one of my jazzy shirts today.'

Fortunately, the boots could have been made for him and Gopiram fastened on his gun belt.

Ray placed his right hand on the automatic's butt. 'Lucky it's my left hand that's out of action.' Then he added, 'OK. But, look, Paul, the fact is that I'm not so keen about travelling in an ambulance. It's not so easy to get out of if it's shot up – and I understand the Japs are no respecters of the Red Cross. And I won't know anybody. I'll just be a bloody Yankee bastard who bombed his own side. So what I am getting at is can I march with you?'

Paul looked doubtful, so Ray went on quickly, 'This injury won't worry me. I'll keep up with you all right.'

'It's going to be hot out there tomorrow,' Paul explained, 'and dusty. There's a shortage of water and I wouldn't be surprised if we were attacked by the Jap infantry.'

'All the more reason for me to be with you. I would respect your experience – you wouldn't have to look after me in an ambulance, then.'

'All right. But providing Doc gives his OK; and, of course, the colonel agrees.'

'That's swell. But what should I do about my leather jacket and the rest of my stuff?'

We'll give it to a medical orderly on one of the ambulances and you can collect it again once we are over the bridge.' He paused and then said seriously, 'There is one other thing, Ray …'

'Sure, anything.'

'You don't wear a Gurkha hat as though you're Nelson Eddy in *Rose Marie*. It should be more to one side, the brim slanting across the head at about 45 degrees. And the strap is a chinstrap; it does not tuck in at the back of your head.'

While 17 Division was starting on its journey to the Sittang Bridge in Rangoon, General Hutton was having doubts about a successful outcome to the Sittang River Front. If the Japanese broke through then the loss of Rangoon was a very strong possibility. A convoy was due in Rangoon but in view of the situation, Hutton advised the navy to return to Calcutta all seventeen ships, except those carrying the armoured brigade, 1 Cameronians and auxiliary pioneers. He then cabled Wavell on the twentieth advising him of his actions.

Malaya had been overrun and Singapore had surrendered a few days earlier, but thousands of miles away in Lembang, Wavell still seemed unable to understand why the Japanese were considered such formidable enemies. Furiously, he cabled Hutton saying that he did not believe the enemy to be superior or the Japanese air force to be a problem. The enemy was obviously tired and had suffered heavy casualties and, as far as he was concerned, there was no sign that the Japanese were in superior strength. There was no need for further withdrawals and Hutton was ordered to attack the enemy with all the air force available.

All the armchair generals were now putting in their opinions. Back in India, the Viceroy, showing an apparent ignorance of the situation, and residing many hundreds of miles from the front line, sent a telegram to Churchill: *Our troops in Burma are not fighting with proper relish. I have not the least doubt that this is in great part due to lack of drive and inspiration from the top.*

The hunt was on again to find scapegoats and Churchill forwarded the telegram to Wavell and asked if he agreed. Wavell did, emphatically, so Churchill said he would send General Sir Harold Alexander, the C.-in-C. Southern Command in England, to replace Huttton and to command, as he put it, 'the considerable army now being assembled on Burma Front.' Churchill was probably under the illusion that two Australian divisions from the Middle East, on their way back to Australia, would be allowed to divert to Burma. But the Prime Minister of Australia had other ideas. He was more concerned about the safety of Australia from possible Japanese attacks. Alexander would certainly not be arriving to lead a large army to victory.

It was after dark on the evening of the twenty-first when 4/12th Frontier Force Regiment and the Malerkotla Sappers arrived at the bridge. Both units were exhausted and shaken by the air attack in which the FFR had suffered some fifty casualties. Little had been done to form a strong bridgehead, but it was decided to leave the readjustment of the bridgehead positions until the next day.

Captain R. Orgill, commanding the sappers, walked over to the bridge with his 2 i/c, Lieutenant Basher Ahmad. General Smyth and the CRE believed that the charges were already in place and had only to be detonated. But when Orgill examined the bridge, he was horrified to find that although the wooden boxes to hold the gelignite had been fitted to three spans, they were empty. The explosives, together with the detonators and the instantaneous detonating fuse, had been removed. The sappers quickly reported to the CRE.

'Well, the bridge has to be ready for detonation by 18.00 hours tomorrow,' the CRE said.

'My men are completely exhausted after the march and the trauma of the bombing,' Orgill protested.

'Just get on with it, Orgill.'

'Yes, sir.'

He gathered his weary men together and led them to the bridge, where they worked through the night of the twenty-first/twenty-second. By 18.00 hours on the twenty-second, Orgill was able to report that two spans of the eleven-span bridge were ready and a third was as ready as the lack of suitable material allowed.

The day before, the troops of Division HQ and 48 Brigade had stretched back along the track. Dry throats and empty stomachs coming on top of the hard-fought four days at Bilin, the hot sun, the dust and the cruel bombing by their own side had drained the energy from most of them. There were no rations at Mokpalin; the soldiers had to forage for food and cooking did not begin until midnight – and in some cases not at all.

Division HQ, the Baluchis and 1/4th Gurkhas were bivouacked at the Mokpalin Quarries, a mile south of Mokpalin village, while the 5th and 3rd Gurkha Rifles Battalions had halted further back along the track because of the water shortage.

The situation was serious and was growing more so by the minute. But at last a decision was made to start sending the transport over as they arrived. The approach to the bridge was thick with dust, the bridge itself had only recently been boarded over for motor traffic and was not as secure as it might have been, and the transport could show no lights. Progress was slow, each driver full of tension as he steered his vehicle onto the bridge and across the rattling boards.

Wireless communication with Rangoon and between Division HQ and its brigades had been tenuous most of the day. So, at around midnight, a staff officer arrived from Rangoon to report verbally that the Japanese might drop parachutists to seize the bridge from the west bank. He also advised the general that 7 Armoured Brigade had arrived in Rangoon, but because all the dock labour had fled, the men were having to unload the tanks themselves and could not get up to the front for at least twenty-four hours.

Smyth decided that the threat of enemy parachutists had to be taken seriously. Sending at once for Lieut. Colonel Lentaigne, commanding 1/4th Gurkhas, Smyth told him to get his men across the bridge by dawn at all costs and be ready to deal with any parachutists.

The general was sending his headquarters across at 04.00 hours and the battalion should follow about a quarter of an hour later.

The early hours of the twenty-second were flying past, but the great bulk of 17 Division had still not crossed the bridge; indeed, it was spread over 15 miles and two of the brigades had not even moved a step. Smyth was prepared to send his HQ forward at 04.00 hours, but about an hour earlier disaster struck when the driver of a 3-ton lorry engaged top gear rather than second, stamped hard on the accelerator instead of the brake in his fright to avoid bumping into an ambulance ahead of him, swerved and ran off the wooden planking, to jam tight in the girders. No recovery apparatus was available and, because the bridge was a girder type, the lorry could not be manhandled over the side. By the light of flares, the sappers laboured for three and a half desperate hours before the traffic flow could be resumed at 06.30 hours.

Unaware of the jam, Lentaigne led his battalion from the Mokpalin Quarries towards the bridge, but on reaching Mokpalin, in the first glimmer of dawn, he found the single village street clogged with transport, engines revving, horns blowing. By perseverance he got his battalion through, only to find that the bridge was completely blocked, but fortunately there was a narrow catwalk for permanent way gangs which ran along the bridge outside the upstream girders.

The Gurkhas crossed as daylight strengthened, the metal catwalk slippery with dew. But the hillmen negotiated it without any disasters. On the other side, Lentaigne established his HQ , digging in some 600 yards from a company of the Duke of Wellington's Regiment whose company commander was most sceptical about the paratroop attack, and he was proved right.

Meanwhile, on the east bank there was chaos. By the time the bridge had been cleared, transport stretched back towards Mokpalin and beyond, double-banked in places, and to add to the snarl up, the vehicles of 16 and 46 Brigades had begun to arrive. There was no traffic control because of a shortage of provost staff. Some drivers cut into the column in no order, while others stopped to collect items which had fallen off their overloaded vehicles, causing more hold-up and confusion than ever reported by an AA Patrol on a bank holiday.

At first light, Smyth moved towards the bridge. On the way he stopped for a moment at the Advanced Dressing Station of 39 Field Ambulance, sited near the east end of the bridge, where the assistant and deputy directors of Medical Services had spent the night in a field ambulance. The general's old friend, Colonel Mackenzie, the ADMS, offered him a cup of tea.

'Kind of you, Mac, but I think I had better push on. I'll see you later on the other side.'

The general crossed the bridge to contact Lentaigne and to select positions for the brigades as they arrived. He then chose to move Division HQ to Abya, some 5 miles to the west, while Brigadier Hugh-Jones of 48 Brigade set up his headquarters about a mile west of the bridge.

At about 08.30 hours, as the Baluchis, much reduced in numbers after their magnificent last-ditch stand at the Salween, were marching through the railway cutting onto the bridge, a savage burst of firing signalled the arrival of the Japanese. A fierce attack out of the jungle north-east of the bridgehead scattered the 3rd Burma Rifles detachment holding the area and for a moment the bridge was wide open to be seized intact by the enemy.

The sappers had just completed their preparation for destroying one span of the bridge and were ordered to stand by to detonate, but the gallant FFR, supported by the remnants of the Baluchis, put in a fierce counter-attack and recaptured the ground east of the cutting, but at a price of fifty casualties.

Hugh-Jones was ordered to take over control of all bridgehead troops. A horseshoe-shaped bridgehead was formed with an intermingled force consisting of the Duke's company and 4th Gurkha Rifles, rushed over from the west bank, the FFR, the Baluchis and the 3rd Burma Rifles. They dug in with their hands as enemy shells fell, but they stood firm, Hugh-Jones extending the bridgehead later to the general line: railway cutting, Pagoda Hill (above the cutting to the north) and Bungalow Hill (about 500 yards south of Pagoda Hill).

In view of the situation, the CRE 17 Division gave orders for the destruction of about 300 sampans, which had been collected on the west bank, and all the power-driven vessels which had been transporting mules and guns north of the bridge.

The Advanced Dressing Station was overrun and Colonel Mackenzie and his deputy were captured. It had been a narrow escape for Smyth: if he had stopped for that cup of tea he would have gone into the cage.

Simultaneously with their attack on the bridgehead, the Japanese had fallen upon the long line of transport jammed up towards Mokpalin and defended by a few baggage guards. The area was soon a shambles of burning trucks, while mortar bombs and shells, rifle and machine-gun fire exploded and cracked about the hills and echoed across the river where the safety of the west bank was so near and yet so far.

Paul knew nothing of these events as he moved his company out of its position outside Kyaikto to at last take the dusty track to Sittang. The transport had driven off in the hours before dawn, no lights, but the whine of the engines as they crawled on low gear seemed loud enough to Paul to awake every Japanese for miles around.

The night before, Brigadiers "Jonah" Jones and Ekin had met at the Boyagyi Rubber Estate to discuss the precarious situation in which they found themselves. Both brigades had remained stationary all day and some of 46 Brigade's rearguard patrols had made contact with enemy patrols. Ekin was most anxious to march through the night, because he felt that every hour brought the enemy closer to the bridge, and Jones was in agreement. Unfortunately, the track was blocked by 48 Brigade. As the next best alternative, they decided to send the combined transport of 16 and 46 Brigades, and in that order, at 03.00 hours, followed three hours later by the troops – in the same order of march, less 4th Burma Rifles, who would withdraw along the railway line on the left flank.

The track passed the rubber trees of the Boyagyi Estate and continued into the jungle. The sun had still not topped the tall trees, but rays slanted here and there through the foliage to etch bright yellow stripes across the dust. The heat was already building up, the swirling dust raising coughs all down the column, men spitting dust onto the side of the track. Soon, there would hardly be enough spittle in the heat-dried mouths and so the water had to be conserved.

In 46 Brigade, 3/7th Gurkhas were in the lead, followed by the

Dogras, next 4/15th Gurkhas and finally the Duke's. Ray Dean marched at Paul's side; a brightly coloured neckerchief across the pilot's mouth making him look like a bandit. Ray's legs seemed to be moving without too much discomfort – he swore the boots could have been made for him, but it was early days yet, Paul thought.

Ray's left hand was in a sling and was not quite as swollen; Doc had given him another injection at around 03.00 hours before going off ahead with the ambulances. Gopiram had found a haversack and water bottle for Ray and had cut him a strong stick.

'Makes me look like Baden-Powell,' Ray complained, but not very earnestly, because he soon found out its value as he trudged along the track.

At around 09.30 hours, the column halted, the head just south of the Meyon Chaung, because Brigadier Ekin wanted to give the rearguard battalion, the Duke's, a chance to catch up. Tony, whose D Company was bringing up the battalion's rear, came forward to have a few words while they lounged at the side of the track.

'How's it going, Ray?'

The American lowered his neckerchief. 'Just fine. I hadn't realised that rinsing out your mouth with red Burmese dust braces you for the rest of the day!'

'You must be missing your Tomahawk.'

'I admit I am. I could give you more assistance from up there than as a crock down here.'

'Consider yourself a liaison officer,' Paul said, 'spreading Anglo–American relations. When we look at you we can at least say that the United States is in the war now, so things can only get better.'

'Things will probably get a lot worse before they start to get better, Paul. We haven't exactly shone as yet in the Pacific. I guess we were caught with our pants down, but one thing is for sure, we Americans don't let our pants lie around our ankles for long. They'll be pulled up soon enough, and the belt tightened, and then the Japs had better look out.'

There was a stir down the front of the column. 'I'd best get back,' Tony said. 'See you later.'

'Sure, Tony. Look after yourself.'

Paul watched his friend's lean figure stride through the dust. Tony looked back once and gave a sort of half salute. Paul felt nervous about him; he looked strained and worried because his company had not yet heard a shot fired in anger.

'Is he a good friend of yours?' Ray queried. And when Paul nodded his head, he added, 'I shouldn't worry about him. I'd say he could look after himself.'

'He's very good with women,' Paul said.

'There you are! Shows he has strong red blood.'

Paul laughed. 'Come on. We're moving.'

They had only marched a short distance, already beginning to feel lethargic in the heat and dust, when a fusillade resounded from the front of the column. When 46 Brigade had halted earlier, 16 Brigade had been unaware of this and had carried on, leaving a gap of about a mile. By ill chance, the Japanese forces had reached the road at this point and had quickly set up a roadblock some 7 miles from the Sittang Bridge.

The 3/7th Gurkhas fought fiercely to clear the block, but the Japanese resisted strongly. Back along the track, Paul had moved his men west of the road, listening to the battle raging ahead as machine-gun and rifle fire raked the brigade column and mortar bombs caused havoc.

Then, the jungle to the east of the road was suddenly full of noisy, chattering, shouting Japanese. They came onto the road in a bunch of about twenty, obviously to build a second roadblock, unaware of C Company's presence. The Gurkhas opened fire, tearing the enemy's ranks apart, the survivors stumbling back into the far jungle. Almost at once the far jungle wall was like a parade of flashing lights as machine-guns retaliated, but the bullets going high. Shrapnel from mortar bombs, whirling like propellers, cut chunks out of the trees. Someone screamed in pain.

The jungle erupted in a thick mass of helmeted, khaki-uniformed soldiers, doubling across the track in two groups of fifteen, shouting with rage, bayonets fixed. They were met with more fierce volleys from the Gurkhas. Those who reached C Company's line were cut down by khukuris. Subedar Tilbir was a fighting machine Paul hardly knew had existed within his quiet exterior. The khukuri was in the hands of a master as he brought it into deadly effect, a whirling wheel of flashing steel that was soon red with blood.

Paul shouted out, 'Amarjit! Attack from the left!' Then he turned to Dilbahadur. 'Quickly, Jemedar Sahib. Blitz attack.'

The Gurkhas raced across the track, over the dead bodies and into the jungle, Bren-gunners firing from the hip, tommy guns and rifles coming together, the stocky Dilbahadur screaming, '*Ayo, Gurkhali!*'

An enemy soldier appeared in front of Paul and then fell away, blood a mask across his face as Paul's tommy gun bullets smashed into his head. The noise was intense: hand grenades crunched, burst casings tearing into flesh and trees, screams and shouts mingled. The Japanese machine-gun position loomed up suddenly, red flashes spitting out brightly in the half sunlight. Paul felt his shirt nicked by a near miss and the Gurkha next to him stumbled into a tree and sprawled over, eyes glazed. And then 10 Platoon was on top of the machine-gun post, the gunner and his crew killed in the heavy, point-blank fusillade.

Paul suddenly sensed danger and turned quickly. A Japanese officer was a few strides away, Samurai sword held high in both hands, mouth open in a cry of rage. But suddenly the sword swung out of his hands, cartwheeling through the air, flashing as sunlight through the trees caught the tempered steel before it was extinguished in the dense undergrowth. The officer collapsed, blood spreading across his chest.

Paul looked quickly over his shoulder. Ray was standing there, appearing quite calm, left hand in a sling, right hand holding the .45 Colt Automatic he had used with such casual accuracy.

Almost at the same time the action stopped abruptly and Paul could now hear shooting further to his right from Tony's direction and much further to his left, but more spasmodic. And he could feel himself breathing quickly as he wondered what toll had been paid in the savage close-quarter action.

He signalled Dilbahadur to return to the main company position, where Amarjit had also returned with his platoon after a successful attack. With the company now together in all-round firing positions, Paul walked among the men with Tilbir to check on the casualties: eight had died, one was seriously wounded and there were several with minor injuries. Japanese bodies littered the road.

Paul was now able to turn to Ray. 'Thanks. A fine piece of marksmanship. I'm glad I had you as my wing man!'

'It was a pleasure, Paul. An experience I would not have missed for the world.'

Paul wondered if Ray was really feeling as cool as his outward appearance implied or, like himself, were his insides churning over? Tilbir coughed politely, which Paul knew was a gentle hint that he had not issued an order he should have.

'Yes, sahib?'

'Should we be moving forward, sahib?'

'Of course.' Jack Hunter was ahead and Paul beckoned to Thandraj. 'Take two men and make contact with B Company.'

The quartermaster slipped away. A moment later, Gopiram said, 'D Company Sahib is coming.'

Paul looked up with relief as Tony parted the foliage and approached. His uniform was crumpled and covered in dust and he did not look as suave as usual. 'You all right, Tony?' Paul asked anxiously.

'Fine,' Tony croaked – no doubt his mouth felt as dry and bitter as Paul's. 'But you!' He looked around at the bodies sprawled everywhere.

'Were you not attacked?' Paul asked in surprise.

'Only a small bunch of five or six. Must have got lost. Bharti Rai's platoon sorted them out. So, what happens now?'

'I've sent my QM forward for orders. If we stay here much longer we could find ourselves a target for their artillery.'

Paul was relieved when Thandraj returned a moment later with a message that Brigadier Ekin was collecting as many of the brigade as possible and marching off to the west. B Company would send word back as soon as the brigadier was ready.

Tony said, 'Right, I'll get back to my company.'

'I'll wait for you to make contact before I move off,' Paul assured him. Tony crashed through the jungle and hurried back to his company. Paul turned to Tilbir. 'What about our wounded?'

'Sadly, the very seriously wounded man has died. As for the other wounded, the medical orderly is patching them up as best he can. They should be able to keep up with us, but we will have to see. If necessary, one or two might have to be carried.'

Paul's mouth really felt dry and he longed for a drink, wondering if the men had been at their water bottles. 'Let everyone have a drink. But in moderation.' He added softly, 'If they have any left.'

Tilbir smiled wryly. Water discipline was very difficult to enforce, especially among the younger Gurkhas.

Paul turned to Ray. 'Have a drink.' The pilot reached quickly for his water bottle – clearly, he had been following orders strictly, but had forgotten he only had one good hand. Gopiram stepped up at once to unclip Ray's water bottle and remove the cork.

The mouthful of water Paul had was like nectar. He could so easily have drunk it all; it was with stern resolution that he put the cork firmly back and returned the bottle to the webbing holder on his belt.

Ray gasped, 'It's been a long time since I appreciated water so much.'

'How's your hand?' Paul asked, remembering and thinking he should have asked earlier.

Ray kept it hidden in the sling. 'Just fine, Paul. Getting better all the time.'

It was probably very painful, but there was nothing Paul could do to help, so he grinned and said. 'That's great.'

The men were growing restless; they wanted to move on. A couple of men from B Company came up breathlessly at that moment. One said, 'The Brigadier Sahib is marching. Hunter Sahib says to hurry.' And just then Amarjit reported that Tony's company had made contact.

C Company moved off at once. Dilbahadur's composite 10 Platoon in front, then HQ, and Amarjit bringing up the rear with 12 Platoon. They followed the path cut through the jungle by the B Company guides. After a while they halted, as contact had been made with B Company. Then they advanced again.

Brigadier Ekin had collected a mixed force of some 500 men with the intention of moving west to bypass the roadblock, but leading a mixed force of that strength in such thick jungle was an arduous task. Paul had his compass, trying to keep track of the direction, because there was every possibility of losing contact. It was hot and close now, the skin on his arms and legs burning where they had come into contact with the undergrowth. That drop of water was already just a faint memory, for his mouth felt dry again, his lips were cracked and there was hardly any spittle left.

His mind began to wander, feeling drowsy in the heat and because of the monotonous stumbling through the jungle. He came alert with a start: somewhere behind there was the crunch of mortars and then the rattle of machine-guns, towards Tony's company or perhaps among the Duke's. Paul stepped out of the column, directing the men to continue, until Amarjit came up, when they both waited. And in the distance there was more mortar and rifle fire.

Paul wondered if he should go back and help D Company. They had the Duke's behind them and he risked losing contact with the rest of the brigade. He decided it was more important to get his own company forward; the brigade might still be an effective force if Ekin had as many men as possible available to him when he came out of the jungle and into Mokpalin, where Paul guessed he must be heading.

Paul hurried forwards again past his men to take up his position in the column, coming suddenly out of the jungle and onto the bank of a dry *chaung*, where the leading section was in a huddle.

'What is it?'

The section leader pointed to the two rear men from B Company who were a link with C Company. One of them looked nervous.

'Huzoor, I do not know what happened. I stopped for a moment because this large clump of jungle snapped back off the man in front and into my face.' Paul could see the blood oozing from the scratch. 'I cut it aside with my khukuri to clear the way and then beyond there was no sign of the others. I hurried forwards, but there were two tracks. The one to the right looked freshly cut, so I followed it and came out on this *chaung*. But no one has been this way.'

Faintly in the distance, Paul could hear mortar bombs and the crackle of light automatics as D Company and the Duke's continued their engagement. He supposed he could retrace their steps to where the man had gone wrong, but then what? How many more blind alleys would he find? The subedar and Ray came forward with Dilbahadur.

Paul said, 'I think we are about a mile, perhaps a bit less, south-west of the road. The course of the *chaung* seems to be heading in the right direction. If we follow it upstream we should hit the road about a mile short of the Mokpalin Quarries, unless it veers too much later on, in which case we shall have to take to the jungle again and follow the compass.'

Paul told the naik of the leading section to carry on along the bank of the *chaung*, which had only a light covering of jungle and was quite dry, and to take the two B Company men into his section. Then the company moved off again. There was no more firing from the last-known position of Tony's company, but shortly afterwards there was the sound of heavy artillery fire from the direction of the bridge.

While Paul was involved in the fierce struggles against the Japanese, and next the dense jungle, events were taking a dramatic turn around Mokpalin and the Sittang Bridge. After the enemy's attempt in the early morning to break through the bridgehead had been checked, other formations of the enemy division had thrust wedges between Pagoda Hill and Mokpalin. In this thick, broken country around the village and the approach to the bridge, Japanese snipers were hidden in the numerous gullies and among the scrub-covered hills, bringing fire to bear on any attempt to break through the roadblocks.

A company of 1/3rd Gurkhas fought its way to the top of Buddha Hill. But their colonel was killed and the enemy roadblocks still proved difficult to break. The battle raged in pockets of action from the twin hills back to Mokpalin, the 5th Gurkha Battalion still holding on to its hill pickets and the scrubland between the village and the hills. Heavy mortar fire was being brought down by the enemy.

On the west-bank bridgehead, Brigadier Hugh-Jones was in a situation which grew more frustrating every minute. He could hear the heavy fighting on the east bank, but was completely in the dark as to what exactly was going on. His wireless operator was unable to raise the rest of his brigade or the other two brigades, for that matter.

At around 16.00 hours, Hugh-Jones realised that he had to restore the situation at the east bank bridgehead and so two companies of 1/4th Gurkhas, sent across the bridge to counter-attack, retook the ground from Pagoda Hill to Bungalow Hill. The brave remnants of 3rd Gurkhas still hung on grimly to Buddha Hill, but there was still no free passage between their positions and the 5th Gurkhas at Mokpalin.

It was in this situation that Brigadier "Jonah" Jones of 16 Brigade arrived in the late afternoon of the twenty-second. He was not a man to let such conditions continue for long and he soon set about his task to restore some order and to achieve his main priority: a perimeter defence around the village of Mokpalin, a sort of fort in the jungle, where he could hold out during the night and break out from in the morning.

Chapter Six
Fort in the Jungle

As Paul followed the *chaung*, the sound of battle could still be heard in fits and starts: a trick of the wind, it sounded like a tunnel in the jungle through which the roar of the guns could travel or the crackle of automatic and rifle fire could suddenly rip across like a belt of spluttering Chinese crackers. Then there would be complete silence until broken suddenly again by more noise of battle.

The afternoon sun baked the jungle and he felt like an ingredient in a recipe being slowly browned with the sweat oozing out like juice in a roasting tray. It was difficult to concentrate. He had to force himself to keep alert as his mind worried about where the march would bring them out. And he thought about Tony and what may have happened to him. And he worried about Ray. Every time he asked the pilot how he was, he always managed to grin and assure Paul that he was just fine, but whenever Paul stole a glance, Ray looked drawn and in some pain. A moment later, Paul had other things to worry about, because the *chaung* took a sharp turn to the right, swinging away to the east. In front was a rough fortification of tangled undergrowth and trees.

Paul did not want to go eastwards, but to avoid doing so would mean forcing a way through the jungle barrier. He ordered two men at a time to cut a way through with their khukuris. For about half an hour they fought the jungle, the men changing over every few minutes, khukuris slashing, until all of a sudden they broke through onto a clear path which looked quite well used; probably, woodcutters from the villagers had beaten it down through the years. What was more, it seemed to be running in a northerly direction. But if they could use it, so could the Japanese.

Paul looked at Tilbir who agreed, 'We must take the risk.' Then he added quickly, 'No, sahib!' as he realised that Paul had planned to go in front. 'I think you should stay back, with one section in front, say 50 yards, to give us plenty of warning.'

Paul saw the sense of his argument, so he ordered a section from Amarjit's platoon to take the lead and for the remainder of the jemedar's men to change places with Dilbahadur's platoon to even out duties – marching was always more difficult for the rear platoon.

After the dense jungle, the little path was like a broad highway and Paul felt his legs urging him to go at a great pace. He had to force himself to keep an even pace. But only about five minutes later, Gopiram caught Paul by the arm and he halted. The Gurkha pointed down the path which turned in a bend, hiding the leading section from view. Paul could hear the sound of voices. The column behind him quickly took up positions on either side of the path and he waited. Couldn't be Japs, he thought. They would hardly stop to pass the time of day.

Presently, the section leader appeared round the corner, accompanied by two British soldiers from the Duke of Wellington's.

'Sergeant Somers, sir,' one of them reported.

He was a big man, in his early thirties, mahogany tanned, his face grimy with sweat and dirt, his khaki shirt and shorts bearing all the marks of a tussle with the jungle and the enemy. Yet, he was obviously an experienced soldier and sure of himself; in spite of the conditions, he carried himself like a sergeant of the Duke's. His companion was around 6 feet 2, shaped like a beanpole, knobbly knees beneath his shorts, bony arms sticking out of his rolled-up shirt sleeves, and he was much younger.

'Is the rest of your battalion in front?' Paul asked.

'No, sir. Just Private Walton and myself. We started off as a battalion until that business back at the roadblock split us up. Since then, it has been a running battle. Some time ago we were in a bit of a skirmish and me and Walton found ourselves separated from the rest of the platoon. Just vanished into thin air. It's the jungle, sir. One moment they're there, you look away and the next moment they've gone.'

'I know the feeling, sergeant,' Paul said, in no doubt that Somers was telling the truth. There must have been similar incidents all over the jungle that day.

'Well, sir,' Somers continued, 'a short while ago we bumped into a party of your Gurkhas with a British officer, about a platoon strong. We tagged on and then hit a small Jap patrol. Killed all the yellow buggers, but the British officer was very badly wounded.'

Paul felt a moment of grave anticipation. 'Where is he?'

'About 100 yards from here. We were just wondering what was to be done when the Gurkhas said that someone was coming. We thought it was more Japs, but were very greatly pleased to see your little Johnnies.'

'You had best lead the way,' Paul said, after explaining in Nepali to Tilbir.

Somers moved back along the path, Walton loping behind him. A short way on, in a small clearing, were about twenty Gurkhas. Amarjit, who as the leading platoon commander had come forward with Paul, said, 'D Company men, sahib. That is Havildar Bharti Rai, commanding 15 Platoon.'

Paul felt himself shiver. Oh God! Not poor Tony. But he tried to hide his anguish as Havildar Bharti came quickly up to meet him.

'Captain Sahib was very badly hurt, sahib,' the Gurkha blurted out, upset and slightly frightened, pointing towards the far end of the clearing. 'But I think he is now dead.'

Paul forced himself not to move, looking around first, noticing the crumpled bodies of some six Japanese, the rest of the D Company platoon sitting in small groups. 'Get your men into a proper defensive position,' he said sternly.

Bharti looked at Paul for a brief moment, surprise and shame mixed in his expression, before he pulled himself together, standing straight. 'Huzoor,' he said firmly and hurried back to his men, moving them into position.

Paul glanced over his shoulder casually, but he need not have worried about his own men. Amarjit had sent some of his platoon further up the path, the rest spreading out on either side with Company HQ. And Dilbahadur had obviously placed his men to watch the way they had come. Paul caught Somers giving him a quizzical look. The sergeant averted his eyes at once. Paul could not tell if Somers was surprised or approving.

There was a hollow just behind the clearing, dipping into the jungle. A little Gurkha jumped to his feet as Paul came up, his face wrinkled in grief. Paul brushed past him and looked down at Tony. Or what had been Tony. He must have taken a burst from an automatic at point-blank range.

Paul came out of the hollow. Tony's Gurkha orderly was waiting and weeping. 'What is your name, *chhora?*'

'Rifleman Josbir Gurung,' sobbed out the battalion's youngest member, who was having to grow up quickly in these desperate conditions.

'He was a good sahib,' Paul said. 'He was my friend as much as he was yours and one day no doubt we will all meet up again when our God calls us. But, meanwhile, I want you to be the Flying Sahib's orderly. Look after him properly; he is not used to our ways. His hand is still giving him trouble, although he will not admit it, but as his orderly you will have the right to force him to take more care. Understand?'

'Huzoor.' Josbir stood to attention.

Tilbir came up. 'Captain Sahib,' he said softly, 'you must move out now with the men. Leave the Davidson Sahib to me. I will see that all is done that must be done.'

Tilbir stood there, lean, upright, his pale eyes seemingly expressionless, and yet Paul could sense the pain, the concern, behind them – for Paul as much as for Tony. The subedar's Gurkha hat was smart in spite of the many times it had been mauled by the jungle, his uniform showing that every effort had been made to keep it presentable; he was every inch a typical Gurkha officer.

Paul returned to the path, Josbir following behind, and sat in the shade for a moment, reflecting on times past with Tony. Then Tilbir approached.

'We have dug a grave under the trees sahib. You will want to bury Davidson Sahib and say a few words of prayer.'

They had been up before the crack of dawn and the subsequent hours had been savage and energy sapping. Paul felt very tired, hot and thirsty. He could imagine how the others felt, particularly Ray and those who had been wounded. He would have to call a halt soon. In fact, he was about to do so when the lead section stopped abruptly. Paul went forward.

The section leader was smiling happily; they had come upon a small *chaung* in which a foot of water gurgled along the stream bed. The urge to rush forwards was great and Paul surmised that those behind him must feel like cattle in a Western reaching water after a hard drive across the desert. But a mad rush could be dangerous. He recognised the section leader as Lance Naik Bombahadur Rai.

'Take your section along the path for about 50 yards, Bombahadur, and set up an observation post. I will send someone to relieve you within, say, half an hour.'

Bombahadur could not help taking a quick glance at the water, but to his great credit he snapped smartly to attention. 'Huzoor, it shall be done.' He growled at his men, reluctant to leave this oasis, but they obeyed him and Paul marked him down as a man for early promotion.

Paul gave similar orders for the last section in Dilbahadur's platoon to set up an OP to the company's rear. Then he said to the subedar, 'We must take a chance, I think, and rest up for a while. But we must be careful, because the Japanese might know about this path, so I want the men to go down to the *chaung* section by section to fill their water bottles and *chagals*. No scramble. Then they can brew up. The first two sections to finish will relieve the two OPs. I think we will have some sentries on the flank, although the jungle looks very thick. Please make sure that they are also relieved within the half-hour.'

'How long will we stay, sahib?'

'Let us see how it goes.'

While Tilbir was giving out orders, Paul walked over to the arbour near the *chaung* where Ray and the two British soldiers had settled down. Paul told Somers and Walton they could fill up straightaway and he was impressed that they had waited for his orders.

'I could sleep for a year,' Ray said. 'And drink a gallon.'

'I take it your orderly is looking after you?'

'Yeah, thanks. He's been a great help.'

Paul took off his pack and squatted beside Ray. Then he pulled out his tatty old map which had not been updated for some thirty years. 'I wish I knew exactly where we were. This path is not on the map and we weaved around a bit after leaving the ambush area earlier today, but I have a hunch we're not far from the Mokpalin Quarries.'

'Let me have a look – I saw a lot of this area from the air.' Ray studied the map. 'My guess, for what it's worth, is that we will hit the railway line between the quarries and the village. If this path has been made by woodcutters, it's more likely to have come from a village. Another mile is my bet.'

Paul knew that the pilots were expert at map reading, much more skilful than himself, and he decided to go along with Ray's thinking. Josbir came up with a *chagal* and began to fuss over Ray, bathing his injured hand. Around them little fires began to crackle. Paul had decided to risk the smoke, weighing it against the morale-booster of hot tea. They also ate the cold rice and dal the QMH had cooked before they had left Kyaikto, wrapped up in small parcels of leaves, one for each man, and a few extra, just in case.

Paul closed his eyes – he was beginning to feel relaxed after the meal and the tea. But at once he saw a picture of Tony lying in the hollow. He opened his eyes quickly, got to his feet and walked back along the path, talking to his men as he did so, attempting to forget by giving them encouragement. The OPs and sentries were being relieved and were trying not to rush to the stream. Paul gave them a *shabash* for enduring the agony of what must have seemed the longest half-hour of their lives. He moved over to the wounded who were being attended to by the medical orderly and stopped to give them some words of encouragement.

When he returned to his headquarters there was the drowsy atmosphere of a picnic. 'Was the rice all right?' he asked the British soldiers, who had no rations of their own and had said they would eat the rice.

'It went down a treat, sir,' Somers said.

'Is that so?'

'Really, sir. I'm an old sweat, been out East a long time. Nothing like rice; sticks to your insides. Should keep the old legs going for a few miles more. And the tea was great – a superb cup of *cha*!'

The long figure that was Private Walton did not stir. Well, thought Paul, it's good to know that he has confidence enough to sleep so easily.

'We'll be moving out in about ten minutes,' Paul told Somers. 'I don't know what we'll meet up with once clear of the jungle, but I'd like you to stay with my HQ as before.'

'That suits me fine, sir.'

Gopiram came up with a filled water bottle which he strapped to Paul's belt. Paul then turned to the subedar, 'Move out in ten minutes, sahib.'

When they set off again about ten minutes later, the sound of battle resumed. A couple of miles ahead, perhaps, Paul thought. The path still led through jungle, a clear path that enabled them to make good time. About a quarter of an hour later, the leading section commander doubled back to report, 'The jungle is ending, huzoor, and we have come out on the railway line.'

Paul went forward with him and after a careful look, he stepped out onto the line. It was obviously the branch line from Mokpalin to the quarries and beyond it would be the road. In the distance, towards the north-west, there was still some desultory firing.

Presently, Paul was joined by Dilbahadur, whose platoon was now in the vanguard, and a moment later by Tilbir.

Paul said, 'I think I would prefer to follow the road. The railway line looks a bit too open for my liking.' The Gurkha officers agreed. 'Then I will take two sections,' Paul decided, 'cross over to the road and carry out a recce. If we get into any trouble, take the column back to the jungle and then perhaps try to break through to Tawgon on the riverbank.'

Tilbir made no acknowledgement and Paul had the distinct feeling that the subedar would do no such thing, but would come storming to their side. But he decided not to emphasise his order.

A moment later, Dilbahadur led the front section across the railway line and into the scrub beyond. When he was in position, Paul came up with the second section and passed through to the road. An abandoned lorry loomed out of the jungle, front wheels into the side of the road. As Paul looked up and down the road the transport stretched as far as he could see, some shattered out of shape, others still coughing puffs of smouldering smoke from a mangled mass of metal. The smell of burning materials and cordite hung in the early evening air – and another smell, which he decided was scorched flesh. But there was no sign of life. When he signalled Dilbahadur to come forward, the jemedar clicked his tongue at the sight.

'We will go towards Mokpalin,' Paul said. 'I shall lead. You bring up the second section. If I want you to take up the lead I will signal. If we meet any Japanese, it will depend on how strong they are as to whether we take them on or return to the rest of the company as quickly as possible.'

Dilbahadur nodded his head and rejoined his section as Paul moved the other one forward. They advanced carefully, nervously; there was something eerie about the empty vehicles as they edged round them and avoided the corpses sprawled in all sorts of positions. There was a buzzing ahead, which grew louder as they approached. Then Paul saw the ambulance tilted over on its side and the bodies of several wounded British soldiers. There was a very obvious Red Cross, but it was all the same to the Japanese, who had riddled the ambulance with machine-gun fire, dragging the no doubt terror-stricken and confused wounded out of the back and onto the road to complete their beastly act by savagely mutilating the British soldiers with bayonets. Paul could feel his stomach rebelling, but managed to keep down the vomit.

They passed the ambulance. 'Huzoor!' the section commander warned. Paul halted at once, crouching beside him at the side of a lorry.

It was a little while before Paul caught the sound of movement ahead and then figures appeared. After what seemed a lifetime, he was able to recognise troops from the KOYLI Battalion. He got to his feet slowly, not wanting to startle them with any sudden movement, and stepped out into the middle of the road so they could see the outline of his Gurkha hat.

'Hello,' greeted the young officer in charge of the patrol. 'From 46th Brigade?'

'Yes – 4/15th GR. I've got about sixty men back over the railway line. The brigade broke up this morning near the Meyon Chaung and we've been making our way to Mokpalin. What's the situation up ahead?'

'Very confusing. Units all over the place. But old "Jonah" Jones has started to organise things, setting up a perimeter around the village. There's no way at the moment that we can get to the bridge, because the

Japs are between it and the village. The brigadier has sent a few patrols to scout around before nightfall. I think the Japs are concentrating to the east and south and you were rather lucky to get through.'

'Are you on your way back, soon?'

'Right now. If you get the rest of your chaps up, we'll head back for the village.'

Paul's Gurkhas were already chatting away with the British soldiers in the camaraderie which has always existed between the British Tommy and Johnny Gurkha – and somehow making themselves understood. Paul sent word for Tilbir to bring the rest of the company forward and soon they were all on their way to the village, the KOYLI officer taking great care as they traversed the undulating scrub-covered land which stretched from the jungle fringe to the wooden houses of Mokpalin.

When they reached the KOYLI position, some 400 yards south-west of the village, Paul was told that Brigade HQ was just to the east of the railway station. Leaving his company, Paul went ahead with Tilbir and a couple of men to report to Brigadier Jones.

He had no difficulty in finding Brigade HQ. The large wooden house and its immediate surroundings was bustling with movement. At the top of the stairs, Paul bumped into a staff officer who said, 'Hello. It's a long way from Kyaikto Railway Station.'

'Why, of course,' Paul said, recognising Peter Grant, the staff officer who had given them their change of orders at Kyaikto. 'Seems 100 years ago.'

'What are you doing here? Is your battalion coming in?'

'No, I'm afraid. Just my company.'

Another figure came into view. 'Who is it, Peter?'

'Captain Cooper, sir. Fifteenth GR.'

'Ah, yes. You're the young man who ambushed those Japs near Kyondo. You seem to have a knack of extricating yourself from tricky situations.'

Paul gave Jones an account of what had happened since the morning. Jones, in return, said that he had no news of Ekin or any of the other members of Paul's battalion.

'Except for their MO, sir,' Grant added, 'Doc Green. He's with an aid post just east of the railway station.'

Paul had hoped that Doc would have got across the bridge earlier, but was glad to know that he was at least still alive.

'Now, what are we going to do with you?' the brigadier pondered. 'Peter. Reserve?'

'We've got a fair amount in reserve, sir,' Grant replied as he looked at the rough sketch map of the perimeter.

Jones had tried to throw a cordon right around Mokpalin, but there were gaps. He had placed his headquarters east of the railway station, 8th Burma Rifles some 400 yards south-east of it with the KOYLIS to their right, and 4th Burma Rifles facing the river further west. North of Mokpalin, the Jats were on high ground south-east of Bungalow Hill. Further east of the village was covered by 5th Gurkhas. In reserve at Brigade HQ were two companies of the Duke of Wellington's and 1/7th Gurkhas. Various stragglers and remnants from the Dogras and 3/7th Gurkhas were under command of 8th Burma Rifles. The artillery – three batteries of the Indian Mountain Battery and 5th Field Battery RA – was placed south and east of the railway station.

'I think they would be rather useful between the 5th Gurkhas and the 8th Burma Rifles, sir,' Grant suggested.

Jones agreed. 'I've no doubt I'll be seeing you on the other side of the river,' was his parting remark to Paul with a smile.

Paul collected his company and led them east across the railway and the road to a suitable position between 5th Gurkhas on his left flank and the Burma Rifles on the right. He quickly set the men to work: his two C Company platoons to the front, digging in amongst a line of bushes and broken bamboo fence; HQ, and in reserve the D Company platoon, were placed behind them, beyond a narrow village track near a small wooden house.

With darkness, the Gurkhas were well dug in, exhausted but more relieved now that they were part of a brigade and would be making a stand. It was dark beyond the perimeter line and the men were alert, knowing how swiftly the Japanese could launch their attacks.

Sergeant Somers and Walton were still in C Company. Paul had suggested they might like to rejoin the two Duke's companies in brigade reserve. The sergeant asked if Paul knew which companies they were and on being told said, 'Neither is my company, sir. If you don't mind, we'd rather stay with you. I've got sort of attached to the company. Rest assured, sir we'll not let you down.'

'Of course, I'm delighted to have you as honorary members of the battalion.' That seemed to please them; they had already been adopted by the Gurkhas.

Earlier, too, Paul had taken his wounded to the aid post near the railway station. It was a gruesome and tragic sight, the many wounded in the makeshift operating theatre and hospital – a Burmese hut – and stretchers, blankets and groundsheets beneath what shade the village trees could give.

He found Doc Green who had just finished an amputation – his third or fourth, he could not remember. There was no anaesthetic. There was also a long line of seriously wounded cases awaiting attention. Normally, he would not have been called upon to perform these operations; but with the Advanced Dressing Station of 39 Field Ambulance overrun in the first moments of the battle, the top medicos captured and no way of evacuating the wounded because the road to the bridge was cut off by the Japanese, he and the other MOs had had to make the decision to operate in urgent cases.

Doc looked shattered: always a tall, thin man, he seemed a shadow of his former self, accentuating the big bony hands which could perform such delicate operations, spattered with blood, his face almost yellow with fatigue, eyes red and angry as well as tired.

'I have some wounded, Doc. My medical orderly thought they needed checking.'

'Right. I will have a look at them in a moment.'

'I've also got Ray Dean here, the American pilot,' Paul said. 'You remember – he injured his hand in the crash.'

'Leave it,' Ray said quickly. 'The Doc has some really serious cases to deal with.'

'Let me be the judge of that,' Doc said crustily, taking Ray's arm and rolling up the sleeve which had been buttoned at the wrist as some protection against the jungle. 'Hmm. Still rather swollen. Coming through the jungle couldn't have helped. But I'll give you another injection which should relieve it.'

When he had done so, Doc asked Paul, 'Who else is with you?'

'Just my company and a platoon from D Company. We broke up at a Jap roadblock this morning. I think the colonel and a large part of the battalion accompanied Brigadier Ekin in a break out to the west. But Tony is dead for sure.'

'I'm sorry about that. I liked him – a good friend of yours, too, I think. Anyway, I've got a lot more work to do. Can't stand here making idle gossip. Look after yourself, young Paul.'

Doc turned away, already thinking of his next patient, walking along the line of wounded. Paul and Ray returned to C Company and waited for what was going to be a long, hard, bloody night.

Paul had both Dilbahadur and Amarjit's platoons in front, alert, anxious for the action to start, but by now well experienced and confident in their ability to match the Japanese in equal contest. Yet, who knew how many thousands of the enemy were out there; in the jungle, on the scrub slopes, in the *chaungs*, hidden in folds in the ground, amply equipped with artillery and mortars.

Paul had made a last visit to the platoons, encouraging the men, making sure that they would not fire on automatic unless absolutely necessary. Where possible, hand grenades and cold steel would be the order of the night. They all seemed excited and he could sense that morale was high in spite of all they had been through and what was yet to come.

When Paul returned to his headquarters he settled down next to Ray. 'Everything all right?'

'Sure. Although I don't deny that I'm shit-scared. But I still wouldn't have missed this for the world. Watching you all this morning – was it only this morning! Watching the way your Gurkhas charged those Japs, that hand-to-hand stuff.'

'You didn't do so badly yourself,' Paul said.

'It's easier firing from a distance.' Ray laughed it off. 'Although, having only one wing, so to speak, my balance was out and I confess my chest was heaving. So I reckon I was lucky to hit the target.'

They lapsed into silence and waited, but not much longer. Paul suddenly sensed that something was about to break, a feeling of being locked in a cupboard with no air, suffocating in the great hatred that surrounded them. Then the night was rent apart by artillery flashes, the blast from exploding shells reverberating around the perimeter, mortar bombs dropping in from their high trajectory. Fierce machine-gun fire opened up from the north-east and the south, the tracer threading the darkness with stitches of red, green and white to indicate the various unit formations. There was the usual rattle of cracker guns to try to locate the defenders' machine-gun positions.

The first wave of Japanese infantry hit the perimeter, rifles unloaded but bayonets fixed and dulled by spreading mud on them, to prevent them from reflecting enemy gunfire. In groups of fifteen, they erupted like apparitions out of the ground a short distance in front of the platoons, having crawled forwards under cover of the artillery barrage and machine-gun fire. The Gurkhas remained steady, meeting them with a flurry of hand grenades. The air seemed filled with the grenades of both sides, thrown or propelled by discharger cups, breaking up, segments flying in every direction. All around the village the noise reached a crescendo as each soldier fought stubbornly to hold back the enemy.

Paul wanted to rush forward to his platoons, but knew he must stay firm. They could be relied upon, they knew what they were doing, but he could feel himself shivering in anticipation.

A mortar bomb exploded quite close. Then another and another, the shrapnel rattling among the trees like children running sticks along railings. Behind him there was a brighter flare of light as a bomb exploded very close, the metal flying past his head. There were cries of pain, but he had to wait, he couldn't investigate just then.

And then, almost as suddenly as they had attacked, the Japanese withdrew, obviously to reform, badly mauled in their first attempt to take Mokpalin. Paul left his slit trench and rushed back to the reserve platoon, where four lay dead and one was seriously wounded. The others were badly shaken.

The little medical orderly said, 'Sahib, the wounded man needs a doctor's attention very soon.'

Paul agreed and told Havildar Bharti, the reserve platoon commander, to organise the wounded man's removal to Doc Green's aid post.

When Bharti and a stretcher party had gone, Paul had the four dead men carried behind some bushes, out of sight for the moment. Then he moved forward to check on the other platoons. Amazingly, there had been no casualties and every man was at a high pitch of excitement, but Dilbahadur whispered, 'Careful, sahib, they are still out there, waiting for the next attack. A bigger one this time, I think.'

Paul turned to the American. 'I think, Ray, you should stay well back, as you are badly handicapped for close-quarter action.'

Ray frowned angrily.

'No. No, Ray. Nothing against your courage. Just being sensible.'

'Sure. OK, Paul.'

Little Josbir stayed at his side, ready to die for his sahib.

At around 22.00 hours, the same build-up of heavy artillery and a hurricane of mortar bombs developed. In the distance, where the road wound its way back towards the quarries, there was a line of flame as many of the lorries were set alight. An ammunition lorry blew up, a billowing balloon of flame scorching the night air.

Towards C Company's front, the Japanese came in again, chattering to each other, and were soon locked in a hand-to-hand struggle. Screams punctuated the night, with shouts of rage and cries of terror, the struggling figures like ghostly shapes. And out of the mass came helmeted figures who had managed to break through.

Paul had equipped himself with a rifle and bayonet. He found himself leaping out of the trench in a sort of dream, rifle at the port and then bringing it down straight and firm and into an approaching Japanese, withdrawing the blade cleanly as the drill sergeant had dinned into him during training, the dead man falling away to his left, mouth open for a scream that was never made. Out of the corner of his eye he saw a Japanese bayonet only a thrust away from his body, but Gopiram's khukuri slashed open the enemy's throat.

To Paul's left his headquarters' group was heavily engaged. Somers and Walton were in among the enemy, fighting for their lives. One of the Gurkhas, the quartermaster's assistant, went down, his head cut open by a swinging sword. Then Tilbir was into the enemy, once again using his khukuri with great skill.

And then, suddenly, the Japanese survivors were retreating, followed by a bombardment from 5th Field Battery, RA and the 3.7 howitzers of 28th Indian Mountain Battery who, earlier in the attack, had been firing over open sights at close range – shrapnel, fuse O, proving of devastating effect – cutting a wide swathe in the enemy's ranks.

And so the night passed, with no long moments to really recover one's breath. And all through the night, further back, the doctors were operating by flashlight as the wounded mounted in numbers, doing what they could, realising, surely, the futility of it all.

On the west bank of the Sittang it had been a night for momentous and agonising decisions: General Smyth had finally given Brigadier Hugh-Jones the order to blow the bridge.

At 04.30 hours, Hugh-Jones began to call in the bridgehead troops from the east bank to a timed programme, the men taking off their boots to run across the bridge: men from 1/4th Gurkhas, the FFR and the Duke of Wellington's, who had all held on so grimly.

Acting as rearguard were two platoons of Gurkhas and with four minutes to go, even these, less two sections guarding the sandbagged emplacements on the bridge, were withdrawn. Just at that moment there was a message on the field telephone: the sappers were not ready and the two sections must hang on. With the Japanese probing in the jungle, a few Gurkhas went forward to keep up the fire they had exchanged all night. Fortunately, the enemy did not know that for five minutes, only two sections stood between them and the bridge.

So in the dark hour before dawn, with the officer commanding the Gurkha detachment and one of his men with a Bren gun giving covering fire, Orgill gave the firing order to Lieutenant Basher Ahmad.

The sapper lieutenant left his foxhole on the west bank and walked along the bridge to light the reserve safety fuse. Then he returned to his foxhole and pressed the exploder for the electric circuit.

Unaware of the fateful moment approaching, Paul sat in the darkness. His mouth was dry, his uniform stuck to his body with sweat and grime, his eyes burning. It would soon to be dawn, but it would only bring more attacks and how much longer could they hold out? He was mulling this over in his mind when there was a blinding flash of light and a blast of red-hot air, which caught the village in a grip, and behind it came the roar of the explosion.

And as the bridge sagged drunkenly into the river there was a strange, brief hush. A moment of complete silence, like an armistice for the dead.

Chapter Seven
A Boat for the Gurkhas

A heavyweight boxer could not have delivered a harder, more energy-sapping punch. The aftermath of the explosion had left Paul dazed and sick to the stomach. The trap was sprung; now, the Japanese had them in the grip of the scorpion's claws and were ready to apply the killing sting.

Around him, Paul sensed that his men were stunned and probably everyone on the east side of the river must have felt the same terror, anger and bewilderment. For the strong swimmers, like himself, the obstacle was not insurmountable; but so many, probably the majority of the men, could not swim or were a length-of-the-baths men. For them, the blowing up of the bridge must indicate that they were doomed to die or be captured.

The silence was abruptly broken by cries of rage from the Japanese surrounding the village, echoing across the hills and the river, and the crash of their artillery signalled a fresh onslaught, a determination to tear the British defences apart and seize Mokpalin.

This was the time for frightened men to break, to panic, but the men held firm, as all round the perimeter the other Gurkhas, Jats, Dogras, the sturdy Yorkshiremen from the KOYLI, the ravaged ranks of the Duke's and the Burma Rifles held together.

As daylight finally pushed aside the night which had seemed never-ending, the stark evidence of the battle was revealed. The Japanese had fought fanatically. The many dead of both sides lay twisted in front of the perimeter while, near the road, lorries were still burning next to others which were just blackened heaps of scrap metal.

Within C Company's sections of the perimeter, CHM Ganesh was making a count of the Gurkha casualties. He reported to Paul, 'Nine killed and four seriously wounded, sahib. There are several not too badly wounded and the medical orderly is caring for them.'

Paul was overcome by the losses, but at last he managed to say, 'Please arrange for the seriously wounded to be taken to the Doctor Sahib.'

'Huzoor.' Ganesh rose to his feet and walked towards the perimeter to make arrangements.

The enemy had pulled back after their last attack, but Paul was not certain if they would return. Now that the bridge was blown there was little to gain tactically as they themselves had suffered heavy casualties. The enemy's most important task, surely, was to find an alternative crossing point further north to continue their advance into Rangoon. In the lull, the wounded were taken to see Doc.

The silence continued for several hours until about 11.15 hours, when there was the drone of approaching aircraft, coming into sight like small blodges, expanding rapidly into more than a score of bombers. A moment later the bombs whistled down, setting several houses alight and finding targets among the abandoned vehicles.

A gun-ammunition truck exploded, discharging black smoke streaked with red flashes into the sky and hurling shrapnel in all directions. The bombers then moved away, slowly becoming smaller and smaller before disappearing from view, leaving behind many casualties. C Company escaped any hits, but Paul shouted a warning to the forward platoons to be on the alert for an infantry attack. But it did not come. What did come was word from Brigadier Jones that he intended to disperse the force at 20.30 hours and attempt to get as many men as possible across the river.

Paul visited the men in their positions, wondering if their mouths were as dry as his, if their eyes were as weary, if they were as afraid of the immediate future. He felt absolutely exhausted, but tried not to show it, which took a great effort and probably was not worth the effort, because the Gurkhas must have damn well known how he felt.

'How's the water situation?' he asked Dilbahadur.

'Not too good, sahib.' The jemedar took off his Gurkha hat and ran a hand over his shaven head which was wet with sweat. 'I have tried to impress on them the importance of drinking sparingly. Maybe each man has about a quarter left in his bottle, some less, some maybe more. The *chagals* we still have; I keep those near me.'

This seemed to be the situation in the other platoon, also. 'I know we have no food,' Paul said. 'But do you think hot tea would help? Using some of the water reserve.'

'We will make tea, sahib,' Dilbahadur said and Amarjit was in agreement. 'It will take our minds off our predicament if nothing else.'

'Do it now, before the Japs decide to pay us another visit.'

'They will not be invited to our tea party, sahib,' Dilbahadur said with a broad grin, which was in itself a morale booster for Paul.

He returned to his headquarters and made the same suggestion to Tilbir. Then he sat down near Ray. 'How's the hand?'

'It's OK,' the American pilot said.

'Can you swim?'

Ray looked at him for a moment. 'I can – but if you're thinking of the 1,000 yards of the Sittang then I doubt if could with this hand. I guess I could get across on my back or maybe a sort of half breaststroke, if it was like a swimming pool, but they say the river has a very fast current.'

Paul leaned across to Somers and asked him the same question. The sergeant shook is head slowly. 'It's the current, sir. As Captain Dean says, I might get across if my life depended on it – at least I hope I could. A lot of my strength has been sapped in the last few days which won't help. But swimming has never been one of my favourite pastimes. And Walton is not very proficient, either.'

'The trouble is that none of my Gurkhas can swim. In fact, I doubt if a count in all the Gurkha battalions here would produce as many as a dozen swimmers.'

'There's plenty of wood and bamboo around, sir,' Somers suggested. 'We could make rafts.'

'I take it you don't expect to find any boats?' Ray queried.

'My guess is that the boats were destroyed to prevent the Japs from using them.'

'Some guy must have put a lot of faith in us holding off the Japs or being able to walk on water,' Ray said.

'I take it you can swim, sir?' Somers said quietly.

Paul nodded his head. Yes, he was a strong swimmer. But he dreaded the thought of putting his men on rafts made in a hurry and pushed out onto a fast-flowing river – and none of them swimmers. They were already tired out and hungry. How much more courage would they have to draw on to overcome the fear of drowning?

Just then, Gopiram and Josbir came up with mugs of tea. Paul took a sip and felt better. But the nightmare of what was to come – what was inevitably to come – still stayed with him. Two wounded returned.

'The Doctor Sahib said we would be all right now for light duty,' one remarked.

Paul smiled. He wondered what "light duty" would involve in the present situation. 'All right. Join your platoons.'

The day passed slowly, the sun swinging across the sky, building up the heat. Then, shortly before 14.00 hours, came word that "Jonah" Jones had decided to bring forward the withdrawal immediately, units to make their way independently down to the river.

The enemy had been fairly quiet for some time, apart from bursts of artillery and mortar activity and a few attacks on the southern perimeter. But everyone was exhausted and Jones knew that they could not hold out much longer – and, indeed, there was no point in doing so now.

When the word came, Paul called his platoon commanders together to discuss the planned withdrawal. 'Can anyone swim?' he asked optimistically. They shook their heads. 'Then I suppose we will have to make rafts. There is quite a lot of wood in the house behind us. We will carry as much as possible down to the river along with any bamboo we can find. And while that is being done, I want to check up on our wounded and the Doctor Sahib. We have five of them at the aid post.'

'Will we take them with us, sahib?' Tilbir asked. 'There is no knowing how the Japanese will treat them after we have gone. And we have seen what little respect they have had for the ambulances.'

Have I not got enough on my plate without trying to get wounded men across the river? Paul thought. But he would have to make a show, if nothing else. 'It depends on how badly wounded they are. We will have to ask the Doctor Sahib. All right. I shall take eight men – no, make it your platoon, Bharti,' he said to the D Company havildar whose charge had been reduced to ten.

He turned to Tilbir. 'Meanwhile, Subedar Sahib, will you carry on here? Collect the wood and bamboo and then bring it and the company to the aid post. We will make the rafts when we reach the river.'

Paul explained the situation to Ray and the British soldiers, before leading Bharti's platoon north-west across the road to Doc's aid post near the railway station. In the distance there was some gunfire. The brigade's main dump of artillery ammunition caught alight and the flames spread to some of the houses and the transport parked along the main village road. Smelly black smoke spread out among the houses and burning bamboo exploded like rifle fire. The fumes made Paul cough as he scrambled through the wreckage, past several bodies, the weapons of the dead and the wounded lying all over the place, until he reached Doc's aid post.

'Glad to see you're still in one piece,' Doc said.

'Thanks, Doc. We're moving out, now.'

'Best of luck, young Paul.' He looked vague, worn down by fatigue. He had been operating all night, doing what he could for the wounded.

'Won't you be coming with us?' Paul asked.

'Coming with you?' He looked puzzled.

'The Japs will be here soon.'

'Thanks for the thought, Paul, but I've got to stay with the wounded. There's still a great deal to be done.'

Paul realised that Doc had made up his mind and it would be pointless trying to press him any further. 'OK, Doc, you must do what you think best. But would it be possible for me to take my five wounded men with me, if you are agreeable?'

The Doc stared at him for a moment. 'I think you are mad. But let's have a look. I don't suppose any of them should be moved. No, not those three. These two? Well, I guess they may have a better chance with you. All the Japanese can't be barbarians. Still, if you think you can manage – go on, clear off.' But he added softly, 'Remind me to buy you a drink when the war is over.'

Bharti's men quickly lifted the wounded Gurkhas on their stretchers, one of them crying out in pain. Bharti spoke to him softly. The man opened his eyes. 'I could not help myself, Havildar Sahib.' He closed his eyes again.

'Goodbye, Doc,' Paul called out, but he was already deep in the examination of another wounded man.

It was with real sadness that Paul turned away, knowing that the chance of their meeting again was very slim.

Gopiram said, 'Sahib, the company has arrived.'

As Paul started to rejoin the company he passed an officer lying on a stretcher.

The officer murmured, 'We really must stop meeting like this.'

Paul crouched beside Peter Grant, stifling an exclamation of surprise. 'I thought you staff *wallahs* kept out of the way of bullets.'

'It was the air raid. Got some metal inside me and the Doc's not too happy about trying to remove it in these primitive conditions.' He hesitated and then said, 'I don't suppose – oh, no, that would really be asking too much. Sorry.' He looked away.

'I don't see why not,' Paul said. 'I'll see if I can ask Doc.'

'No, don't bother him. It was selfish of me to ask.'

Paul said, 'I can get you as far as the river. But what happens after that is, as they say, in the laps of the gods.'

'I'd rather take that risk than hang around for the Japs. No need to ask Doc. He'll be too busy to notice I've gone.'

Paul called to Bharti. 'Two men to carry the sahib.'

C Company had obviously dismantled a number of houses – the timber and pieces of bamboo were spread out as loads among the men. Paul just hoped that the rafts would prove successful.

He led the way down towards the river with a section from Amarjit's platoon. The smoke was quite thick now, forming an excellent screen, enabling them to make their way unobserved, while exploding ammunition was loud and fearsome enough to form a rampart which the enemy hesitated to approach too close. Paul did not know at the time that this was owing to some splendid and unselfish work by the men from 5th Gurkhas and the Jats.

There were shouts coming from all around, disembodied voices in the smoke and jungle, and some heavy firing from the Indian Mountain Battery as C Company crossed the railway line and climbed beyond it, past huts and trees for about a quarter of a mile. There was a lot of noise in front and Paul halted the company.

'I am going to scout forward to the cliff's edge,' he told Tilbir.

'I think I must come with you, sahib,' Tilbir said determinedly.

Accompanied by Tilbir, Gopiram and Somers, with a couple of men from the leading section, Paul moved carefully to the edge of the cliff and from the cover of some thick shrubs, they looked down onto the river.

The sight which met Paul's eyes would be with him forever. Thousands of British, Gurkha, Indian and Burmese troops were packed tightly along the beach like day trippers on a hot summer's day. Only there was no happy laughter, no frolicking in the water. Out on that beach were many vulnerable men because they were leaderless, hungry, exhausted, wounded and very frightened. But there were many others who showed courage and leadership, organising groups to cross the river in or on just about everything that could float: planks, logs, water bottles, petrol tins, bamboo, *chagals* blown up like Mae Wests, all made into some sort of raft or lifebelt. Most of the soldiers had abandoned their weapons – like litter after a football match – and rifles, tommy guns, Brens, mortars, revolvers and hand grenades were strewn along the river's edge. Many of the men had discarded most of their clothes and quite a few were in the nude to improve their chances when attempting to swim the treacherous river which stretched a sickly green colour for almost a mile to the distant bank. There were obviously no boats; Paul was not aware of the CRE's previous order.

The river was already full of bobbing heads. In some units officers were maintaining a good discipline, keeping their men close together, taking as many weapons as possible on improvised rafts, the swimmers helping the non-swimmers. Many, who could swim a few lengths of a swimming pool, found the width of the river too much for their strength and were swept away by the current or just vanished beneath the surface. It was also a time for heroes, supporting friends who could not swim; the strong swimmers crossing the river two or three times to take the wounded over on makeshift rafts; men giving up their places on rafts to their wounded comrades. The cliffs afforded some protection, but now and then a Japanese sniper found a target, a bobbing head disappearing in a froth of blood.

Southwards, pockets of 17 Division troops were still holding out – or maybe trapped, Paul thought – because behind the smoke which hid the river from the village came spasmodic bursts of automatic fire and the crump of mortar bombs. In fact, the amended message to disperse had not reached all the units and two companies of the KOYLI, 8th Burma Rifles, some Gurkhas from the 3/7th and the remnants of the Dogras were holding on grimly against a late enemy attack. It was their courage and determination which was keeping the enemy away from the river and allowing so many men the chance to escape.

The Indian Mountain Battery had taken up a final position on the beach, firing their last gun while, from the rest, breechblocks and sights were removed and thrown down wells or into the river.

Paul felt shattered, frightened and in despair. A roll-call showed that he had altogether fifty-one men to get across the river, including the non-Gurkhas, the wounded and himself; and he was the only swimmer. The sight that greeted them of those desperate men down there was disheartening. He knew most of the Gurkhas could not swim, but from the look of it, very few soldiers from any of the regiments could swim strongly enough to conquer the river without the aid of some improvised lifebelt or a raft. Every time a non-swimmer launched himself out onto the river on a makeshift raft, or clutching a length of bamboo, it was a leap into the dark, and he almost instantly came to grips with that vicious current. How could Paul put his own men in such a dangerous, desperate situation? Perhaps there could still be some boats on the far bank.

'We will go back now,' Paul said, trying with all his strength not to show his fear. But he could sense Tilbir's own fear and that of the others at the thought of what lay ahead. They had faced the Japanese with great courage – for what lay ahead they would have to delve much deeper into their mettle.

Back with the rest of the company, Paul said bluntly, 'We have seen what it is like and it is not promising. If we make rafts the chances are – well, uncertain. The crossing is bound to be perilous, I cannot lie about that – anyway, the Subedar Sahib has seen with his own eyes. But what is the alternative? We might be able to slip through the enemy lines, head east and then north and cross the river further upstream, although I fear that we have left it too late. We could, of course, surrender.'

Tilbir shook his head violently and there was a general murmur of disapproval from all the men. 'We would rather die fighting or take our chance on the river. You, sahib, must get across.'

'And leave you!'

'Perhaps you could get us started, give us some assistance in the water. But you have the means of escape and you must do so.'

'Not me! Before I submit you to that devil's river, let me try to find a boat. I will swim across and search the far bank. The only difficulty might be in bringing it back alone, but we have nothing to lose except time.'

'Then we will put our trust in you, sahib.' This time, there was a general murmur of approval from the ranks of the company which moved Paul deeply and in a way it gave him a feeling of confidence.

'Right. We will move forward and hide in the jungle near the river, on that cliff. It will soon be dark and I think I would prefer to wait until then.'

'It shall be so, sahib. But what about the other sahibs?'

'The American Sahib's hand prevents him from swimming. The Sergeant Sahib and his comrade would probably volunteer, but they cannot swim very well and would be more of a hindrance than a help.'

'I'm with you whatever you do,' Ray said when Paul told him of the plan.

'We would come with you, sir,' Somers said, 'but you are right, we could be a hindrance if we got into difficulties in the middle of the river. If ... no, not if, sir, I have great faith in your finding a boat ... so when you bring it back, we can then help in paddling it to the west bank. After all, more than one trip will be necessary, could be three, to get all the men across. There is also another point, sir, which I am sure you have thought about. If you can't find a boat, no doubt we will have to use rafts and then Walton and I swim well enough to help look after the Johnnies crossing the river. Sort of give them some encouragement.'

'Of course you could –'

Somers cut him short. 'I hope, sir, that you were not going to suggest that I should make my own escape.'

'It never crossed my mind, sergeant.'

Somers grinned, knowing full well what Paul was going to suggest. 'That's good, sir. After all, I know you think a lot of your Gurkha Johnnies – so do we, come to that – but the Duke's have a reputation, too, going back a long way. It was the Iron Duke himself who took over the old 33rd Regiment of Foot and added to its already great reputation. Corunna, Waterloo, Ypres, the Somme and Dunkirk, that's just some of our battle honours, sir.'

'I think the regiment's traditions are in good hands, Sergeant Somers,' Paul said.

They waited in the cover of the patchy jungle astride the cliff which overlooked the Sittang. Darkness had come at last and Paul had decided to give it another hour before he attempted his swim. The odd shot could still be heard, with the occasional cry for help; a soldier drowning out in the river or wounded waiting on the beach for help from someone who had promised to return. And many a brave man kept the promise. But it was a frustrating, seemingly hopeless situation.

Paul had no illusions as he lay on the ground. God, he thought, why did it have to come to this? How much more can men give of their courage and determination, with belief in their commanders and a sense of pride in the traditions of their regiments? Must everything be a waste: all that marching and fighting come to an end on some stinking Burmese river because of other men's incompetence?

Miles away from the front there were men who, as they dined in the mess, in their smart, clean mess kit, or in the banquet halls of their palatial government residences, drank expensive wines and talked of a poor show by the troops in Burma. Of course, Paul was not aware at that time that the Viceroy of India had condemned the troops in his cable to Churchill.

The troops they criticised had no previous experience in jungle warfare and were starved of much essential equipment, pitched against an enemy trained on the battlefields of China. Yet these troops had fought hard and almost non-stop for five weeks, often facing the enemy in close-quarter combat – like those young Baluchis on the Salween, who had held out for eight terrifying hours, or the FFR at Moulmein. They had shown high courage, fortitude and stubbornness during those vital days on the Bilin.

And all this to what purpose? To delay the Japanese advance and allow reinforcements into Rangoon, so it was said; only he damn-well knew that there wasn't much to pour into Burma. A trickle at the best. Then they had tied General Smyth's hands behind his back and by the time he was allowed to move his division to the Sittang, it was already too late.

That was why they waited here, why some 4,000 men who deserved so much better had to pit their wits and their lives against a mile-wide river with two enemy divisions breathing down their necks.

He could hear the others stirring, restless like himself, wondering about their fate. After all they had been through: Kawkareik; Moulmein. Yes, Moulmein. And Sue Whitcomb. The civilians were also all caught in the trap. Where were they now? Sue and her parents? Probably not in Rangoon. Driving north, he supposed, to get as far away from Rangoon as possible. He tried to form an image of Sue in his mind. He had only known her for so short a time and yet he felt he had known her always, and he certainly wanted to know her always. Not much time had elapsed since their meeting and yet there had been so much blood spilt and tragedy between to mar the picture. He squeezed his eyes tighter and she was there for a moment. The last night on the veranda at Moulmein. A smiling face. The blonde hair. The lips he had kissed. But the vision vanished quickly because someone was shaking him by the leg.

'Sahib!' Gopiram alerted him. 'Someone comes, sahib.'

There was a low murmur of voices and then a figure crawled towards him in the near darkness. 'Corporal Steel, sir, 2nd KOYLI, and two men from the Burma Rifles.'

Paul could not see him very well; he could just make out that he was around average height and he had a young voice. 'Where is your unit, corporal?'

'Lost it, sir. Or rather, they lost me when we broke up to try to reach the river.' Paul learned from him then of the three or four units who had held out on the perimeter. 'The colonel decided we had best move out, as everyone else seemed to have gone. It wasn't easy breaking off from the Japs and in the darkness I got separated. Then I bumped into two Karens from the Burma Rifles. We were making for the river when challenged by your men. You about to cross, sir?'

Paul explained the situation and Steel murmured, 'It's pretty tricky out there, sir. And not much chance of finding a boat.'

'How do you intend to get across?'

'The two Karens. They live by a river and are like fish in the water. That's what they say. So we are going to have a shot at swimming across.'

'No doubt you can swim, corporal?'

'Yes, sir. Army champion, once.'

'Then you won't have any trouble,' Paul muttered bitterly.

The corporal moved uncomfortably in the darkness. 'It will be hard on you, sir, going over on your own.' He started to say something and then seemed to hesitate. Paul felt a moment of apprehension, wondering if some hope was about to be offered. At last Steel said, 'Why don't we help out, sir?'

'Of course, I would be grateful,' Paul said quickly, 'but would it be fair, perhaps stifling your chances of escape. And, after all, you have no connection with this battalion. There is too much risk, really, as we don't know when the Japs will come down to the river.'

'You've got two Duke's men; had a quick word with the sergeant as I came through to your HQ.'

'They are different. They've been with us a long time now.' Did yesterday afternoon qualify as a long time? It certainly seemed like it. 'They are almost part of the unit and they volunteered to stay with us.'

'At times like these, we must try to help each other, sir.'

Paul was suspicious, wondering if the corporal was being too considerate. Well, he had given the corporal a chance to back out. Now, he had to grab the chance. 'And what about the Karens?' The Karens were one of the indigenous Burmese tribes that were particularly loyal to the British. A tough, determined race, in many ways like the Gurkhas.

Steel called the men forward. They were mere shadowy figures in the darkness and he noticed they still carried their rifles.

'Do you speak English?'

One of them replied, 'A little, thakin.'

'What is your name?'

'Maung Gyi. My friend is Ba Saw.'

'I am going to swim the river to find a boat to help my men to cross the river as they cannot swim.'

'We come with you, the Corporal Thakin and us. Much easier for you. The river is like a home to us; we have no problem in crossing.'

Paul explained the changed situation to Tilbir and Somers. Tilbir gave an uncharacteristic sigh. Somers said, 'What a piece of luck, sir.'

'I hope it turns out that way,' Paul said, more to himself than to the others.

The four swimmers crawled out of the jungle patch and climbed down to the river's edge, together with Tilbir, Gopiram, three riflemen, Somers and Walton. By this time, most of the other trapped soldiers had either crossed or drowned or given up the attempt in favour of infiltrating north to seek another crossing point where there might be boats or a ford. A few hundred had managed to cross via the bridge – the Japanese having abandoned the bridgehead – by means of a rope lifeline across the gap left by the demolition.

Paul and his swimmers stripped to their underpants, leaving their clothes with the beach party who would wait at the river's edge. The rest of the company remained in the jungle with Dilbahadur in charge and Ray.

'We will try our best,' Paul said to Tilbir. 'But get Dilbahadur to start the men building as many rafts as possible while they are waiting. It will keep their minds occupied, anyway. If I have to return without boats, at least we won't be wasting time and then we can cross as best we can. Give me, what, a couple of hours. If I am not back by then, you must start getting the men down to the river and onto rafts. Sergeant Somers and Walton will help. If you do not intend to surrender then you must take the risk.'

'If you do not find a boat, sahib, do not come back,' Tilbir said.

'What do you mean?'

'The battalion will have to be reformed. They will have need of officer sahibs like you.'

'They will need much finer men like you,' Paul said. 'I will return one way or the other.'

'Then may God go with you, sahib. I know you will not fail us.'

To Paul's surprise, Tilbir seized his hands and held them for a moment, passing a message of friendship and respect. Then Tilbir released Paul's hands and was once more the dependable company subedar.

Paul stepped into the river with the others. Each of the Karens had a Burmese dah in a bamboo sheath slung over his head and down his back, tight against his body. Then he noticed that Steel had strapped a knife around his waist. Perhaps he was also expecting trouble. A moment later, Paul was in the water, which was colder than he had expected, and he forgot about the knife.

They began swimming in pairs – Steel and Paul forming one pair, the Karens the other – each man to keep an eye on his partner and help if he suddenly found himself in difficulty. Behind them, the sky was lit by dozens of fires which flickered about Mokpalin and beyond. Now and again came the sound of a shot, a burst of automatic. Ahead it was all darkness and quiet.

Ahead also lay the river's power. Paul felt the current embrace him and begin to take him away from the shore down towards the sea. He kicked furiously, fighting against its force, his arms beginning to ache as with powerful strokes he escaped from its embrace and suddenly found himself in calmer waters. Then he heard Steel cry out, 'Sir! Sir!'

The corporal swept past, twisting over in the current in his attempt to fight it but not succeeding. Paul felt a surge of panic and for a moment he was trapped in the water, his limbs not wanting to move. He was through the current and could at last make the shore. Steel's voice, further away now, carried across the water, 'Sir! Sir!' Then the shame of it struck Paul. What was the matter with him! He broke free, but as he turned to swim back into the current, he saw two dark blobs launch from the bank further downstream and move rapidly towards a third blob which was Steel. Then the three blobs merged into one large one as the Karens dragged the corporal towards the bank.

Paul's feet touched the river bottom and he waded ashore, struggling up onto the bank. He sat down abruptly, feeling the ground and the sky whirling like a merry-go-round. He thought the sensation would never stop. Then, gradually, his vision cleared and he was able to stand up, although his legs were still trembling. He took stock of his surroundings. Westwards from the bank, the ground seemed to be a vast stretch of open fields, while north and south there were patches of trees and lengths of open bank. He wondered how far south the current had brought him.

Presently, the Karens approached, Ba Saw supporting Steel, who looked very shaken as the Karen lowered him to the ground.

'Are you all right, Captain Thakin?' Maung Gyi asked.

'Yes, thank you, Maung Gyi. How about the Corporal Thakin?'

'I'll be all right, sir. Just a bit shaken up.'

Paul turned to Maung Gyi. 'That was a very brave thing you did.'

'Yes,' Steel said. 'I cannot thank you enough.'

'Oh, it was nothing,' he waved aside any praise. 'We were brought up on the river; it was everyday thing to do.' He turned and pointed southwards. 'I think there is a fishing village that way. It a bit far, so I think no boats taken by army. Ba Saw and I must go now. We go quickly. I think, thakin, you and Corporal Thakin wait for us.'

Paul hesitated for a moment. 'I think the corporal and I should go the other way.' He pointed north. 'There may be boats in that direction.'

'OK, thakin. But if you find boat, please wait for us. The river not easy for boating. You probably find it very difficult.'

Paul agreed and the Karens set off quickly, their figures becoming dark blobs and then disappearing into the far darkness.

'Ready, corporal?'

'Yes, sir. Thanks. I … I am sorry about that. I thought I could swim the river without any trouble. Can't understand it.'

'The last four days have been pretty tough,' Paul said. 'Sapped more of our energy than we realised, I suppose.' But he wondered if Steel really had been a swimming champion or had he only said that to make sure somebody would be on hand to help him across the river? Anyway, it was too late to wonder now; they must move on and find a boat.

They walked along the bank, the absence of boots making itself known at once as stones and grit cut the soles of their feet. But they struggled on, cursing, not making very good progress.

Paul kept thinking about the moment he froze on the river. He felt ashamed and puzzled. He had fought hand-to-hand with his enemies and yet the river had stolen his courage, if only for a moment. But he felt certain he would not have been able to save Steel and most likely they would both have drowned. Then who would have found a boat for his Gurkhas? It was something he would have to live with and not dwell on.

He emerged from his thoughts abruptly as the rough ground gave way to a well-used footpath, where they were able to move along quickly. They kept looking out for boats, but there was only the naked shore.

They covered another half a mile before reaching a thick clump of trees with jungle spreading out behind it and westwards. As they came under its dark, ominous cloak, Paul could see the outline of a small creek. His heart was thumping as they approached and then he saw a large boat pulled halfway out of the creek. It looked to be in good order, but what was it doing there? They halted behind a tree, searching the area carefully, suspecting a trap. After about five minutes, Paul decided to go up to the boat. Steel reached it first and he jumped aboard to look inside the bamboo cabin. He signalled that it was empty and then he rejoined Paul on the bank and they put their shoulders to the boat. It seemed as though it would never move and they had to use much more force before it began to slide down the bank, slowly at first and then with a sudden rush into the water. Steel climbed aboard and brought the boat alongside.

Paul stood on the bank for a moment, hands on hips, getting his breath back. Suddenly, the night was split by the rattle of a tommy gun and a cluster of bullets whipped past his right shoulder and into the trees beyond. He whirled, horrified, to face a Burmese man who had come silently out of the jungle. He wore a *longyi* – the Burmese waist cloth – and what looked like a khaki shirt. All this way, with bayonets, shells, mortar-fire, and then to end up in the hands of a bloody Burmese dacoit. If the man intended to kill him, he was obviously not familiar with tommy guns, for the gun had jumped in his hands, the bullets ending up high and missing Paul by a fraction.

But the dacoit did not fire again, instead shouting out in Burmese; probably telling me to stand still, Paul decided. Then the man turned his head slightly and shouted again – to the rest of the gang, Paul supposed. In that instant he felt the wind of something flashing past his face, the thump of a knife entering the dacoit's throat. The man dropped his tommy gun, his hands grasping at the knife's handle, frantically trying to withdraw it.

Paul ran forward and picked up the tommy gun. The dacoit was rolling on the ground in his death agony, hands around the handle of the knife. Paul bent down to retrieve the knife, but Steel shouted, 'Leave it, sir! Quick! he will have mates, I'm sure.'

There were shouts in the jungle and two Burmese emerged from the jungle, *dahs* ready to strike. Paul hesitated, not knowing how much ammunition remained in the magazine, and decided to await their move. Suddenly, the leading man shouted angrily and rushed towards him. Paul fired a short burst and the dacoit crumpled like a bird hit in flight and crashed to the ground almost at Paul's feet. The second man turned abruptly for the shelter of the jungle. Paul fired again, thankful that there were still bullets in the gun. The dacoit clutched his side, screamed in pain, bumped into a tree, rebounded and then fell spreadeagled, half in and half out of the jungle. His feet kicked for a moment and then he became still.

'Come on, sir!' Steel shouted.

Paul hesitated for a moment. 'What about the Karens? They asked us to wait.'

'How do we know they are coming back?' Steel asked anxiously. 'Or how long they might be.'

'They could walk straight into the dacoits,' Paul said. He unclipped the magazine on the tommy gun. It was a twenty-shot magazine. 'There are three bullets left.' He set the control lever to single shot. 'I should be able to get in a few shots'.

'Sir, we don't know how many there are. It is too dangerous. We must get out of here.'

'They saved your life, corporal.'

Steel leaned back against the boat. He was breathing heavily. 'Of course, sir. I am really sorry, sir.'

'My gut feeling is that this was just a small gang,' Paul said, to ease Steel's concern. 'We will give the Karens say, half an hour. We really cannot wait any longer; there are the men waiting anxiously on the other side to consider.'

Time seemed to creep by. The river was full of noise; and the jungle rustled alarmingly. There was a shout in the distance and the reports of a couple of shots. Paul held the tommy gun tightly and was beginning to wonder if he had done the right thing, when Steel whispered, 'I think there is something moving on the river.'

They waited anxiously, until a boat glided into the creek and was brought alongside the shore.

'Thakin. Thakin.' Maung Gyi stepped out of the boat. 'Oh, you found a boat.' Then he saw the dead bodies. 'What happened, thakin?'

'Dacoits. But no sign of any more.'

'But you had a boat. You should have gone.'

'We had to warn you.'

'Oh. What can I say, thakin. But now we go quickly. You and me in one boat and the Corporal Thakin with Ba Saw.'

'Where did you find the boat?' Paul asked.

'Fishing village, downriver. Army not get there. Two or three boats pulled up on beach, village very quiet, no dogs. Ba Saw and me take boat into river.' A broad grin spread over his face. 'We are experts, thakin.'

Paul laughed. 'On the river or stealing?'

'Both, thakin.'

Paul and Maung Gyi climbed into their boat, which rocked for a moment, righted itself, and they paddled furiously out of the creek and onto the vastness of the river. Steel quickly retrieved his knife then he and Ba Saw boarded the second boat. Now the big boats were difficult to handle, caught in the current, twisting and bobbing like a hooked swordfish on the end of a line. But Maung Gyi and Ba Saw steered the boats through with the experience of years, with Paul and Steel paddling furiously.

The dark outline of the eastern shore came into view, then the boats straightened and Paul realised they were out of the current. The boats grounded on a sandbank and he wondered where they had landed. To his surprise he heard Gopiram's voice. 'Here, sahib! Here, sahib!'

There were shadowy figures on the sandbank and Tilbir assuring him that all was well. Gurkhas were running across the high bank above the river, leaping down onto the sandbank.

'We caught a glimpse of the boats, sahib,' Tilbir explained, 'and realised you were quite a way south, so we have been running along the top to meet you.'

'How long till daybreak?'

'About four hours, sahib. You have found two boats.'

'We were very lucky. What about the wounded?'

'Regrettably, one has died, from D Company. The Captain Sahib and the remaining rifleman are being carried forward now. They seem to be holding out well. We have seen no Japanese nearby, but Jemedar Amarjit's platoon has formed a rearguard.'

Maung Gyi and Ba Saw sprang nimbly from their boats.

'*Shabash!*' Tilbir exclaimed. 'Well done, indeed!' And there was a murmur of approval from the Gurkhas lining the bank.

'I do not think, Maung Gyi, that we could have brought the boat across without your help,' Paul said. 'And certainly not fully laden.'

'It was nothing, thakin. Now, we help you take Gurkhas across.'

'There will be fifty-one of us – no, one poor wounded man has since died, so including the two wounded remaining, plus you, Ba Saw and the Corporal Thakin, the total will be fifty-three.'

'No problem,' Maung Gyi said confidently. 'Three times crossing OK.'

'There may be more dacoits on the other side, so I will send Dilbahadur's platoon first to establish a bridgehead.'

Dilbahadur led his men onto the sandbank and Maung Gyi and Ba Saw arranged them in their respective boats. Then the boats were pushed out into the river. At once the Karens had the boats under firm control, although heavily laden, and as they met the current and seemed to glide through it, Paul at last felt a great sense of relief.

The skilled Karens, born to the task, brought the boats smoothly to rest on the west bank, a bit further south of the creek. Dilbahadur quickly disembarked his men and placed them in their defensive positions.

The boats then returned to the east bank again and the wounded were carried aboard, together with Somers, Ray, Walton and some of Amarjit's platoon. The remainder of Amarjit's platoon, Tilbir and part of his headquarters remained on the sandbank for the final trip, Tilbir insisting he would stay till the last.

As the boats set out on their final return journey to the east bank, Paul heard shots and mortar fire up towards the bridge. He was not aware that it was a group of Gurkhas and KOYLI in a desperate rearguard in the course of which the colonel of the British regiment was killed.

Paul was thankful that this would be the last journey. A faint glow was touching the jungle-covered hills beyond the eastern shore and the beach was not so shadowy. In fact, there seemed to more men than he had estimated. But the reason was clear when he stepped ashore to be met by an excited Tilbir.

'The Colonel Sahib is here!'

Paul had mixed feelings for the moment. Although pleased that Osborne was safe, his mind was working out figures of loads and the time of approaching dawn.

'Well done, Paul,' Lieut. Colonel Osborne said. 'A very good show. Tilbir has filled me in with the details of your activities as we waited.'

'How many men have you got, sir?' Paul said abruptly. Praises could keep. He was only concerned in shipping everyone to the west bank. He didn't want the bloody Japs to walk in now and beat them into final submission.

The adjutant said, 'Cooper!' in a forceful way, mindful of him being disrespectful.

But the colonel said quietly, 'Steady, Robin. Paul must get his priorities right. There are eighteen of us, Paul, including the wounded … er, Subedar Major.'

'Yes, sahib, two seriously wounded.'

'It will take two trips to clear the beach,' Paul said.

'Then you get your men away first. We'll wait for the next trip.'

Paul knew it would be useless to suggest that the colonel should go first – even if he had recognised that Paul was in command on the beach! – but he did include the two wounded cases with the last of C Company.

Loading up without more delay, the boats set off on the third trip, did a quick turnaround on the west bank and headed back as fast as possible. The Gurkhas on the sandbank were standing out clearly as daylight began to slip over the far hills and spread down towards the river. Machine-gun fire chattered from the direction of the bridge and some rifles made a brief comment, then silence. The Japanese must be closing in on the river to see what pickings they could find, while the colonel was organising his men in a defensive position. The boat crew were paddling furiously, but it seemed to Paul as though the far shore would never be reached.

And then they were there; the Gurkhas running across the sand, loading quickly into the boats, but in an orderly fashion. In a matter of seconds, both boats were pulling out, the east bank beginning to recede, and Paul thought they had made it until the unmistakable figures of Japanese soldiers suddenly appeared on the beach and rifle shots whined overhead. A couple of Japanese soldiers were running forward with a machine-gun, setting it up on the ground.

The first burst of machine-gun fire snapped overhead, while the next ricocheted off the water, like skimming stones from a boy playing ducks and drakes, and Paul tensed, waiting for the arrival of the next burst. But the subedar major seized a rifle and opened fire from the stern. He had won at Bisley and his first shot must have almost ruffled the enemy gunner's hair, because the next burst was wild, well away from the boats. It was the last shot from the Japanese, for the subedar major's next shot split open the machine-gunner's head and the third flung the other Japanese soldier onto the sand.

As the boats were being unloaded, Paul paused for a moment to take a last look at the river. Its dark, ominous water was beginning to take on a touch of yellow as the sun rose above the trees. But two bodies twisting their way down to the sea belied any change in the river's character. It was still hungry, still savouring the orgy of the night. He cursed the river and was filled with sadness at the thought of his men who had given their lives.

But as he climbed up the bank to rejoin his company, he might have felt better if could have known that Fate had a vicious sting in its tail. In three and a half years' time it would be General Sakurai standing on the riverbank in the rain, looking into the darkness where the river, swollen by the monsoon, roared its way down to the sea. No longer a triumphant general, his division would have been smashed by a revitalised 17 Division, the Japanese Army defeated. And this time, Sakurai would not be seeing the bodies of the Allies but hundreds of Japanese soldiers, bobbing and twisting in the current of the still-hungry river as they were swept out to the sea. And it would be his men who would be screaming out for help.

Chapter Eight
Rangoon in Danger

After a tough march, the group from 4/15th Gurkha Rifles reached the railway line at Waw, where they had been told to rendezvous. Gopiram had brought over the swimmers' clothes, so they were suitably attired again.

Looking at the soldiers from other units, Paul realised how lucky it was that he and the Karens had found those sampans, because C Company had been able to bring over all its weapons and the men, although dishevelled and weary, were at least still in their uniforms.

Fortunately, the Japanese seemed to have lost interest in 17 Division and they had moved some 10 miles up the river to build a temporary bridge. Their main objective now was to capture Rangoon and obviously they did not wish to suffer more casualties in clearing up. As a result, the British were able to run trains freely into Waw and even lorries within a mile or so of the riverbank to pick up exhausted and wounded survivors.

There was good work done at that small railway station. Trains had been assembled, and blankets and tea provided. There was a contrast in assistance: on the one hand local Burmese inhabitants helped the bedraggled and hungry survivors with food, and clothes for the naked, while on the other, Burmese dacoits murdered several soldiers struggling to reach safety on their own.

The wounded were handed over to a medical team. Grant was still conscious.

'You did a great job, Paul,' he said as they parted.

'Just you get better soon,' Paul said. 'See that they remove all that metal inside you – my Gurkhas complained that you weighed a ton!'

Grant smiled faintly. 'See you in Rangoon, or Delhi, or somewhere ...'

The Gurkhas stumbled onto one of the trains, every move taking a great effort. The guard blew his whistle and Paul was glad that they were moving further away from the Sittang. But when he closed his eyes there were pictures of Japanese with swords and bayonets dripping blood, until at last sheer exhaustion drove them away.

He awakened to find the compartment in darkness and to hear the train rattling over the points as it came into Pegu Railway Station. Somehow, Paul managed to raise enough energy to jump down from the train and organise the men on the platform. They, on their part, did their best to look smart as they awaited the colonel's orders.

Shortly afterwards, they were loaded into lorries and driven some 3 miles out of Pegu, completely disorientated in the darkness, and set down at their allotted area in the defensive perimeter around the town. There was nothing they could do that night. Everyone just found some sort of shelter and fell into the sleep of the dead until daybreak of 25 February.

The Burmese roosters hardly had time to clear the sleep from their eyes, when a jeep squealed to a halt outside the cluster of huts where the Gurkhas had spent the night. The driver, in his baseball hat, with an unlit cigar hanging from his mouth, was easily identified as an American. Paul shook Ray awake.

'They've come for you.'

'Who?' Ray asked sleepily.

'The redcaps.'

Ray sat up with a start. Paul laughed. 'No. It's one of your chaps from the AVG. They haven't taken long to track you down.'

Ray walked over to the window. 'Bob!' he called out.

The American in the jeep looked up. 'Hi, Ray. You've got ten minutes to get off your arse.'

'That's not very friendly,' Paul remarked.

Ray smiled. 'It is for Bob.'

'You're going back to the squadron?'

'I guess so, Paul. In a way, I'd rather stay here. It's been a great experience for me.'

'There is a precedence for an American to join the Gurkhas. There have been one or two others.'

'Don't make it harder for me,' Ray said. 'I'm going to miss the Gurkhas one hell of a lot. But at the moment, my skill as a fighter pilot is more useful and in demand. Bob would never have come here this morning – he's probably been searching all night! – if I was not needed. Now, where are my clothes? Hell!' He put a hand to his forehead. 'My flying gear!'

'Even if you are not going to stay in a Gurkha Regiment,' Paul said, 'it looks as if you are leaving in a Gurkha uniform.'

'What will they say when I get back to Mingaladon?'

Paul couldn't help laughing at the picture he had in his mind of Ray arriving back among his pilots, complete with puttees and Gurkha hat.

But there was nothing else for it; his flying gear was probably a small pile of charred material in the middle of a burnt-out truck on the east bank of the Sittang by now.

Ray put on a brave face and reached for his borrowed clothes. Josbir came in and was fussing around, making sure Ray was properly turned out.

'I don't suppose I could take him with me?' Ray asked.

'I'm afraid not. But if you ever decide to return to us, no doubt something can be arranged.'

'Blackmail,' Ray complained.

The rasping sound of a jeep's klaxon came from outside.

'I'd best be going. Shouldn't I say goodbye to the colonel?'

'He'd like that.'

Shortly afterwards, Ray left the hut and walked to the jeep. A large crowd of men from C Company and the colonel gathered round to wish him goodbye. He would surely be remembered as part of the battalion's history.

Bob looked at Ray as he climbed into the passenger seat, Gurkha hat at a right angle. 'Gees!' Paul heard him mutter. And that was all – the rest would come later, Paul thought as the jeep moved away, Ray waving, the Gurkhas cheering.

It was a time for goodbyes all round. Sergeant Somers and Walton returned to the Duke of Wellington's, Corporal Steel to 2 KOYLI and the Karens to their Burma Rifles battalion, all of them taking the Gurkhas' thanks and letters to their commanding officers from Osborne, praising them for their fine work. Somers had been upset by the news that his colonel had been murdered by Burmese dacoits while resting in a hut after swimming the river. It made Paul realise how lucky he had been – and all thanks to Steel.

When Paul finally saw Steel in daylight for the first time, he found the corporal was much younger than he had supposed. A short, stocky man, the corporal had made an effort to put his uniform in order, and Paul imagined he had earned his stripes. Whether he had really been a champion swimmer was debatable. But his skill with a knife had been of significant value. He had been shocked to learn that his colonel had been so tragically killed on the beach. As he turned to go he said, 'I will keep an eye on the Karens, sir, and see they get back to their battalion.'

And there was good news for the battalion with the return of Major Kennedy and Jack Hunter with about sixty men from their A and B Companies. After the ambush on the Sittang Road, they had also lost touch with Brigadier Ekin, but managed to avoid the Japanese, turning north to eventually reach the Sittang some miles upstream of the bridge where the crossing was easier, although they had had to make rafts and had unfortunately lost several men in the process.

Osborne gathered his officers around him to put them in the picture. He was down to five, including himself, and there was little chance of reinforcements in the near future. But he had a good complement of Gurkha officers who would have to fill in and he had no doubt that they would be reliable. Because of this he had included the senior Gurkha officers in the meeting.

'The heavy losses of men and equipment have almost rent 17 Division asunder,' he told them. 'I understand that only some 2,000 officers and men managed to escape to the west bank, bringing with them 500 rifles or so, a handful of Bren guns and tommy guns. The Gurkha battalions have suffered badly, apart from the 1/4th who, of course, crossed the bridge early and have a very healthy strength of some 680.

'The roll call for the other Gurkha battalions is around 100 each; 46 Brigade has been broken up and the division now consists of 48 and 16 Brigades. Our battalion has been attached to 48 Brigade for the time being.'

Osborne looked over his officers. He was sure that some tough fighting lay ahead and he was going to have to rely heavily on the few he had available. But they had proved themselves over the past weeks and he felt certain they would not let the regiment or himself down.

Meanwhile, in Rangoon, the situation was frenetic as plans were made for the evacuation of the thousands of civilians in the city. The plan was to run one train daily from Rangoon direct to Mandalay for privileged evacuees – those guaranteed a safe passage out of the city. Rangoon Station was a through line to the west proceeding to Prome, and to the east to Pegu.

Captain Tony Mains, GSOII at Headquarters Burma Army, was responsible for the Field Security Sections and he was ordered to take over the loading of the daily train. The first thing he found was that all the railway subordinates had decamped and he had only a handful of railway officers, mostly British or Anglo-Burmese, to rely on, plus his own Field Security men. He reconnoitred the station and found it consisted of four platforms connected by a footbridge from the main entrance with offices on the north side. It was well fenced in, being in the centre of the city, which made the task of crowd control easier.

Each day he was given a list of passengers by Colonel Brewitt, the Deputy Director of Railways, and an estimate of the numbers. The passengers were a mixed bag, ranging from civilian residents, business people, government clerical staff and subordinate officers to coolies and hospital sweepers. And as the privileged train, the *Number One Up-Mail,* ran straight through to Mandalay, everyone wanted to get aboard, whether they had a right to or not. The train was due to depart at 15.00 hours and by noon, the forecourt was a seething mass of passengers and luggage.

A very efficient officer, Mains quickly secured firm control to prevent a mad scramble, organising a strict procedure. First, the senior official in charge of each party was called inside the station to give the exact number of his group. He then rejoined his party, waiting until 13.00 hours, when he returned, accompanied by a reliable person who was to act as guide. As soon as the train was alongside the platform, Mains personally allotted the accommodation, marking on the compartment doors in chalk the name of the party. Leaders and guides were brought to the entrance gate when loading was due to begin. The leader of the party stood by the gate through which the evacuees had to pass in single file, supported by two Field Security men, and personally identified each member of his party. The guides then led the evacuees to their allotted compartment.

The Whitcombs and the Stevens drove to the station, where Jack managed to find a space among the crush of vehicles jamming the station entrance. The Whitcombs had sensibly decided to take only their packs, but Celia had insisted that she could not manage without a suitcase of what she termed "essentials". That this would probably cause problems later did not occur to her. Jack locked the car, although he knew he would never see it again.

They had decided that George would be nominated as leader and he was called inside to give the exact number of his party.

'As there are only five of you, I think you can act as guide as well,' Tony Mains said. 'Come back at one.'

George rejoined his party in the jam-packed forecourt. Celia was sitting on her suitcase and George, experienced after his escape from Moulmein, was concerned about her ability to stand up to what he was certain would be a gruelling journey. She looked somewhat bewildered in the heat of the forecourt, but he was more confident of the others. Mary and Sue were seasoned refugees now and Jack seemed to be bearing up well, although he was still complaining about the abandonment of his car.

At 13.00 hours, George was called forward. The train was alongside the platform and Mains had marked the compartment doors. Now, he showed the guides their allotted carriages. When the time came for loading, George stood by the entrance gate to identify each member of his party as they passed through; he then led them to their compartment.

Loading was a problem because a metre-gauge third-class carriage was designed to seat eighty persons, but at least a hundred were being crammed in and several had brought more luggage than was sensible.

'My God!' Celia exclaimed as for a moment she stood frozen at the door.

'For Christ's sake, get in!' somebody shouted and Jack pushed her inside, the suitcase swinging alarmingly.

'Mind that bloody case!' a passenger already inside shouted in alarm.

Then Jack managed to bodily lift his wife to the far end and dump her on a window seat. George pressing on behind also managed to find Mary and Sue seats by a window.

In a moment, a horde of passengers shoved their way into the compartment, fighting for seats, the unlucky ones standing pressed against each other. George and Jack stood with backs against the seats occupied by the women. The heat in the compartment was almost unbearable. Fortunately, there was not too long a delay before *Number One Up-Mail* pulled out of the station and as it built up speed some air drifted through the windows.

The Mandalay line ran through Pegu and for a considerable distance on both sides of the town the line was very close to the Japanese. From her window, Sue looked anxiously across the rooftops of the town and out to the distant countryside as she wondered about Paul. Was he somewhere out there? Had he escaped from Sittang?

And then the *Number One Up-Mail* had passed through the town safely and was heading north for Mandalay.

Major General Jackie Smyth was also on the move, having put in a request for leave. During the campaign he had literally run himself to a standstill and the recurrence of his fistula trouble had not helped. On 7 February 1942, before the crucial battle for the Sittang had begun, Smyth was surprised by a visit from Major General Treffry Thompson, the Deputy Director Medical Services to the Burma Army, who insisted, despite his protests, that a medical board should be convened for him immediately.

It was fixed for the eleventh, but the President of the Board went sick and Smyth's ADMS, Colonel Mackenzie, was appointed in his place. Beforehand, Smyth had begged Mackenzie to let him carry on, at least until the critical battle for the Sittang was resolved, so the colonel gave him some arsenic and strychnine injections to keep him going.

The Board pronounced Smyth fit to carry on, provided he took two month's rest at the first available opportunity. Only Hutton and Thompson saw the report before it was lost with most of the other documents at AHQ in the hasty withdrawal from Rangoon.

On 25 February, believing that he could now take the leave recommended, Smyth wrote to Hutton for his permission to leave as early as he could be spared, pointing out that "Punch" Cowan was a really efficient substitute to step into his shoes. The request was strongly recommended by General Thompson and Hutton took immediate action on it. Smyth was informed on 1 March that he had been granted a month's leave in India, Cowan taking over as acting major general. Smyth was upset at leaving his division and his officers who had supported him so well and agreed with his views and tactics. He was especially concerned because he was certain Rangoon would fall and 17 Division faced hard times ahead.

To Smyth's surprise, he was told that he would be travelling with Wavell and they took off from Mingaladon Airport on 2 March. But the two generals sat at opposite ends of the aircraft. Incredibly, Wavell had not said a word to Smyth since his visit to his HQ on 6 February and neither was he to speak to Smyth again during his lifetime. Smyth could almost feel the hatred, the contempt, across the space between them. If only, Smyth wished, Wavell had let him cross the river those four days earlier. But it seemed that nothing would make the general change his mind. But I hardly deserve to be treated like a leper.

They landed at Lashio and stayed overnight while Wavell had a discussion with Chiang Kai-shek. The next day they flew to Calcutta, still at opposite ends of the aircraft. Almost as soon as they had landed, another aircraft wheeled up alongside. As the passengers descended, Smyth recognised the unmistakable figure of General Alexander. Quickly, Wavell joined Alexander on the tarmac and led him briskly away to the rest house. Obviously, Smyth was not to be allowed to speak to Alex.

What could they be discussing? Must be his instructions on taking over command in Burma, he thought. Smyth was anxious – he was well aware of Wavell's view that Rangoon could be held. But what Smyth did not know was that twenty-minute discussion in the rest house was almost to lead to the complete destruction of the Burma Army.

Smyth was standing on the tarmac when the station commander approached him somewhat diffidently. The C.-in-C., it appeared, wished to continue his journey to Delhi alone. Smyth's baggage was unloaded and piled on the tarmac. Shortly after, Wavell returned to his plane, walking straight past Smyth and his luggage without any sign of recognition.

Smyth was now informed that because of the great shortage of aircraft, the only plane available to take him on to Delhi was a rather antiquated two-seater Camel, flown by a Sikh. Smyth was not concerned about being flown by a Sikh – after all, he had served with a Sikh regiment during World War I – but he was concerned about the plane. A concern which proved justified when the aircraft failed to take off, losing a wing in some bushes and ending halfway up a tree. The station commander rushed over in a car and was relieved to find Smyth unhurt. Another Camel was wheeled out and this one made it safely to Delhi.

By the time he reached Delhi, Smyth was exhausted, his mind in a turmoil after the events that had unfolded over the past few days. Fortunately, his beloved wife, Florence, was waiting for him. But the alleviation of his exhaustion, and the return of some tranquillity to his mind, soon vanished with morning, when he received an official letter from the Military Secretary at Army Headquarters by express messenger.

'What is it?' Florence asked in alarm as she saw the expression on his face.

'I … I am deprived of my major general's rank forthwith and have been immediately retired from the service on Wavell's orders'

Florence took the letter from his hand, but before she could read it, he exclaimed, 'My God! it has just occurred to me. I was to become a substantive major general within the next few days. Now, I shall be deprived of my rank and my pension.'

'Wait, there is more. You have to explain to Wavell why you applied for leave when your division was in action. How that man must hate you!' Florence said bitterly.

'I do not know for sure. I always thought him a fair man. Of course, he had very fixed ideas about the Japanese and even after the fall of Singapore, he had no respect for their capabilities. But I have to wonder how much he might have been influenced by the reports he received from Hutton. Did he know that I had asked to be moved to the Sittang six days before?'

'Whatever the reason, are you going to take the matter further?'

'I do not suppose he will grant me an interview, but I shall try. Though, this business of my leave will have to be sorted out.'

Smyth's request to see Wavell was refused, but General Treffry Thompson came to the rescue by clearing the question of leave and medical reports.

Smyth's health began to deteriorate and he was confined to bed. He received no medical treatment from service doctors, but when two civilian doctors considered his condition to be serious, Florence wrote to General Hartley, the Deputy C.-in-C. As a result he was medically boarded and granted three further months' sick leave.

At last, on 27 September 1942, he and Florence sailed from Bombay on the troopship *Malaya* for an unknown future. There was little doubt in both their minds that Smyth had been made the scapegoat, but he learned that he had many friends. All his military colleagues, from Bill Slim downwards, had come to visit him in hospital and to give him their support.

It was only after the war that he was able to clear his name. Meanwhile, his life could have been in ruins, but he was able to make a new career in journalism and he eventually became a Member of Parliament.

Chapter Nine
Escape from Rangoon

Lieutenant General Sir Harold Alexander, KCB CSI DSO MC, was visiting the coastal defences in the Isle of Wight on 19 February 1942, when he received a message to report immediately to the CIGS, General Sir Alan Brooke, who told him he was to assume command of the army in Burma as soon as possible.

'As soon as possible means at once,' Brooke emphasised.

But because the weather was too bad to fly Alexander had to wait a week, driving to the aerodrome every evening, only to be turned back, until at last he eventually took off on the night of 27 February in a Flying Fortress. It was so bitterly cold that icicles formed on his oxygen mask. He spent twenty-four hours at the British Embassy in Cairo before taking another plane to India. Engine trouble caused a forced landing in the Persian Gulf, but at last he reached Delhi on 2 March, continuing the next day to Calcutta, where he met General Wavell at the airport.

As he stepped down onto the tarmac, he thought he saw Jackie Smyth, but there was no chance of exchanging greetings, because Wavell stormed up and led him off to the nearby rest house.

At this fateful meeting, Wavell filled him in with the situation in Burma and gave him his orders. Wavell still believed that the Japanese were second-rate soldiers and he could not understand why they were causing so much trouble. Even though Singapore had fallen, he felt assured that the depleted 17 Division, ill-equipped and half trained, could hold Rangoon.

'The Japanese must be worn out by now and probably short of supplies,' he told Alexander. 'Rangoon must be defended to the last. A determined stand must surely be successful.'

After Alexander had taken off for Burma, Wavell sent a cable to the CIGS: Have issued instructions that Rangoon is not to be given up without a battle as aggressive as our resources will permit.

Alexander continued his journey to Burma, flying into Magwe Airfield on 4 March. A day later he flew on to Rangoon, the last plane to land there. He was disturbed to see the permanent pall of smoke from burning buildings which overhung the city. Sir Reginald Dorman Smith, the Governor of Burma, had given orders for the evacuation of the civilian population several days earlier and some demolitions had already begun, although the destruction of the port and oil installations had been held up pending Alexander's arrival.

Making his way to AHQ, Alexander found that Hutton was at the front. But he learned enough from the staff to realise that the situation was serious. The *33* and *55 Divisions* were encroaching quickly on Rangoon. They were in strength in Waw and the neighbouring villages north and north-east of Pegu and troops were infiltrating under cover of darkness across the Sittang River between Pegu and Nyaunglebin.

Alexander drove the 40 miles to 17 Division HQ to meet Hutton and Brigadier "Punch" Cowan, who had relieved Smyth as commander of 17 Division. Now, Alexander took over official command of the Burma Army, with Hutton reluctantly agreeing to remain as his chief of staff. Hutton filled him in with the situation. The defence of Rangoon was untenable and his advice was to withdraw 17 Division immediately from Pegu, evacuate Rangoon and pull back the Burma Army to Prome, taking up positions in the Irrawaddy Valley. Hutton had already put into place instructions for the necessary demolition of vital installations and he had outlined the action to be taken after the withdrawal. They were all agreed that the most likely manoeuvre by the enemy was to move round on the left flank and seize Rangoon behind their backs.

In fact, General Iida, the commander of the Japanese *15 Army*, had issued an operational instruction to *33 Division* to first effect an early capture of Rangoon and secondly to destroy the British forces around the city. Meanwhile, *55 Division*, after the capture of Pegu, was to send one infantry regiment to pursue the British towards Rangoon, while the other concentrated their efforts in Pegu in preparation for a concerted northward drive. General Sakurai of *33* Division decided to cross the Rangoon–Prome road and try to enter Rangoon from the north-west.

Alexander was in a quandary. Hutton had given a very clear picture of the situation, but Wavell had been so emphatic at Calcutta. Now, Alexander decided he should follow Wavell's instructions.

'I believe we should defend the city for as long as possible,' Alexander said.

Hutton looked at his chief of staff, "Taffy" Davies. They were both taken aback and horrified.

'I don't think you are fully aware of the situation, sir,' Hutton said. 'Seventeenth Division is defending Pegu with great difficulty and is very much reduced in numbers and equipment. It is really only the presence of 7 Armoured Brigade which is holding things together.'

'Rangoon is too important to give up so easily,' Alexander persisted. 'Sixty-three Brigade has just arrived. And I must say I am not happy about the huge gap which appears to have opened up between 1 Burma Division and 17 Division. I believe we should hold on to Rangoon for as long as possible. I want that gap closed and an attack launched in the area between Pegu and Waw, and the demolition plans should be postponed.'

Commanded by Brigadier John Wickham, 63 Brigade was only partially trained and was still awaiting the disembarkation of its transport. But Alexander ordered Wickham to reinforce 17 Division and 7 Armoured Brigade in the planned offensive. Wickham decided to go forward to reconnoitre the area in which his brigade would operate, taking with him his three battalion commanders. They travelled in two Bren carriers provided by 1/4th Gurkhas, to contact 4th Gurkhas. The group moved in single file led by a tank, then a Bren carrier, another tank, a second Bren carrier and lastly a third tank. The first carrier, driven by a subaltern of the 4 Brigade, contained Wickham, Lieut. Col. Leonard, CO of 1/10th Gurkhas, the Brigade Major and three Gurkhas of 1/4th. The second carrier held the commanding officers of the Sikhs and the FFR and one of their adjutants.

As they moved up the line they came across an abandoned British 30 cwt. truck. The leading tank roared past it along the right-hand ditch, while the leading Bren-carrier driver considered the other side of the road better going and drove on the very verge passing below a tree where a Japanese sniper was in hiding. The carrier was armoured front and sides but had no head cover. The sniper waited until the carrier was below him, the occupants clearly visible and unprotected, and then opened fire with his light machine-gun. Bullets flew in all directions, rattling and ricocheting around the interior. The brigadier was hit in an eye, which he later lost, and blood pumped from his leg. Lieut. Col. Leonard was badly wounded; he later found he had sixty-eight bullet holes and was fortunate that none had proved fatal. The brigade major was temporarily knocked out by a blow on the chin and a couple of the Gurkha riflemen were hit, blood pouring from the leg of one and from a hole in the head from the other; both survived. But the Gurkha lance naik, who had been sitting on top, unprotected, was untouched. Spotting the Japanese sniper in the tree he promptly dispatched him with a burst of automatic fire.

The carrier driver had escaped with just a cut face, but he decided to turn back to Pegu, as the wounded obviously needed urgent medical attention. The second carrier had continued down the road on the far side. The next day its burnt-out remains were found with the charred remains of its occupants. Within a short time of its arrival, 63 Brigade's brigadier had been wounded, two battalion commanders killed and another badly wounded.

For Alexander, the news added to his difficulties, which were mounting. The attempt to link 1 Burma Division and 17 Division had failed, as the enemy were too strongly entrenched in the gap. Fighting in the Pegu area was also not going well and by noon of 6 March, a considerable body of troops was cut off in the town. Alexander also heard that the *33 Division* was heading for the Prome road and the oil refinery at Syriam was in danger of being seized. A demolition squad was waiting there for the order to blow the installation.

At nightfall on 6 March, Alexander at last reached the conclusion that it was not possible to hold Rangoon any longer. At midnight, he gave the orders to evacuate the city and for his forces to regroup north of the city at Tharrawaddy on the Prome road in the Irrawaddy Valley.

At dawn the following morning, the advanced guard reached Tharrawaddy without incident. At the same time, the Rangoon garrison moved out from the city in a convoy stretching some 2 miles in the bright, hot sunlight. The forces in Pegu had orders to break out and then join the convoy which was taking the road to Prome.

The convoy passed the deserted and bomb-cratered Mingaladon Airfield until reaching approximately Milestone 11, where the road forked north to Prome, with Hlegu and Pegu to the right. The convoy followed the Prome road for half a mile until, just past the village of Taukkyan, heavy firing broke out as the vanguard came up against a roadblock. By now, the column was out of the city confines and the road was narrow with thick jungle on both sides.

Supported by tanks of 7th Hussars, 1st Gloucesters attacked, but the Japanese were well established. A second attack by 2/13th FFR of 63 Brigade fared no better and with night approaching fast, they dug in along the south side of the block.

When night fell, Alexander found himself, with Hutton and the administration staff of his headquarters, stuck on a narrow Burmese road, in an area of about a square mile, hemmed in by the jungle, while the whole convoy bivouacked for the night alongside the road. The force in Pegu was also bottled up and Hugh-Jones was given orders to cut his way out at all costs and join the rest of the Burma Army.

To Alexander, it felt like being stuck in no-man's-land and he was well aware of the army's desperate situation. But, as was characteristic of him, he seemed the most unconcerned person in the whole set-up, sitting quite imperturbably in a Burmese house that was dimly lit by a few oil lamps his staff had managed to find. Tactically, the column was so badly placed that a powerful attack by the enemy could destroy it; and Alexander's command of the army in Burma appeared unlikely to last for more than a few days.

He ordered 63 Brigade, supported by all available armour and artillery, to clear the block in the morning. The plan was for the Sikhs and Gurkhas to attack the block on the east and west of the road respectively, while tanks and the FFR broke through on its axis. The attack was to be preceded by an artillery concentration at 08.35 hours.

The two battalions set off for their forming-up places. In the darkness, the Gurkhas had great difficulty in passing through the congested village of Taukkyan and they did not reach their goal till the small hours of the morning, tired and hungry. The Sikhs reached their rendezvous somewhat earlier. As they waited in the thick jungle they were aware of a large enemy presence in the area. The Gurkhas west of the roadblock heard the creaking of bullock-carts and saw a large enemy force to their left, moving south to Rangoon. A message was sent to 63 Brigade HQ on the main road, but it was treated with scepticism. So Alexander, passing a fitful night, did not learn what was happening.

General Sakurai had moved his *33 Division* north of the city and he planned to cross the Prome road after dark on the seventh and then turn south and advance on Rangoon from the north-west. On the morning of the seventh, the advance guard of *111/214 Battalion* reached the Prome road some 5 miles north of Taukkyan, to find British troops in considerable numbers moving north. In order to protect the flank of his division as it crossed the road, the advance-guard commander cut the road and by about noon had established a strong roadblock. When Colonel Sakuma, *214 Regiment,* was informed, he left his HQ to report the incident to Sakurai.

Sakurai, who assumed that the British planned to hold Rangoon, was concerned that this encounter on the Prome road would cause the British to strengthen their defences against an attack from the north-west, which might jeopardise the success of the operation of his division and deprive him of the glory of a triumphant entry. Sakuma was sent back to his HQ with instructions to continue his regiment's encircling movement on Rangoon.

On his return, he found *111/214 Battalion* under heavy pressure at the roadblock and he ordered it to disengage as soon as it could after dark and follow up the main body of the regiment. So it was that during the hours of darkness Japanese troops were seen to be crossing the Prome road and moving south within 200 yards of 1/10th Gurkhas.

On the morning of the eighth, shortly before the attack of 63 Brigade and 7 Armoured Brigade, 2nd Royal Tank Regiment reported that the roadblock was unoccupied. Hardly believing his luck, Alexander ordered the convoy to move out. At 10.00 hours the Rangoon garrison, with 16 Brigade as rearguard, passed through the roadblock and headed north towards Tharrawaddy. The Burma Army had escaped by the skin of its teeth, thanks to the Japanese character of sticking firmly to orders. Behind them, the wharves, warehouses and dockside cranes lay smashed by the demolitions which had been set off at 14.00 hours on the seventh. The power station was alight and the oil refineries lay in ruins. A thick pall of black smoke hung over the city.

At about midday on the eighth, *215 Regiment* entered Rangoon to find, to its surprise, that the city was deserted. Sakurai was furious and he immediately sent a regiment in pursuit of the convoy. The regiment reached Taukkyan after the British rearguard had moved north and having covered over 30 miles in some seventeen hours, it was then forced to halt through lack of supplies. Meanwhile, the Burma Army continued northwards, with no interference by the enemy apart from some high-level bombing, which did little damage. By 23.00 hours on the eighth, the last of the marching troops were clear of Hmawbi.

During the ninth and tenth, covered by 7 Armoured, they were moved in motor transport to the Tharrawaddy area. In Rangoon, General Sakurai realised that he had lost a great opportunity to destroy the British Burma Army.

Paul waited in the dark for the order to move out. The narrow road running through the centre of Pegu was crowded with the troops, transport and tanks of 17 Division and 7 Armoured Brigade. Somewhere in the vicinity, the Japanese were no doubt waiting to attack as the British attempted to break out of the town. Earlier, on the evening of 6 March, Brigadier Hugh-Jones had received orders from Alexander to move out of Pegu. The plan was for 7th Hussars to cross the Pegu River that night followed by 48 Brigade and all the transport. The Japanese had established a roadblock at Payathonzu, some 5 miles south of the town on the Rangoon road. The Hussars were to break through and then the whole column would follow. Once the tail of 48 Brigade was across, the sappers would blow the bridges over the river and railway. In position west of the river near the railway station, 1st West York and 1st Cameronians would tag on behind the column as rearguard.

At around 22.00 hours, Paul heard the tanks start further down the road and cross the bridge over the Pegu River. As his company was not at the front of the column, he did not expect to move forward for a while. Anyway, the Hussars had decided to postpone their attack on the roadblock until daybreak and so had harboured for the night.

In the early hours of the seventh, 48 Brigade started to move out to join up with the Hussars. With 1/7th Gurkhas as advance guard, the column passed through the West Yorks and Cameronians, 1/4th Gurkhas on the right and 5/3rd Gurkhas on the left, to form a box with the transport on the road between them.

When the advance guard contacted 7th Hussars the column halted, the transport closed up on the road and double-banked and the flank battalions disposed on each side and close to the road. It was a cold morning and the mist from the river almost enveloped the waiting column. Then, at 06.30 hours, the sappers blew the bridges over the river and the railway. The explosions were still echoing eerily around the mist when the enemy attacked the rearguard battalions. The West Yorks and Cameronians, reacting quickly, at close quarters with the shadowy figures of their enemy, used their bayonets to good effect, forcing the enemy back.

Meanwhile, the Hussars launched their attack against the roadblock, which was defended with great ferocity by the Japanese. The Hussars lost two tanks before eventually smashing through the enemy defences and clearing the road. But, owing to a misunderstanding, the tanks then moved on along the road without leaving picquets to keep it open. Japanese infantry immediately closed in again and two Gurkha battalions at once attacked head on, while a third made a wide hook and came in behind the block.

The Japanese waiting in ambush were hidden in culverts and were well dug in among the orchards and jungle which lined the northern line of the road. The morning mist was still curling about the road as they opened up with fierce fire. Flashes of red streaked the mist as mortar bombs seemed to drop suddenly from above, to explode with deadly accuracy among the crowded line of transport, machine-gun bullets pursuing their targets across the road. Pandemonium broke loose on the road, which was jammed with double-banked traffic. Some drivers fled from their vehicles, others tried to pass vehicles in front. A group of the enemy attacked the line of ambulances and the sitting patients took to the nearby jungle. Those seriously wounded, lying on the stretchers, were easy targets for the Japanese machine-gunners, their bullets ripping into already devastated flesh and limbs, bringing them ghoulish enjoyment as their helpless victims screamed in terror and pain.

The Gurkha battalions swung swiftly into action to flush out the enemy. Paul moved from the far side of the road, finding a way to the opposite side through the tangle of vehicles spewed across it. In the clearing mist he could just make out the trees of an orchard, where a Japanese force was in position. Bullets made their presence known, ricocheting off the road, smacking against the vehicles with metallic snaps.

On his left, Amarjit plunged into the orchard with his platoon, Bren-gunners firing from the hip, section leaders blazing away with their tommy guns, grenades flashing in the mist about the trees. Then the Gurkha riflemen were into the Japanese with their bayonets. A Japanese officer was beating the road with the flat of his sword to rouse his men into action. He was caught in the crossfire of bullets and somersaulted onto his back in a heap. Dilbahadur, on the right, saw a group of Japanese who had taken up position in a ditch. His platoon enfiladed them, the bullets catching them in a line, toppling them over like ninepins.

All along the road the Gurkhas attacked with bayonet, tommy gun and Bren guns fired from the hip. Lieut. Col. Lentaigne, commanding the 4th Gurkha Battalion, personally led his men with rifle and bayonet straight into a large orchard, where they attacked a company of Japanese – and with great efficiency and courage, wiped out seventy of the enemy. Further along the road, Lieut. Col. White of 7th Gurkhas was in the fore when he was killed by a sniper. The snipers were active and Lieut. Col. Cameron was hit in the leg. But as he lay on the ground he still shouted out orders to his men.

By early afternoon, determined and courageous action by the Gurkhas had cleared the road and the transport continued with little difficulty to reach Hlegu. Once the vehicles were cleared, the rest of the brigade infantry formed a hollow square and struck off south-east across the paddy fields and then followed the railway to Tawa Railway Station, from where they took the rough track which brought them back to the road. They continued their march with only two breaks from 16.00 hours until 13.00 hours the next day, on the eighth, when they reached Hlegu. Lorries were waiting there to take them to the Taukkyan road junction and then onward along the Prome road.

It had been a tough fight and losses, especially among senior officers, had been severe; but the force had fought with great determination and considerable skill, inflicting heavy casualties on the Japanese, who did not attempt to follow up.

The British Burma Army at last arrived in the Irrawaddy Valley, where it intended to make its next stand. In Prome, 63 Brigade was there to cover the main road from the south, 16 Brigade was in Hmawza to hold the south-east approaches and 48 Brigade was in reserve in the Wettigan area, also covering any hostile move around the flank, while 7 Armoured Brigade harboured with 48 Brigade in the rear.

As the lorries carrying the men of 4/15th Gurkhas arrived in the village of Wettigan, guides directed them to their positions. Dusty and with uniforms black with sweat, many spotted and streaked with blood, the men debussed, a few of whom had soiled bandages on various limbs and covering their heads. Paul led the way to his allotted position on the perimeter, his HQ sited in a wooden Burmese house, and set the men to digging defensive positions.

A Gurkha came up and saluted. 'Colonel Sahib Order Group, sahib. GOs also, sahib.'

As darkness settled on Wettigan, Paul led Tilbir, Dilbahadur and Amarjit across the main village street and then down a narrow lane leading to the colonel's HQ. A bamboo stockade encircled the compound of the large house, which was raised off the ground on massive teak poles. The owners had long since departed and a number of the HQ staff had commandeered the ample space beneath the house. Paul and his party climbed the steep, slatted staircase onto the veranda and entered the main living room. There was a faint smell of kerosene oil from a newly lit lantern hanging from a hook on a rafter. The lantern cast only a small pool of light onto the colonel, who sat at a low, round table in the centre of the room, leaving the corners in shadow, where the other members of the battalion were already sitting cross-legged on the wooden floor.

'Sit yourself down,' the colonel said in English and then he changed to Gurkhali for the benefit of the Gurkha officers. 'First, I must congratulate you and your men on the splendid show at Pegu. It was a tight situation. Sadly, we did not escape unscathed. Several gallant men died and others have been seriously wounded.

'We now have five British officers and twelve Gurkha officers. We will all have to do the work of two men, I fear. Although, of course, we have several very good NCOs, some of whom should be promoted. The difficulty is that we will continue to grow fewer in numbers, as will all the battalions. And with Rangoon now closed to us, there is almost no chance of us obtaining reinforcements.'

He paused for a moment, looking over his officers, and then he continued, 'But we must make the best of what we have and I know I can rely on the battalion to continue its high standard. We will certainly have to if we are to survive. There are going to be many more tight situations. At the moment, 48 Brigade is in reserve, but it won't be long before we are in action.

'You have obviously realised by now that the only way of escape for the Burma Army is north and out through India. I do not believe that we can hold on to Burma, so the plan must be to detain the enemy for as long as possible and to inflict as much damage as possible. It will be a fighting retreat. We will fight all the way to the border with India, of that I am sure.

'We might not get any reinforcements, but if we can delay them long enough, nature could come to our aid with the arrival of the monsoons. I am sure we will be racing the monsoon, to leave the Japanese stuck in the mud, their communications badly stretched. Then we will have several months to re-equip and train and build up our forces for the day when we retake Burma.

'Fortunately, General Hutton had the foresight to transfer supplies from the godowns at the port to the Irrawaddy Valley area, so we probably have sufficient supplies for a couple of months. That is all I have to say. Have you any questions?'

'Have we managed to find a replacement for Doc, sir,' Major Arthur Kennedy asked.

'Fortunately, there was a spare doctor at Brigade HQ and he has joined us. In fact, I think by the time you get back to your companies, you should find he has already begun attending to the wounded.' He looked around. 'Anything else?'

Somewhat diffidently, Paul asked, 'Have you any news of civilians, sir?'

The colonel hesitated for a moment. He had heard of Paul's meeting with the Whitcombs in Moulmein. 'I think most of the civilians

150

were evacuated from Rangoon earlier. I have to say that I doubt if there were any fixed plans to get them away safely. I fear it is going to be every man for himself. The only way out would be north by road if they had transport or, if anyone is lucky enough, to find a place on the few aircraft available. I am sorry I cannot be more helpful, Paul.'

'It's all right, sir. I understand.'

'Well, if there is nothing else, then you may dismiss to your companies.'

He watched Paul disappear into the shadows on his way out. He had enough confidence in the young officer by now to feel certain he would not let his concern over the girl cloud his judgement as a company commander.

When Paul awoke in the morning he was surprised to hear birds singing in the trees. He stepped out onto the veranda, feeling stiff and not yet fully refreshed from sleep. It all seemed strangely peaceful. He looked northwards, where a line of hills topped the dark shadow of the jungle, and he wondered about Sue and her parents. If they were on the road, they must have covered a fair distance by now. He had doubts about their chances of having found seats on a plane out of Rangoon, but there was always the possibility of finding a plane at one of the upcountry airfields.

He descended the rickety staircase to where his men were busy improving their trenches. Otherwise, there seemed for the moment to be no indication of a war at hand. But it wouldn't be long, he thought, before he would have to pick up his tommy gun, put on his equipment and go out to do battle. One thing was that he had heard there was a new general in charge in the name of Slim. Perhaps he was the man to turn defeat into victory.

Part Two

The Scarecrow Army

Chapter Ten
The Bullock-cart Ambush

The road led north through the Dry Zone to Taungdwingyi, HQ of 17 Division: a waterless brown countryside of low, undulating stony hills cut up by *chaungs,* which had long forgotten the feel of water lapping against their banks, and occasional patches of parched jungle. Touch a branch and it would fall off in the hand and crumble to dust. The road was crowded with a slow-moving mass of Indian and Burmese refugees, trudging in the overpowering heat, clinging to what few possessions they owned, fleeing from the invading Japanese Army which was advancing north from Rangoon.

Captain Paul Cooper, leading a small reconnaissance patrol of Gurkhas from his company, felt overcome by the sight of this living tragedy, women struggling with their children of all ages, families trying to keep together and support the elderly members, the sick trying to keep up. How many of them would escape? Would they reach their goal: the safety of India, hundreds of miles in the distance? They were running from the Japanese, but many other perils awaited them on the road: cholera, marauding Indian and Burmese gangs seeking plunder and the ever-present threat of rape for the majority.

With the capture of Rangoon, Japanese reinforcements and equipment were now being shipped into Burma to strengthen their advance northwards, their first main objective being the oilfields at Yenangyaung, and only the depleted, but still resolute, British Burma Army stood in their way. The Japanese would obviously attack quite soon. Meanwhile, they were infiltrating small groups disguised as Burmese to cause disruption. Looking over the refugees, Paul wondered how he could tell the difference. The bona fide refugees would probably know, but would they take the risk of warning him?

He noticed a young Burmese boy at the roadside holding his leg as though in some pain. Paul kept moving on; he couldn't stop to help every refugee. But the boy seemed determined to attract his attention, touching his mouth and his ears and pointing back along the road as though he had some information.

Paul turned back and bent down as though to look at the leg while the boy whispered in broken English, 'Thakin. Bullock-cart. Japan machine-gun.'

Paul glanced down the road. He could see three carts creaking along.

'The middle one, thakin. I point out.'

Jemedar Amarjit came up alongside and Paul explained. 'It could be true,' he added.

Amarjit agreed, 'But with so many refugees around the cart we would have to make a careful approach.'

'I was about to give the order to return,' Paul said. 'Let us have a break now and then turn back along the road as though patrolling normally. I think we should catch up with the cart quite easily.'

The Gurkhas relaxed by the side of the road, drinking sparingly from their water bottles, lighting up cigarettes.

Paul asked the boy for his name.

'Tun Hla, Thakin.'

He looked about fourteen. Could be older. Hard to tell with Burmese faces.

'Where is your family?'

'Village bombed. All killed.'

A common enough story, Paul thought. He had seen enough evidence of burnt-out villages and bodies strewn across the road. 'How many people in the cart?'

'The driver and one, plus two in back.'

'All right. We will go back now along the road. You stay with me and point out the cart. Carefully.' Paul then turned and said to Amarjit, 'I think we should form two groups. You take the lead one and I will follow with the other. There are three carts. Walk alongside the third one, exchange a few friendly words. Then move on to the middle cart. Engage the bullock-cart driver in conversation while the rear section examines the back of the cart. There are four to take out, but we have to make sure the boy's story is correct before we take action.'

Amarjit hesitated for a moment. 'Excuse me, sahib, but I think you should go in the front group. And let me take charge of the rear, because we will have to move quickly.'

Although Amarjit was young for his rank he had already proved his worth on the long retreat north and he felt it his duty to protect his commanding officer.

Paul smiled. 'You are probably right. We will do it your way.'

The Gurkhas formed up again and walked back along the road, weaving their way through the refugees. The carts were still in sight and were creaking along at a slow rate. In a short time, Paul and his group of four caught up with the third cart at the rear. It was drawn by two bullocks. The driver was a middle-aged Burmese, with a younger man and a child sitting beside him. The back of the cart was overloaded with what seemed to be all the family possessions and the rest of the family were perched precariously on the top: grandmother, mother and three children of various ages. All looked nervous as Paul approached. He smiled in what he hoped was a friendly fashion, greeting them with the few Burmese words he knew. They all replied in chorus. He moved on, Amarjit dallying at the back of the cart and looking it over, which made the occupants even more nervous.

Paul and his group of Gurkhas, with Tun Hla, came alongside the middle cart. Did the driver look Japanese? He seemed a genuine Burmese man, stocky, wearing a *longyi* tucked between his legs as he sat cross-legged on the driving platform, controlling the bullocks. Next to him was a young man with a headband. Sitting in the back, facing the road, were a woman and a youngish man, his legs dangling over the back of the cart. There was not as much luggage as on the previous cart, just a tarpaulin which covered part of the back of the cart.

Paul nodded at the driver as he kept pace with the bullocks. He noted with relief that there were no refugees walking alongside the cart and there was a good gap between the three carts.

The driver was watching Paul so intently he failed to notice a large rut in the road. A wheel caught in the hole, the cart lurched and the bullocks became nervous, pulling the cart into the middle of the road. The tarpaulin shifted slightly as the object under it moved. Amarjit, at the back of the cart, was sure he noticed the shape of a machine-gun. He leaned into the back of the cart and at that moment the woman's hand came up with an automatic pistol and a bullet missed Amarjit's head by the narrowest of margins. Rifleman Tikajit Pun, by the Jemedar's side, raked the woman with his tommy gun. The bullets hurled her back against the tarpaulin and caught the man, who fell like a sack into the road. The driver and his companion tried to reach for weapons, but Naik Bombahadur Rai fired instantly. The driver sprawled forward between the shafts, hanging down, his head smashing against the road. The other Japanese man, bowled over by the bullets, somersaulted onto the road at the other side.

The bullocks lurched forward, their eyes popping out with fear, but Tun Hla rushed in front, hands spread, calming them down in Burmese as he must have done many times in his village. But the leading cart took off at high speed, careering across the road. All down the road, the refugees broke up with shouts and cries.

Amarjit made sure the Japanese were dead and then he turned to Paul. 'The woman was a man.'

'Search them.'

They found some letters and family photographs, but no military material. Under the tarpaulin was a standard Japanese 6.25 Nambu light machine-gun, similar to the British Bren gun in appearance. There were also three Arisaka 6.5 rifles and an automatic pistol.

By now, the refugees had recovered from their panic, realising there would be no more shooting, and were beginning to crowd around and gape in astonishment.

'We will take the weapons with us.' Paul said. 'What about the bodies, Jemedar Sahib?'

'The Japanese Army will surely be along here before long, sahib. Perhaps we should leave them at the roadside, covered with the tarpaulin. They were not proper soldiers, sahib. There have been many cases of this sort of treachery.'

'Very well. But what about the bullock-cart? We cannot take it with us and to just leave it by the roadside seems wrong.' He noticed an Indian family coming up the road: a man and his wife, an old mother who was hobbling with a stick and three or four children of various ages. He said to Tun Hla, 'Ask them if they would like the cart.'

The family had a moment's discussion and the man seemed very pleased with the deal, but his wife was disturbed.

'It is the killing, thakin,' Tun Hla explained. 'The blood.'

'I should have thought they would have seen enough killing and blood by now,' Paul said. 'If they do not want it I will offer it to someone else.'

The old woman must have caught the gist of the conversation, because she hobbled up to the cart with the children and they quickly placed their belongings in the back.

'Well, that's settled,' said Paul with a grin and the Gurkhas chuckled. Paul turned to Tun Hla. 'What about you?'

'I come with you, thakin. Make good servant.' Paul hesitated. The boy said anxiously, 'I no eat much, thakin.'

Paul caught him by the arm. 'Come along, then. You will do.'

The patrol turned off the road and entered Kokkogwa village, threading its way through the wooden houses that were still standing but had been abandoned following Japanese air raids and the prospect of an approaching battle. Paul moved past the tanks in harbour and the ranks of 48 Brigade spread out strategically about the village, standing by for the approaching enemy. The depleted ranks of the 4/15th Gurkha Rifles were in position not far from Brigade HQ towards the centre of the village.

As the patrol approached, Lieut. Col. Lionel Osborne called out from his position in the shade of a tree, 'Hello, Paul, what have you been up to?'

Paul signalled to Rifleman Manbahadur Gurung, who had been detailed to carry the Japanese machine-gun, to show it to the colonel. Paul narrated the event. 'I get the feeling we will see quite a lot of fifth-column activity. It is really quite easy for them.'

Brigadier Cameron, commanding 48 Brigade and whose headquarters were in earshot, had watched the approach of the patrol with interest. Now, he came forward to inspect the machine-gun and other captured weapons.

'Well done. Too many of these bastards about. And not always easy to spot.'

A few months earlier, Cameron had commanded a Gurkha Rifles battalion. At the Pegu outbreak he had been shot in both legs, but armed with a rifle and a bottle of rum, he had continued to command, first from a stretcher and then from a Bren carrier. A resolute, unpredictable man, he had subsequently been promoted to Brigadier to command 48 Brigade.

In the aftermath of the retreat from Rangoon, Osborne's battalion had been reduced drastically in numbers, down to just above 100. He had approached Cameron to find a home in his brigade for the battalion. The brigadier was desperately short of men, but true to his nature he kept Osborne waiting.

'I imagine they have been bashed about a bit,' he said.

'Who has not, sir,' said Osborne. 'But it has made them the better soldiers for it.'

Cameron was well aware of the fine reputation Osborne's battalion had achieved at the Sittang Bridge and Pegu and he certainly was not going to let them go to some other brigade, but he carried on in his seemingly disinterested way, which did not fool Osborne who, as a regular officer, had known him in his subaltern days.

The Scorpion Trap

'What is your strength?'

'One hundred and twenty, sir, which I have divided into two companies of forty each; A, commanded by Major Kennedy, and C by Captain Cooper. In addition, there is a small support group with a mortar and medium machine-gun. And a small battalion HQ.'

'Hmm. I have a rather reduced brigade defence platoon and little in the way of reinforcements if fully engaged.' Then he smiled, 'I think, Lionel, that your little lot would be very useful as emergency reinforcements, and attached to my HQ.'

'Thank you, sir,' Osborne said, thinking, bet the little bugger had that in mind all along.

Paul left the colonel and moved over to his company's position. The men had dug defensive positions because it was always possible that the enemy could infiltrate into Brigade HQ. The patrol was greeted excitedly by the rest of the company, keen to find out what had happened. Tikajit Pun and Bombahadur Rai were well to the fore, making the most of their part in shooting the Japanese spies.

Gopiram relieved Paul of his pack and weapons and looked curiously at the Burmese youth.

'This is Tun Hla,' Paul explained. 'It was he who pointed out the Japanese in the bullock-carts. As he has no family, I thought he could join us. Perhaps you could look after him. I am sure he could be of help.'

Gopiram and the Burmese boy looked at each other for a moment, the one quizzical and the other anxious. Then Gopiram's pleasant and friendly nature asserted itself and he grinned. They could not speak each other's language, but in the way of the East they would find a way to communicate. Gopiram took Tun Hla off to his place in Company HQ and Paul gave a sigh of relief.

Gopiram had constructed a small shelter of branches and leaves for Paul as some cover from the sun and he sank gratefully onto the groundsheet which covered a bed of leaves beneath a bamboo matting awning. Subedar Tilbir was nearby, and presently Dilbahadur and Amarjit walked over to join them.

'Is there any news, sahib?' Dilbahadur asked.

'I am waiting to hear from the Colonel Sahib. There has been a patrol out to the east and it should be back soon with some up-to-date news.'

'Another fight, sahib.' Dilbahadur shook his head. 'And more men to lose.'

'Is there no hope of reinforcements?' Tilbir asked.

160

'I have to say, none at all.'

Paul was concerned about the attitude of his Gurkha officers. They had been such a source of strength to him during the arduous retreat through the Sittang and Pegu. But with the continuous pattern of withdrawals up the Irrawaddy Valley after the engagement at Prome, the paucity of proper medical attention for the wounded, the knowledge that the Japanese invariably bayoneted wounded prisoners rather than go to the trouble of looking after them: it was little wonder that morale was beginning to suffer.

Paul was aware that he had to assert himself more than before. With another fight looming, the thought of losing more men was one he found difficult to bear. At the same time, he felt sure that it was only a temporary malaise and that a victory of sorts this coming night would change everyone's attitude.

Just then, Gopiram appeared bearing mugs of tea, with Tun Hla assisting; the young Burman had changed his *longyi* for khaki trousers. Paul decided the tea break would be a good moment to try to insert some confidence into his officers.

'I know you are worried about the situation we find ourselves in,' he said. 'I know I am. The withdrawals seem pointless, but my belief is that we will eventually escape into India, doing as much damage to the Japanese before that as we can, and then build up our army and return to drive the Japanese out of Burma and all the way back to Japan.'

The Gurkhas remained expressionless.

'Maybe this sounds like a dream. But I have good reason for my optimism and that is our commanding officer, General Slim. I feel he will see us through. After all, he does speak Gurkhali.'

This time the Gurkhas chuckled.

Paul continued quickly, 'Of course, he has a tough job. Only a brief time to organise matters. As we say, he came straight into the deep end.'

'What does that mean, sahib? Into the deep end?' Amarjit asked.

'It is like a swimming pool, which starts shallow and gets deeper at the other end. When you are learning to swim you keep to the shallow end, so that your feet can touch the bottom; in other words, you can stand with your head above water. When you are proficient, you can move to the deep end. But if you start straightaway in the deep end then obviously you are going to be in great trouble.'

Dilbahadur exclaimed, 'I know all about deep ends! When I was a rifleman my company commander, Robinson Sahib that was, decided we should learn how to swim. He took us to the swimming baths and being a young fool, sahib, I got mixed up with deep end and the shallow end and jumped straight into the deep end and the water went up my nose, but Robinson Sahib pulled me out. That was my last swimming lesson, or for anyone else in the company, because Robinson Sahib was transferred and none of us ever went back to a swimming pool. Which is why we caused you so much torment at the Sittang River, Captain Sahib.'

'Well,' said Paul, thankful to Dilbahadur for his analogy, 'like you, the General Sahib has found himself in at the deep end. But he has the experience of being a general and I am sure he would not panic and let the water run up his nose, instead learning very quickly how to swim out of trouble. And so, of course, keep us out of too much trouble as well. So we must do our best to help him.'

Chapter Eleven
The Deep End

Major General W. J. "Bill" Slim, commanding 10 Indian Division in Iraq, received a telephone call from his army commander.

'You are to leave for India within the next three days.'

Slim gripped the phone harder. It seemed an abrupt way to tell him he had been sacked.

The army commander explained, 'You are wanted for another job, but I cannot tell you the details because I do not yet know them myself.'

Slim had enjoyed commanding the division and he was not pleased at being moved to an unknown position, unaware that he was following in the footsteps of Smyth and Alexander. He got ready to leave, but was held up by sandstorms – with Alexander it had been ice – but finally he took off from Habbaniyeh Lake in a flying boat. Arriving in India, he landed on the lake in Gwalior and then took a train to Delhi where, to his delight, he was met by his wife. So the move had provided one bonus.

Next morning, he reported at General Headquarters India, where no one seemed to know what his job was, adding to his puzzlement by informing him that he was to fly to Burma almost at once with Lieut. General Morris, Chief of General Staff in India. Morris was visiting the front to learn at first hand what was going on in Burma.

Why they should want Slim to go as well was not explained, but he had always been a good soldier and he did what he was told. In 1914, he had been commissioned in the Royal Warwickshire Regiment and was with them at Gallipoli, where he had his first experience of Gurkhas when he fought alongside 6th Gurkha Rifles. Severely wounded at Gallipoli, he was discharged as unfit for further service, but by sheer willpower and determination, he fought back to complete fitness. He was determined to make his career with the Gurkhas. As a first step he obtained a commission in a West Indian Regiment, but never joined them, instead serving with another Royal Warwickshire Regiment in Mesopotamia. In 1919, he transferred to the Indian Army and to his great joy was accepted into 6 Gurkha Rifles, being made adjutant in 1922. After coming top at Staff College, and by the time he was forty-seven, he was commanding a 7th Gurkha Battalion. With World War II he was given command of a brigade and then 10 Indian Division in Eritrea.

Now, he was in Delhi on his way to some new command. He left early with Morris, spending the night in Calcutta before flying on to Akyab, a port on the Arakan Coast of Burma. Here, they had a long session with Air Vice Marshall Stevenson, the Air Officer Commanding in Burma, discussing the situation late into the night. None of it was very promising: Rangoon had fallen a few days earlier and the Burma Army was reorganising and resting in the Irrawaddy Valley.

The next day they continued their journey to Magwe, now the main air base in Burma. They landed on the Irrawaddy River at Magwe and then transferred to a smaller plane which took them on to Mandalay. From there, they were driven up the winding road to Maymyo, the summer capital of Burma.

At Maymyo he met General Alexander, who had just arrived from Rangoon, outwardly seeming as calm as ever, but obviously worried over the situation. It was a short meeting, as Alexander had to leave to attend a conference with the governor. Slim was not aware that before long he and Alexander would be working together as a close team.

After a brief stay in Maymyo, Morris and Slim returned to Mandalay and started their return journey. But during a stopover at Calcutta for breakfast in Government House, Slim was sent for by Wavell. They met in one of the visitors' sitting rooms. Wavell was his usual calm, placid self; it was almost a repeat of his interview with Smyth a few months earlier.

After asking Slim some questions on his recent trip to Burma, Wavell lapsed into one of his silences. Slim wondered anxiously what was coming next. He prayed he would not be offered Hutton's job, because he did not think he was cut out to be a staff man.

Then the silence was suddenly broken. 'I want you to command a corps that is being formed in Burma.'

Slim could hardly believe what he had heard. Promotion to Lieut. General and to command a corps was very far from his expectations.

'General Alexander has a difficult task. I do not suppose yours will be any less difficult, but two heads are often better than one. I am sure that working together will bring about the much-needed success.' He paused for a moment and then continued, 'The sooner you are on your way the better.'

Slim said he could leave the next day.

'Well, good luck.'

They shook hands and Slim left to start what would be a momentous journey, not knowing, not imagining, to what fame and fortune it would lead.

General Sir Harold Alexander looked at the map of Burma spread out on the wall and considered the situation. Since his escape from Rangoon by the skin of his teeth, he was now in a temporary vacuum. It was a case of anticipating the next move by the Japanese.

He turned away from the map and walked over to the window, although he did not expect to get any inspiration from the view. He could almost draw the map by heart and was all too aware of the problems ahead. Always sprucely turned out, quite fearless, he had a reputation to live up to, because he had made a great name for himself at Dunkirk.

He returned to the map. He was sure the Japanese were intending a two-prong attack. The two routes into Central Burma were obviously by way of the river valleys. To the east, the Sittang Valley led north by rail and road through Toungoo, the important junction for the Karen Hills, and on to Mandalay and subsequently to the Shan States, Lashio and Myitkyina. To the west was the great Irrawaddy Valley; not so extensive a road and railway system as in the east, but an obvious route north into the vital oilfields of Yenangyaung. That the Japanese would have sufficient forces and equipment to carry out their intentions was without doubt. With Malaya and Rangoon in their possession, they could pour troops into Burma at will.

He was quite right in his calculations. General Iida, his Japanese counterpart, had planned accordingly: *33 Division* would advance along the Irrawaddy route to the oilfields and *55 Division* would fall on Toungoo and Meiktila on the road to Mandalay. The Japanese Army would be greatly strengthened by the convoys heading for Rangoon.

So far, there had been no action along the Irrawaddy Valley where 17 Division, still not fully re-equipped after Sittang, was reforming some 30 miles south of Prome. On the other side of Burma, 80 miles across the densely jungled Pegu Yomas, 1 Burma Division had been embroiled in several heavy actions. Now, the division was consolidated on a line astride the main road and railway about 3 miles south of Nyaunglebin and extending across the Sittang River to Shwegyin.

To Alexander's relief, the Chinese Army was to join the Burma Army, while V Chinese Army was on its way south and its 200 Chinese Division, dispatched in advance, was nearing Toungoo. Alexander's plan was to create a general defence, running from Tharrawaddy in the west to roughly Nyaunglebin in the east. The Chinese would cover the east and the British would be responsible for the west. As soon as the Chinese arrived they could take over from 1 Burma Division, which could then move over to the west to join Burma Army. But to Alexander's chagrin, he now learned that the Chinese refused to advance further south than Toungoo. This would leave a gap where the Burma Division had been and Alexander's defence line would now have to stretch further north than he had intended, from Toungoo to the west.

Because of the conditions, Alexander had felt that he could not satisfactorily undertake the dual role of C.-in-C. Burma and Commander of the British Forces, and he had asked for a Corps Commander. So it was that Lieut. General "Bill" Slim landed at Prome on 13 March 1942 and drove straight from the airfield to meet Alexander and the two divisional commanders: Major General Bruce Scott of 1 Burma Division and Major General "Punch" Cowan of 17 Division.

Alexander was pleased to welcome Slim. 'Sorry to drag you straight into a conference, Bill,' Alexander said. 'But matters are moving very rapidly, and not quite as expected, and I wanted to put you in the picture as quickly as possible. Also, it seemed a good opportunity for you to meet your divisional commanders.' He paused and smiled. 'Although it seems that you know each other already.'

'Indeed we do, sir,' Slim agreed.

By sheer luck, both the generals had served in Slim's old regiment, 6th Gurkha Rifles. The three of them had soldiered together for twenty-odd years, their wives were close friends and their children were brought up together. The fact that they were on such good terms was to mean a great deal in the dark times to come.

Alexander explained the situation and the location of the various British forces to Slim. 'Well, gentlemen, the main battle for Central Burma is clearly about to take place. How long we are expected to retain control of Central and Upper Burma I really do not know. The C.-in-C. believes a stage might soon be reached when we will have to decide whether to withdraw north-east into China or north into India. Meanwhile, we will have to impose the maximum delay and make the enemy work hard for their gains.'

Following the short conference, Alexander left after lunch for his HQ in Maymyo. Slim was now able to get to know his command. Burcorps HQ was situated in the bombed-out Law Courts in Prome, a river port on the east bank of the Irrawaddy. He found it was very much a skeleton headquarters, consisting of a handful of officers and men, a few clerks and a very small detachment of Burma Signals. His chief of staff, Brigadier "Taffy" Davies, was a brilliant staff officer and the remainder of his team were to serve him well throughout the campaign.

Having inspected his HQ, Slim set off with Cowan to visit 17 Division. It was an opportunity to look over the division and to meet some of the men. He thought they looked tired, which did not surprise him considering what they had gone through, and he was pleased that their spirit remained good. But he was surprised at the shortage of equipment and the state of their boots and uniforms. He also visited Brigadier Anstice's 7 Armoured Brigade, which was under Cowan's command and which had already done sterling work and showed their mettle.

The rest of Slim's Burcorps consisted of 1 Burma Division, which was making the long, hazardous journey from the far Sittang Valley to join him on the Irrawaddy. After several clashes with the Japanese, the division had disengaged, leaving the Toungoo area in the hands of the Chinese 200 Division. By rail and road, the Burma Division had crossed the country to concentrate in the Dayindabo–Kyaukpadaung–Allanmyo area some 50 miles north of Prome.

When Slim returned to his HQ he was still concerned about the shortage of equipment and so he tackled his chief of staff.

'Of course, sir, from now on, without Rangoon, we have become completely dependent on stocks already in the country,' Brigadier Davies told him, 'and what we can get locally. But we were fortunate that General Hutton had the foresight to order three quarters of all the reserve stock held in Rangoon to be moved to the Mandalay area. That was as far back as 22 January, so he was certainly thinking ahead. And the transfer was completed before the fall of Rangoon.

'We were also fortunate that General Goddard was put in charge of administration and he has certainly got things moving.'

Davies then told Slim that a hospital and medical stores depot was being established immediately at Shwebo, an ammunition depot near Shwebo, an ordnance stores depot at Myinmu and an engineer stores depot at Monywa.

'What about petrol?' Slim asked.

'Supplies of petrol and oil are satisfactory, provided, of course, that the oilfields can be held. And if they should go, arrangements are in hand to move supplies further on to tie in with our movements, whatever they might turn out to be.'

He added that there was a six-month supply of medical stores and the ammunition was expected to last until the rains.

'What do they base that on?' Slim queried. 'I wonder how much fighting they expect us to do! And what about transport?'

'I hear that 17 Division is down to seventy-two vehicles, mainly 3-tonners. I believe, also, that all available river transport craft have arrived at Prome. Things are moving; the wounded and sick have been sent upstream. Military stores of all kinds, which includes locally purchased rice, have also been sent upstream to new depots.'

'As you say, General Goddard has certainly got things under control. But what about clothing, boots and so on?'

'A great deal was lost through enemy action, so I was told. Bombing, I presume.' Davies grinned. 'I think our boots will have to last a long while still to come, sir!'

It was obvious to Slim that he was taking over a situation which was not going well. He had definitely been landed in the deep end, but it was not the first time and no doubt would not be the last. But experience had taught him not to start rushing about and giving orders, sending people in all directions, until he knew what it was all about.

If there was a master plan, what was it? A last-ditch stand to hold part of Burma? Or to get the army back to India more or less intact by a series of well-planned withdrawals?

General Wavell had already realised he was unlikely to hold on to Central and Upper Burma. For now, communications and the location of reserve supplies in the Meiktila–Mandalay area were the predominate factors. Eventually, Wavell would have to consider an exit from the country. But which way? To India or China? Was the decision going to be political or military?

In fact, it seemed to Slim there was no master plan, except to prevent any further loss of land to the advancing Japanese. In this, he was in agreement and he was in favour of counter-attacking at the earliest opportunity. But, as he was to find quite soon, unfortunately, the best laid plans would certainly go astray.

When the fall of Rangoon was imminent, an air base had been established at Magwe, on the Irrawaddy River some 300 miles to the north of the capital. Named Burwing, it consisted of four squadrons of fighters and bombers from the RAF and the AVG.

On the afternoon of 21 March, Captain Ray Dean of the AVG was reclining in the officers' mess at Magwe Airfield. The previous day, air reconnaissance had disclosed a concentration of about 100 Japanese aircraft in the Rangoon area. Early on the twenty-first, nine Blenheims, escorted by Hurricanes, had made a surprise attack on Mingaladon Airfield, destroying or damaging many Japanese aircraft on the ground for the loss of one British aircraft. Now, Ray was helping the excited pilots to celebrate.

Suddenly, the building was rocked by the blast of bombs and everyone rushed out of the mess. The sky appeared black with aircraft as some 250 Japanese bombers, escorted by fighters, blasted the airfield in revenge. There had been no warning, so the base was taken completely by surprise.

As shrapnel was scattered across the field, the pilots raced for their aircraft. When Ray reached the AVG parking area he realised the bombs had done serious damage. To his dismay, he found his own Tomahawk badly damaged. It was probably flyable, but certainly not fit for a dogfight.

He could hear several Hurricanes roar into life. Some twelve of the RAF's fighters were serviceable and a few managed to take off, shooting down four enemy aircraft. But the weight of the attack was too great and there had been no pens and dispersible areas for the British aircraft.

The next morning found only three P-40s of the AVG squadron and three Hurricanes able to fly; and of these only the Hurricanes were fit to fight.

The AVG squadron commander consulted his pilots. 'I guess we are not doing any good over here,' he said.

'They are sure to attack again today,' Ray said.

'I reckon we should leave with what we have got,' his commander decided. 'Especially as there is no early warning system.'

He reported to Group Captain Broughall at Burwing HQ and that morning they left for Loiwing. As Ray coaxed his aircraft away from the airfield, he looked down at the destruction. He felt as though he were running away, but there was really no other option. And with a new plane he could get back at the Japanese from China.

At around half past four, a final enemy attack by fifty bombers in two waves completed the destruction of the whole of the British Air Force, apart from a few planes that could still fly, and these were flown to Akyab, the British not realising that it was to be the Japanese's next target.

Early the next morning, Burwing HQ and the personnel of its squadrons left hurriedly for Lashio and Loiwing. That same day, the Japanese destroyed Akyab which was abandoned. The last of the RAF had left Burma. From then on, Slim was totally without air reconnaissance defence or support.

The Japanese were now lords of the skies; but instead of using all their overwhelming strength to harass the Burma Army, they attacked the chief centres of rail and road communication in the rear of the Allies and launched a bombing spree that saw the devastation of the major towns and villages. Nearly all were of wooden buildings and they vanished in flames.

Although the effect on morale was at first serious, later the troops seemed in some way to become accustomed to the constant air assault and they adjusted themselves to it. But the actual casualties to fighting troops inflicted by the Japanese aircraft were surprisingly small.

On 4 March, Lieut. General J. W. Stillwell had arrived in Chungking to fill the post of the generalissimo's chief of staff and commander general of the USA forces in the China–Burma–India theatre of operations, and he set up his HQ in Burma. His rudeness and unjustified criticisms, especially aimed at the British, earned him the nickname of "Vinegar Joe", but both Alexander and Slim found that they could work with him.

Stillwell thought he had full command of the generalissimo's troops in Burma, but Chiang Kai-shek had not given him the Kwan-fang Seal as C.-in-C., but only as chief of staff. All orders of a major nature had to pass through General Lin Wei – Chinese General Staff Mission – and could be carried out only with the sanction of the generalissimo, who constantly changed his mind. The combination of the British and Chinese forces, which should have been a valuable strength against the Japanese, was therefore fatally flawed. And it was not long before Stillwell found to his chagrin that his command of the Chinese forces was more illusory than real.

The Chinese 200 Division, having taken over from 1 Burma Division, placed its forward troops near Pyu and its main perimeter defences around Toungoo. By 19 March, the Japanese had made contact with the Chinese forward troops. After stubborn resistance, the Chinese fell slowly back to their main perimeter. On the morning of the twenty-third, a motorised column from *143 Regiment*, making a wide enveloping movement west of the town, occupied Kyungon Airfield and cut off 200 Division from V Chinese Army.

Now on its own, 200 Division put up a strong resistance against *55 Division* and the Japanese were forced to hurry forward advance elements of their *56 Division*, which had arrived in Rangoon on the twenty-fifth.

General Stillwell, watching the situation closely, determined to organise a counter-attack in strength southwards. The Chinese 22 Division had arrived in Pyinmana and he ordered it to advance to the aid of 200 Division. It was now that Stillwell realised that his command of the Chinese armies was more illusory than real, because the division made no attempt to obey his orders.

Stillwell, looking for a way to relieve the situation, was wrongly under the impression that the Japanese were being reinforced by their division in the Irrawaddy Valley and he believed an attack in that area would help the Chinese in Toungoo. In desperation, he sent a message to Burma Army HQ, as well as two of his staff officers, to put his case more strongly to Slim personally.

Alexander was in Chungking on 28 March when he met Chiang Kai-shek, who had received Stillwell's plea to persuade the British to take the offensive in the Irrawaddy Valley. The request put Alexander in an awkward predicament. He knew that Burcorps was not ready to take the offensive following its withdrawal to Prome. He also recognised the strategic necessity to hold Toungoo. To fail the Chinese in their hour of need would allow Chiang an excuse to withhold assistance to Alexander at a time when it might be vital. But how? The only option, Alexander surmised, was to mount an offensive sweep from Prome in the hope of engaging forward elements of *33 Division*.

Slim was not happy about the order. He was certainly keen to counter-attack, but not at this stage. All he could do was send a mobile force to stir up the enemy.

Accordingly, Major General Cowan formed a striking force of a regiment of tanks, a battery, three infantry battalions and a field company of sappers and miners, under the command of Brigadier Anstice, and sent them north towards Paungde. It was not as strong a force as it might seem, because the battalions were each only the strength of two companies.

Unknown to Cowan and Slim, who did not have the advantage of air reconnaissance, the move coincided with a Japanese advance up the Irrawaddy to seize the riverside village of Shwedaung. When Cowan became aware of this he realised that Anstice would be cut off from Prome and so he promptly ordered him to return. But the Japanese had reacted quickly and the force found itself hemmed in by roadblocks and became involved in a fierce, bitter conflict. Attempts through the evening of the twenty-ninth against the block at Shwedaung failed; attacks the following morning burst through the block, but the transport was held up again by a further block at the north side of the town and by trucks and ambulances loaded with wounded jammed up along the road. Shwedaung itself was now burning fiercely. There was nothing for it but break off the engagement and escape as best they could across country to Prome.

Slim could hardly hide his emotions as he saw the mobile force stagger into Prome in dribs and drabs. The conflict in and around Shwedaung had been savage; both sides had suffered heavy casualties. The British had lost over 350 killed and missing, and many more wounded, also two 25-pounders, ten tanks and numerous vehicles.

Of course, war was a horrendous experience, he thought, but at least one expected certain rules of conduct, especially to prisoners of war. But a report he had received disturbed him considerably. A detachment of marines had been ambushed in Padaung village across the river and they had put up a brave struggle against an overwhelming force of Japanese. There were twelve British Marines, all wounded and taken prisoner, who were kept till the next day, when they were tied to trees and used by the Japanese to demonstrate bayonet fighting to an admiring audience of Burmese villagers. Slim would find in due course that this behaviour was repeated throughout the Burma Campaign. It was hard to understand why soldiers who fought so bravely and intensely, could also perform such bestial acts.

Slim could ill afford the losses to Burcorps. But what he found bitterly hurtful was the fact that the whole manoeuvre was an unnecessary disaster.

On 30 March, in the face of ever increasing enemy pressure, 200 Division was forced to abandon its positions in Toungoo and cutting its way out of town, they passed through 22 Chinese Division, whose advanced troops were at Yedashe, and went into reserve north of Pyinmana. It had put up the most stubborn defence, at a cost of heavy casualties, against superior Japanese forces, and an unchallenged Japanese air force, for nearly a fortnight. But, when forced to withdraw northwards, it failed to blow the vital bridge over the Sittang River, which carried the Toungoo–Mawchi–Bawlake road. The Japanese gained immediate use of this road, which led into the heart of the Karen Hills and the Shan States. The loss of Toungoo and control of the Mawchi–Bawlake road was to have as serious an effect on the future of the campaign as the Sittang Bridge had done earlier.

The problem facing Alexander and Slim now was whether or not they should hold on to Prome. The eastern half of the line across Burma had gone. Prome, stretching a couple of miles along the east bank of the

Irrawaddy, surrounded by scrub jungle, would need a long perimeter to defend it. Already, the Japanese were closing in and had occupied parts of the opposite west bank. The town was almost completely burnt after a particularly heavy air raid and cholera had spread among the refugees. But there were large dumps of stores, mainly rice, lying on the riverside quays. Every effort was made to backload vital stores, the order of priority being 87/90 octane, spirit lubricants and ammunition. But many reserves had to be abandoned. There was no railway out of Prome to the north and available road transport was negligible. The only route out was by river and the civilian crews were loath to come south of Allanmyo because of Japanese air raids. The river was also dangerously low, making night navigation dangerous, and during the day, Japanese aircraft had a free hand. But, thanks to the ability of General Goddard and Burcorps personnel, considerable progress was made.

Slim decided to move his HQ to Allanmyo where, on 1 April, he was visited by Wavell and Alexander. A map was spread out on a table in the Burmese house where Slim had established his HQ and the three generals studied it carefully.

Wavell looked up and stared into space for a moment while the others waited for him to speak. At last, he said, 'Unfortunately, I believe another withdrawal is necessary if we are to defend the oilfields.'

Alexander ran his fingers over the map. 'Around this area, would you say, sir?'

The others agreed that Burcorps should now concentrate in the area around Allanmyo, covering Kyaukpadaung about 30 miles to the east and Thayetmyo west of the river just south of Allanmyo. Slim was glad the decision had been made.

Alexander now asked Wavell if he could release more air support. 'Air attacks are a daily nightmare, sir.'

Wavell did not hesitate in his reply. 'No. I am sorry, but I believe all available aircraft should be held for the defence of India.'

When Wavell and Alexander had departed, Slim gave orders to speed up backloading and prepare to move out of Prome.

Before the evacuation of Prome had begun, the Japanese jumped the gun by launching an attack on the evening of 1 April. Cowan had placed 63 Brigade in the town and south of it, 16 Brigade around Tamagauk some 5 miles to the north, with 48 Brigade about Hmazwa 4 miles to the east on a road out of Prome.

The village of Hmazwa, surrounded by scrub jungle and bamboo groves, was situated adjacent to the main railway line from Prome, which ran straight to the village and then curved south towards Rangoon; but no train had used the line for some time and the villagers had fled into hiding following the air raid on Prome and the likelihood of a fierce battle in the vicinity. But there was plenty of activity in the village and the immediate surrounding countryside, as 48 Brigade settled into position. Although the houses in the village were available, the Gurkhas were digging in, feeling safer in a trench than a wooden building, and were prepared for the attack they felt certain would come before the night was out.

Paul stood with Subedar Tilbir Gurung at the front of his company position on the southern fringe of the village. Behind him, his men put the final touches to their defence trenches. Paul looked past the houses through a gap in a bamboo grove and across the scrub jungle to the railway line and beyond to Prome.

Practically every house there had been smashed to splinters by the Japanese air force or burnt to a cinder in the many fires. Some were still burning; he thought he glimpsed a flicker of red in the distance. He almost believed he could smell the acrid odour of the burning town. There was no wind and the atmosphere was heavy and close after the heat of the day; away to the south-west the ruins of Shwedaung village still puffed out smoke, adding to the polluted air. Night was not far off and the hot, cloudless blue sky was beginning to pale and send out strands of yellow and red.

Paul and Tilbir turned back to C Company's position and settled down on the edge of a trench. Gopiram and the subedar's orderly came up with a meal of rice, dal and vegetables. Obviously, even the resourceful Gopiram had not found a chicken lurking among the houses. While they were eating, night had fallen quickly and the moon was now dominating the sky and everywhere was as bright as day.

Lieut. General Sakurai, well supplied with lorries discarded by Burcorps, brought *33 Division* up from Shwedaung to attack Prome. It was just before midnight when *215 Regiment* launched its attack in bright moonlight against the Indian battalion of 63 Brigade, holding the south of the town. The Indians retaliated fiercely, driving the Japanese back. Then a second attack followed, but this time the Japanese managed to infiltrate between the holding force into the town. Pouring through the gap in the south, the enemy attacked the other defenders from the rear and there was confusion amidst the ruins of the town. The enemy threatened to overwhelm 63 Brigade HQ and the gun positions, forcing the withdrawal of the brigade to positions astride the road and railway on the eastern exists.

At about the same time, Sakurai had launched *214 Regiment* against 48 Brigade in Hmawza. Alerted by the firing in the town, the brigade was ready.

Paul and his company waited in their trenches. As brigade reserve they were not in the front line, but sat ready in case the enemy managed to infiltrate or if they were required to move forward as reinforcements.

The Japanese artillery opened fire, shells exploding in the village. A house crumbled under a direct hit, earth from a nearby shell showering Paul's trench. Now, 1st Indian Field Regiment returned fire, their shells soaring out of the village and catching the approaching Japanese infantry. The Gurkha battalions on the perimeter opened a fierce fire, the Japanese clear targets in the bright moonlight. Some of the enemy reached the railway line and Paul could hear the bullets ricocheting off the tracks and the shouts and screams. Sitting in his trench, unable to join in the attack, was frustrating. But the reserve was not needed as the enemy scrambled away, leaving dead and wounded in the scrub jungle and garlanding the railway lines.

For a couple of hours the brigade remained on stand-to. Then, at around 03.00 hours, Paul was called to an order group.

'Well,' Osborne observed, 'we seem to have sorted that lot out. Although, we played no real part ourselves. That is how it goes sometimes. Anyway, we are on the move again.'

General Cowan, expecting the enemy to attack from the eastern end of Prome, had decided to pull back the division north to new positions astride the main road, on the general line of the Nawin Chaung, while 48 and 63 Brigades were to disengage before dawn and move back to selected positions through 16 Brigade, and 7 Armoured Brigade was to cover the left flank along the Wettigan road.

It was a dark dawn after the moonlight as 48 Brigade began to move out of the village. They had not gone far, when the battalion on the right was surprised to see a Japanese column moving parallel, obviously in an attempt to come round the flank. Launching a quick attack, the Gurkhas caught the Japanese unaware and after a short, sharp engagement the Japanese dispersed.

At 10.30 hours that morning, Cowan phoned Slim to say he had received reliable information of a strong enemy force moving round to his left on Dayindabo, 16 miles on the road ahead, which could cut him off. Was he to hold or fall back on Allanmyo? If the Japanese got between 17 Division and Allanmyo there was little to stop them going all the way to the oilfields except two weak brigades of 1 Burma Division, so Slim told him to continue and sent 1 Burma Brigade to Dayindabo to defend it if threatened and to help 17 Division through.

An hour later, 17 Division began its long, harrowing 60-mile march to Allanmyo. There would be a break at Dayindabo that night and then the division would continue the next 30 miles or so to Allanmyo.

Already coming up to the middle of the day, the sun from the cloudless blue sky radiated a terrible heat on the marching men. Paul tied his handkerchief more firmly across his mouth as the dust from marching feet swirled up into his face. He was reminded of the road to Sittang, but this was more horrendous, because it was the hottest time of the year. The heat seemed to burn into his eyes and the men ahead appeared, for a moment, as silhouettes and then as though enmeshed in a yellow glow. His mouth felt like it was full of grit and his lips were scorched by the lack of water. He could feel the weight of the water bottle at his hip; there had been enough water, if muddy, in the Nawin Chaung to at least start the march with full water bottles. But the problem was safeguarding the contents by enforcing strict water discipline, which was never easy. There were few water holes on the way and preventing men from crowding around them was particularly difficult. Osborne had warned all his officers beforehand and Paul was pleased that the men of the battalion were kept on a tight leash by the Gurkha officers and NCOs.

For the first part of their march to Dayindabo they passed through 15 miles of the forest reserve. Although the trees on either side of the road gave some shade, they failed to lower the temperature of the scorching heat. The trees themselves looked as though they were crying out for water and waiting desperately for the saving battalions of the approaching monsoon. They also gave some cover from the marauding Japanese aircraft.

It was not long before the Japanese planes discovered the long, retreating line of 17 Division with its attractive target of marching men, lorries and tanks. Whistles blew frantically as the enemy fighters were observed speeding out of the clear sky. The column scattered, seeking shelter in the forest or in any ditch at the side of the road. Machine-gun bullets ricocheted off the road, slashing at the trees. Then, as quickly as they had appeared, the fighters vanished. Remarkably, there had been few casualties. The division reformed and continued its weary march.

The men had been in action for most of a night and day and legs and bodies were protesting.

By nightfall, 17 Division had reached Dayindabo, where there was the relief of a night's rest. The Japanese infantry had not followed them out of Prome and 1 Burma Brigade was in position around the village. Osborne and his officers walked around the battalion, congratulating the men on their performance, spreading more encouragement. Most of the men had probably already fallen asleep and whether they heard was doubtful.

The next day, the division continued its march, which followed the same pattern, except there was no forest, and the land stretched hot and barren into the heat haze. Japanese aircraft attacked again. Then at last the division marched into Allanmyo.

Alexander now decided to place his forces along the new east–west line running from the Irrawaddy through Loikaw to the Southern Shan State. The line ran through the towns of Taungdwingyi and Pyinmana. The plan was for the Chinese to garrison the left flank of the Taungdwingyi line and Burcorps the right. Slim was told to place his forces in Taungdwingyi itself to protect Mandalay and to maintain a firm link with the Chinese. Slim felt this to be a mistake, as he might find himself fighting two separate divisional battles: one at Taungdwingyi and the other at Magwe. But Alexander was plagued with the need to keep on good terms with the Chinese, so Slim had to shorten his line. He withdrew to Magwe and the Japanese immediately occupied Allanmyo.

Burcorps was in position on the Taungdwingyi line by 8 April. Because of the water shortage, Slim was forced to locate his forces near village wells. He had 13 Burma Brigade at Thityogauk, 17 Division had its HQ at Taungdwingyi and 48 Brigade and 7 Armoured Brigade was at Kokkogwa. But there was no sign of help from the Chinese and Slim found himself having to hold the whole of the right flank by himself, including Taungdwingyi and the oilfields.

Chapter Twelve
Storm Over Kokkogwa

Dark clouds had been gathering above the village and night came early. In the gloom of Company HQ, Subedar Tilbir Gurung said, 'It is going to be an uncomfortable night, sahib.'

Sitting above the rim of his weapon pit, Paul replied, 'The consolation is that it is going to be just as bad for the enemy. They must be gathering right now somewhere out there to the south for their attack.'

'But they will have the advantage of coming out of the dark.'

'But they are expected.'

Earlier, Osborne had called the British and Gurkha officers together to impart the information and instructions he had received from Brigadier Cameron. A company of 2/5th Gurkhas had encountered the Japanese some 15 miles south of Kokkogwa and a full-scale attack on the village was imminent. The various Gurkha battalions which formed the brigade were in positions around the perimeter of the village and Osborne had been told to keep his battalion alert for any call for assistance.

As Paul waited, a huge clap of thunder resounded above the village, making him jump involuntarily. In the distance, vivid flashes of lightning opened up the sky providing instances of lightness as a violent storm enveloped the village. There was more thunder, and then the Japanese artillery joined in with a massive barrage as shells and mortar fire exploded on the perimeter, the fiery streaks from approaching shells mingling with the flashes of lightning. In the confusion of storm and shellfire, a black mass of enemy emerged from the south and launched a very heavy attack supported by considerable artillery and mortar fire. A couple of Gurkha section posts were overrun by sheer numbers and a desperate call was made to Brigade HQ for help. The Brigade Defence Platoon and a platoon from 1/4th Gurkhas were

179

thrown into the battle. But the action was fierce and Osborne's battalion was rushed forward.

Paul's company hurried through the village into the bedlam on the perimeter as artillery and mortar fire, and bursts from machine-guns and rifles, and the crumps of grenades still competed with the rolling thunder and the sizzling lightning. For a moment Paul would find himself in blackness and then the lightning would light up the whole area. He brought his company into position on the perimeter. The road ran east and west across his front and in a flash of lightning he saw a *chaung* running to his left. Sensing that the enemy might use this to try to infiltrate, he sent Havildar Bharti with a Bren group to cover the *chaung*.

It seemed that the first fierce onslaught had been held. But now the noisy chink of bayonets being fixed made an ominous sound. Paul alerted his men as a mass of figures loomed out of the night, to be met by fierce fire from all the Gurkha units. There were screams and shouts as bullets struck home and he could see squads stumbling across the skyline as the ravaged enemy retreated beyond the village limits. Then there was silence for a moment, until Bharti's Bren-gunner opened fire: one burst of five and then silence. The gun must have jammed. A grenade exploded inside the *chaung* with a hollow thump. Paul jumped to his feet and stumbled across the broken ground, followed and overtaken by a section of his men who rushed to Bharti's aid. There were a few rifle shots and then shouts as a melee ensued. Khukuris and bayonets clashed and then, abruptly, the surviving Japanese scurried back along the *chaung* and into the night. The Gurkhas emerged from the *chaung* carrying two wounded who were taken to the Regimental Aid Post. There were no further attacks and the thunder had also rolled away, sounding a few final peals in the distance. There was little sign of dawn at 05.00 hours because it was now pitch-black with the end of the storm.

In that pitch-darkness a battalion of *215 Regiment* launched a second attack on the smaller village of Thadodam, situated a short distance to the west of Kokkogwa and held by 7th Gurkhas. Despite suffering severe casualties, the enemy managed to occupy the village, taking up strong positions along the line of thick cactus hedges which bordered the village. A Gurkha counter-attack was held by heavy fire, causing a number of casualties. The situation was critical as there was nothing left between the Japanese and the guns of 1st Indian Field Regiment. But as dawn began to break, the gunners sensed the danger and calmly dragged their weapons out of the gun pits and in the half light, they slewed them round and opened fire at 400 yards over open sights, leading to severe casualties to the enemy. The Japanese retreated into a dry *chaung* with a flat bottom covered in pebbles and deep enough to form a natural anti-tank defence. A Japanese 37 mm anti-tank gun brought heavy fire onto the area, but heavy retaliatory fire killed the gunners and tanks drove over the gun.

At Brigade HQ both companies of 4/15th Gurkhas had returned to their previous positions. Osborne called the company commanders to his headquarters to report on the night's action.

Arthur Kennedy reported two killed and one wounded in A Company. Paul was surprised at the change in Kennedy's physical appearance. A large, florid man, he looked pale now and his uniform seemed to hang on him as though he had lost a lot of weight. Paul wondered if he had also changed. The continuous pressure. The intense heat. The seeming lack of purpose. All this must be beginning to tell.

'I had two wounded, sir,' Paul reported. 'Not too bad, thankfully, but they were hospital cases, so we are two down.'

In the distance they could hear the noise of battle at Thadodam and as a further reminder of that action, a runner came from Brigade HQ to hand Osborne a note: The fourth are going in with tanks. Some backup could be useful.

Who will I send? He made up his mind at once. 'Paul, will you take your company – 4GR are moving up now with tanks.'

Did they really need back-up? The thought flashed through Paul's mind. Well, even they must be feeling the pinch of casualties.

The attack was led by a 4th Gurkha Company with nine tanks under command and the village brilliantly cleared of the enemy. With three tanks acting as a stop behind the village, the Japanese were flushed out of the *chaung* by the Gurkhas and finished off by the tanks.

Paul was talking to the Gurkha company commander, when two Gurkhas came running up from a belt of trees in the near distance.

'Sahib! Sahib!' one cried out, a look of horror on his face. 'Over there, sahib. By the trees.'

The major and Paul followed the men and the sight which greeted them filled them with unbelievable repugnance. The bodies of three 7th Gurkha riflemen, who had been captured earlier, were tied to the trees, their hands secured behind their backs. Then, in an act of sheer brutality, the Japanese soldiers had bayoneted them to death and the eyes of one of them had been gouged out. Paul felt the bile in his throat and with great difficulty he managed to control himself.

Paul and the major rejoined their men after the bodies of the three Gurkhas had been cut down and returned to their battalion. A few moments later, the Japanese laid down a heavy artillery barrage on the village, shells skimming over the top of the trees and exploding among the tanks and men. One of the tanks was hit and it burst into flames and the adjutant of 4th Gurkhas was mortally wounded while assisting the crew. Paul and his men jumped for their lives into the *chaung,* from where he could see flashes above the rim and hear the roar of the explosions, and he hugged the ground. Gradually, the explosions grew fewer and then there was silence apart from the cries of the wounded.

There were intermittent skirmishes during the night. A large number of Japanese were found in a nearby village by a Gurkha patrol which inflicted heavy punishment as the village burst into flames.

Jack Hunter had brought his 3-inch mortar team forward, for on a nearby ridge an enemy gun was being a persistence nuisance. His jemedar gave a slight cough and Jack realised he must assert himself and have more faith in his ability. He led his team as they stalked the gun, using what cover there was in the undulating ground. Within range, they destroyed the gun with just one bomb. Then, in the approaching daylight, they saw a Japanese patrol caught in the open and annihilated it with a barrage of bombs.

'That was well done, sahib,' the jemedar said.

For the first time Jack felt his confidence gathering.

With daylight, Japanese aircraft bombed the village of Kokkogwa, setting alight the still-standing houses and destroying some vehicles, but they did not follow up with an infantry assault. And on the afternoon of the fourteenth, 48 Brigade moved out of the village and joined the rest of 17 Division at Taungdwingyi.

For *33 Division*, which had been such a devastating force at Sittang, it was a salutary lesson in not underestimating one's enemy – 48 Brigade had repulsed every attack, rebuffing the Japanese attempt to capture Kokkogwa. But although *215 Regiment* had been defeated, General Sakurai had managed to infiltrate *213* and *214 Regiments* past Burcorp's right flank and they were now racing towards the oil wells at Yenangyaung.

Chapter Thirteen
Hell's Cauldron

Lieut. General Sakurai, commanding *33 Division*, was racing north through the Irrawaddy Valley, following his troops who were advancing to seize the oilfields at Yenangyaung. The captured jeep he was travelling in bounced in the ruts of the rough track, but he was grateful to the British for leaving it behind for his use. The Japanese had done quite well from the mounting bonanza of abandoned supplies. Moreover, he was able to drive without any fear of attack from Allied aircraft.

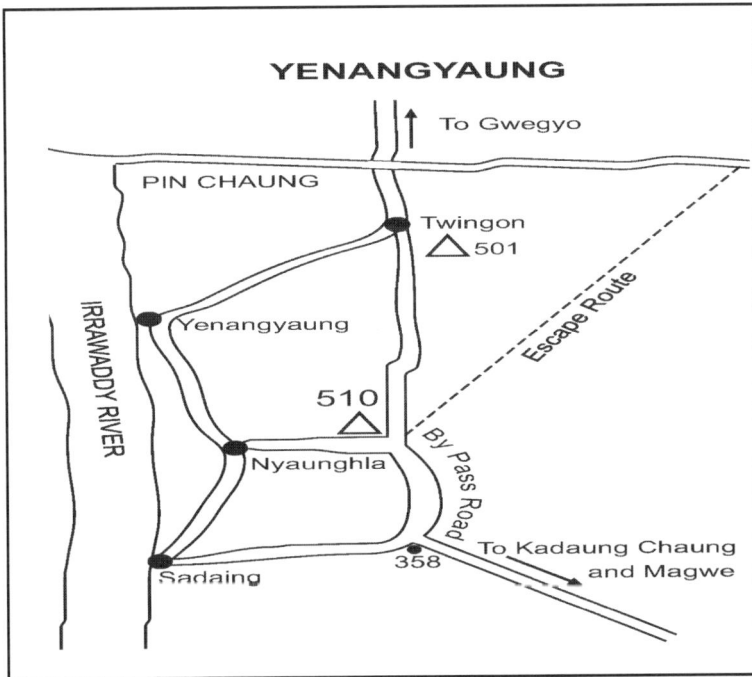

YENANGYAUNG

To Gwegyo

PIN CHAUNG

Twingon
△ 501

Escape Route

Yenangyaung

510
△

Nyaunghla

IRRAWADDY RIVER

By Pass Road

358

To Kadaung Chaung
and Magwe

Sadaing

He was as determined to take the oil wells as he had been to trap the Burma Army at Sittang. Although he had caused great damage to 17 Division, he had not been able to prevent the bridge from being destroyed. The British did not seem to mind blowing things up, like the general at Sittang, and no doubt they would not hesitate to send their oil wells into oblivion. This time, he must get there first.

Yenangyaung, situated on the banks of the Irrawaddy, was an oil town of 5,000 oil wells, three gasoline plants and the largest power station in Burma. The output was in excess of 250 million gallons a year. It was a prize the Japanese wanted desperately to win and the British were equally as determined to make sure they would not.

Between Sakurai's division and Yenangyaung stood 1 Burma Division and 17 Division. Against the British left wing he had launched *215 Regiment*, only for it to be badly mauled by 48 Brigade at Kokkogwa.

Slim was well aware that 1 Burma Division was sadly depleted and more weight was needed to defend the route to Yenangyaung. If he were able to move 17 Division from Taungdwingyi, he could have built up a more solid wall of defence. Unfortunately, Alexander was still tied by political demands and he refused because it would upset the Chinese.

With the intense build-up of pressure along the British right flank, Slim decided he had no alternative but to pull 1 Burma Division back north to take up a position along the deep, but dry, watercourse of the Yin Chaung, which started just north of the Irrawaddy and then ran east to west to enter the river some 8 miles south of Magwe.

At 12.30 hours on 12 April, Slim met Major General Bruce Scott at Magwe and they concluded that the Japanese were attempting to work around the left flank. Scott would have to pull back his division along the line of the Yin Chaung.

While the division was pulling back, Slim visited the area on 15 April and he realised all too well that the chances of holding on to the oil wells were so remote as to be almost nil. He certainly could not let them fall into Japanese hands. At 13.00 hours that afternoon he gave the order to blow up the fields; the production of fuel continuing until the last possible moment because of the needs of the Allied forces.

In anticipation of the demolition, all the British women and children, numbering some 400, had already been evacuated by river steamer to India. Leslie Foster, a former engineer of Shell Mex, and Captain Walter Scott, RE, who had both destroyed the oil depot in Rangoon, had been instructed to prepare the Yenangyaung depot for demolition. On Slim's orders, with an ear-splitting blast, one million gallons of crude oil caught fire; machinery, generators, buildings and the power house were all destroyed.

The Japanese forces aproaching Yenangyaung could see the column of black smoke ahead of them.

Back at his headquarters, a furious Sakurai studied the map and realised that he could lure 1 Burma Division into a trap. If he forced them across the Yin Chaung, the division's only way out would be over the Pin Chaung to the north. Behind them would be the Yin Chaung where his troops waited and to their right would be the Irrawaddy; and the whole area in between was almost a desert. All he had to do was move up the Irrawaddy and take Yenangyaung, while other regiments would sweep past the enemy's left flank, blocking off the Pin Chaung ford at the village of Twingon, and also the escape road beyond the *chaung* which led to Gwegyo. Trapped between these barriers, desperately short of water and low on ammunition, they could be bombarded at will, accounting for those who did not die first from thirst. It would be the perfect Scorpion Trap.

Over the next two days, Scott pulled back his division to the waterless Yin Chaung, covered by 7 Armoured Brigade. He had been ordered not to relinquish the line of the Yin Chaung except under extreme pressure and he knew that if he had to do so the next line, owing to lack of water, would have to be 40 miles north on the Pin Chaung in order to survive. In between was a waterless semi-desert of small hills covered in twisted brown scrubland of bushes and bare of trees; and with deep, dry *nullahs* or watercourses. He would have to keep to the road and the temperature would be well over 100°F.

On the night of 16/17 April, the Japanese attacked 1 Burma Brigade in position along the Yin Chaung. The brigade fought gallantly, but finally had to withdraw; at that time its battalions were very weak, some having as few as 300 men, tired, ill-fed and lacking equipment. Now, the Burma Division had no alternative but to pull further back towards Yenangyaung and start its hazardous journey towards the Pin Chaung. But General Scott was disturbed by the physical condition of his division. The sight of his exhausted men, who had managed in spite of all the tribulations to fight with such spirit, filled him with dismay. Slim had told him to delay his withdrawal for as long as possible, as he was expecting the Chinese to attack the Japanese right flank advancing northwards. All the same, an immediate withdrawal would have been advisable, but that afternoon of 15 April, Scott had allowed his weary men a breathing space of half a day. The delay was to have serious consequences.

Taking full advantage of Scott's compassionate move, Sakurai infiltrated a whole regiment through the weakly held defences and *214 Regiment* was able to move round the left flank and block the way to the Pin Chaung. This was Scott's only escape route out of the Yenangyaung area and now he would have a desperate fight on his hands.

At 09.30 hours on 16 April, Scott at last withdrew his division, heading for the Kadaung Chaung, about halfway to Yenangyaung. The whole way across the arid land they were harassed by low-flying enemy aircraft, having to scramble out of their vehicles to take what cover was available, then carrying on, stop-starting in the crippling heat, until evening brought some relief and they were able to harbour astride the Kadaung Chaung. The Japanese had not followed up.

Scott decided to send Rear Division HQ and all transport not required, with a 7 Armoured Brigade escort, to Gwegyo. The transport column passed through Twingon village and crossing the Pin Chaung, headed 5 miles further north to harbour that night. But 213 Regiment, having infiltrated the left flank, had cut the road and established a roadblock, trapping the advance guard of the British column and the main body of transport. At the same time, the enemy seized the Pin Chaung ford behind the column's rearguard, and established a second roadblock at Twingon. The Japanese also came upriver and attacked Yenangyaung, driving the small garrison of 1st Gloucesters to the south end of the town.

The only good news for Slim was word from Alexander that he was sending him 38 Chinese Division, commanded by General Sun, from the newly arrived VI Chinese Army. Slim asked for it to be concentrated at Kyaukpadaung as soon as possible.

Later in the day, Lieut. General Sun Li Jen of 38 Chinese Division arrived. As he spoke good English, with a slight American accent, having been educated at the Virginia Military Academy, no interpreter was required. Slim realised that the general was suspicious and it was essential to gain his confidence. The Chinese had no artillery or tanks of their own and were going to be supported by Burma Army artillery and all the tanks available. On the spur of the moment, Slim told Sun that the support would in fact be under his command. The Chinese general's attitude changed appreciably; Brigadier Anstice of 7 Armoured Brigade was not so pleased. But, fortunately, the brigadier and Sun got on famously and Slim had, in private, advised Sun to always consult with Anstice before employing him. Which he wisely did.

On the seventeenth, the Burma Division started to withdraw to Nyaunghla on the southern outskirts of Yenangyaung, the rearguard not getting in until midnight. The shortage of water made it necessary to position the division near the Irrawaddy and some of the force was positioned at Sadaing; 13 Brigade was immediately south of Nyaunghla and 1 Burma Brigade at Milestone 358.

Meanwhile, earlier that day, the armoured escort with the trapped transport had managed to clear the roadblock north of the Pin Chaung and the bulk of the transport had reached Gwegyo in the afternoon. But the Japanese still held the Pin Chaung ford and Twingon. Sakurai had achieved his aim. He might have lost the oilfields, but he had the Burma Division trapped and if he could smash it that would be a fatal blow to Burcorps.

With his division spread out on the outskirts of Yenangyaung, Scott waited to receive orders from Slim. Their only link was by radio from Tank Brigade HQ to the small tank signals detachment Scott had with his squadron. Security could not be guaranteed, but the two generals had the advantage of having known each other for so long and both having served in Gurkha regiments. Furthermore, both of them had the advantage of using Gurkhali and a code – such as their children's ages – so as not to reveal the gist of their conversation.

'*Sunnos,*' Slim began in Gurkhali. '*Yoh hukkum chha. Aile khola ko bato banda chha. Boli bihana, hamro sahti haru hamala garcha, aru khola kholdai chha. Tes bela ma timi tel ko gaon deki bhagnu parchha.*'

He added some code using the children's ages and Scott got the gist of the plan: 1 Burma Division was to break out north, while the Chinese came down to the Pin Chaung, cleared the roadblock at the ford and attacked the Japanese who were trying to block Scott's division. The Chinese would attack at dawn on 18 April and Scott was to break out under cover of the attack.

The division, stretched around Nyaunghla in harbour, was trapped in Sakurai's Hell's Cauldron. It was going to be a long night. At Milestone 358 on the Yenangyaung bypass road, the 150 survivors of 2nd King's Own Yorkshire Light Infantry hoped that the setting sun, which was like a huge red ball ringed in dust beyond the Irrawaddy, would bring some relief from the heat.

Sergeant Steel, curled up under a blackened shrub, could find little comfort on the hard earth. His mouth felt dry and his lips were burning, with hardly a drop of water all day, and what he had left in his water bottle would have to last the night and probably well into the next day. It was bound to be a similar day, too, with the temperature well over 114°F and with little shelter in the grim surroundings. It was like living in hell, with the treeless, undulating land, covered with shrubs that had forgotten what green leaves should look like, blackened by heat and the spread of oil from the demolitions. The skyline was of wrecked derricks and shattered machinery and in the distance some of the buildings still seemed to be burning. There was also a smell in the air like burnt cork.

It was Sod's Law, he thought, that the last time the KOYLIs were trapped in a dangerous situation at the Sittang there was more water than they wanted. He had hardly thought of Captain Cooper and the Gurkhas for a long time. He had been lucky at the Sittang; indeed, one of the few survivors of the devastated battalion. But thinking of that made him think of water and he could almost feel the Sittang's cold current around his body. God! he would have to pull himself together or he certainly would not last the night. Even to think of what awaited them the next morning might also not be wise.

He was awakened early the next morning, having managed to get some restless sleep, as the division prepared to attack. The Cameronians reached their first objective, to capture the ridge northeast of Nyaunghla with little opposition, and 7th Burma Rifles passed through and gained enough ground to prevent the Nyaunghla road from coming under small-arms fire, but neither it nor 12th Burma Rifles could make any further progress. The two battalions had received little artillery support owing to the shortage of ammunition; 5th Mountain Battery could keep only one gun in action. By afternoon the Cameronians had succeeded in preventing the Japanese from working southwards along the riverbank, but it was at the cost of heavy casualties.

Earlier, 13 Brigade had led the assault towards Twingon and the Pin Chaung also under cover of limited artillery because of the shortage of shells. A bypass road was cleared and a good deal of the transport got down almost to the Pin Chaung itself, only to be held up by the Japanese on the south bank. The British and Indian troops fought doggedly over low ridge after ridge, the Japanese defending each one to the last man.

They then gained Point 510 and 13 Brigade continued to advance on Twingon, but the leading battalion, 5/1st Punjab, found the enemy holding the high ground above Point 501 east of the village. The Punjabis gained a precarious foothold on the ridge and held it until mid afternoon, when a strong counter-attack forced them back with heavy casualties.

The Royal Inniskilling Fusiliers, on the left, failed to break into Twingon. There were two companies, however, which worked round the village and reached the Pin Chaung, but they fell into an ambush when they mistook the Japanese for Chinese and were taken prisoner. On the right, 1/18th Royal Garhwal Rifles were held up by wire fences and suffered severely. But by nightfall they had managed to enter the village, which was now in flames and could not be held.

During the afternoon, the remaining division transport had moved forward along the bypass road, the head of the column halting at the road junction a mile north of Point 510. By evening, the whole division was concentrated south of Twingon.

The division had done everything they could possibly be asked, but where were the Chinese? Earlier, the Chinese attack had reached the Pin Chaung and cleared the north bank, but they had failed to take the strongly held roadblock at the ford. Even the tanks, prevented from closing by the soft sand of the river bed, could not drive the defenders out. As a result, the enemy still held the roadblock north of the village and was firmly established on both sides of the Pin Chaung.

Scott was in a desperate situation. The blinding glare from the sun, and the suffocating airless atmosphere which he had been subjected to all day while trying to maintain a cool head to gauge the changing situations, had left him exhausted. He could imagine how his men were feeling: the continuous marching and fighting while caged in by the heat, suffering the torture of unquenched thirst. And as for the wounded – what torment they must be going through, the stifling heat adding to the agony of their wounds. Could his division hold out another night? Did he feel he himself could hold out? That was the yard stick. Of course, he had no other choice but to hold out, but by the morning he felt sure he would be much weaker and so would his men.

At half past four that afternoon, Scott contacted Slim on the radio and asked permission to destroy the guns and transport and fight his way out that night. Slim hesitated. He could imagine the desperate situation the division was in and how the men were suffering, but generals have to make seemingly cruel decisions and as he sat in the radio van with the headphones on, he realised that he had to order Scott to hold on. The Chinese had promised to attack the next morning with all available tanks and artillery. If the Burma Division attacked at the same time they could break through.

'You must hang on, Bruce,' Slim said with finality.

Scott managed to stifle a sob in his voice. 'All right, Bill.' Which Slim, knowing the man from such long personal acquaintance, was sure he would say. 'But get those bloody Chinese to attack,' Scott added as he signed off.

Steel knew it was going to be a horrendous night and he made certain that the men of his skeleton platoon had dug slit trenches in preparation for the onslaught which would surely come. The setting of the sun had not brought much relief from the heat and a mouth without saliva that was crying out for water was no help. It did not exactly encourage men to keep up their courage when they could hear the wounded weeping in the night, either.

Outside the perimeter, the Japanese were closing in from the north and south, seeking a final kill. Throughout the night they flailed the division with shells and mortars. Scott's guns did not reply; they were down to about twenty rounds per gun and needed them in the morning. Just before dawn 13 Brigade, holding the northern face of the perimeter, repulsed an attack from the direction of Twingon.

Dawn did not bring any relief, either, as, with targets in sight, the enemy machine-guns and mortars increased their fire, causing casualties and damage to some of the vehicles. Dawn also brought a severe blow for Slim, when he was told that the Chinese attack had been delayed yet again. It was eventually promised for 12.30 hours. How could he tell Scott to hold on?

Meanwhile, in the perimeter, the heat began to build up and through lack of water men began to die. The whole area was criss-crossed with machine-gun bullets and splattered by mortar shrapnel. Steel crouched lower in his slit trench and felt certain that this day would be his last.

Scott, trying to keep his wits about him, was wondering how to get out of this dreadful situation when a tank commander came up with a possible way of escape. A squadron of his tanks had discovered and cleared a track leading away to the east, down to the Pin Chaung which, it was hoped, would take vehicles.

The Chinese had postponed their attack again: to 15.00 hours. Scott had had enough. Communication with Slim had been cut and so coordination was now impossible. To hell with it, Scott decided. Let us go! He formed up the column, guns in front, wounded in ambulances and trucks next. With a spearhead of tanks and infantry, the column lurched down the narrow, uneven path through the low hillocks. The column soon came under mortar and gunfire. A tank, two anti-aircraft guns and several vehicles were knocked out. But Scott led the column on steadily until, suddenly, the trail turned to sand, the leading ambulances became bogged down and the column stopped.

But Scott was determined to go on. He ordered the wheeled vehicles to be abandoned and the guns to be put out of action. As many wounded as possible were piled on the tanks and Scott gave the final order to fight a way out on foot. Despite machine-gun fire from a nearby village, the division reached the Pin Chaung about one and a half miles north-east of Twingon. At the sight of the water in the *chaung*, the mules who had come out with them went mad, and the men flung themselves face downwards into it. The haggard, red-eyed British, Indian and Burmese soldiers who staggered up the bank were a terrible sight. But every man Slim saw was still carrying his rifle.

The two brigades of the division had reached Yenangyaung at a strength of not more than one; subsequently, they had lost in killed and wounded 20 per cent of that small number, along with a considerable portion of their guns, mortars and vehicles. None of these losses could be replaced. After its ordeal, the division could be of no fighting value until it had rested and, as much as was possible, reorganised. They collected that night about Gwegyo.

The Chinese finally attacked at about 15.00 hours on 19 April, too late to help Scott's division. Crossing the Pin Chaung they advanced with dash, taking Twingon late that evening and rescuing the men of the Inniskillings captured earlier. There was further heavy fighting the next day, with the Chinese penetrating into Yenangyaung. But there was danger of a really heavy Japanese counter-attack at dawn on the twenty-first and Slim agreed with Sun that the Chinese had done enough and should withdraw over the Pin Chaung. The Chinese fell back to Gwegyo and covered 1 Burma Division, which was being reorganised in the Mount Popa area, north-east of Kyaukpadaung.

Unfortunately, there had been no choice but to leave a number of the badly wounded in the ambulances when the column had finally broken out. A young gunner officer volunteered to go back to discover their fate. Under cover of darkness, he reached the ambulances which were still standing on the track. But when he looked inside, the gruesome sight filled him with horror: every man either had his throat cut or had been bayoneted to death.

191

THE WAY OUT: MANDALAY-IMPHAL

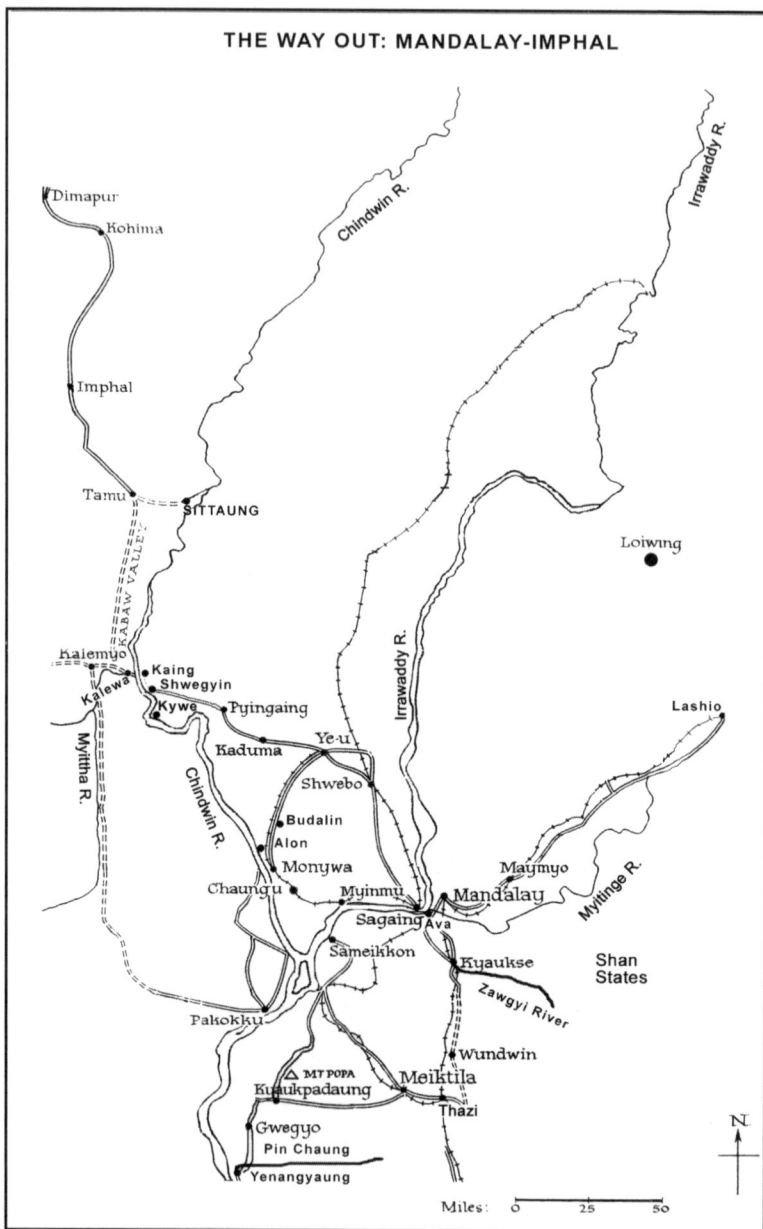

Dimapur

Kohima

Chindwin R.

Irrawaddy R.

Imphal

Tamu

SITTAUNG

Loiwing

KABAW VALLEY

Kalemyo

Kalewa

Kaing
Shwegyin

Kywe

Pyingaing

Myittha R.

Chindwin R.

Kaduma

Ye-u

Irrawaddy R.

Lashio

Shwebo

Budalin

Alon

Monywa

Chaungu

Myinmu

Maymyo

Mandalay

Myitinge R.

Sagaing Ava

Sameikkon

Kyaukse

Shan
States

Zawgyi River

Pakokku

Wundwin

△ MT POPA

Kyaukpadaung

Meiktila

Thazi

Gwegyo

Pin Chaung

Yenangyaung

N

Miles: 0   25   50

Chapter Fourteen
Rearguard at Kyaukse

As his company marched with 48 Brigade towards the Burmese town of Kyaukse, Paul looked over his men and felt both pride and sorrow. He was proud of the way his Gurkhas had behaved during the past three months or more against daunting odds, but he was sad at the way the ranks had dwindled. There were fewer every day. So many of his men had been killed or injured, suffering the hardship of the rough ride in the back of lorries to receive medical treatment.

He missed their faces, their individual mannerisms. Manbahadur with his laughing moon-face, nicknamed Mr Moto because he always seemed overweight, but was able to move quickly, finally catching a burst from a machine-gun he was charging. And Josbir Gurung, little Josbir, the youngest of the men, really just a boy, who had been Ray Dean's orderly at the Sittang. Finding his body in a ditch had been a dreadful moment which had shaken him in spite of all the dead he had seen. And … No! No more! Paul shook his head. He had to let them go in peace and give himself some peace as well. But his mind was distracted again, seeing the condition of his men's uniforms. Somehow, they kept their clothes on their backs and an appearance of smartness about them, even getting more wear out of their boots. He could feel the hard surface of the road through his own soles, but there was no possible means of obtaining supplies of new equipment. The countryside through which they marched also had a worn-out look and a smell of decay about it. Everywhere were burned-out villages and signs of the destruction caused by the indiscriminate bombing by Japanese aircraft.

At nightfall on 26 April, the brigade reached Kyaukse and the units started to take up their allotted positions. In the darkness the town had an eerie appearance, its blackened, ruined houses looming among the shrapnel-scarred trees.

The situation in Burma had reached a critical phase. Disaster had struck the Chinese forces when the Japanese broke through in the east at Loikaw and Pyinmana, VI Chinese Army falling apart at alarming speed. With the complete disappearance of VI Army, and the almost certain disintegration of the other Chinese armies, it was obviously time for the British to withdraw from Burma as soon as possible, as intact as they could and with as much as they could.

The last thing Alexander wanted was to be caught on the wrong side of the Irrawaddy at Mandalay, to face another Sittang disaster. He had been in touch with Wavell earlier with regards to the policy to be adopted in the event of a total withdrawal to India and Wavell was still determined to keep in touch with the Chinese. He did not want to give them any grounds for accusing the British of running away to India.

Alexander had ordered his senior commanders to meet him on 25 April at Kyaukse, a village some 25 miles south of Mandalay.

'As I see it,' he said to Stillwell and Slim, 'there are two possible routes back to India. One would be via Mogaung or Myitkyina through the Hukwang Valley. The other would be the cross-country route leading north from Shwebo to Kalewa on the Chindwin, through the Kabaw Valley to Tamu in Manipur and thence to Imphal. Personally, I prefer the second choice.'

Both Slim and Stillwell agreed with him. The Hukwang Valley was mountainous, interspersed with rivers, and was therefore a considerably difficult terrain. It was to prove the graveyard for thousands of refugees who tried to escape along that route.

Alexander then put forward the plan he had formulated with Wavell: 1 Burma Division would cover the approaches to India via Kalewa, 17 Division would withdraw to India, but lose a brigade which, with 7 Armoured Brigade, would accompany V Chinese Army to China via Lashio, while VI Chinese Army would withdraw to China by way of Lashio and Kengtung.

Slim felt his hackles rise: the idea of breaking up Burcorps and sending British troops into China appalled him. Keeping himself under control as much as he could, he pointed out that the C.-in-C. had said he wanted the Burma Army to get back in shape to help defend Assam. Well, the splitting up of 17 Division would lower morale considerably, just when full support from all ranks was so vitally important. At this time, too, Yunnan was in the grip of a severe famine and airlifts to supply the British troops with essential rations would be nigh on impossible.

Alexander was not pleased, but he realised that Slim had put forward valid points and so the original plan was dropped. But that was a later step. It was much more important now to withdraw the Allied forces north of the Irrawaddy. The Chinese were obviously not able to look after themselves during such a move, so Slim's corps was to act as rearguard to the fugitive V Chinese Army as it made its escape.

Retirement was to begin at once, for the Chinese Army was already in full flight; 7 Armoured Brigade was ordered to make for Meiktila with all speed and 17 Division was to be interposed between the Chinese and the Japanese. Speed was essential in order to get all the British and Chinese across the Irrawaddy via the Ava Bridge before the Japanese could catch them with their backs to the river.

With the Chinese clear of the Meiktila area, Slim ordered Cowan to move 17 Division to Wundwin, which he was to hold until 16.00 hours on 27 April, and then withdraw through Kyaukse, where 48 Brigade and 7th Hussars were to provide the final rearguard.

Taking up positions in the southern part of Kyaukse was 48 Brigade. Kyaukse had been an attractive little town, the western part studded with trees. The small Zawgyi River ran through the town and from it, irrigation channels flowed alongside the road to the open fields, the banks of the waterway thickly covered with gardens and banana groves.

One Gurkha battalion watched the open fields to the west; the Gurkhas opened a water sluice to flood the fields, and to their surprise hundreds of snakes came wriggling out. Another held the ridge to the east with pickets, while between these two, the third battalion covered the road and railway approaching from the south on a narrow front. There were two companies placed forward either side of the road and in between them they established a roadblock covered by anti-tank guns and 3-inch mortars.

Osborne moved his battalion into its position near Brigade HQ. Paul and his Gurkha officers were directing the men in digging their weapon pits when they heard the hum of approaching transport as the rest of 17 Division moved through the town on its way to the Ava Bridge. The Chinese had been allotted first place in the crossing, with 7 Armoured Brigade and 17 Division to cross after them and then blow up the bridge.

At around midnight there was a further disturbance as 63 Brigade approached and passed through the town and beyond, to occupy positions covering the road and rail bridge over the Myitinge River, south of Mandalay, as 48 Brigade's rearguard.

Hoping that was the last of the disturbances, Paul settled down on his groundsheet. He still felt nervous before an attack. After the first time at Kawkareik he thought he would become, well, not blasé, but certainly accustomed. If anything, knowing what would be in store, he felt more anxious. But so far, once the action started he usually felt cool and ... not brave – no – what was the word he wanted? Composed? Collected? Unperturbed? No, certainly not that. More like controlled. In control. Yes, that was it. He surprised himself at times by the complete self-control he seemed to have.

Gopiram suddenly crouched at his side. 'Anything I can do for you, sahib? Tea, perhaps.'

'No, Gopiram. I am quite comfortable. I will sleep soon.'

The orderly slipped away. Around him, Paul could hear the various snores and grunts of the sleeping men, curled up in all sorts of positions. Well, they seemed relaxed. He closed his eyes and sleep came to him at once.

There were to be three crossing points across the Irrawaddy. Apart from the Ava Bridge, ferries would be used at Sameikkon and west of Mandalay. But Slim was doubtful about the ferries and he drove down to check for himself with Brigadier Swift, Chief Engineer of 1 Burma Division. At one ferry point there was no sign of any craft. At another there was a battered barge aground some yards from the beach. At the third, just some small craft capable of taking one or two vehicles at a time. They looked at each other.

'This will not do,' remarked Slim.

'Wait a moment, sir,' Swift said. 'I believe they are planning to sink the Irrawaddy Flotilla fleet today. I had better get there quickly.'

Living up to his name, Brigadier Swift drove at speed to Mandalay and was in time to save some of the steamers, bringing them back downstream to the ferry points. Barges were pulled off the sandbanks, approaches improved and ferries of a sort provided.

On 27 April, Slim decided to visit the more dangerous 17 Division flank, stretching west to east across the secondary road to Kyaukse, where 48 Brigade was taking up position. There was increasing evidence of attacks and atrocities by gangs of Burmese against Indian refugees, Chinese stragglers and, on occasion, Indian troops trying to repair signal wire.

On the way he fell in with a mobile column from 17 Division and was accompanying them back to Kyaukse, when they came abruptly upon a Burmese gang attacking an army signal team. Being beaten up mercilessly were two of the signallers. The arrival of the mobile column put an end to that and the gang was promptly eliminated.

He continued on to Kyaukse and found 48 Brigade in a strong defensive position. Brigadier Cameron told him there were four weak battalions, a troop of anti-tank two-pounders, twelve guns and some sappers, plus about 1,800 men. Burcorps was shrinking fast, but the brigade had shown its mettle at Kokkogwa and Slim felt confident that he could rely on it in this critical phase of the withdrawal across the Irrawaddy.

The crack *18 Chrysanthemum Division,* which had spearheaded the invasion of Malaya, had arrived in Burma through Rangoon and it now moved north to attack Kyaukse. The division reached the outskirts of the town on 28 April, full of confidence, believing that it would experience little difficulty in knocking over the town.

The Japanese decided to put in an attack that night and the first wave of infantry approached the village in bright moonlight, showing an arrogance for which they would pay dearly. The Gurkhas allowed the Japanese to approach up the road until at almost point-blank range, when they opened a withering fire, cutting down the enemy who fled in confusion, leaving their dead and many wounded screaming in pain.

There followed a lull of some two hours, during which small parties of Japanese crept forward to remove the dead and the wounded. Then, at around a half-hour after midnight, the enemy put in another heavy attack. The moon was now at its fullest point, making the enemy easy targets. The Gurkhas allowed them to come even closer, before once again decimating them by close-order fire and a bombardment of 3-inch mortars, which accounted for some forty killed and many wounded.

With a waning moon and drifting clouds towards dawn, the Japanese tried again at around 05.15 hours, but once again they were sent tumbling back with heavy casualties. The *Chrysanthemum Division* was not accustomed to being treated in such a cavalier fashion and judging from the shouts and screams of distress heard in the dark, they were thoroughly demoralised. On other fronts, strong enemy patrols had also been driven back. At daybreak, the 7th Hussars' tanks swept the front and found a small burnt-out hamlet, in front of a Gurkha company, still occupied by the enemy. The Gurkhas attacked, supported by artillery. At first they could see no sign of the enemy and then one of the Gurkhas, like a bloodhound, pointed at a culvert and there, cowering together, were some forty members of the elite division. In a moment, the Gurkhas started hurling grenades into one end of the culvert, while tommy gun fire was directed into the other end. A few Japanese bolted down the *nullah* and were killed by grenades, but the remaining thirty-eight were found packed tight and stone dead in the culvert.

Humiliated, the Japanese pressed their attack, intending now to seize Kyaukse in a pincer grip. Gurkha patrols discovered strong forces infiltrating into the jungle and neighbouring villages. An artillery duel developed, with heavy enemy fire landing direct hits on Brigade HQ. Paul and his men crouched in their weapon pits as the shells exploded all around, shrapnel flying in all directions. To Paul's relief he suffered no casualties, but a shell had landed near A Company.

Cameron realised he would have to reinforce his forward ranks to meet the new threat. The Brigade Defence Platoon was already in action, so both companies of 4/15th Gurkhas were ordered forward.

Paul led his men past the crumpled black skeletons of the town houses, the acrid smell of burnt wood still hanging in the air, a pitiful sight in the light of day. There was fierce machine-gun and small-arms fire ahead and the crunch of grenades came echoing back through the town. Irrigation channels flowed through, lined with gardens and banana groves and the bright flowers which had survived the bombing, for a moment bringing some life again to Kyaukse. But in the banana groves a deadly, close-quarter fight was in progress.

Amarjit to his right, Dilbahadur to his left, Paul led the rush into the grove to come to the aid of the other Gurkhas, Gopiram sticking closely to his side as he found himself in the centre of the melee. The shiny green trunks of the banana trees were torn open by grenade shrapnel and where a khukuri had sliced through one, the trunk bent, serrated leaves above fell to the ground and the flowers were trampled underfoot as the two groups fought savagely. In front of him he saw a Gurkha strike out with his khukuri, but the Japanese target managed to turn it aside with his bayonet. The Gurkha toppled to his side, his khukuri biting into the trunk of a banana tree, and then the Japanese infantryman brought his bayonet into the Gurkha's body. As the Gurkha crashed into the tree and slithered to the ground, Paul lurched forwards, thrusting his bayonet into the now exposed body of the Jap. As he removed the bayonet, Gopiram rushed past him to meet an oncoming enemy and dispose of him with a fierce slash. Now, Paul found himself hemmed in as his men formed a shield around him as they fought the enemy. The noise of weapons and shouting seemed to reach a crescendo and then die away as the enemy at last broke, retreating out of the village.

Japanese aircraft now appeared to dive-bomb and machine-gun the area. Then, at around 15.30 hours, the Japanese advanced again, but battalion machine-guns opened up onto the banana groves and screams of pain and shouts were heard as the enemy withdrew.

*　　*　　*

Back in Brigade HQ, Cameron at last received information from Division HQ that the Chinese were safely across the Ava Bridge and his brigade was then ordered to withdraw from Kyaukse at 18.00 hours. A couple of tanks crossed the main bridge southwards and at 17.30 hours they raked the Japanese forward positions with belt after belt of fire. Under this cover, 48 Brigade withdrew north over the Zawgyi River, where 63 Brigade was in position.

Paul led his company across the bridge where, with the rest of the brigade personnel, they quickly bussed into the waiting lorries and together with 63 Brigade, they drove into Mandalay on their way to the Ava Bridge, destroying the final road bridge over the Zawgyi halfway between Kyaukse and the Myitinge River.

Mandalay was a heap of smouldering ruins after the constant Japanese air attacks, the business and native quarters reduced to ashes. Over the whole city hung a cloud of smoke and the stench of decay. The moon was just beginning to rise and its light fell on streets blocked by telephone wires hanging like garlands, dead bullocks, abandoned bullock-carts and burnt-out vehicles. Bloated corpses floated among the lily ponds in the moat which surrounded Fort Dufferin.

Flies and bluebottles rose in swarms as the lorries disturbed them and the Gurkhas had to smash them aside with their hats. Paul could see rats scurrying alongside the road. When Paul's lorry drove through to the bridge, the moon had risen enough for him to be aware of the whole ghastly scene. But he did not know that Sue Whitcomb had been in the city a few days earlier, making good her escape across the bridge. Slim waited in his jeep, watching his men cross the bridge. The Chinese were already across along with all Burcorps, with the exception of 63 Brigade, which still held the approaches to the bridge. On the south side, the general noticed a line of tanks, their officers in worried consultation, and he went across to them. A Stuart tank weighed 13 tons, alarmingly a notice warned that the roadway running across the bridge only had a maximum capacity of 6 tons.

Slim asked who had built the bridge and was shown a tablet with the name of a well-known British engineering firm. In his experience, any permanent bridge built by British engineers would almost certainly have a safety feature of 100 per cent and he ordered the tanks to cross.

He watched nervously as the road sagged when the first tank made its way warily over the bridge. But the bridge remained secure. At last, all the tanks were across and 63 Brigade motored over. And, finally, Slim made his way across before giving the order to blow the bridge.

At one minute to midnight on 30 April 1942, the bridge was blown and its central span fell neatly into the river.

A significant sign, Slim thought, that the British had lost Burma.

Chapter Fifteen
A Perilous Journey

When the Whitcombs and the Stevens arrived in Mandalay, they were told they would be continuing by road to Maymyo. But because of delays, they would have to stop over in Mandalay for a day or two.

The day or two turned into three or four and it was 8 March when they finally took the winding hill road to Maymyo. While waiting for the convoy to start, they were given the news that Rangoon had fallen.

Maymyo, the summer capital of Burma, was 3,500 ft above sea level and was more European than Burmese in character with its Western-style houses. Situated in the hills above Mandalay, it was where the government established itself in the hot weather.

Normally, at this time of the year it would be crowded with government officials and the wives of businessmen escaping the heat of the capital and the plains. Although the general exodus had been somewhat curtailed by the war, it was still teeming, but with evacuees and military. The two military hospitals were crowded with wounded soldiers and Generals Alexander and Stillwell had established their HQ in the town. The governor was also in residence.

Celia, however, came to the rescue as she had very good friends who were only too happy to put them up. The Jacksons had a large, attractive house with a typical Maymyo garden, which displayed a gorgeous array of multicoloured cannas, bright zinnias, dahlias and marigolds; there were also plum and cherry trees, and strawberries when in season.

Peter and Julia Jackson were a friendly couple in their early sixties. They had lived in Burma for more than twenty-five years and had decided to retire in Maymyo rather than return to England. They had always adopted a British way of life, but preferred the climate of Maymyo to England. Besides, there was no shortage of servants, which made life so much easier.

'It is so kind of you to put us up,' Celia said.

'It is lovely to have you,' Julia replied. 'We do not have many English visitors these days. And I should imagine you need some rest and comfort.'

'Oh, yes! It was horrible. Trapped on that crowded train; hardly any air and suffocating in the heat. Then four days in Mandalay in an awful transit camp. And tossed to bits in the back of a truck on that hilly road to Maymyo.'

'You will be all right now, Celia, dear. Fortunately, we have a large house. Something Peter insisted on, thank goodness. Now, U Thant will show you to your rooms and the boys will take up your luggage – is that all you were allowed? And I am sure you would like a hot bath. Just leave your dirty clothes in the basket in your room and they will be washed.'

'No hurry,' Peter said. 'Come down when you are ready and join us for a drink before dinner.'

George and Mary looked round the double bedroom they had been given. It was comfortably furnished, with a few paintings of English villages on the walls.

'You know,' said George, 'we will have to be careful. This is all too comfortable. We must not be taken in; common sense tells me we will have to be on the move again quite soon. We have to get to India.'

'Yes. They do seem to live in cloud cuckoo land,' Mary agreed.

'So does Celia. Getting her to move on is going to be difficult.'

Sue was the last to come down to the lounge. She felt really refreshed after her hot bath and she had changed into some clean clothes. She was glad to see the dirty travel clothes whipped away by a servant.

The lounge had a definite English atmosphere, with its comfortable settees and armchairs, occasional tables and chairs, and there were plenty of table lamps with bright shades. The only acknowledgement of the fact it was in Burma were some excellent paintings of pagodas and countryside; otherwise, the paintings were typically British.

She sat down in an armchair and Peter offered her a sherry which was served on a brass tray by a servant in an expensive-looking *longyi*.

'Now, you must make yourself at home,' Julia said. 'It has been a terrible experience, I am sure. And losing your home – I cannot think of anything worse than that.'

'That really was dreadful,' Celia agreed. 'And being shoved from pillar to post.'

'Well, you don't have to worry about that, any more,' Peter said. 'You are very welcome to stay here as long as it takes.'

George looked up anxiously. 'Have you not made any plans, then, for leaving?'

From the look on the faces of their hosts, Sue decided that her father had thrown a veritable hand grenade into the room.

At last Peter spoke. 'Oh, I do not think it will come to that.'

'But Rangoon has fallen.'

'Yet, General Alexander and Stillwell have their headquarters here and the governor is in residence. I am sure we will be quite safe.'

With a warning glance from Mary, George decided it would be pointless to continue. These people lived in their own little world.

The next day George went to Army HQ and on his return, he gathered his group together.

'I learned that the evacuation of women and children started last month. While there are no plans at the moment to evacuate Maymyo, the hospitals are filling up with wounded and many more are sure to arrive. They will have to be got out via Shwebo, where planes from India are still available, but probably not for much longer. Of course, the army spokesman tried to be optimistic, but there is no doubt in my mind that eventually the Japanese will force their way up north. With Rangoon now available to them, they must be pouring in reinforcements and supplies. We really should be ready to move.'

Celia was quite upset. 'You heard the Jacksons. We should not do anything in a rush. It is so peaceful here. And why should we have to face some horrible journey for no good reason. I have no intention of moving until it is definite.'

Jack said, 'Perhaps Celia is right. We should give it a bit longer. And this is a good opportunity to recharge our batteries, as you might say, before we have to face the unknown perils that may lie ahead.'

George knew that Jack would not leave without Celia and he guessed Mary would be reluctant to do so without her brother, so any decision was postponed for a later date. Passing the time was going to be difficult.

'What about the hospitals?' George suggested to Sue. 'Perhaps they could do with some help.'

'I am not trained –' Sue began.

But her father cut in, 'There are other ways to help in a hospital. With all those wounded soldiers, I am sure they would be grateful for any assistance.'

Sue decided to give it a try and she went to the nearest hospital of the two in Maymyo. The building was crowded, with many ambulances coming and going. She climbed up onto the front veranda and through the open doors she could see a long ward packed to capacity and more, all the beds occupied.

She wondered who she should speak to and her courage began to fade, but as she turned away a Sister came out of the ward. A tall woman in her late thirties with a cheerful face, she looked efficient in her crisp uniform.

'Hello, looking for someone?'

'Well ...' Sue hesitated. 'Well, actually, I was wondering if I could be of any help and I did not know who to report to. And perhaps you don't really need anyone,' she added tentatively.

Sister Dexter saw an attractive young woman, maybe twenty, she guessed. She looked quite fit. 'Have you any hospital experience?'

'No. But I did first aid at school.'

'Well, that is a good start,' Sister Dexter said encouragingly. 'As you can see, we have a lot of poor wounded soldiers. And we do need help. Not necessarily medical, but there are lots of ways you could help, if you are willing.'

Sue said she would like to help and Sister Dexter said, 'Good. Come along with me.'

The next few weeks were a busy time for Sue as she saw to the patients' needs, and kept them happy, often going round with their meals. Then she was promoted to helping in changing bandages. She would return home weary, but sometimes found sleep difficult. Seeing all those wounded men every day made her think about Paul and at nights she worried about him.

And Mary was worried about Sue and she wondered if she should persuade her to stop going to the hospital. Although she did not think that would be easy.

'Oh, Mother, when you see all those poor wounded soldiers, you know they want all the help they can get.'

'But I do not think it is those wounded who are giving you sleepless nights?'

Sue held her mother's gaze for a moment. 'Oh, am I being stupid to be so worried about someone I have known for so short a while? In fact, I suppose I hardly know him at all. And yet I know I love him. And I feel certain he loves me. Do you have to know someone a long time to feel the way I do about him?'

'Well, I suppose love at first sight is not as uncommon as all that. Indeed, I think it could have been love at first sight between your father and me.'

Sue looked keenly at her mother. 'Do you mean that?'

'I met your father when he was on leave in England. We were at a dance and he was without a partner, so my cousin introduced us. Was I stricken with him? I know he asked me out a few days later. And then he returned to Burma. And to my surprise, a short while later, I received a letter from him asking me to marry him. Well, dear, it must have been love at first sight, because to my family and friends' astonishment and alarm, I caught a ship to Rangoon. And I think it has worked out very well, don't you?'

'Oh, Mother, I don't quite believe you.'

'Well, it is near enough to the truth. The Fishing Fleet they called us. We travelled out on the P & O shipping line to the East and there were usually a fair number of brides-to-be on every sailing, going out to marry men they hardly knew and not always realising what sort of life they might have to lead in out-of-the-way places. I think most of them worked out all right in the end. Of course, there were a few scandals aboard ship when a bride-to-be met a bachelor tea planter on his way back to his tea garden and found she loved him more than her would-be husband.'

She caught Sue by the arm. 'Not me.' She laughed. 'I was certainly not the flighty type. But seriously, dear, I found Paul an attractive, pleasant young man and I'm sure his Gurkhas certainly think highly of him. In that short time I noticed the same relationship between them as I have noticed between your father and his men. An unlikely recommendation for marriage, but the Burmese and Karens are quick in judging a person's character and I am sure the Gurkhas are the same; they neither tolerate fools nor charlatans gladly. Just let us hope he comes through safely and you have a second chance to appraise him.'

A second chance! But would there ever be that opportunity? It was so difficult to get news. There were any number of wounded Gurkhas on the wards, but none of them knew Captain Cooper Sahib. Then, one day, when she was replenishing a wounded Gurkha's water jug, he suddenly called out, 'Memsahib.' Then added, 'Moulmein, memsahib.'

She almost dropped the jug. 'You were there? Captain Cooper Sahib?'

He nodded his head and said in broken English, 'Big house – two *memsahibs*.'

'How is Captain Sahib?' she asked breathlessly.

'OK.'

'When did you last see him?' she asked anxiously, but he did not seem to understand.

'When wounded?' she asked desperately, pointing at his bandages.

He thought for a moment and then held up five fingers. She knew that she could not rely on his idea of time being accurate, but at least it seemed that Paul was all right about a week ago.

Meanwhile, George was growing worried and frustrated. The news from central Burma was bad. He was sure it would not be long before the Japanese poured into Maymyo. Then Sue returned from the hospital one evening to tell him that plans were being made to evacuate the wounded to Shwebo.

The Jacksons were not impressed. 'That really does not change anything for us,' Peter said. 'We are too old and set in our ways to face the rough journey which surely awaits all evacuees.'

'Do you think a Japanese prison camp would be more comfortable?' George asked.

'I am sure the Japanese will abide by the Geneva Convention and treat us correctly. They are civilised people.'

George was astounded at his naiveness. Then Celia said, her voice rather high, 'I think everything is exaggerated. You know what it was like on that horrible train. I am not going through that again.'

'Perhaps we should give it a day or two,' Jack said. He knew how strung-up Celia had become and he was not really sure how to handle her.

Mary, not wanting to abandon her brother, said tentatively, 'Well, maybe we should see what happens in the next day or two.'

George knew it would be pointless to press the matter. They would have to go, of that he was certain; he would just have to wait for an opportune moment. And that moment came the next day, when Colonel Peterson called. He was an old friend of George's.

'I had to come and see you, George, because I am rather concerned to find you still here.'

'So am I,' George said. 'But I have not been able to convince everyone.'

'Look, the whole town is emptying fast. Wounded are being evacuated. The army is clearing off. Alexander and Stillwell are also on their way out. I would have gone myself, but had to attend to some important matters first. But I am off tomorrow, by road. I have an old coach, but in good condition with comfortable seats. We will see what the situation is in Mandalay and whether or not it is more convenient to continue by train to Shwebo. But we have to be quick. I am sure Burcorps is going to blow the Ava Bridge and then try to escape to the Chindwin and out to India. The Chinese are collapsing.' He looked around the room. 'So, what about it?'

'It is kind of you, Colonel Peterson, to make the offer,' Peter said quietly. 'But my wife and I are staying on. It is pointless trying to change our minds.'

Celia cried out, 'And I shall stay with them!'

'No, you will not!' Jack said suddenly to everyone's surprise. 'I certainly do not want to end up in a Japanese POW camp. And you are not going to, either. I have supported you so far, but we cannot play games any more.'

Celia started to cry and Jack helped her upstairs.

The next day, the colonel picked them up as arranged: the three Whitcombs, plus Celia and Jack, and two Indian servants. The Jacksons, two forlorn figures, waved them goodbye.

They left the cool of Maymyo, down the hilly, winding road and then out onto the plain, the heat meeting them. The coach was reasonably comfortable and they drove into Mandalay late afternoon. The city bore stark evidence of previous air raids as the colonel drove through the litter-strewn, almost deserted streets and past crumbling buildings, finally coming to a halt a few streets away from the railway station.

The colonel got out of the coach. 'I am just going to make some enquiries,' he began. 'I will –' He stopped, as an air-raid siren sounded, and looked up at the sky. The warning was too short; already there was the hum of approaching aircraft. 'Get out of the coach!' he shouted.

As the passengers scrambled out of the coach, the sky above them was dotted with Japanese aircraft. The Japanese unloaded their cargo of bombs as Sue grabbed her mother and pushed her into a shallow ditch at the side of the road, crouching down beside her. The salvo whistled down and exploded all around them and she could feel the earth tremble. There were screams and shouts and then sudden silence for a moment. Then again shouts, but in the distance.

Sue helped her mother out of the ditch and was horrified at the sight which met her. The coach was tilted over on its side and the front was just a crumpled tangle of metal. All around the ground was strewn with bodies. She staggered forward, looking frantically for her father. Celia was lying on the road as though peacefully asleep, but quite dead from the blast. Jack, lying near her, had his legs blown off. The colonel was certainly dead and so were the Indian servants lying in a crumpled heap. At last, she found her father's smashed body. He had been blown some distance from the blast.

Mary came up. 'George! George!'

Sue put an arm around her. 'Nothing we can do, Mum.'

'Oh my God! there must be something.'

'He is dead, Mum. And so is everyone else.'

'What are we going to do with the body? The funeral?'

Ever more practical Sue, although her heart was almost breaking, bent over her father's battered body and removed his passport and wallet. Her mother had sat down in the middle of the road, her head in her hands. Sue could feel her own body trembling with the shock, but she knew she had to take charge if they were to get away. Her mother had always been the guiding hand, but now she had to take over.

She walked over to the coach and looked through a window. The seats were tilted, but she thought she could see her rucksack. The front of the coach had been blown open and she managed to scramble through, creeping on her side, feeling the coach move as she did so. She hesitated for a moment and then crawled a bit further. Locating her rucksack, she pulled it out and then went back for her mother's. She considered looking for the other passengers' luggage, as she felt there could be some essentials she might need, but the coach groaned and tilted further and she lost her courage.

She returned to her mother and helped her to her feet. 'Come on, Mum. We've got to get help. Find out how to get to the railway station.'

There was silence all around them, no sign of people, just ruined buildings and a lot of shouting in the distance. Sue had no idea where the railway station could be and there was no one to ask. They would have to find someone. She hoisted one rucksack onto her back and held the other in one hand as she half dragged her mother along the road.

Dark shadows were spreading quickly over the ruins and the road. Sue continued, avoiding with difficulty the rubble which lay everywhere. Then she thought she heard voices and turning a corner she saw a small Burmese tea shop which had escaped damage and its oil lamp beamed a welcome. A couple of men came out and stared at them for a moment before hurrying up the road. There seemed to be no other customers and the Burmese woman proprietor looked at Sue and her mother suspiciously. But Sue had spent her whole life in Burma and when she spoke in fluent Burmese the woman immediately became interested.

'Come. Sit down.' The woman pointed to some tables. Sue sat her mother down on a bench and laid their packs on the floor. 'I will get you some tea.'

'Do you know where the railway station is?'

'It is too dark to go now. Dangerous. A lot of bad persons around after the air raid. I show you in the morning.'

The Burmese woman gave them some tea and then cooked a meal of rice and curry with some *balachan*, the national pickle. Afterwards, she pointed to a corner of the room. 'You can sleep there,' she said, laying down some bamboo matting.

Sue had managed to get her mother to take some food, but she was still suffering from shock. The Burmese woman told Sue where the toilet was and Sue led her mother to the back of the cafe. It was a very primitive outside loo, with a not-too-clean hole in the ground.

Afterwards, she led her mother to the matting beds and took out a blanket from her rucksack, making her mother as comfortable as possible. Mary was sobbing quietly but eventually, completely exhausted, she fell asleep.

The Burmese woman said, 'I will wake you in the morning. Sleep well. Nothing to be afraid of here.' She disappeared into the back of the shop, taking the lamp with her.

Sue lay down beside her mother, wondering if it were safe to sleep. The woman seemed honest and helpful. In the end, Sue was so tired she fell asleep.

Sue awoke with a start. The cafe was filled with daylight. For a moment she could not remember where she was and then the Burmese woman appeared carrying two cups of green tea and some small cakes.

Mary was awake and Sue took her to the toilet. There was a tap where Sue was able to wash her face and help her mother clean up.

Afterwards, the Burmese woman gave them a breakfast of noodles. 'Do you wish to go to the railway station, now?' she asked.

Sue said they would. 'And how much do I owe you?' She was glad she had taken her father's wallet. At least they would have money.

The Burmese woman led them out of the cafe onto the road and gave Sue directions. It seemed they were not far from Central Station. But when they came out of a side road onto the main street opposite the station, they stopped in despair. The whole area was packed with Indian refugees, all pressing into the station precincts.

Sue took her mother by the arm and they leaned against a wall while Sue wondered what to do next. 'We'll never get in the station, Mum, much less on a train.'

'Then what are we to do?' Mary said plaintively. 'If only your father were here.'

Sue looked down the road and saw an army truck parked nearby. The driver seemed to be staring at them. Then he started the engine and drove slowly up to them. A corporal, Sue noticed, probably in his late twenties, with fair hair and full face; he looked stocky behind the wheel. He leaned out of the passenger window.

'Were you hoping to catch a train?'

'That was the intention.'

'Then I think you will have to wait a long time.' He had a voice with an accent.

Sue, not used to English dialects, was not sure where he might be from.

'I'm going to Shwebo,' he said.

Sue waited, but the soldier did not follow up with an offer of a lift. She was not sure what to do. She was desperate to get her mother to Shwebo. But could she trust this young man?

He suddenly grinned. 'Do I look a disreputable type?'

'Oh, no. It's just – well, yes, we could certainly do with a lift.'

'I'm Colin,' he said.

'And we're Sue and Mary.'

'Right. Your mother – I presume – can sit in the front. There are seats at the back.'

He opened the passenger door and Sue helped her mother into the seat. Then she clambered into the canvas-topped back with the rucksacks and sat on a bench seat. There was a canvas flapped opening behind the driver and he peered through it.

'You all right?'

'Yes, thanks. There's lots of room in here –'

'Too risky to offer a lift to the refugees. Before you know where you were you would be swamped.'

He drove off, heading south towards the Ava Bridge. Crossing it, he then turned north along the 50 mile road to Shwebo.

About halfway, Colin pulled up at the side of the road. 'There's some water in the back. And you can stretch your legs for a while.'

Sue and Mary were glad of the water, parched in the hot weather. And Sue was thankful to get down from the back.

'Were you caught in the air raid yesterday?' Colin asked.

'We were in a coach. Everyone was killed except for us. My father was among those killed.'

'I'm really sorry to hear that,' Colin said, realising now why Mary was so void.

'And you?' Sue asked.

'I came up from Shwebo with the major and the captain for a meeting. I was parked outside the building when the Japs attacked. The whole place took a direct hit and was practically demolished. I tried to clear the rubble with some others, but it was an impossible task and no doubt they had all been killed, anyway. I spent the night in the truck, waiting for the morning. And then I saw you.'

They got back into the truck and headed for Shwebo. 'I'll take you to my HQ, first,' Colin said. 'And find out what arrangements there are for refugees.'

When they arrived in Shwebo it was to find it packed with refugees, army personnel and some 2,000 or so wounded soldiers waiting to be evacuated. At his HQ, Colin left them in the truck while he went to report and make enquiries.

On his return he told them, 'It seems as if all the British refugees and their servants and various government officials were dispatched to the Chindwin, to be taken by steamer to Kalewa. My colonel suggested you should go to the temporary hospitals, which are bound to be understaffed and would welcome helpers. And you could be taken on the strength, so to speak. Before that, come into HQ for a wash and a meal. Then I'll take you over.'

About an hour later, after a refreshing wash and a good lunch, Colin drove them to the hospital.

'I'll introduce you to the Sister in charge,' Colin said as they walked up to the entrance.

But a voice called from the veranda above, 'Hello, Sue. What are you doing here?'

'It's Sister Dexter,' Sue said with delight.

'Oh, you know each other,' Colin said, surprised.

'Come on up,' Sister Dexter said. 'Yes, Sue was a great help to me in Maymyo. Have you come to help me here as well?'

'I hope so,' Sue said.

'Well, I'll push off, then,' Colin said.

'Oh, Colin! I can't thank you enough,' Sue cried, giving him a big hug and a kiss.

Colin looked a bit embarrassed. 'I'll see you around.'

'He just about saved our lives,' Sue said. 'Oh, I never asked him his surname!' But Colin had already driven off.

'We'll catch him later. Now, is this your mother?'

'My husband was killed,' Mary said.

Sister Dexter glanced at Sue and then put an arm around Mary. 'Come along, my dear, and we'll get you settled.'

Sue followed, carrying their packs as Sister Dexter took them to a large room with several beds and mattresses on the floor.

'It's all a bit chaotic at the moment,' she said. 'The army is planning to move out of Burma and we have to take the wounded with us. A few thousand. But General Alex is determined to leave no one behind. So you see how every helping hand is doubly welcome.'

Over the next few days, Sue worked overtime assisting the wounded, the hard work helping to keep her mind off the tragedy at Mandalay. And then they heard that the Ava Bridge had been blown and the Burma Army had made its escape over the Irrawaddy.

Sue realised how fortunate she and her mother had been to get across in time. And yet she was sad about her father and Jack and Celia. Poor Celia, perhaps they should have left her in Maymyo.

And then she was overwhelmed with work, getting the wounded ready for their departure, until eventually the hospital was cleared. Transport was also provided for the hospital staff and Sister Dexter had arranged for Sue and Mary to travel in a bus with some of the Indian helpers and their families. The bus might look as though it could do with a coat of paint, Sue thought, but I have a feeling it could be more comfortable than travelling in the back of a lorry.

She settled her mother into the front passenger seat and then took her place at the back. As the bus moved off to join the long convoy of oddly assorted vehicles, she wondered where she would end up this time.

Chapter Sixteen
Racing the Monsoon

After crossing the Irrawaddy, 48 Brigade took up position in the village of Myinmu on the banks of the river and by the railway track. As Paul's company moved into its allotted positions, he could not help but notice that his numbers were down again. At Kyaukse, he had lost two killed and two wounded, who were now on their way to hospital in Shwebo.

When the battalion was in position, Osborne called the British and Gurkha officers together to explain the situation and future plans.

'As you must be aware, the decision has been made to withdraw to India. Well, we have come a long way, almost a thousand miles, and now it seems we are on the last lap which, I am sure, will not be an easy one.'

He studied his officers. The British officers looked … was scruffy the right word? No, they had tried to keep up appearances as best they could. They had tried to shave regularly. Their uniforms, the holes in their stockings, had been diligently patched up by dedicated orderlies. The boots were beginning to take on odd shapes, though, and he did not suppose he looked very different. Of course, not only their attire had been ravaged by climate and rough treatment, but their faces bore the marks of the horrendous experiences of the past few weeks.

Robin, with that inner belief in himself, did not look much changed except, the colonel thought, he detected a slight tick in the cheek. Paul was the youngest and he still bore himself well, although there was sadness in his eyes which Osborne put down to the many losses in his company. Paul would have felt each one very personally. Hunter … well, Jack was Jack – and he was still the same, still appearing to lack confidence in himself, which was strange after he had shown at Kokkogwa what he was capable of achieving. He just did not seem to believe that he could do it again.

And Arthur, Arthur Kennedy. He was really worried about Arthur, for they went back a long way. Arthur had handled his company well and he still showed no lack of courage, but he had lost a great deal of weight and his face was almost yellow. Doc Forster had told Osborne that he was certain Kennedy had picked up a virus for which he had no medicine. Robin had suggested he should take over the company, but Osborne considered Robin too important as his right-hand man. And Kennedy had begged the colonel not to send him north to hospital, so he was keeping going on aspirin and was still able to handle his company.

The Gurkha officers, as he expected, somehow managed to keep up appearances. How they did it he never knew. They would emerge from a close-quarter jungle clash looking as battered as anyone else. Yet, in a short while, there they were, marks of war obliterated, even their Gurkha *topis* still stood upright on their heads. His own, he knew, was almost a battered relic in spite of the efforts of his orderly.

He continued with his talk, more for the benefit of the Gurkha officers, who would not be as fully aware of what lay ahead.

'As you know, our gateway out of Burma into Assam and India is at Shwegyin, on the east bank of the Chindwin. To get there we follow the road from Ye-u, but I must warn you, it is a very rough road and not one in regular use. It ends at Shwegyin and the only way beyond is by steamer some 6 miles upriver to Kalewa on the west bank, where the army disembarks. Then there will be a long trek, through the malaria-infested Kabaw Valley and dense jungle, to reach Tamu and the all-weather road which is being built from Imphal.'

He paused for a moment, 'In a way, it is going to be a second Sittang, as we have to reach the river and get across well ahead of the Japanese. But this time we have a second enemy: we also have to race the monsoon to the river. The rains are due to start on 20 May – forecasters seem quite certain of the date! – so it really is going to be a race against time. And one we must win. You can imagine the chaos if we are caught in torrential rain and miles of glutinous mud, falling easy prey to the enemy; although, of course, even the Japanese would be badly hindered by the weather. So, all in all, it is going to be a really tough journey. But I expect the battalion will come through as usual.'

On the evening of 28 April, Lieut. General Slim left his headquarters in a monastery at Sagaing to make a quick tour of the river line. He realised only too well that the Burma Army must move quickly on the next and final stage of its retreat if they were to survive. With the Japanese pushing rapidly north and east of the Irrawaddy, and the Chinese Army in the state it was, he could not maintain his position west of Mandalay for long.

In any case, he must start before the monsoon. Regardless of the weather, the route would obviously need drastic and urgent improvements.

He ordered a reconnaissance party, with engineers, to take a column consisting of one of each type of large vehicle, tank, anti-aircraft gun and lorrry, over the route to check its feasibility. Meanwhile, Burma Army HQ was also working as hard as possible to improve the track and to stock it with supplies and water.

The Japanese having failed in their attempt to trap their Allied Armies in the loop of the Irrawaddy, General Iida now ordered his four divisions to strike at the rear of the Allies and cut their lines of retreat, destroying them in one block. The *56 Division* was to capture Lashio and advance to the Salween, *18 Division* was to move to Lashio and *55 Division* was to clear the Mandalay area, while *33 Division* was to move on Monywa and Shwebo.

The nemesis of 17 Division, General Sakurai of *33 Division*, was once again seeking a way to destroy the British. He knew the escape route was to the north via Shwegyin and Kalewa and it was imperative that he get there before Burcorps. From Monywa, on the Chindwin, he would have a clear run up the river right into the heart of the British escape exit at Kalewa.

Slim and Alexander were also aware that they had to get to Shwegyin first. That was the obvious centre of attack, but Slim was also concerned that the Japanese, as was their fashion, might well try a hook on the left up the Myittha Valley and reach Kalewa from that direction. He decided to send 2 Burma Brigade to block the punch.

It was also important to hold Monywa, on the east bank of the Chindwin, so as to block any attempt by the Japanese to use the river road. But by dispatching 2 Burma Brigade from Pakokku, the way had been left open to Monywa. The remainder of 1 Burma Division was to fill the gap, but having crossed via the Sameikkon ferry on 28 April, the exhausted state of the men had delayed its advance for twenty-four hours, not continuing the withdrawal to Monywa until late on the thirtieth.

General Sakurai left Yenangyaung on the twenty-sixth, heading for Pakokku and Monywa. His *215 Regiment*, coming up the west bank of the Chindwin by motor transport, reached Pakokku on the evening of the twenty-eighth. The regimental commander was surprised to find it unoccupied. Suspecting that Monywa might also be an easy target, he continued with an advance guard until reaching a point opposite the town at dusk on the thirtieth. A battalion of *214 Regiment*, and an engineer battalion, were moving up the Chindwin in landing craft with the intention of helping *215 Regiment* to cross the river. But, carried away in his enthusiasm, the regimental commander did not wait. Instead he attacked Monywa that night from across the river with artillery, mortar and machine-gun fire.

On 30 April, 17 Division was still in position along the riverbank, but Slim had moved his HQ back through Monywa and was now established some miles north of the town in a grove of trees around a small Buddhist monastery.

He was at his headquarters, having dinner under some trees, when a couple of officers suddenly appeared out of the gloom and reported that the Japanese had taken Monywa.

Now, Slim and his staff could hear the distinctive crunch of Japanese mortars in the distance. They immediately sprang into action. Scott was ordered to concentrate 1 and 13 Brigades at Changu, 15 miles south of Monywa, while 63 Brigade was sent by train to join them there and 48 Brigade was ordered to send one battalion at once and follow as quickly as possible with the reminder. Meanwhile, Slim moved his HQ to Ye-u.

Knowing that Shwegyin was now in real danger, Slim packed 16 Brigade into lorries and sent them with all speed up the road to protect this exit point. The brigade placed a battalion in Shwegyin, one in Kalemyo and two in Kalewa, ready in case the Japanese made a quick advance upriver.

Meanwhile, counter-attacks failed to restore the situation in Monywa, so the force was withdrawn to Alon and then moved with all transport available through Budalin to Ye-u, to join the general exodus. The refugees waiting at Alon were sent quickly upriver to safety. Now, Alexander gave the order for the withdrawal to start.

The road was, in reality, just a cart track with no bridges and frequent steep gradients and narrow cuttings. There were many *chaungs*; obstacle courses through sand, where many of the private cars making their escape had got stuck, including the governor's black Rolls-Royce which he had abandoned. Long stretches were completely without water and it was the hottest time of the year. For 140 miles, it led from Ye-u to Kaduma, and then to Pyingaing and finally to Shwegyin on the east bank of the Chindwin. The sappers tried to improve the track by laying corduroy racks across the soft sand, where watercourses crossed the track, and improved the traffic-control system.

To maintain Burcorps during the withdrawal, thirty days' supplies were available for 6,500 British, 2,200 Gurkhas and Indians, 4,000 Burmese and 1,600 animals. Stocks of ammunition were considered adequate. The fuel situation had to be watched carefully. The sole remaining stocks were 25,000 gallons of MT and 1,000 gallons of 87/90 octane fuel at Shwebo, and 20,000 gallons of 87/90 octane with 65 Company RASC and B Echelon 7 Armoured Brigade. Bullock-carts, mules and ponies were purchased locally. Although the forces were placed on half rations from 4 May, there was never any real shortage of supplies and stocks of petrol were sufficient for all the remaining vehicles to get to Shwegyin.

For the wounded it was a nightmare journey: with a shortage of ambulances, they were packed into lorries and a few civilian buses, ill-sprung vehicles, and the jolting of the vehicles added greatly to their suffering. With no more evacuation by air possible, there were some 2,300 wounded to transport and many did not survive the journey. They had to stay in their vehicles for the whole passage, because they could not be taken off except for the crossing of the river. It was an agonising time, trapped in the searing heat, and, because hastily applied dressings could not be changed except in an emergency, a stench pervaded the vehicles.

At the last moment it was discovered that a number of wounded had been overlooked and they were got out just in time. There were also thousands of refugees, mainly Indians, riddled with disease and half starving, who had come a long way, losing many members of their families. Alexander was determined to rescue all casualties. The refugees were fed by the army and given lifts where possible, but most had to walk.

That the vast majority of wounded and refugees reached Shwegyin safely was owing to superhuman efforts by the line of communication staff, led by Major General Eric Goddard and the LOC commander, Major General A. V. T. Wakeley, who provided staging camps at intervals along the track, with dumps of food, medical posts and evacuation points for the sick, both military and civilian, and additional water points.

Paul's truck seemed to jump from one rut to another, sinking into hole after hole as it was driven as fast as possible along the track which was supposed to be a road. He found himself leaving his seat after every jolt and he hoped he would not hit his head on the cab roof. He felt concerned about his men in the back, but they were so jammed together that they probably cushioned each other against the violent motion. The heat was suffocating and it enveloped the truck like a furnace.

Ahead rumbled and swayed a variety of transport of all shapes and sizes, many of which had seen happier days. Alexander had tried to find room for refugees in the transport, but with so many thousands of them, many hundreds were trudging along the side of the road.

At first the countryside was bare, apart from a dotting of trees, and the road was cut by cracks in the surface; there were also dry *chaungs* with no bridges. But, gradually, the trees grew thicker until, at Kaduma, the track plunged suddenly into dense jungle, which kept out the sun, but not the heat, trapped in the narrow corridor between the trees, stretching for some 100 miles into the distance.

Rushing to get into position on the outskirts of Shwegyin was 48 Brigade. Although a great number of the wounded and the refugees had set out earlier, there were still enough of their vehicles to get snared between the army vehicles, and the great cracks in the road surface held up progress.

There seemed to be a longer delay than usual. Then, coming round a bend, Paul saw a bus jammed into the side of the road and people were running in panic, women clutching their babies and children screaming. He jumped down from the cab as his driver brought the vehicle to a halt and rushed over to the bus. A refugee ran past, shouting, 'Dacoits! Dacoits!'

He noticed a path crushed out through the bank and he followed it into a glade. A crowd of refugees was huddled together in one corner, while several Indians, obviously deserters still in their uniforms, were sorting roughly though the meagre belongings. On the other side, to his horror, he saw another group had stripped some young Indian girls and were already beginning to rape them.

But to his immediate front was a white woman, with long blonde hair and ripped clothes, lying in a heap and looming over her was a large Indian soldier unbuttoning his trousers, reaching for his penis.

The man looked up. 'Get away, soldier boy,' he snarled, moving towards the tommy gun he had laid to the side of him.

Paul was aware of the woman stretched out on the ground but did not hesitate. Switching to single shot, he lifted the gun to his shoulder and fired; three aimed .45 bullets pumped into the rapist's stomach, splitting open his belly, blood and matter seeping into the black pubic hair, lifting him off his feet to sprawl on the ground.

Paul's Gurkhas were now flooding into the glade and the Indian deserters were preparing to flee, one or two hurriedly discarding their trousers for quicker flight. They were caught and quickly dispatched by khukuris. A few shots whistled overhead from the far trees. The Gurkhas opened fire, killing some of the men, the rest disappearing into the jungle. Gurkhas were gathering the discarded clothing of the two Indian girls and were quickly covering them up, trying to comfort them.

Paul moved over to the English girl and then staggered back suddenly in horror and disbelief. He was pushed to one side and there was the dependable Gopiram with a blanket to cover the girl and help her up, while in Gurkha style he diligently applied the blanket.

'It is your memsahib,' Gopiram said.

'Sue,' he muttered. Then louder, 'Oh, Sue, darling. What have they done to you?'

She was helped to her feet, her hair hanging like strings, her face bearing a vivid bruise and dirt running down her cheeks.

'Oh my God! Paul!' She tried to pull the blanket more securely around her body.

Then Gopiram was there again, holding a shirt in his hand, one he had obviously treasured to keep for Paul at some later date. Another Gurkha produced a pair of shorts. The shirt was much too large, but the shorts seemed to be a good fit. Gopiram produced a length of string and Sue was able to use this as a belt. Paul wanted to take her into his arms, but the men were watching. Oh, to hell with them!

Her mind was in a whirl. What was Paul doing here? She could see the dead Indian on the ground, blood and matter everywhere. She wanted to vomit, but Paul was holding her tightly. Something was wrong, Sue knew. What was it? She began to push him away, looking around in alarm.

'My God! My mother!' She saw the crowd of refugees clustered at the side of the glade. 'There,' she cried. 'There.'

She hurried over with Paul and knelt down before a woman sitting bewildered among the scattered belongings.

Was that Mary Whitcomb? Paul wondered in surprise. He could hardly believe what he saw. She looked quite old and thin and her hair had turned quite grey. What must she have been through? And where was Sue's father? He helped raise Mary to her feet.

'Oh, it's that handsome young Gurkha officer, Paul,' she said, her voice husky and barely audible. 'Oh dear, we are in a mess. What strange clothes you are wearing, dear.'

Her mother's confusion brought Sue to her senses. She had to pull herself together. Her body still trembled, but she had to hold out. 'It's all right, Mummy. The Gurkhas are here.'

Paul's men were quickly gathering the other refugees together and helping them sort out what remained of their belongings. Mary's pack was untouched, but there was no sign of Sue's few belongings. Paul and

Gopiram helped Sue and her mother down the path and onto the road, the rest of the refugees following.

'This is the driver,' Tilbir said. 'He is not hurt and should be able to drive the bus. We will get it back onto the road.'

In a moment, a gang of Gurkhas heaved and pushed the bus back onto the road. The driver climbed into the cab and to everyone's relief, he managed to start the engine.

Paul could see Osborne standing by his jeep with Robin, looking over but not saying anything. What was he to do? Could he leave his men and go with Sue? But Tilbir had realised the situation.

'Sahib, we will send Tun Hla with the memsahibs.'

'Yes, thakin. I look after them well.'

Paul was surprised at the change in the Burmese boy. He had grown up quickly among the Gurkhas and he looked very capable in the uniform they had given him.

'You will have to wear Burmese clothes. We do not want you being shot as a deserter.'

'I have my *longyi* in my pack, thakin. Do not worry. I look after them much. I defend them with my life.'

Paul hid a smile. 'Yes, I am sure you will.'

The bus was loaded and the Gurkhas helped Mary into the passenger seat by the driver.

Holding Sue by the arm, Paul said, 'I wish I could go with you.'

'No, Paul. We'll be all right. We are almost at the river. No real harm has come to me. And I am sure your Burmese lad will take care of us. He reminds me of our boy at Moulmein.'

'Just a moment.' Paul took out his field notebook and quickly wrote: *To whom it may concern – my fiancée Sue Whitcomb is travelling with her mother Mary Whitcomb. I should be most grateful for any help you could give her. Paul Cooper, Capt. 4/15 Gurkha Rifles.* He handed the note over to Sue and helped her into the bus. The other passengers had returned to their seats.

'Sahib.'

Paul looked around in surprise as one of his men pressed past him to hand Sue a well-filled haversack through the window. At the last moment Paul unbuckled his Smith & Wesson and passed it to Tun Hla and then the bus pulled out, Sue waving as did the passengers, thankful at their lucky escape. He watched the bus drive up the road, hidden in a moment by clouds of dust, before returning to his truck. The men had already climbed into the back.

Osborne had still said nothing. He knew he could not give Paul permission to go with Sue and he hoped he would not have to stop him forcibly. He felt he had enough confidence in Paul to be spared that order. And then, in their usual way, the Gurkhas had taken the matter out of his hands. Now, he climbed back into his jeep and drove off down the road. Paul followed and shortly afterwards, overtook the bus and passed it. The brigade was in a hurry to get to the river.

As the lorry passed the bus, Paul realised that he had not asked about Sue's father and she had said nothing. A tragedy must have happened, as with so many refugees, somewhere along the way. He could find out later, no doubt, and also learn what they had been through.

Lieut. General "Bill" Slim drove down the approach road into the Shwegyin Basin, an area of flat ground some 1,000 yards wide, surrounded on three sides by a precipitous limestone escarpment rising some 200 feet, its sides covered by jungle and thick scrub. From the top, Slim reckoned there would be a clear view into the Basin, making it a death trap.

The Basin was a veritable bottleneck; apart from a journey upriver by steamer, the only other way out was by a rough footpath, leading from the entrance, across steep hills, to the river opposite Kalewa.

Driving down to the bay, he had to negotiate his way past soldiers, tanks and army vehicles waiting for their turn on the steamers. There were also hundreds of derelict cars, abandoned by refugees regardless of obstruction, and the thousands of refugees trying to get a passage on the steamers. Among the cars lay sick and dying refugees and parentless children. How many would find room on the steamers was going to be a lottery.

At first there were six steamers available, each able to cram some 500 or 600 passengers, but only one lorry, two or three guns and a couple of jeeps. There was a single rickety, improvised pier which was submerged by a sudden rise in the river in the middle of the evacuation and it had to be rebuilt. There was no direct crossing; the steamers had to go 6 miles upstream to Kalewa on the west bank, unload and return – a round trip of several hours.

Loading was particularly hard and a stalwart team of corps "Q" staff, sappers, marines, spare officers, indeed anybody available, worked with hardly a break. Every gun had to be manhandled onto the deck, where stanchions and fittings seemed to go out of their way to thwart stowage. To manoeuvre lorries and tanks required great patience, as a slight mistake and a vehicle could block the gangway causing hours of delay. Slim decided that only four-wheel-drive vehicles would be taken aboard.

Embarking men was easy, as they had only their weapons to carry; but the men also had to cut or collect wood and as they came aboard, each man threw a log onto a pile for the engine.

Slim got out of his jeep and looked around to work out the defence of the Basin. All about him were Indian refugees, crowded around the derelict vehicles, with children and babies crying. Alexander had said he wanted to get the refugees to safety, but it was going to be difficult to fit them all in together with the troops, even though the army's numbers had been drastically reduced. His attention was caught by a blonde head and to make sure he looked twice at the young woman crouched over another, who was obviously not too well and seemed to be helped by a Burmese lad. He hesitated. He did not really wish to get involved with refugees; he had enough on his plate.

'Do you need help?' he asked tentatively.

Sue looked up and then got to her feet, brushing aside her hair. 'I'm trying to get my mother onto a steamer,' she said. 'It's proving difficult.'

'How did you get this far?'

'We managed to find a place on a bus out of Shwebo to Ye-u and on to here.'

She wondered if she should show him Paul's note. Then she handed it to him. He read it and looked at her for a moment.

'Do you know where he is?' Slim asked.

'With his battalion, down the road; 48 Brigade, I think.' She told him briefly how she had got the note.

He looked around and saw a fatigue party nearby and summoned the officer over, who saluted smartly, wondering what the general might want. 'Yes, sir?'

'Do you think you could get this young lady and her mother – and her bodyguard – onto a steamer?'

'Of course, sir.' He saluted and then helped Sue with her mother.

Slim watched them thread their way through the crowds. Well, he thought, smiling, sometimes being a general can be an advantage.

But now he had to turn his attention to the defence of the Basin, which would not be easy, surrounded as it was by dense jungle running right to the top of the escarpment. He sent a Gurkha commando detachment downriver to watch the most likely approach upstream by the Japanese, had a floating boom built bank to bank about 2 miles south of Shwegyin to stop Japanese naval craft and positioned a battalion and a small marine flotilla to cover both sides of the river at the boom. Along the escarpment, two companies of the 1/9th Royal

Jats battalion were in position, with some detachments. Units were weak, the defence thin, but nearly always there would be troops waiting to embark who could be used as reserve. He would have to rely on the outlying defence screen for an early warning. He was concerned about the danger from air attacks, especially with the tight concentration of people and vehicles in the Basin, and he centralised all the AA guns, few though they were in number.

On 7 May, the Japanese made their first air attack, and again on the ninth. But the casualties were not as heavy as might have been expected in the narrow space; as experienced troops, the men had already dug slit trenches for protection. A good many vehicles, however, were destroyed or damaged. The boom was broken twice, but was repaired during the night.

No steamers were lost, but the Indian civilian crews refused to continue to bring their ships downstream of Kalewa. A guard of soldiers was formed to force them to work, but it was impossible to prevent the Lascars from slipping overboard. Only through the courage of the British ships' officers and a few loyal Indian subordinates did any steamers get to the Shwegyin jetty. But both the number of ships and rate of turnaround decreased alarmingly.

The various units began to arrive for embarkation. On the night of 8/9 May, 1 Burma Division and 13 Brigade were shipped out. Then 2nd Royal Tanks of 7 Armoured Brigade arrived and 63 Brigade and they were moved out that same night, but minus the tanks.

The HQ of 17 Division and the rearguard of 48 Brigade were stopped by Major General Cowan some 2 miles down the track from Shwegyin to avoid congestion. And on the ninth, Cowan very wisely sent 7th Gurkhas to reinforce the troops holding the escarpment. The Gurkha battalion was a slim version of its full strength, like all the other formations which had lost heavily in the long retreat north. Osborne approached Cameron and suggested that his battalion, or maybe part of it, might as well go as backup. They were only sitting on their hands.

'Take the battalion,' Cameron said without hesitation.

They moved out after dark, marching into the Basin, 7th Gurkhas leading. Even in the darkness Paul could make out the shambles within the horseshoe. Masses of wrecked vehicles, jagged shapes in the night light. The men had to be careful where they were walking. There were also several dead bodies – some poor refugees who had found death the only relief. He felt a wild urge to look for Sue. Could she still be here or … no, she must have found a place on a steamer.

He almost went stumbling into the dark, but remembered all too well his responsibilities.

There were already several trenches, but the Gurkhas dug some more before settling down for the night. Lying back on his arms, Paul could see the top of the escarpment against the night sky and the dark patches of jungle spread across the Basin wall. The Jat battalion was up there – the first line of defence if the Japanese attacked. Maybe they would be too late and everyone would have got away. But there was not much chance of that; although the majority of the troops had been embarked, the 25-pounders and most of the administration staff and a few miserable refugees still remained.

So long as Sue had got away, he thought. She must have found a berth on one of the steamers and by now be safe in Kalewa. But it would be a tough journey up the dangerous Kabaw Valley to Tamu. Even with Tun Hla to help, there was her mother who would be a great handicap and the monsoon due anytime now, to consider.

Gopiram had tried to make him a comfortable bed of leaves, covered by a groundsheet, near an expensive-looking car, but he still felt uncomfortable and the nearness of the river brought a chill wind around his shoulders. The sharp cries of the waterbirds and the rustle of animals going down to drink sounded clearly. He really should try to get some sleep. Around him his men already seemed sound asleep, apart from bursts of coughs, and snores and grunts and, as usual, someone talking in his sleep.

Every time he closed his eyes, Sue came into view and into his mind. At least he had met her again, even if in horrendous circumstances, no longer just daydreams in the jungle. She was dishevelled and there had been terror in her eyes, but he admired the way she had pulled herself together when handling her mother. But, now alone, the attempted rape would surely be lying in her mind, in her dreams. Tun Hla was a capable young lad and she could speak his language, but he was inexperienced and could hardly help her.

If only he could be near her now. To comfort her. My God! how he loved her. She was everything he had imagined in Moulmein. And he wanted her. But after the attempted rape would she be brittle? She would need careful handling and he was far from experienced. He had learned how to kill, but what did he know about sex? He sighed. Just the once. Would that be enough?

It had been poor Tony Davidson's fault, that one occasion. After they had heard the news about Burma, he had come to him saying, 'You've got to come with me, Paul. We'll go tonight. I don't want you dying a virgin; so many young men – really just boys – killed before they have had time to taste the pleasure of love.'

They had crossed the racecourse and found a taxi to take them into Poona Cantonment.

'This is not one of your ordinary Indian brothels. It's a high-class establishment. Very high class and,' he added with a chuckle, 'very expensive.'

Paul could still visualise the villa and the smartly uniformed doorman, who greeted Tony as a regular customer with a big salute and wide smile. Inside the house in the smart reception room they were met by Rita, the proprietress, an attractive Indian woman in a beautiful and expensive sari.

'Good evening, Tony Sahib. Always glad to see you, especially as this could be the last time for a while.'

'How on earth did you know that?'

She laughed, 'Oh, there are no secrets in India. But I see you have brought a guest.'

'This is my dear friend Paul who, I am ashamed to say, is still a virgin.'

Rita made a face. 'Oh, we cannot have that.' She looked Paul over and he had the distinct impression that she was stripping him naked to discover his capabilities. 'Now, what can we do about it? I think Jasmine is the answer.'

Yes, Jasmine. She was certainly attractive … and young – probably very young, he guessed. She had jet black hair with large black eyes to match, a narrow face and voluptuous red lips. She was wearing a silky slip, he well remembered, which revealed the lines of her slim, supple body and small breasts.

She had appraised him for a moment and then said in English, 'You have rubber?'

Tony had slipped him a packet earlier. Removing her slip, she tossed it over a chair as she moved with a natural, graceful agility to the bed.

'Come,' she beckoned, sitting with her knees up.

Paul undressed quickly and when he reached the bed she suddenly opened her legs to receive him which caught his breath. After that it was a bit of a haze; he remembered lying between her legs and it was a rousing experience. But to her it was obviously just a job and there was no feeling of romance. And had he really learned anything? It had all seemed so quick.

He was distracted as a light flashed suddenly up on the escarpment, a match being struck, and then for a moment he saw the red glow of a cigarette end which was quickly extinguished; by the smoker's hand or the furious intervention of his section commander at this rash move. It made Paul feel the urge for a cigarette, but he had to uphold discipline and Japanese snipers had a habit of creeping their way into forward positions.

A cigarette would have helped him to relax. He couldn't go on thinking of Sue and forming pictures of Jasmine. He must get some sleep. Perhaps if he walked around for a bit. He moved carefully between the sleeping men and found his way down to the river. Below him was a small sandbank; on the far side there seemed to be fields and further on, the hill ranges were in dark shadow.

He turned to go back, but stopped abruptly as he heard movement to his left. He dropped a hand to his side, but the Smith & Wesson was not there. For a moment he felt alarmed as he realised he was not armed and then the figure came closer and he recognised Major Arthur Kennedy, the battalion second in command and temporary A Company commander.

'Hello, Paul. Couldn't you sleep, either?' Kennedy asked.

'Hello, sir. No. I thought a little walk might help.'

With his eyes accustomed to the darkness and some light in the sky, Paul was able to see Kennedy reasonably clearly. He thought the major looked thin and stooped. Kennedy was a senior major, much older than Paul, so there had not been much personal contact between them. And, of course, there had not been much contact over the last few weeks as there was no communal officers' mess, and so they only saw each other at order groups, where they spoke little. Kennedy was inclined to be sparse with his words.

'But you sleep all right normally, I presume,' Kennedy asked.

'No trouble, sir.'

'I wish I could say the same. But this bug is slowly killing me.'

'We'll soon be in Imphal, sir. Should be able to get you right at the hospital.'

Kennedy turned towards the river. 'I love rivers,' he said to Paul's surprise. 'So peaceful, so soothing. A distinct atmosphere as you approach it. I'm sure you noticed … a different sound, an invitation almost to stand on its banks and take in all its beauty and friendliness. And all the wildlife it encourages.'

This was a Kennedy Paul did not know. How much of it was really him or was it the virus attacking his body and mind?

'What about the Sittang, sir?' Paul could not help asking.

'Ah, yes. But you must realise that a river is a living creature, with moods and problems like ours. The blowing up of the bridge presented a problem it could do nothing about. It couldn't shrink suddenly in size or reduce its current, to protect the soldiers in the water. Further upstream, the Sittang is a lovely, meandering river.'

Kennedy moved to the bank and slithered down a rough track onto the sandbank. Paul thought he had better follow him, his feet sinking into the sand.

Kennedy stood near the edge of the sandbank, the water lapping gently against it, trickling into the sand. Further out, towards the far side of the river, the water sped past in a fast current, rippling with little waves tinged with white. It was cooler by the water and Paul had to admit, there was certainly a peaceful feeling. But he was beginning to feel tired and he wondered how he could get away. He certainly did not want to stay on the sandbank all night, which it seemed Kennedy might do. But was it safe to leave him? Well, he was running his company efficiently. Just because he had ideas about rivers did not mean that he could not look after himself.

There was a sudden movement on the bank above and three Gurkhas came down onto the sandbank. Paul recognised Ramesh Thapa, Kennedy's company subedar, a senior Gurkha officer of long service. He was obviously worried at the absence of his company commander, wandering about in the night, unaccompanied.

'Good evening, Captain Sahib,' he said to Paul as he passed him and approached Kennedy.

'It is time for lights out, Major Sahib,' Ramesh said.

Kennedy laughed. 'All right, Ramesh. I'll come quietly.' He climbed up onto the bank followed by the Gurkhas.

The subedar turned to look back at Paul, 'Your orderly is here, sahib.'

'Oh, then I guess it is lights out for me, too,' Paul said.

The subedar smiled. 'It is better so, sahib.'

Paul climbed up onto the bank where Gopiram was waiting. Behind him, the Chindwin River was flowing down to join the great Irrawaddy River. He had to admit that it did look quite peaceful, but what he did not know was that about 8 miles downriver, a Japanese force in boats was preparing to launch an attack on Shwegyin.

General Sakurai, angry and frustrated because he had not been able to cripple the British forces at Monywa, allowing them to get away to Ye-u, believed there was still time to catch up with them at Kalewa.

From Monywa, *8 Company* of *213 Regiment* embarked in forty engineer boats and proceeded up the Chindwin, covering their boats with banana and palm leaves, although there were no British aircraft to spot them.

They landed at night on the east bank at Kywe about 8 miles south of Shwegyin and moved inland along a jungle track, to avoid contacting the guards on the boom. But they bumped into the Gurkha commandos unit who, for some reason, did not send out a warning; it was presumed later that their wireless set must have failed. They also did not attack but started to withdraw and became separated in the dark. Their commander was drowned trying to swim the river.

A second company from the same Japanese regiment came upriver some hours later, landing at the same spot and marching through the jungle behind the first group. Altogether, the attacking group numbered some 700 and included guns, mortars and machine-guns. Their orders were to attack the heights and command the Basin.

Early in the morning of 10 May, Slim boarded his launch and left his HQ at Kalewa to visit Shwegyin and find out how the evacuation was progressing. He reached the jetty at about 05.30 hours just as daylight was beginning to lighten up the Basin. A steamer was alongside, but loading had been interrupted while the sappers repaired the pier which had been damaged by a lorry.

At the same time, in the strengthening light of day, Paul had a clearer view across the Basin and of the wreckage which cluttered it. His mouth felt dry after a fairly restless night, curled up near what must once have been an expensive car, and he hoped that Gopiram was about to make tea and that perhaps there might be some rations available for breakfast.

His thoughts were rudely shattered as mortar shells suddenly exploded all around the Basin and machine-gun bullets criss-crossed overhead, spitting sparks off the wrecked vehicles, ricocheting in all directions. Everyone dived for whatever cover was available.

Slim had just disembarked onto the jetty when red tracer bullets snapped overhead as *8 Company* of *213 Regiment* raced through the jungle and attacked 1/9th Royal Jats on the escarpment. Caught in heavy return fire, the Japanese suffered several casualties as they clung to the rocky slopes. On the craggy slope and on the escarpment edge a fierce fight ensued, both sides suffering heavily. The Indians made a valiant effort, but some of the enemy worked their way along the ridge dominating the eastern side of the Basin and captured a prominent knoll. One squad managed to break into the Basin, but was quickly dealt with.

Heavy mortar fire targeted the Basin, but 7th Gurkhas sprang to their feet and rushed towards the cliffs, climbing up in the face of fierce fire, meeting their foe hand-to-hand in the tangle of jungle.

'Go after them,' Osborne ordered, 'and help with the wounded.'

Paul climbed up the rocky face; ahead of him a crescendo of shots, screams and shouts could be heard. He soon came across wounded. Those who could manage to walk were helped down the hillside, while others were carried. There were a lot of dead. The Japanese wounded were ignored; there was certainly no room for them on the steamers.

Amidst the battle, a steamer was alongside the jetty, held there only by the courage of the skipper. The 25-pounders of the Armoured Brigade were being embarked and as the guns were brought down to the water's edge, they were kept firing until the last moment, the shells causing havoc among the Japanese.

Wounded coming down the escarpment were being helped or carried aboard and when the steamer was fully loaded it departed up-river. The likelihood of more steamers arriving was very slight.

Major General "Punch" Cowan had now entered the Basin with the rest of 48 Brigade and Division HQ as he took command of the operation. Slim, therefore, returned to his launch and visited the steamers lying upstream, wondering if he could possibly ask them to once more face the perils of the Basin. In turn, three of the skippers gallantly brought their ships inshore a few yards above the jetty under a cliff, which gave shelter from mortar fire while they embarked wounded and administrative staff for what would prove to be the last trip.

On the cliff tops, where the fierce fight had been going on throughout most of the day, *8 Company* had secured several holds, but it had almost been wiped out. Both sides had been hit heavily.

The second party of *6 Company* now infiltrated and headed for the heights on the left front. One section got to the highest point, and others followed, and after one and a half hours of fierce contest they finally occupied the hill. British tanks fired continuously, cracking the rocks of the hill, and Japanese soldiers lying flat in shallow depressions were hit in their stomachs and killed one by one. Unable to care for their comrades, the survivors just pulled at their legs to drop them over the cliff face down into the Basin.

The Japanese carried a mountain gun to the top of the hill and its first shot hit a tank. But six shells from the Bofors' gun of an Indian light anti-aircraft battery burst about the Japanese gun, turning it over and wiping out the crew.

The 7th Gurkhas, who had already lost a considerable number in killed and wounded, put in another counter-attack at about 14.00 hours and as they raced for the perilous cliffs, their ranks thinned. Osborne sent his men after them as backup, but this time to fight.

As Paul led his men towards the hill face, bullets whipped across, and from the corner of his eye he saw two of his men stagger and roll over. Then he was into the jungle. Out of the dark greenery came a flash of light and he heard the crack of a bullet as it sped past his head. Then he saw the outline of a Japanese soldier and killed him with a burst. He moved forward and up, slipping on loose stones, branches brushing against his arms and face. Around him were shouts, screams and shots, sounding dulled by the jungle. Where was Gopiram? Some men were fighting on either side of him, khukuris flashing, bayonets sliding through. A Gurkha at his side cut down a soldier and then gasped as a bayonet took him in the chest. Paul fired at the Japanese, watching him stumble to the ground. Beside him, the Gurkha was down. Who was he? My God! it looked like Bombahadur Rai! He could now see daylight and he was near the top. Ahead of him, a group of Gurkhas and Japanese were in close combat.

Away to Paul's left, Arthur Kennedy was gasping for breath, every step agony as he forced himself up the cliff with his A Company.

'Are you all right, sahib?' his orderly asked anxiously.

'Yes. Yes. Go on.'

But a man came up on either side and took him up effortlessly. One fell away as he was hit. Then there was jungle and Kennedy found himself alone for a moment.

Above him was a ledge and a machine-gun opened fire, knocking him against a tree. He felt a great pain across his chest, but at the same moment relief. It was all over, no more struggling against the virus, trying to keep up his position. And then came oblivion.

His company tried to take over the hill, but were unable to dislodge the enemy. All along the hill, now, Gurkhas and Jats were recalled, trying to take their wounded with them, not wanting to leave them for the Japanese.

Down in the Basin, Major General Cowan summed up the situation. He considered another counter-attack, but it seemed pointless with no more steamers awaiting. And he realised that the Japanese were being steadily reinforced. If he was going to escape with what he had it would have to be soon. The only way out was via the Kaing track: a precipitous route which skirted the east bank of the Chindwin. But only the minimum amount of equipment could be carried.

At 17.00 hours the guns and mortars began wasting down the remaining ammunition. Jack Hunter found contentment at last, firing his mortars and machine-gun. The Basin echoed with the continuous blast and chatter and up in the escarpment the Japanese dug deeper, suffering more casualties. The layback positions were established by 2/5th Gurkhas to protect the final withdrawal of the covering troops through the northern exit of the Basin, while the 7th Gurkha battalion moved wearily towards the track; it had lost eighty killed and wounded. The two gallant companies of the Royal Jats, greatly reduced, also took to the track. Behind them, in the last glimmer of daylight, the gunners put down a fierce concentration of fire. They fired all the shells they had in twenty minutes and under cover of the heaviest barrage of the campaign, the last troops passed through the rearguard.

Slim took one last look from his launch. The Basin was a firework display of explosions and roaring flames and shrapnel screaming off the wrecked vehicles, sending sparks whirling into the night. It was a sad moment for him, thinking especially of the loss of his tanks, which had been the backbone of the retreat. Still, at least he had saved about a third of the guns and a fair proportion of the four-wheel-drive vehicles. He had seen enough; he gave the order for the launch to move upstream.

The track to Kaing was narrow, curving its way across the hills bordering the river. The weary men, heavily burdened, many carrying those wounded who could not walk, stumbled over the rough surface of the track; even the mules found it hard going. At times, the precipitous sides fell away into the jungle below. In the darkness progress was particularly tricky as obstructions and obstacles were overcome with curses and sometimes pain. Behind them, they could hear explosions from time to time as flames reached un-expended ammunition or a mortar bomb, or perhaps a box of grenades, exploding into the night. The flames soared into the night sky, reaching towards the top of the escarpment.

Paul marched in a part dream, stumbling more than he might have expected, his mind not on the track at all. He was devastated by the sad losses to his company right at the end. So many brave men, good companions through rough, perilous days, giving of their best to the end. Many had been wounded, some being carried along the path, the others had been taken to the steamers and he prayed they had reached the safety of Kalewa. Even then, they faced a long, agonising journey through the Kabaw Valley, the Death Valley as it was fearfully called. But he believed that a number of lorries had been saved, so there would at least be transport for them. There was a good chance that he might see the wounded again, for they might rejoin the company, but the others … such bad luck after what they had been through. So unfair. Bombahadur Rai was gone, and Bharti Gurung and Tikajit Pun, and so many others, and poor Arthur Kennedy, their faces swimming in front of his eyes. He knew he shouldn't grieve so badly, but to hell with it, he would allow himself to do so in the blackness of the night on the trudge along the track. In the morning, he would have to face the future without them, and turn his mind to looking after those who remained. All brave men, too.

With daylight, the track at last descended into Kaing to the river's edge and there they were met by steamers and ferried across to Kalewa.

The Japanese made no attempt to follow up. It had been Burcorps' last encounter with the enemy. In the sky above, a single Japanese aircraft hovered but did not attack.

When the guns had ceased dealing out death and destruction across the ridge, the dazed Japanese waited for another attack. But there was no sign of approaching troops. Scouts sent down into the Basin reported that the enemy had slipped away. There was a track leading out of the Basin, but the Japanese were too exhausted and stunned by their losses to move off the ridge.

In the morning, General Sakurai came to see for himself. There was a great number of dead bodies scattered about the Basin, from both sides, and plenty of vehicles – some with their engines still running. There were also stocks of food piled up in various places. The hungry Japanese soldiers settled down greedily to a feast and suffered the consequences later, when many of them were laid low by diarrhoea.

Sakurai was upset that so many of the enemy had escaped, but they had obviously suffered grievously. And to make up for the disappointment, there was always the great amount of booty. He returned to his launch; behind him, the white mosquito nets left by the British swung in the wind.

Chapter Seventeen
Death Valley

Sue walked down the gangway with some trepidation, wondering what lay ahead. She had got to Kalewa, but she knew her problems were only partly resolved. Ahead lay some 90 miles of jungle track, rough and hilly. And how was she going to get her mother to Tamu? She at least had Tun Hla to help; she could never have managed at all without him. He was now assisting Mary onto the pier and she joined them.

The whole area was packed with refugees, soldiers and vehicles. Somehow, she had to get her mother onto a lorry. She could not see the general, but felt she had already used up her goodwill with him. The note might help if she could find the right person. But how to get through the mob?

Tun Hla had found a stout stick for Mary and with this and his supporting arm, she was able to make reasonable progress.

'We have to pick up the track north through the Kabaw Valley, ma,' he said to Sue in Burmese. 'I think for just a short distance,' he added.

A motorable track had been bulldozed through to Kalewa from Tamu within the last few days, enabling staging posts between Kalewa and Imphal to be stocked with rations for 36,000 men by 6 May. Some trucks rolled past, quite a few of which would be reserved for the wounded, Slim had decided, and the rest to send some units forward. But most of the soldiers would have to march. Later, there could be some change around for the exhausted and the sick. Although, Slim thought, I wonder who is not ready to drop.

Tun Hla said, 'I think, ma, we should try to find somewhere to camp for the night. In the morning, as we walk, we might be seen or we might meet someone who is willing to help get your mother onto a truck. But first we must get some water.'

Watering points had been established by the sappers on the route north and Tun Hla found one close to the pier. But he had to queue and struggle in a thirsty mob for over an hour before he was able to fill his water bottle and an empty whisky bottle he had found.

He returned to the others and they walked along the crowded road. Some refugees had already collapsed by the roadside, their desperate families trying to encourage them to continue. A great number of them would leave their bones in the valley.

Mary was making a great effort, but Sue knew it could not last. They kept going, stumbling along slowly as steadily as possible until they reached the turn-off to the valley track.

Daylight was beginning to fade when Tun Hla led them off the track and found space in a small clearing in the jungle. For the time being the weather was still warm and dry, although Sue, with her long experience, knew that with the arrival of the monsoon it would turn quite cold and treacherous in these jungle hills; and there would be the mosquitoes to contend with.

Tun Hla quickly cut some branches with his khukuri and made a small shelter and a bed of leaves, onto which he helped Mary. Then he opened his pack.

'The men tried to put various things in here,' he said, 'but they did not have much time.' He looked inside. 'There is some tea and powdered milk. I think a small bag of rice. And what is this ... a box of matches, most useful. Already, I have my blanket, groundsheet and mess tin. What have you got, ma?'

Sue opened the bulging haversack she had been handed on the bus and had not as yet examined. 'Oh, the lovely people! They have put in a comb and a small mirror, and a sliver of soap.'

How like a woman, the young Burmese boy thought, interested in toiletries when food is more important.

'What else ... there is a packet of biscuits and a towel, and an army jumper.'

'Hmm. I think I must do foraging. There is ration dump nearby, but whether they give me anything I do not know. I try. You be safe here for a while.'

'Of course.'

But Tun Hla, still thinking of the attempted rape, reached into his pack and took out Paul's Smith & Wesson revolver. 'You know how to use this, I think?'

'Yes, I do. But where did you get it?'

'It is all right. The Captain Thakin gave it me.'

Sue took the revolver gingerly and broke open the chamber. It was loaded. 'I am sure I shall be safe now. But you be careful. Do not try to steal. The mood of everyone is unpredictable.'

'I will be very careful,' he promised as he slipped away.

As the light began to fade, Sue wished she could light a fire. But brought up with servants she had no idea how to start one. Then it grew darker and she could see fires burst out into flames all around her as the jungle was lit up by the refugees and some of the army personnel, settling in for the night.

Mary was muttering on her bed of leaves. Sue bent over her; she seemed, however, to be asleep. It would be best to leave her like that. Sue stood up again and walked around the little campsite. She thought she had managed to overcome the trauma of the attempted rape, but she knew she had not done so. It was not something she could overcome so easily; only the responsibility of looking after her mother kept her from dwelling on it continuously and the knowledge of being near Paul gave her some more strength.

There seemed to be dark shadows all around and she gripped the revolver. She felt frightened and she wondered if she would even be able to pull the trigger. Was that somebody lurking in the bushes? Suddenly, the whole incident seemed to flash in front of her: being seized by the evil Indian soldier, the strong smell of country liquor, the struggle ending with the fierce blow which sent her spinning onto the ground and the sound of ripping clothes. Then he was standing above her, lowering his trousers, making lewd remarks as he fumbled for his penis. And suddenly he swung round and she heard the loud whacks of bullets driving into his body. She shut her eyes and his screams penetrated right into her head before suddenly cutting off abruptly, followed by the thud of his sprawling body. And when she opened her eyes, Paul was there!

She shivered. Was she never going to forget? What was that? Somebody was out there now!

Tun Hla appeared and she let out a great sigh of relief. He did not remark on it, but said, 'You have not lit fire.'

'I do not know how to,' she admitted reluctantly, thinking he would laugh scornfully.

But he just said, 'Oh, do not worry, I get one started. A nice big one.'

In a short while he had a fire burning merrily. The sight of it made Sue happier and somehow she felt more secure.

'Were you frightened, ma? Perhaps I should not have left you alone.'

'I was just being stupid,' she said quickly.

'Ma it is not stupid to feel frightened after your experience. But you be all right now. It will all turn out right, you will see, and you have the Captain Thakin waiting for you. And, meanwhile, we have your mother to look after.'

She hugged him. 'Oh, Tun Hla, you are wonderful.'

'I know, ma,' he said with a laugh. 'Just look what I have brought for you. They are feeding the refugees, so I was able to get a few things. There are a lot of mouths to feed, but they were being quite generous. I have a good supply of rice, some more tea and powdered milk and some tinned food.' He held the tins out to Sue.

'These two tins are corned beef,' Sue said. 'There is a tin of fish – sardines. Some beans. And this looks … yes, meat and veg.'

'What should we eat tonight? I think we should have the rice.'

'We have no cutlery,' Sue pointed out. 'Have you anything?'

'Only my khukuri. Will you be able to eat with your hands? I will have to try to find some spoons and forks tomorrow.'

'We will be all right with hands,' Sue assured him. 'But it means we'll have to avoid the messy food like sardines. I think the corned beef is the answer with the rice.'

With the fire well set, Tun Hla filled one half of his mess tin with water and brewed tea.

'We have to be careful with the water. In the morning I must try to find another empty bottle or some container.' He produced a couple of mugs from his pack and filled them with tea. 'How is your mother? Is she ready for tea?'

Mary had awoken and she spoke from her bed of leaves. 'Oh, yes, please. I am dying for a cup.'

As she and Sue drank from the mugs, Tun Hla drank the remains of the tea from the mess tin and rinsed it. He then filled both halves of the mess tin with water and cooked the rice.

'Tomorrow, I must try to find a cooking pot and some spoons or forks. People are discarding their belongings quite freely.'

When the rice was cooked, he served some into each mess tin and the remainder onto a large leaf. 'Good as a plate,' he said with a chuckle. He then added portions of bully beef.

Sue handed a mess tin to her mother who had sat up on the bed, the leaves crackling beneath her. 'Can you manage?'

She laughed, 'Oh, with my hands. But I have done that before. And I do feel hungry. I think I can manage.'

She finished the meal which pleased Sue, because her mother had to build up her energy and there seemed to be little signs of a slight recovery.

'Now, you had better get some sleep,' Sue said to her mother.

Tun Hla added some more leaves and smoothed them out as much as possible. He took out his blanket and folding it, he placed it under Mary's head as a pillow. She leaned back and was so exhausted she fell asleep at once.

'I will make you a little bed, now,' Tun Hla told Sue.

He gathered some more leaves and Sue brought out her army jumper to make a pillow. The night had not brought a great drop in the heat.

'Now your mother is asleep I will tell you something else I learned. I understand they will offer lifts to some refugees. Depending on the amount of room available.'

Sue felt a moment of relief and then common sense took over. 'It will be a matter of luck.'

'Oh, ma! You must not give up hope.'

'That is easily said,' Sue rejoined bitterly.

'How easily you forget, ma. Did you not meet the General Sahib? And the Captain Sahib?'

'You are quite right. Tun Hla, how old are you?'

'Not very old in years, perhaps, but I have been through such distress, such adversity, such heartbreak, that I think I am much older.'

'Heartbreak?' Sue wondered.

He hesitated for a moment. 'My whole family was killed by Japanese bombs. Mother, father, little brother –' He paused and looked away.

'Oh, Tun Hla!' She put an arm around his shoulder. 'I never knew.'

'It is all right, ma. It has happened. Nothing I can do. Anyway, now I feel I have a new family. The Gurkhas and the Captain Thakin have made me feel so welcome.'

He straightened up abruptly and trying to keep his voice firmer, said, 'And now I think you should go to sleep – hard day tomorrow.'

'How about you?'

'I will stay awake a bit longer. It is best to find out the lie of the land. How safe it is for us. Perhaps, ma, I should take back the revolver.'

Sue awoke at the first sign of dawn, after a night of mixed dreams, for a moment not quite sure where she was. Then realisation returned and she got up quickly, going over to her mother who was awake.

'How are you this morning?'

'Oh, Sue, I am bursting!'

Sue looked around. There were plenty of bushes and the nearest party of refugees seemed a long way off. She helped her mother to a suitable spot and then took advantage of the occasion herself. Then the two women returned to the campsite.

'I feel so dirty,' Mary complained. 'I wish I could wash.'

'There's no water at the moment, Mummy.' She noticed that Tun Hla had emptied his pack and gone off with it and the water containers. 'I think Tun Hla is getting some more.'

A short while later Tun Hla returned, looking quite jovial, although staggering under the weight of his pack. Tied to it was a saucepan and in his hand was a large kettle. He took from his pack his water bottle and one bottle of water.

'The kettle is also full,' he said.

'Where on earth did you get it?'

'People are discarding things as they go, finding them too heavy.'

'I wish you could find some clothes,' Sue said. 'I think this shirt is going to get off my back and walk it is so filthy. And as for my mother, I am sure there are little crawly things in her linings.'

'We will have to keep our eyes open this morning. Meanwhile, I have this little bowl, a couple of tin plates and ...' he lifted a hand triumphantly, clutching a couple of spoons and forks. He filled the bowl with water. 'You can now have a little wash.'

While Sue and her mother had a wash, Tun Hla lit the fire and put the kettle on. Later, he made tea.

'I do not know what to give you for breakfast. There is rice and some biscuits. Can you eat the fish?'

'Leave the fish for later. I am sure rice and biscuits with tea will be all right,' Sue assured him.

After breakfast, they worked out a plan of action. Many of the refugees were already on the move, leaving behind more bodies and a clutter of discarded belongings. The military seemed to be getting ready to march, having their breakfast first, and some lorries were already moving out.

'It is going to be very hot,' Tun Hla said. 'We should try to cover as much distance as we can before the sun gets really strong.'

They decided to move off at once. Tun Hla shouldered his pack and then helped Mary to her feet and handed her the stick. Sue slung the haversack over her shoulder and carried the kettle in her hand. Soon, they were in the middle of a throng of refugees, mainly Indians, some Burmese.

It was to be a day that Sue would always remember. Growing hotter and hotter all the time, the jungle on either side seemed to reflect the heat and send it everywhere. She was upset at the sight of her mother struggling to cope, having to take many stops to rest. Although, around her, everyone seemed to be struggling: the Indian families persuading grandparents to keep moving, children to find more strength, the sick to rise up from the ground and make an effort to reach the evening camp, combined with cries and weeping. She kept an anxious eye on the few passing vehicles, hoping someone might take pity. But they were just three people in a pathetic crowd of refugees.

Sue was not sure how many miles they had covered, but it could not have been many. Perhaps six or seven at a great struggle, which was by no means enough. Somehow, she would have to get her mother onto a lorry. She was relieved when the sun dipped at last below the far hills and a cool breeze suddenly sprang up.

'This looks a good spot to camp,' Tun Hla said, 'and we had best camp now. It is a few miles to the next water point. Your mother will never reach it today. You can rest here and await my return. Probably be a few hours I should think.'

'Poor Tun Hla. I am sorry.'

He was getting them settled down when he noticed an old tin trunk and some bags lying among the bushes. Some refugees must have made a camp there. He walked over to the trunk and Sue joined him, excited. It was a cheap, battered trunk and was padlocked.

'Soon get that open, ma.'

He found a stone and smashed the lock, and then lifted the lid. Inside was a jumble of clothes and ornaments which looked as if they had been packed in a hurry.

'There is a *longyi*,' Sue said. 'And another.'

She took out the *longyis*. The trunk must have belonged to a woman, because the *longyis* had a wide black cotton band at the waist. Then she rummaged through the rest of the contents, ignoring the jewellery and bangles, which might have been valuable but were of no interest to her.

'Oh, this looks like a blouse … and another. They are Burmese or Indian and probably too small. We shall see. Unfortunately, there are no undergarments. What else? A blanket. This looks like a waterproof sheet, for a child, I suppose.'

'Let me see,' Tun Hla asked, taking the sheet. 'Yes, this could be very useful, I think.'

She slipped on a *longyi* over her shorts. 'That's all right and the other should definitely fit my mother. The blouses I am not so sure about.'

She went behind a bush and removed the dirty shirt. The blouse was close-fitting but not too tight. The trouble was that the style had narrow sleeves which were meant for slimmer arms. Sue knew she had lost weight, but the sleeves would just have to be split open. She would show most of her waist, not that it mattered. She then tried the garments on her mother and they fitted well, she having lost so much weight.

'What do you think, Tun Hla?'

He agreed. 'Now I must go for water,' he said, leaving them the bottle which was still full. He also passed her the revolver. 'Just in case, ma.'

The next morning was 12 May 1942 and it started raining. The monsoon had arrived early, at first just a few drops, tap-dancing on the leaves. The sky had lost its deep blue shade and was a grey colour with patches of black which grew wider all the time, filling up the sky until it was an ominous, threatening mass. Lightning streaked across it, thunder rolling and echoing about the hills. Then the rain grew more forceful and rapid, speeding up the valley, drumming on the leaves and bouncing off the ground, the noise so loud that conversation was barely possible. The hills disappeared behind the clouds and a wall of rain. In a moment, the hard ground began to soften and then turn into liquid, squelchy mud, the track becoming a bog.

Tun Hla, anticipating the early morning rain, had gone deeper into the jungle where the canopy gave them some shelter. He had taken out his groundsheet and stretched it between two trees, tying the ends, before moving their belongings under it, covering them with the waterproof sheet. And the three of them huddled together to sit out the storm. They placed Mary in the middle, arms around her to keep her as warm and dry as possible.

The rain seemed to go on for an eternity, thunder crashing alarmingly overhead. It was quite dark, the sun obliterated, but lightning sizzled as it illuminated the jungle. The rain was blown into the shelter from time to time, but the thick canopy above kept them relatively dry albeit damp.

After a couple of hours or so the rain started to ease off, with the occasional flash of lightning in the distance, followed by a rumble of thunder. The hard rain turned to a drizzle and then to drops, and finally it stopped.

Slim came out in his jeep across the slushy road. The rain had arrived in the nick of time and was all the better for being early. The condition of the track told him emphatically what would have happened if they had lost the race against the monsoon. What was more – it now worked in reverse and would hold back the Japanese if they were planning any further pursuit.

His soldiers might be spared a running fight with the Japanese, but they would be facing another enemy in the weather. The hard track would just be a permanent layer of thick mud, several inches deep, through which his men would have to plunge and slither, most of them with boots worn down to the sole and in clothes which were in tatters. He wished he had more transport; he had managed to save around fifty lorries, but a great number of these would be used to carry the wounded and the very sick. Sometimes, there may be a few to give a detachment a lift forward to earn a short rest. Several days of torment lay ahead, in the rain, attacked by mosquitoes, seldom being dry, passing restless nights and some stricken with fever. But in spite of what they had gone through, there was still a strong spirit running through the whole corps and Slim was confident that they would fight their way through to Imphal, with the same stubbornness and determination that had helped them all the way up Burma without disintegrating into a terrified rabble.

It was the refugees he really felt sorry for as they struggled on, riddled with fever, weighed down by young children and old parents. But there was little he could do to help. At least there was no shortage of food and water.

Tun Hla came out from under the groundsheet with Sue and they walked to the track, where hundreds of other people were also now emerging.

'Do you think your mother will be able to cope with all that mud?'

'Well, we cannot stay here forever. Even if we can cover some ground it would be better, surely.'

'After the first monsoon rain, quite often we get a day or two of quiet,' Tun Hla said optimistically.

'You mean, take a chance and wait until tomorrow?'

'Oh, ma, what to do!'

It was the first time that Tun Hla had shown his anxiety and Sue was not surprised. He had been so strong for a young boy, but it would be left to her to bolster him up this time.

'What to do? What to do? Let us ask Mummy. Oh, Mummy, how do you feel about it? Do you think you are well enough to press on?'

Although Mary was physically weak, she had been showing signs of a return to more normality.

'Please, let me try. I think I could go a short distance at least.'

You're trying to be brave, Sue thought. But regardless, we must make an effort. Yet she knew that unless they could get a lift quite soon, her mother would not survive. Now the monsoon had come this would no longer be a picnic. Malaria and the cold, and trying to keep dry, and struggling to move her poor feet through the thick mud would surely be just too much for her mother.

'Right, Mummy. We will go,' Sue said.

Tun Hla quickly took down the groundsheet and packed up. He then helped Mary to her feet and handed her the stick. They moved out of the jungle and to the track, joining the throng already on the move. They were soon surrounded by the hundreds of refugees stumbling along, many with great difficulty. Sue tried to keep to the hardest and clearest part of the track to avoid the mud, but it was not easy, hemmed in as they were from time to time. Mary struggled valiantly, determined to keep going, Tun Hla holding her firmly.

Then the crowd began to spread out and Sue, looking back, saw a military unit approaching along the track. They were not moving smartly as though on parade, obviously as tired as she was, and they looked scruffy and some had beards.

They kept to the track as the crowd hustled out of the way, some pushed aside, though not too roughly. Tun Hla held Mary firmly as he moved her to one side. Sue was helping when she was brushed aside and she slipped on the muddy surface, ending up sitting in the mud.

She looked up and saw several British faces staring at her as they passed. She thought they were grinning and shouted, 'You bloody shits!' How had she remembered the words? she wondered.

The shout caused the soldiers to pause and the rear section halted for a moment, not believing what they had heard, merely looking down at the woman who had come out with the expletive.

Sergeant Jennings, more from curiosity than anything else, pulled Sue to her feet. To his surprise, he looked into the deep blue eyes of an obviously attractive young woman, if at the moment she was in rather a mess.

'You're not Indian,' he said unnecessarily. He glanced at Mary and Tun Hla.

'My mother and our escort.'

'I am very sorry about the fall and for messing up your clothes. Look, come along with us. We are going to camp in a moment. Let us see what we can do to make amends.'

Tun Hla set up camp a little way from the soldiers, so that Sue and Mary could dry themselves with the single towel and change into their longyis. The day was drawing to a close as Sergeant Jennings walked over. Tun Hla had spread the groundsheet and blanket over the damp leaves for Sue and her mother to sit on and he now produced a log for the sergeant.

'If you send your lad up to my QM he will give him some rations. We are short, but a change in variety might be welcome for you.'

After Tun Hla had moved over to the army camp, Jennings asked, 'How did you ladies get into this situation?'

Sue filled him in with the background and then she showed him Paul's note.

'Well, I do not know how your mother has managed to get this far. You've been lucky with your Burmese boy, but from now on, in the rain, it's going to be hell. I think you must have transport if you are going to reach Tamu. And that, I think, I should be able to arrange. We expect to be picked up tomorrow for a turn in a truck. There should be room for you. It won't be comfortable, but it will be a lot better than trudging through mud. I do not know how far our stint will be and then we will have to march again, but I will try to get you shifted onto another truck.'

Sue hoped she would not break into tears and she wondered afterwards how she had managed not to do so. They talked for a while and Sue asked if he knew anything about Paul and his regiment.

'Well, I know there was a big final battle in the Basin and then 17 Division HQ and 48 Brigade escaped along the Kaing track to Kalewa. I believe they then went upriver to Sittaung, intending to march overland to Tamu.' He hesitated for a moment and then said, 'I can't tell you if your captain was on that steamer but, if he was, you should meet up with him in Tamu or maybe in Imphal.

At Kalewa, after crossing over the river from the end of the Kaing track, Paul had hoped the brigade would take the Kabaw track, giving him a chance to look for Sue. But that very night, 48 Brigade, the Duke of Wellington's and some other units were given orders to board the steamers and sail north to Sittaung, 70 miles up the Chindwin. From there, they would march to Tamu and pick up transport to Imphal.

For Paul it was a blow. As the steamer puffed its way north, he looked back at the blinking lights of Kalewa disappearing into the night and with that, any hope of tracking down Sue.

Dawn found the steamers sailing up the river in convoy and above them a darkening sky flashed lightning, sending out great claps of thunder, before letting loose the first monsoon rain with a vengeance.

The soldiers swore as they tried to find shelter, having hoped for a pleasant river cruise and a chance to rest.

The rain eased off by the afternoon and a dry night was followed by a bright dawn, which saw them steaming up an attractive stretch of the river, with fish popping up with splashes, tree-lined banks and glimpses beyond of fields and distant hills. There was relief at not having to cope with bullets, shells and bayonets, but the sky was a danger and close watch was kept for Japanese aircraft. But none appeared; the rain the day before may have put them off.

Paul was sitting on the upper deck with Osborne and Robin when Tilbir and Dilbahadur appeared, beaming with pleasure, and behind them the stocky figure of Sergeant Somers and the long length of Private Walton of the Duke of Wellington's.

'Morning, sir,' Somers said, saluting. 'Glad to see you are still with us.'

Osborne smiled. 'You, too, Somers and Walton.'

'It has been a great pleasure to meet your battalion again, sir, and talk to good friends among the Johnnies.'

They shook hands and found a place to sit. Osborne said, 'The battalion remembers you both very well.' He could see several Gurkhas peeping up the gangway. 'How have you fared?'

'Not too bad, sir. Although we suffered up at Prome. That was a hard fight and we lost a lot of men. Since then, like everyone else, we've been on the route march. Then we were rushed with 63 Brigade to Ye-u and on to Kalewa and Shwegyin to defend against any Japanese advance.'

'Ah!' Osborne interrupted as several orderlies appeared carrying mugs and kettles. 'Looks as though we are going to get some refreshments.'

As tea was served, Somers asked, 'You were in the Basin, sir?'

'Yes, I'm afraid we lost a lot of men, many probably familiar to you. But we managed to get away up the Kaing track in the nick of time. Well, what will happen to you now?'

'I reckon we'll be sent back to India to reform, sir.'

The next day they steamed into the waters of Sittaung and disembarked by the village; the steamers were then sunk to prevent them from being captured. It started to rain again when Osborne led his drastically reduced battalion from Sittaung, across the open muddy fields, away from the river and towards the hills. Then they trudged along a precipitous, rough track to Tamu and on to Palel, where they found transport awaiting to take them to Imphal on the newly created all-weather road.

*   *   *

As Slim drove along the track he passed units on the march and chatted to individuals, encouraging them as they ploughed through the mud, which was up to their knees in places. Many were shivering from the fever which had spread quite rapidly. Others were shivering from the cold weather that came with the rain. Their nights were restless, disturbed by dripping trees and the cries of the refugees. But they carried on, never breaking down.

To Slim's delight, a couple of marches short of Tamu, they were met by an Indian mechanical transport company. But the drivers were frightened and they refused to drive further south, taking their lorries into the jungle to hide. Slim, however, overcame this difficulty by putting a man from 7 Armoured Brigade beside each driver and there was no longer any trouble. The transport was of great value ferrying the wounded and the sick, and sometimes whole units forward.

At last, on 17 May, they reached Tamu, and on the nineteenth, the rearguard marched into India. The Burma Army had retreated nearly 1,000 miles in some three and a half months. The remnants numbered some 30,000, having lost around 13,000 killed, wounded and missing during the campaign.

Slim got out of his jeep and stood on a bank beside the road to watch them march in: British, Indian, Gurkha, Burmese, so gaunt and ragged they reminded him of scarecrows. But they carried their arms and kept their ranks.

Well, they might look like scarecrows, Slim thought, but they looked like soldiers. And he did not think he had ever felt prouder of any body of men as these.

Epilogue

Imphal, May 1942

The Imphal Plain, with its level rice fields and grassland, dotted with clumps of trees and villages, was rimmed by low hills rising about 3,000 feet above, and here and there were distant peaks reaching 10,000 to 12,000 feet.

When Lieut. Colonel Osborne reached Imphal he expected that arrangements would have been made for the battalion's reception, but a supercilious young officer pointed to an area of jungle on the steep hillside.

'You can camp there,' he said.

Osborne contained his temper. 'What about tentage and water arrangements?'

'Oh, you can't expect anything like that. You'll just have to do the best you can.'

Robin was furious at the insolence of the young lieutenant, but Osborne just shook his head slightly. It would not get him any tents. One day soon, the young man would no doubt find out the facts of active service for himself the hard way.

It was the reception meted out to all the military of the Burma Army. For almost four months the Burma Corps had fought every inch of the way to India's frontier. They had been defeated but never conquered or disintegrated into a terrified, screaming mob, and they had brought back their personal weapons.

Major General "Punch" Cowan was proud of his 17 Division which, against all the odds, had emerged from the ordeal of Burma as a top fighting formation, and its morale was, he believed, 100 per cent.

They had prevented the Japanese from sweeping straight into India and it was because of this that the British were able to expand and train and, within a few years, to smash the Japanese Army. But the crescendo of misinformed criticism, which was levelled at them from far afield, spread a false reputation and what was a valiant performance was condemned as a disaster. When the 30,000 survivors finally reached Imphal, they expected a decent reception; instead, they were treated like pariahs. There was no decent accommodation to shelter from the monsoon rain, no cooking pots and no mosquito nets – Imphal was swarming with mosquitoes – and there was a shortage of rations.

The reception had been so different at Dunkirk, where the troops had been welcomed as though they had won a great victory, admired for their courage in retreat and looked after with compassion. Of course, Dunkirk was only just across the Channel, whereas Burma was some unknown place on the other side of the world and could surely have no effect on the war in Europe. But the loss of India would have had serious repercussions across the world.

Osborne quickly called an order group. 'We can show them that we will not just lie down and die,' he said icily.

The Gurkhas moved onto the hillside and soon began to show their skill. Khukuris were applied and the undergrowth was cut back, a cleared space allocated for each unit, and very soon an encampment of brushwood shelters appeared. With groundsheets and roofs of intertwined branches, they managed to provide reasonable protection from the rain. But blankets were in short supply and those carried by the men were almost all wet through. Everyone was longing for a break in the rain.

Several of the men were down with malaria and Doc Forster was striving to look after them and the other sick men. The fatigue parties had erected a basha as a makeshift hospital, so at least the men were relatively dry. But the doctor was drastically short of medical supplies. Rations were also scarce and Robin and the Quartermaster Jemedar had gone off to find out where they could get supplies.

The next day there was a break in the rain and the sun came out sufficiently strong enough to turn blankets and sodden garments from wet to damp. Robin, with a fatigue party, had brought back rations from a supply point organised mainly through the unstinted efforts of generals Cowan and Scott and General Savory of 23 Indian Division.

Paul was watching his company quartermaster havildar and Tilbir organise the distribution of rations when he heard his name being called. Looking up, he saw Osborne with a civilian standing by his side and he moved further up the hill to join them.

The colonel was smiling. 'There is someone here to see you, Paul.'

Paul moved closer. 'Dad!' He could hardly believe it to be true. 'How on earth …'

He got no further before his father's arms were around him. 'Thank God you are safe, Paul. I have been searching all the units trying to get information about you. And then I met your colonel. Let me look at you. You have certainly lost weight. And you definitely need some new clothes.'

'Take your father down to the mess,' Osborne said.

The Gurkhas had built a bamboo basha on which they had fixed a board: Officers' Mess. Inside were stools they had fashioned and with a wry sense of humour, even a sort of bar, although there was, unfortunately, no alcohol available.

'You must tell me how you got here,' Paul said as they sat down on the roughly made stools.

Mike Cooper told his son, 'The Indian Tea Association and the Assam tea planters are assisting with supplies and the planters are coming with thousands of their coolies to help in the construction of the Imphal road; others are putting up relief camps for the homeless refugees and I felt I ought to play my part.'

'Nobody else seems very interested in our welfare,' Paul said.

'Well, we were certainly worried about you, your mother and me. Somehow, I have got to get word to her that you are safe.' He caught Paul by the arm. 'You are all right? I mean, you have not been wounded?'

Paul smiled. 'Do not worry, Dad, I managed to dodge all the bullets.' He looked up as Gopiram appeared. 'I was going to apologise for not being able to offer you any refreshment, but I should have known I could rely on Gopiram.' His orderly approached with two mugs of tea. 'This is Gopiram, my orderly, bodyguard and friend. He has looked after me and saved me, I am sure. Gopiram, this is my father.'

'*Namaste*,' said Mike, speaking in Nepali. 'From what I have heard, I owe you a great deal for taking care of my son.'

Gopiram looked surprised for a moment. 'You speak Nepali, sahib. But, of course, I should not be surprised as he is your son.' He handed them their mugs of tea and then backed away.

Paul said, 'Look, Dad, there is something I have to tell you. I need your help.' Paul then told his father about Sue. 'I don't know if she's even alive or where she is. If she got through the Kabaw Valley then she must be somewhere in Imphal. Probably in some refugee camp.'

'And I don't suppose you've been able to carry out a search. But I will do so for you. There are quite a few camps around. Leave it with me. I'll get back to you in a day or two. You are not moving?'

Paul laughed. 'No, I think we are stuck here forever.' He showed his father out of the mess. 'How did you get here?'

'I left my truck on the road below the hill. I have a boy looking after it. Right, Paul, I will try my best.'

Paul watched his father climb down the hill and disappear behind the trees.

The next morning Paul was roused by an excited Gopiram. 'Look, sahib! Look who is here!'

Paul sat up on his bed of leaves. There was a figure beside Gopiram. For a moment Paul was puzzled. The figure was not clear in the gloom and the individual was wearing a *longyi*. Then he came fully awake. 'Tun Hla!'

The Burmese boy crouched by his side.

'Where are they?' Paul asked, frantic to know, looking beyond Tun Hla, hoping to see Sue and Mary.

'They are in camp,' Tun Hla said. 'Refugee camp. They all right, thakin, no hurt, no sick. I look everywhere for you, thakin. Only now I find you.'

Paul got to his feet. 'And you, Tun Hla. You are all right?'

'I am OK, thakin.'

He looked drawn, Paul thought. He had been given quite a responsibility. His *longyi* and shirt were grubby. Paul wanted to set off at once for the camp, but he realised it was far too early to disturb the colonel. He would just have to be patient.

Gopiram brought tea and Tun Hla squatted on the ground while Paul questioned him about his adventures.

'What happened after you left us?'

'We got to river. Very crowded. But how to get on a boat? Ma talked to big General Sahib and we got on boat.'

'Slim!' Paul wondered how Sue had managed that.

Tun Hla told of the hard times in the Kabaw Valley. 'And then, thakin, very lucky. British soldiers put us on lorry. Some trouble Tamu, but we get another lorry to Imphal. More trouble. No one know what happening. But we taken to camp. Not very nice camp. And I think I must find you soon.'

'It must have been very hard for the ladies.'

'Very hard for old lady. One time I thought she die. If not meet soldiers it would have been impossible, so much rain. Then she gets better. Still hard for her, I think, thakin, but now I think OK.'

Paul decided it was late enough to tackle Osborne, so he and Tun Hla walked further up the hill, past the Gurkhas getting ready for morning parade. After a night of rain the ground was oozing mud and slush, although by now everyone was becoming used to the mess. There was a haze around the trees, but Paul thought he caught a glimpse of the sun trying to burn its way through.

Osborne was having his tea and he looked up as Paul approached. Seeing Tun Hla, he knew at once the reason for Paul's visit.

'You've obviously found her,' he said.

'Yes, sir. Tun Hla says they are in a refugee camp about an hour from here.'

'Well,' said Osborne at once, 'you had best go and see her.'

'Thank you, sir.' Paul saluted and hurried back to advise Tilbir to take over the company.

'Gopiram will go with you, sahib. And I think two men.' Paul did not query the bodyguards, but Tilbir continued, 'And I think, sahib, maybe you should take some rations or some items for the memsahibs.'

'How stupid of me,' Paul said. 'But my mind is miles away, Subedar Sahib.'

'It is understood, sahib. But let us ask Tun Hla.'

'A groundsheet and perhaps a blanket, sahib.'

'We are short of most things ourselves, but maybe we can manage that, even if you have to take mine,' Paul said.

'No need, sahib,' Tilbir said quickly. 'I will see to it.'

'Anything else, Tun Hla?'

Rather hesitatingly, Tun Hla asked,' The ladies are missing their tea.'

'We can't have that, Subedar Sahib.'

'No, sahib,' Tilbir agreed, smiling. 'Tea and some powdered milk it will be.'

When the various items had been collected, Paul set off with Tun Hla and the rest. Fortunately, it was not raining and the sun seemed to be winning its battle against the circling black clouds, but the ground was muddy and slippery and undulating. They passed several camps spread on the hillsides, many of which looked in a bad way. After an hour or so Paul could see a large, sprawling camp and he could hear screaming children and shouts echoing across the hills. There was a strong smell as he approached. Must be passing the ablution area, he thought, which were crude bamboo enclosures. They passed through and came into the camp, with one or two tents for the lucky ones, the rest trying to get some comfort in crude shelters.

'This way, thakin.' He led Paul towards the far end.

The two women looked up at his approach and then they got to their feet in half belief. But Paul ran forward and took Sue into his arms, feeling the warmth of her body against his. She moved out of his embrace.

'I'm not exactly presentable,' she said.

He tried visualise her. Up to now his memory had been restricted to Moulmein and the incident on the road to Shwegyin. Was she tall? A bit shorter than him. Was she beautiful? As if it really mattered. In spite of the ravages of the sun and rain, exhaustion and insects, he knew he still found her attractive, and he loved her.

'We managed to do some laundry, if you can call it that, in the rain,' she joked.

Paul moved over to Mary and kissed her on the cheek. 'I am so pleased to see you, Mary. You must have had a terrible time.'

Mary looked quite thin and there was a yellow tinge to her complexion, but her eyes were much more alert than before. 'I was lucky to have such great helpers.'

Paul looked around their little camp. It was rough, but Tun Hla had done his best to make it habitable. 'We have brought you a few things.'

'There is tea and powdered milk,' Tun Hla said excitedly. 'Shall I make tea?'

'Of course,' said Mary.

They sat on the large stones which Tun Hla had gathered as seats. Paul noticed a small fire burning.

'Tun Hla does his best to keep that going so we have instant heat,' Sue said. 'And it will be a real treat to have some tea.'

While Tun Hla was heating the water, Paul asked, somewhat tentatively, 'You know, I have not heard what happened to George, your father.'

Sue told him of George's death in the air raid.

'Were you staying in Mandalay?' Paul asked.

'No, we had come from Maymyo,' Sue said. Then, with Mary interjecting, she told him the story of what had happened after they had left Moulmein.

Afterwards, Paul said, 'Now, we've got to get you out of here.'

But he wondered how it could be done. He didn't want to embarrass Osborne by suggesting they should be taken into the battalion camp. Though, maybe they could make a separate camp nearby.

His problem was sorted out when Gopiram touched his arm. 'Your father is here, sahib.'

Paul looked around with a great sense of relief as his father approached.

Mike Cooper said, 'So, you found them first. I've been searching for them everywhere.' He looked over Sue. She was obviously not at her best, but it did not hide her attractiveness. The older woman must be her mother.

Paul made the introductions and explained his father's presence.

'I was wondering what to do, Dad. I thought I could move them closer to our camp.'

'No need. What I would suggest is that I take them to my camp. No, not tents; it's actually a house. There are many empty buildings, because most of the Manipuris fled after the last air raid. There's plenty of room and they could have a chance to get cleaned up.' He turned to the women. 'And you'll need some new clothes, I guess.'

'Oh, yes!' they said in unison.

'Well, I'm sure that can be arranged. We brought a huge quantity of clothing with us, donations from people all over Assam. Most of it has gone, I'm afraid, but there is still quite a lot to choose from. But first let's move you out of this dump.'

Gopiram and the bodyguards quickly gathered their pitiful belongings together, including the kettle which had been their most valuable find on the trek. A half-hour's walk, with the Gurkhas helping Mary, brought them to Mike's truck.

'Paul, you had best come with us so you know where to find me. Then I'll drive you and your men back to near your camp. It's quite a distance.'

Mike's HQ was in a cluster of buildings at the edge of town and when Sue and her mother, with Tun Hla, had settled in, Mike said, 'I'll take Paul back. Give you a chance to freshen up. And then we'll find you those clothes.'

Mike drove off. On the journey he said to Paul, 'Would they have any relatives in India?'

'I rather doubt it,' Paul said.

'Then we must try to get them to the tea garden.'

Paul was too stunned to reply for a moment. 'Dad, I don't know what to say.'

'Well,' his father said quietly, 'I presume they are family?'

'Of course, Dad. Very much so, I am sure.'

'We'll ask them later. Although, getting them to Darjeeling won't be easy. Transport facilities are really buggered up at the moment. Can't rely on the railway men. Especially as there have been air raids. I would have to take them to Dimapur and see about getting them on a train to Calcutta. Then, from Calcutta, they would have to get a train to Siliguri, which I don't think will be difficult. The problem is contacting your mother.' He paused for a moment. 'I'm hoping it will be possible to send a telegram to Joan from Dimapur. Then she can meet them at Siliguri.'

'If Sue knows the day and train time, Dad, I'm sure she would have no trouble sending a telegram from Calcutta. The only problem is that I have no money to give her. I bet there isn't a field cashier within miles.'

'You leave that to me. Right, this is where I drop you off. Can you meet me here tomorrow afternoon? Good. Then I'll fill you in with the progress report.'

The next morning, Osborne called an order group.

'I have some news at last. We are to return to Dehra Dun for rehabilitation. I am sure you will all agree that it will be a great pleasure to have our battalion back to full strength. You have done wonders and we have also suffered great losses, and now we should have the opportunity to make all that tribulation worthwhile.

'I have no actual date of departure, but I understand it should be within the next week. It is just a matter of arranging transport, which at the moment is very unreliable.'

Paul asked, 'Will there be an opportunity for the men to go on leave, sir?'

'The men certainly deserve it,' Osborne agreed. 'But I think we will have to wait until we get to the centre to see how the land lies. I will do all I can to arrange it.'

Later that day, having been granted permission, Paul met Mike and was driven to his father's camp.

He was surprised in the change in the two women, particularly Mary. She seemed much more alert. The sadness at the loss of George was still there, to get over that would take much longer, but she was happier and they were both wearing colourful cotton dresses.

'It was like walking into a shop again,' Sue said, 'and we were able to find a number of necessities.' She laughed. 'Knickers, for example! Not exactly ladies lingerie, but still very welcome. No stockings, but serviceable socks.'

'And no shoes our size, unfortunately,' Mary said. 'But we did find some strong, well-made sandals.'

'And you have no idea how good it is to brush one's teeth with a toothbrush and toothpaste instead of using a twig,' Sue said feelingly.

Tun Hla had discarded his *longyi* for a khaki shirt and trousers and he looked much more relaxed now that he was relieved of his considerable responsibility.

They settled down in Mike's HQ office to discuss the situation and both Mary and Sue were astounded at Mike's offer. They had no relations in India and were delighted to accept. Paul had asked Tun Hla if he would like to go as well and he was certainly pleased with the idea.

'There have been trains to Calcutta,' Mike said. 'I believe Bill Slim managed to get on one. But we will go down to Dimapur and gauge the situation on the spot. May have to wait a bit or we might strike lucky.'

'I have heard this morning that the battalion will be moving out soon,' Paul said.

'No need to worry, Paul,' his father said. 'I shall take the girls,' he smiled at Mary, 'and Tun Hla down to Dimapur as soon as possible. We don't want to be trapped here by a landslide on the road. And I will see them onto a train.'

'You've done such a lot already, Dad.'

'I told you to stop worrying. You can leave everything to me. It's easier for me. You are tied to your battalion and military discipline.'

Mike explained that the train was a metre-gauge and would cross the Brahamaputra River before continuing to Parbatipur, where they would change to a broad-gauge train for the final run to Calcutta. It would be a long journey of over 300 miles.

'I hope to be able to send a telegram from Dimapur to alert Joan. In any case, Sue could telegraph from Calcutta and give Joan the train time from Calcutta to Siliguri, where Joan will meet them.'

'They will be alone in Calcutta,' Paul began to protest.

But Sue said, 'Oh, Paul, we know how to look after ourselves in a civilised city.'

'Sorry. I just ...'

'I know.' She touched his arm.

Mike said, 'They will probably have to stay a day or two in Calcutta, but I shall give them the name of a good hotel where I am known. And I will make sure they have enough funds. I have a bank account in Calcutta.'

They came out of the room and Paul and Sue wandered off to one side. 'You know how I feel about you,' Paul said, taking her into his arms.

'And ...' she began impishly. Then, seeing his face, she said, 'And me, too, of course, darling.'

'Can you be sure?'

'Can you?'

'I thought of you so much, especially during the dangerous moments.'

'You think I never thought of you? After Moulmein there was no news. Just hoping against hope. And then in Maymyo I met one of your wounded men who recognised me, so I knew that you were alive at that moment ... And meeting you again on the road to Shwegyin – what a meeting that was.'

'That was horrendous. But thank God I was there. But your feelings ...'

'Don't worry, Paul, darling. I do love you and I need you.'

She pushed him away slightly and then took his hands, placing them against her breasts. Their eyes met and he knew it would be all right. He heard voices approaching and, slowly dropping his hands from her breasts, he took hold of her around the waist.

'I'll get leave and meet you in Darjeeling. Nothing is quite certain these days. They are reforming the battalion. But they will have to chain me to the orderly room to stop me.

'Don't do anything rash. I'm sure your parents will look after us.'

The others were approaching and he kissed her, not wanting to let her go. But finally they joined the others.

Mike watched Paul and Gopiram climb up the hill from the road. Paul turned and waved and then was wrapped up in the jungle. For the moment, thought Mike, he is safe. But God knows what lies in the future. This war will last for a very long time.

As he drove off, he thought, Meanwhile – meanwhile I will most surely arrange happiness for Paul and Sue for how short a while it might be in Darjeeling.

Selected Bibliography

Regimental Histories:

3rd Queen Alexandra's Own Gurkha Rifles. Edited by Brig. C. N. Barclay, CBE DSO. William Clowes & Sons, 1953.

4th Prince of Wales' Own Gurkha Rifles. Vol III (1938–1948). By Col. J. N. Mackay DSO. William Blackwood & Sons, 1952.

5th Royal Gurkha Rifles (Frontier Force) Vol II (1929–1947). Gale & Polden, 1956.

7th Duke of Edinburgh's Own Gurkha Rifles. By Col. J. N. Mackay DSO. William Blackwood & Sons, 1962.

Official Publications:

Major General S. Woodburn Kirby. CB. CMG. CIE. OBE. MC. *The War Against Japan. Vol II India's Most Dangerous Hour,* London, 1958. HMSO.

Bisheshwar Prasad. D. LITT., General Editor. *Official History of the Indian Armed Forces in the Second World War 1939–45. 'The Retreat From Burma 1941–42'* (Combined Inter-Services Historical Section, India and Pakistan 1952).

Books:

Allen, J. *Burma: The Longest War.* Dent, 1984.

Carew, Tim. *The Longest Retreat: The Burma Campaign 1942.* Hamish Hamilton, 1969.

Connell, John. *Wavell: Scholar and Soldier.* Collins, 1969.

Connell, John. *Wavell: Supreme Commander.* Completed and edited by Michael Roberts. Collins, 1969.

Evans, G. *Slim as Military Commander.* Batsford, 1969.

Grant, I. L. and Tamayama, K. *Burma 1942: The Japanese Invasion: Both Sides Tell the Story of a Savage Jungle War.* The Zampi Press, 1999.

Lunt, J. D. *A Hell of a Licking. The Retreat From Burma 1941–42.* Collins, 1986.

Lyman, Robert. *Slim, Master of War.* Robinson, 2005.

Mains, Tony. *The Retreat From Burma.* W. Foulsham, 1973.

North, J. (Ed). *The Alexander Memoirs 1940–45.* Cassell, 1962.

Pownall, Sir H. *Diary. Vol II 1940–44.* Edited by Brian Bond. Leo Cooper. 1974.

Scott, R. L. Jnr. *Flying Tiger: Chennault of China.* Greenwood Press, 1973.

Slim, Field Marshall Sir W. *Defeat into Victory.* Cassell, 1956.

Smyth, Brigadier Sir J. *Before The Dawn.* Cassell, 1957.

Smyth, Brigadier Sir J. *The Only Enemy.* Cassell, 1959.

Smyth, Brigadier Sir J. *Leadership In War (1939–45).* David Charles, 1974.

Smyth, Brigadier Sir J. *Milestones.* Sidgwick & Jackson, 1979.

Tamayama, Kazuo and Nunneley, John. *Tales by Japanese Soldiers of the Burma Campaign 1942–45.* Cassell, 2000.

Williams, Lt. Col. J. H. *Elephant Bill.* Granada, 1982.